Mostly True GHOSTLY Stories

Natasha J. Rosewood

Mostly

True

GHOSTLY

Stories

By

Natasha J. Rosewood

GHOSTLY is a collection of ten spooky, fictionalized tales inspired by the real-life experiences of ex-flight attendant, psychic and author, Natasha J. Rosewood.

Whether set in a haunted youth hostel in France, a ghost town in Death Valley, California, over the Alps at 35,000 feet or in the alien-invaded English countryside, every story will have you teetering on the edge of the abyss between reality and illusion.

Queries regarding rights and permission should be addressed to:
Natasha J. Rosewood
Box 1426
Gibsons, B.C. V0N 1V0
Canada

Website: www.natashapsychic.com

Printed by:	Amazon CreateSpace
Cover Art	Heather Waddell
	(www.waddellart.com)
	Picture: Sechelt Watch
Cover Design:	Natasha J. Rosewood/
	Christine Unterthiner
Book Concept & Design:	Natasha J. Rosewood
Graphic Art:	Christine Unterthiner
Book Layout:	Suzanne Doyle-Ingram
Substantive Editing:	Betty Keller

Note for Librarians: A cataloguing record for this book that includes Dewey Classification and US Library of Congress numbers is available from the National Library of Canada. The complete cataloguing record can be obtained from the National Library's online database at: www.nlc-bnc.ca/amicus/index-e.html

ISBN 978-0-973-4711-2-0

CONTENTS

MORE BOOKS
by
Natasha J. Rosewood

Aaagh! I Think I'm Psychic (And You Can Be Too) ...

... is a sometimes humorous, sometimes heartbreaking account of Natasha's reluctant psychic awakening. Her story is accompanied by metaphysical endnotes to help the reader recognize and develop his or her own inherent intuitive ability, and to offer a deeper understanding of the psychic forces that were at play when Natasha magnetized these events to her. Prepare for a sense of déja vu. Aaagh!

Aaagh! I Thought You Were Dead (And Other Psychic Adventures) ...

. . ."**Do you see dead people?**" a potential psychic client once asked me. "**Oh, yes. All the time,**" I responded. "**And so can you . . . if you are open.**" But seeing spirits is only a small element of Natasha Rosewood's life as a psychic development coach, spiritual healer and writer.   Join Natasha in *Aaagh! I Thought You Were Dead (And Other Psychic Adventures)* as she shares just some of the fun and fascinating-true life experiences from her personal and professional life as a psychic.   Her fast- paced, light-hearted storytelling entertains as it empowers us all to explore our greatest mind potential. The "Dear Natasha" responses that follow each out-of-this-world tale answer the questions that many of us would all love to ask a psychic.

TAKE A PEEK

Mostly True GHOSTLY Stories

PREVIEWS

"What do y-y-you think that is?" David was pointing into the belly of the quarry. A vague, dark, metallic shape was barely visible in the growing dark.

"A dead robot?" I offered, laughing. "I don't know. An old car?"

"I w-w-want to ssss-see." David grinned at me mischievously. Let's go in."

It was 1968. Sarah, an 18-year-old relative newcomer to this northern English town, had fallen in love with the tall, gentle David. Even his stammer was endearing. In the spring dusk, the young couple went through the hilly Pennines for what should have been an innocent country drive. But by the end of this surreal evening, Sarah needed to know—for her very survival—what had really happened in the quarry?

Then the banging suddenly stopped. There was a long silence followed by a confusion of sounds. Thumps, raised voices. Tools dropping. Swearing. Eve looked up from her magazine and frowned at me. My stomach lurched. I knew something was terribly wrong.

Samantha is a young woman who has given up on love and decides to buy a cottage in the Buckinghamshire countryside. Despite believing that *she* has chosen her quaint new home, it soon becomes apparent that the haunted house has picked *her* for its own devices. Only after repeated, unexplained horrific events does it become clear why it is Samantha the ghosts want.

3. SUMMER DREAM Page 58

"Where are you?" she screamed, hoping to defy the deafening silence. But on the dock the stillness only became heavier and heavier, threatening to crush and swallow her. Her voice simply echoed around the empty inlet.

Diane is enjoying a lazy afternoon on their summerhouse patio while her husband takes their two daughters fishing on the inlet and her parents relax inside. Before lapsing into a nap, the thirty-eight year old agonizes over her unraveling marriage. What happens next is not a wake-up call Diane had ever imagined. Only later does the true threat become apparent.

4. DEADHEADERS Page 74

It was Tuesday. A thick early morning mist lay over the fields in front of my house. My coffee had gone cold at my computer desk. While on my way to the kitchen to top it off with hotter liquid, I heard a tentative knock at the door. I stopped, put the mug down on the kitchen counter and listened. Another knock, firmer this time.

When Alicia's fiancé dies suddenly, she isolates herself in a remote country house where she chooses to be alone in her grief. When there's an unexpected knock at the door, she is surprised by her willingness to open up to these visitors. She welcomes them—at first—letting them into her world and even sharing some of her own stories. But too late she realizes nothing could have prepared her for this spine-chilling reality.

5. INTO THE VALLEY OF DEATH Page 85

I glanced over my shoulder to see if Joanna was still sleeping. Then I turned again and blinked my eyes, not sure of what I was seeing.

"Ben?" I wanted him to confirm that I wasn't insane. I forced myself to control my encroaching panic. "Stop the car!"

"What?" he asked puzzled, pulling over. And then following my gaze, he saw for himself. "What the hell . . .?" And looking at me, "Where the hell . . .?"

During a vacation driving through California, a brother and two sisters find themselves driving into Death Valley at night. Their tank is less than half full but looking for a gas station in the hottest desert on the planet becomes the least of their worries.

6. KNOCKING Page 111

The woman sitting in the aisle seat instantly paled, craning her head around the back of her seat to try and see what Charlotte was seeing. "Meine Gute!" she exclaimed. "Was ist los, Fraulein? Are vee going to crash?"

"N-o-o-o!" Charlotte shrieked at the rear door.

Just two weeks. Annie, her friend and flat mate who also worked as a flight attendant had died only two weeks earlier in a fatal air crash over the Alps. Today was Charlotte's first flight back at work. And now she had to fly the same route where Annie and others had perished. While Charlotte dreaded going through the same motions of her friend's final moments, she couldn't have anticipated the horror of a never-ending nightmare that was just beginning.

7. SOUL MATES Page 124

Another grinding noise. What was that? Oh no, the chairlift was stopping again. A sudden shadowy movement on the outside of the cover made me jerk back. A large dark amorphous shape was floating just in front of the plastic. What could it be fifty feet above the ground? Oh God. The thing was coming at me! Thud! against the cover. I screamed. What the . . . ?

For this professional psychic, the evening should have been just another gig, reading for a corporate group at the top of Whistler Mountain. But as the night unfolded, the behavior of some people—colleagues and clients—became eerier and eerier. Now she was frozen and stranded in the black, cold night, but not completely alone on the swaying chairlift.

8. CARMEL FOG Page 145

Where was everybody? Except for one lone figure attached to a leash and a dog further down the long curved sweep of sand, the beach was completely deserted. The scene was uncannily silent. How long had she been asleep? And where was Gary?

Nine months after their three-year-old son's abduction, a young Canadian couple decide to get away from a voracious media and drive to California for a much needed break. But when the infamous Carmel fog rolls in over a sunny ocean and her husband also goes missing, Cheryl wonders if she is going insane—or is something trying to send her a message?

9. CLOSING TIME Page 196

We peered into the darkness. I shivered as a thick cloak of cold air swirled around me and then passed through me. There, strewn on six rows of two-tiered bunk beds were sleeping bags. Backpacks, similar to ours, some half-unpacked sat at the end of each bunk. Neatly placed pairs of walking shoes were parked under the narrow beds, but there were no occupants. Where had they gone?

When three young female travellers arrive just before closing time at a French youth hostel, they expect the place to still be open and occupied. It is only the first night of their European hitchhiking adventure and the large country *maison* is occupied—but not in the way they could have possibly imagined.

10. CHARLIE ECHO Page 222

The next envelope Paula laid her hands on was sealed. It was beige, old and crinkled around the edges. Maybe they are photographs, Paula thought. She flipped it over. "Do Not Open Until After my Death," was scrawled across the front in her mother's flowing script.

When Paula's abusive mother dies, the 25 year-old is stunned by the revelation of her family's deep secret. She decides to find out more about the troubled woman. But when Paula begins her new career as a flight attendant, she discovers that her mother was not the only family member who had connections to aviation . . . and who was disturbed. Now she can't escape—not even at 35,000 feet.

Dedication

To my wonderful husband, Lorne, for all that he does,

especially coming up with the title of this book.

And to all the spirits, alive and er . . . not alive, who make these stories possible.

DO YOU BELIEVE IN GHOSTS?

The Intention of this book is to challenge readers to question their sense of illusion or reality, to affirm the eternity of their spirit and for them to revel in the magic of their own minds so they may use universal energies for the highest good. In the process, I hope to empower and enlighten as well as entertain. Each story asks the question: What is possible from a metaphysical, spiritual, psychological, quantum-consciousness point of view? And what can *we* do to clear the ghosts from our lives?

Your Beliefs. I have not written this or any other books to beat you, dear reader, over the head with my beliefs, nor to discredit any religion or credo. These stories are inspired by my personal experiences and imagination. And like you, I only see my experiences through the lens of my current perceptions. Our beliefs, whatever they may be, serve as a filter until they are no longer valid and then we change them. If this book offends you, therefore, know that it was not the author's intention. (Just donate it to your friendly neighbourhood ghost buster.) And whether or not you believe in ghosts, I hope these stories entertain you.

Need a ghost buster? If you have questions about ghosts; in your home or *your* own ghosts of the past, please refer to my first two books: ***Aaagh! I Think I'm Psychic (And You Can Be Too)*** and ***Aaagh! I Thought You Were Dead (And Other Psychic Adventures)*** or contact me for a consultation. Both books offer instructions on how to help, or shoo away, ghosts. You can also learn how to commune directly with loved ones—alive or dead. Most importantly the underlying theme is about forgiveness and healing old hurts so you never have to deal with ghosts—or become a ghost yourself. Hopefully my writing will inspire you to live freely in the moment, without guilt, and to know that no one is dead, because life is eternal. It is never too late to forgive, to love and to be loved—even in death.

Spirit Appreciation

Divine Thanks and Gratitude go to:

- ❖ My dear husband, Lorne, who came up with the title!

- ❖ The spirits of the adults, children, and other beings who have appeared in my life and inspired the stories in this book.

- ❖ My family and friends for being there through the great and the not-so-great times. You know who you are.

- ❖ All the talented people who have contributed to the final production of this book:

  > * **Betty Keller**, Writing Guru Extraordinaire and Substantive Editor

  > * **Heather Waddell**, Cover Artist whose beautiful and intriguing art work continue to draw people to my writing

  > * **Suzanne Doyle-Ingram**, Book Layout and Designer

  > * **Christine Unterthiner,** Graphic Art

- ❖ All the readers of my first and second books; *Aaagh! I Think I'm Psychic (And You Can Be Too)* and *Aaagh! I Thought You Were Dead*

(And Other Psychic Adventures), especially those who sent me wonderful testimonials and thereby inspire me to keep writing.

❖ My own spirit guides, angels, deceased friends, and other divinities who protect, guide and channel healing wisdom through me.

1

BREATHE

"What is that?" I asked David as we drove past the towering expanse of a satellite dish overwhelming a large field.

"Oh, that's J-J-Joddrell Bank," he explained. "I'm not sure but I think they m-m-monitor what's happening in outer sp-space. Some people believe that it's th-the reason why we attract ssss-o many UFOs around here."

"UFOs?" I was skeptical. Not that I didn't believe in UFOs, I did. But I was new to the area and David, my boyfriend of just two months, was known for his practical jokes as well as an endearing stutter and a wicked sense of humor.

"I'm s-s-serious." He gave me his serious look. "A couple of years ago people driving through the hills near here reported that their c-c-car engines suddenly died and their car radios went on the b-b-blink. Then, lo and behold, ssss-some flying sss-saucer appeared."

David switched to his Alfred Hitchcock voice. "N-not many people b-b-believed them, of course. Not until a UFO m-made a star appearance over Macclesfield in f-f-f-full daylight. At least ten thousand p-p-people saw this noiseless round disc appear, with its pulsating orange lights, and then d-disappear and reappear again. All th-th-those people couldn't be crazy. Or could th-th-they?"

"Very funny," I retorted. And he was. That's what had attracted me to David, that he could make me smile and the fact that he was tall and gentle and emanated a kind of inner strength. "Have you seen any UFOs?"

"Not yet, but I keep l-l-looking!" He grinned.

On Wednesday, May 17, 1968, life was good. I was seventeen, free of any immediate pressure to study, and I was in love. On this rare, clear, blue-skied evening, David wanted to take me for a drive up into the Pennines to show off his newly acquired, second-hand, gray Humber.

"It's very comfortable," I commented as we drove. Though the car's plump seats were all cracked with age, the interior still smelled of leather.

He seemed pleased that I approved.

Around us the Cheshire countryside appeared serene in the golden light of summer. Sheep and their lambs grazed in the fields. In the distance the land rose up into a wall of dark green hills, and a soft pink haze drifted over the horizon. We drove on through the small mill town of Bollington and then found our way onto a narrow country lane, rising up and up, winding through the village of Pottage Hill. Soon we were in the Pennines following the meandering road that cut a line between the upper side of the slopes and the lower fields as they rolled downward. David suddenly pulled over to the left, parking the car in what seemed like a well-used spot.

"Let's go and t-t-take a l-l-look at the v-view," he urged, jumping out of the car. He grabbed my hand and pulled me across the road to look down the hillside. In the encroaching darkness, as we stood before a low, dilapidated stone wall, we were just able to make out the shadowy outlines of villages now clusters of glistening orange and yellow lights, snuggled each into their own hollows.

David suddenly turned around to face up the slope

on the other side of the road. "Oh, l-l-look," he said, pointing to something beyond the spot where he had parked his car. "Looks like an old cottage built into the hill."

I swiveled and peered into the shadows to see what took his interest.

"C'mon." David took my arm, pulling me across the narrow country lane. "Let's go see."

I saw what had been a dwelling sheltered in the lee of the hill. The roof was completely gone and the stones that made up the walls remained precariously balanced one on top of the other.

"I think this is a miner's cottage, and that," David said, pointing to the right, "m-m-must be the quarry."

I followed his focus. "Or was," I corrected. What in the old days must have been the mining site was now just a flattish grassy area enclosed in a semi-circular wall of undergrowth. The dimension of an undersized football field, black patches of trees, bushes and other tangled plant life hung down as if bending over to listen to something—or as if crushed by some great weight. A two-stringed barbed wire fence was loosely slung across the front of the area.

"What do y-y-you think that is?" David was pointing far into the belly of the quarry. A vague shape, dark and metallic, was barely visible in the growing dark.

"A dead robot?" I offered, laughing. "I don't know. An old car?"

"I w-w-want to ssss-see." David grinned at me mischievously.

I hesitated. The quarry was darkening rapidly, the greens turning to varying shades of black. As we stood in front of the pit, I was reminded of a huge gaping mouth, as though a dinosaur had taken a large bite out of the

3

hillside, leaving just this murky cavernous hole.

"Let's go in," he said grabbing my hand and pulling me forward. David held the top line of barbed wire high for me while I carefully pulled myself through. Then, deftly, he did the same.

We hadn't walked far when I heard a noise. I stopped to listen, peering upward into shadows.

"What *is* that?" I turned to David but he was already bounding ahead of me in the direction of the pit.

Someone or something was breathing. But it was too loud for a someone; it had to be a some*thing*. Where was the noise coming from? Could a huge animal be crouching in the trees? Was the breathing coming from up there on the right toward the top of the quarry? No. Not specifically, anyway. The whole hillside appeared to be heaving. The noise was getting louder and louder. I spun around. The breathing was coming from everywhere now: the trees, the grass, the quarry wall. The whole area was pulsating, heaving with breath.

I swiveled in David's direction. He wasn't there! I opened my mouth to scream but nothing came out. Then all around, the sound of the breathing ceased. A strange thick silence rang in my ears. I was paralyzed, trapped in it, as if time had come to a halt. Or was it sheer terror? Then suddenly the silence was gone. The air lightened and cleared. Then the breathing began again, this time overwhelming, deafening. I had to get away. I spun, terrified, and lurched into a sprint back toward the road.

Just get through the fence, I told myself. *It's not far.* The ground was clumpy beneath my feet, and my shoes weren't made for running. The pounding in my ears couldn't drown out the breathing that was closing in around me, threatening to swallow me up.

"Please God, get me out of here," I rasped as I

reached the fence. I bent down. *One leg through, bring the other through. I've made it!* I thought

But then *I* was jerked backward as the hood of my jacket caught on the fence, holding me captive between two lethal strands of barbed wire, forcing me to stare downward at the ground. A panicked sob escaped from my throat. I thrashed from side to side, attempting to unhook myself. But it wasn't letting me go. Then I sensed someone standing over me. Suddenly freed, I could straighten up. David, his tall form barely recognizable in the shadows, was planted there motionless. "Thanks a lot for waiting for me," I hissed, both relief and anger spewing out of me.

"Come on," he urged. "Into the car!" He was right. We didn't have time for recriminations. We both scrambled into the Humber. I banged down the stiff button lock on my door. David fumbled as he hurriedly tried to insert the key into the ignition. Even in the darkness, I knew his hand was shaking.

"Hurry up!" I whispered loudly.

"I'm trying!" he snapped.

I stared into the quarry half-hoping, half-terrified that whatever it was would make itself visible. But only a still black void stared back at me.

Finally David found the ignition. The car groaned—and choked. *Oh, no! What if this thing had control of the car?*

He muttered something and turned the key again. The car coughed and sputtered and then, oh, joy, the engine hummed!

David crunched the gear stick into reverse and banged his foot on the pedal, nearly backing into the fence. The tires squealed as he turned the big car sharply on the road and accelerated back toward Pottage Hill.

The high beams illuminated only hedgerows as we sped down the otherwise black lane. The road was only wide enough for a single car and David was driving too fast for the narrow space, but I didn't want him to slow down.

Until we saw the familiar lights of the village, we didn't speak—or exhale. Now, with a reasonable distance between the quarry and us, I glanced over at David. His face broke into a grin and I giggled.

"Let's go for a drink," I suggested, laughing but still shaking.

"Good idea."

We pulled into the Lamb's Inn, perched on a steep rise of a hill on the village outskirts. Its brightly lit alcoves were decorated with antique knickknacks displayed on yellowed, tobacco-stained walls. The place was empty except for two young businessmen who leaned against the bar, chatting while fixated on a television suspended above the bar. An oddity for a pub, I thought. But now that we were around people and lights and normality, I breathed deeply.

"What'll it be then?" the rotund barman asked David.

"Two ciders, please."

I found a seat in the corner and, pulling my jacket around my shoulders, I huddled on the hard wooden bench, I could still hear the sound of that breathing. I shuddered. *What on earth could it have been?*

David brought two small tankards over to our table and sat down. He grinned. "Gerr it down ye," he said, raising his glass to mine, "as they say around here."

"David, what do you think that . . . thing was?"

"I don't know, but it was *big*."

"It sounded like the whole quarry was breathing."

6

The barman started gathering up used glasses from the tables near us, emptying ashtrays, and wiping the wood surfaces with a frayed rag.

A vague angst began to settle over me like a dark cloud. *Strange*, I thought. *David hadn't stuttered since we left the quarry.* "And, by the way, was that your idea of a joke?" I sniped. "Leaving me like that?"

David's glass banged down on the table. "I wasn't playing a joke on you, Sarah." His face flushed a deep pink. "I looked for you and I couldn't see you. I thought *you* had left *me!*"

"But I was standing right there in the middle of the quarry!"

The barman was hovering. "Yer not from 'ere, are yer?" he asked, addressing David.

"No. Brighton." My boyfriend had only been in the north for a few years longer than I had.

"Oh, aye." The man was standing over us now. "Well, I 'ope yer not thinkin' about goin' up into those 'ills tonight."

David sputtered on his drink.

"Strange things 'ave 'appened up there 'bout this time of year, I can tell 'ee." Now *he* sounded like Alfred Hitchcock.

"Really?" I peered up at him.

"Oh, aye." He sat down at the table opposite, wheezing slightly.

"Like what?" David asked.

I glanced at my boyfriend's features. Maybe it was just the harsh yellow lights of the pub but he looked different somehow, paler, drawn. And he still hadn't stuttered. Who was he . . . really? Coward, trickster—or innocent?

"Things that really can't be explained," the

barman was saying, turning to peer out of the window into the night.

"Can you tell us?" I asked.

"Aye, but you might not believe me."

"Tell us anyway . . . please," I urged.

He scratched his chin. "Well, there were one young couple. Came in early evenin' 'bout this time o' year."

David and I leaned in closer.

"Well, they looked, you know, like a nice pair. Americans. Said they were traveling aroun't' country. Then the strangest thing 'appened. They asked me 'ow long it would take to get from 'ere to Bangor in North Wales 'cause they 'ad to be there by Wednesday lunchtime. 'Well,' I said, 'yer goin' to be a bit late, aren't yer? Today's Wednesday.'"

The barman sat forward, the buttons on his thin cotton shirt straining.

"Now, I know we can all get our days mixed up. I do it all t' time. So I said, 'You've just got a bit confused, that's all.' Well, she gave me a look that would 'ave skinned a cow! So did 'e! 'That's not possible,' 'e said. 'I know that when we left Yorkshire this morning, it was Tuesday. I still have the paper I bought at the hotel before we left.'" The man shifted his weight on the bench. "And blow me down if he didn't plonk it on' t table to show it to me. Yesterday's *Telegraph*. Tuesday it said. 'E wouldn't lie about summat like that, now would 'e?"

I leaned back against the wall. A trembling had started somewhere in my body.

"'I'm not 'ere to argue,' I said," the bartender continued, "'but I'll get *my* paper.' I showed 'im the *Sun*. There it were in bold print—Wednesday, May 11, 1967. Some'ow they'd lost a day." He shook his head at the memory.

"Do you know if they ever found out what happened?" I asked quietly. The trembling had progressed to my legs now.

"Oh, aye. The lady rang me up just before she went back to America." He stroked his rough chin. "Said she couldn't tell me 'ole story but she wanted me to promise that I would warn people not to go to t' quarry."

"Why?" The question came out of my mouth involuntarily.

"Well, for t' rest o' their trip, she said, 'er 'usband acted really strange-like. So strange that she were afraid to be with 'im. Told me she'd left 'im and she were goin' back to America on 'er own."

His bulbous eyes rested on David.

"Apparently they'd decided to take a detour on their journey an' stopped at quarry just up road. Do you know old quarry?"

David barely nodded.

"Just to admire t' view, she said, when they 'eard this strange noise, like breathin'," the barman went on oblivious to the fact that my whole body was now quivering. "And when they were there, 'er 'usband disappeared." I sat up straight, pulling my jacket tight around me. "For a while, anyways."

Just like David.

"And that night she'd found some red marks on 'is neck that weren't there before." He pointed a chubby finger to a place behind his shirt collar.

"What do you think happened to them?" David asked softly.

The barman took a deep breath and scrutinized both of us.

"Well, I'd deny it if anybody asked, but I think

9

they were used for experiments."

"Experiments!" I blurted. "For what?"

A scraping noise came from the front of the pub. Two elderly gentlemen had come in, pulled stools out, and parked themselves at the bar.

Suddenly grinning, he said, "Oh, better get back to work." Instantly reverting to his role as bartender, he pulled his bulk off the bench. But before he moved away from our table, he turned and said, "Oh, by the way, a few days after bein' in t' quarry, she found out she were pregnant."

"So?" David's tone was more defensive than cynical.

"Nought unusual, but she'd always been told by doctors it were impossible for 'er to 'ave children."

We both watched him as he shuffled back to his position behind the bar. I shivered and pulled my jacket even tighter around me. David was staring into his drink.

A roar of laughter came from the front of the pub. Suddenly I didn't feel comfortable being alone with my boyfriend. "Shall we go and watch TV?"

David shrugged and stood up. Taking our almost empty glasses, we walked over to join the regulars at the bar. Several stools were vacant at one end.

"'Nother round?" the barman asked, polishing a wineglass.

David nodded.

A comedy had just ended. Now the news was on. I wasn't really paying much attention to the stiff newscaster, Reginald Bosinquet. Familiar images appeared of shell-shocked children in Ireland, tanks rolling through Israel, ongoing apartheid violence in South Africa, but they didn't register. Something was odd, though. Maybe it was just the uncommon act of watching television in a pub. Our ciders appeared and we drank in silence. Then the announcer on the television said something. His words made me freeze.

"When did he say Martin Luther King died?" I turned to David. He was frowning.

"Last year."

We listened again. Now Reginald was talking about Apollo Two landing on the moon in July, just two months away. "But I thought they weren't going up till next year." I was aware that my voice was rising. *Breathe,* I told myself.

"Yer a bit out o' touch, aren't yer, chuck?" The barman was pulling a pint. "They 'ave to put a man on t' moon this year, just like Mr. Kennedy had promised, before the end o' t' decade."

David and I stared at each other. Nothing made sense. The news was ending. Reginald was shuffling papers and signing off.

"And that's the end of the nine o'clock news for today, May 17, 1969."

I inhaled sharply. David let his tankard slam down on the bar.

"But today is . . . ." My eyes scanned the wall behind the bar, desperately searching for a calendar. I frowned at David. Why hadn't I noticed that red mark on his neck just visible above the collar of his pink shirt? And how come he still hadn't stuttered? The paralyzing fear that made my stomach clench was validated by his answer.

". . . supposed to be May 17, 1968," he said softly, finishing my sentence.

As he turned to look at me, the gentleness in his eyes had been replaced by a cold, emotionless stare. When his hand grasped mine and he said, "We should go

11

now," I realized that the person who would be driving me home was someone—or something—I didn't know at all.

2

WEEPING WILLOW COTTAGE

When I look back on that time, I realize that, although I thought I had chosen Weeping Willow Cottage, I was wrong. The house had chosen me.

Just one year earlier, I had returned from a ten-month adventure traveling around Europe with my now ex-boyfriend, Tom. We had been sitting in our blue and white VW camper at the northernmost tip of Finland, sipping instant coffee and munching on digestive biscuits when he told me that he didn't want to marry me. As if my parent's abuse wasn't enough, they had made sure that no man would want me either. I was officially unlovable. Crying all the way through Sweden and Norway. I had finally acknowledged—by the time we got off the ferry at Dover— that Tom and I really wouldn't be settling down together. I decided—miserable or not—I would buy my own home.

And so there I was a year later— twenty-five years old and a special events coordinator for a large hotel near Heathrow Airport—standing in the entrance of Weeping Willow, the last 400-year-old cottage within my price range. From the outside the cottage was deceptively small. The single oak front door opened into a low-ceilinged vestibule that led to a spacious living room. On the left was a square, modernized kitchen. At the top of the spiral wooden staircase I discovered one large and two medium-sized bedrooms off a small landing. As I strolled through a light-filled dining room to the back of the house and into a budding garden where a weeping willow dominated the small patch of grass, I felt that this cottage, tucked away in a cozy corner of Haddenham, Buckinghamshire, was meant to be mine.

My friends Julie and Di, who had come with me, cooed at the large fireplace and the coziness of the rooms. Despite the fact that the cottage needed major renovations as in levelling the floor in the large bedroom and installing central heating, two months later we—Di, Julie and I—moved in— just the three of us, or so we thought. The date was March 13, 1976.

Diane and Julie were air stewardesses, based at Heathrow working for an airline that took them all over the world while I slogged away at the hotel nearby. For me summer months were about dealing with muggy London heat and dense traffic jams while accomplishing highly stressful organizational feats and using my various languages on multinational tourists. So there wasn't much time to pay attention to the pesky idiosyncrasies of my new home.

One night, ensconced in my large bedroom, I was drifting off to sleep when I thought I heard a noise. Both Julie and Di were away and the house was otherwise silent. *Sounds like someone is breathing,* I thought. Yes, it was definitely deep breathing . . . heavy and rasping . . . as if . . . a *man* . . . was in my room. I sat up in bed and listened. Was it emanating from the wall near the closet? Or was the heavy breathing *in* the closet? The sound, though coming from that side of the room, was difficult to place.

Maybe it's something else, I thought. How could breathing be coming from the closet . . . unless . . .? I didn't want to think about the possibility of a ghost. I decided I must be imagining things, or perhaps it was some strange noise from the house itself . . . the pipes maybe? Eventually exhausted, I succumbed to sleep.

When the heavy breathing started up again the next night and the next, I decided the noise must be something to do with the water tank on the tiny landing. I could live with that.

Then Di returned from Dubai. "Bloody 'ell, Sam," she exclaimed the next morning in her pronounced northern accent. "When did you start snorin'? You're loud enough to wake the bluddy dead!"

"You can hear it, too?" I asked, alarmed.

"Nice try!" She laughed. "Tryin' to blame it on summat else, are yer? Or have yer got a man stashed in yer room?"

"Ha-ha," I responded, drily. Since Tom and I had broken up, my life was devoid of men and romance. "There's something in my room, but trust me, it's not a live man. I want you to come to my room and listen to it." Di knew I wasn't kidding now. "It's giving me the creeps," I continued. "But the noise only starts later on, around eleven o'clock."

"Sounds like it's comin' from *within* the closet near the floor," Di said later, as she sat on my bedroom chair listening. "Like an older man in a deep sleep."

I slumped down on the bed. *Great! I had bought a haunted house.*

"Maybe the previous owner knows summat about it," Di suggested. "You should give 'er a ring."

I took Di's advice the following week and called Wendy.

"Breathing? No, I never heard any breathing." She sounded distracted, unwilling to be called back into her previous life. "There were some other noises . . . scraping sounds." I held my breath, feeling somewhat vindicated. "But I decided they were coming from next door."

"Oh," I murmured, disappointed. *Scraping sounds*? Like me, Wendy obviously preferred to believe that the breathing wasn't something supernatural. I *knew* that whatever the sounds were, they were not coming from the adjoining cottage. My neighbors were a newly married young Anglo-American couple. The walls were thick between the two cottages, and the only sound I ever heard from next door was the occasional peal of laughter from the Texan wife.

So I learned to live with the breathing. Six months later, just as I was getting used to it, the nocturnal noise suddenly stopped. Shortly afterwards I awoke in the middle of the night. A dream had left me with a gnawing unease that something terrible was about to happen. I tried to recall the details but the disturbing images had already retreated into my subconscious.

In September Julie's husband-to-be returned from overseas and she left Di and me to get married. Derek, a twenty-six-year-old pharmaceutical salesman from Hampshire, moved into her room. His penchant for wearing pinstriped suits and peering out into the world through huge glasses that overwhelmed his slim face always struck me as slightly comical. We got on famously.

One night after Derek had gallantly assisted me in painting over the orange walls of the living room with two layers of cream latex, we sat by the glow of the fire, rewarding ourselves with a bottle of wine, and admiring our handiwork.

"Good job," I commented, smiling, "but you've got more paint on you and your glasses than on the walls."

Derek grunted and reached for a clean rag. While

picking the paint smears off the lenses, he said, "I've been meaning to tell you somethin'," he said, his country accent even stronger after imbibing wine.

"Is that right, my dear?" I teased.

"Aye." He wasn't smiling.

"Getting married?"

"Nah." He grinned bashfully. "Not bloody likely, my love."

Normally I bristled at being addressed as dear or love but the way Derek said "my dear" was somehow . . . well . . . endearing. I breathed a sigh of relief. "Well, what is it?"

"I 'ate to tell you, but I think there's a ghost in this 'ouse." He sat back and exhaled as if relieved of his burden.

"You mean . . . haunted?" I repeated a little too sardonically. Di and I had not spoken of the breathing since the noise had stopped and definitely hadn't mentioned it to Derek. "What makes you say that?"

He took a sip of wine, the orange glow from the fire reflected on his cleaned glasses. "One day, I were alone in the 'ouse. You and Di were away somewhere. Well, you know 'ow 'ard you 'ave to pull on the airing cupboard door? It doesn't open by itself like, and when it's open you can't get past the door into the bathroom?"

I nodded. That door always caught on a ruck in the carpet. Another thing to fix.

"Well, when I went into the bathroom, the airing cupboard door were closed shut. I 'ad me shower and when I came out, I went smack bang into t' airing cupboard door!" Derek clapped his hands together for emphasis. I struggled to keep a straight face. Whenever he was serious, I always felt an urge to giggle. Or maybe I was nervous. "If there was nobody in the 'ouse, you tell me 'ow did that door open?"

"Is that it?" I asked.

"No." He sat up in his chair, warming to the topic. "Sometimes my bedroom door suddenly swings wide open, like somebody's mad. I expect to see you standing there, but there's nobody."

I took a sip of wine. I didn't have an answer. Why would it occur to Derek that I would be mad at him? But that wasn't important now. If this was true, if the place was haunted, what was I supposed to do? Sell the house? I could just see the real estate sign on the lawn with a large *HAUNTED!* sticker slapped across the red and blue lettering.

"But it feels so peaceful here," I reassured Derek. I didn't want to lose him. He was such a wonderful tenant and he was fast becoming a good friend.

"Aye, that's true," he nodded. "Maybe the ghost just doesn't like men."

"Maybe . . ."

I continued to believe that if I didn't pay any attention to the ghost, it would go away.

I dreaded Christmas. Capital Radio was already counting down shopping days like a ticking time bomb. Volunteering to work every day over the holiday was an option. To come home to an empty house—devoid of celebrating relatives and the smell of turkey—I knew would be too lonely. So while my intuition was screaming at me to avoid spending Christmas with my mother, I didn't listen.

Instead of gathering at Weeping Willow as I had proposed, my older sister insisted that we go to her house up north for the holiday. Anyone who drove up the M1— a motorway that stretched from London to Manchester with kamikaze drivers careening at a hundred miles an hour in dense fog, often causing deadly pile-ups—knew it was a dice with death, even with a good driver. And my mother's driving, even when she was sober, was erratic. As tactfully as possible, I offered to drive. But as usual, her dominance prevailed.

On that foggy Christmas Eve, in cold and rainy weather, with my mother at the wheel of her aging white Fiat, Grandie, my beloved seventy-eight-year-old grandmother sat in the front while I silently prayed in the back. In the shadows, occasionally illuminated by the yellow flickering lights of oncoming cars, I could see the strain in Grandie's face. We sat hunched and still, while my mother barely negotiated the perilous, crowded motorway—until the car broke down in the rain just north of London. My mother was able to coax the squeaking Fiat along the motorway's narrow hard shoulder to the next service station at Watford. While we waited in the starkly illuminated motorway cafeteria for the fan belt to be replaced, my mother not-so-surreptitiously produced from her coat pocket a bottle of Schweppes tonic water, "to calm her nerves," she said. Grandie and I exchanged worried glances realizing that the bottle no doubt contained a large ratio of gin.

Later, after an additional three harrowing hours of her inebriated and neurotic driving, when we finally drove into the gray, drizzly, bleakness of Preston, *our* nerves were shredded. Was it the dark, small industrial town, with its depressing rows and rows of blackened terraced houses, the myriad of unhappy childhood memories that surfaced or simply the permeating drizzle that dampened my spirit? The sense of dread was in my bones. I shivered.

As we entered my sister's festively decorated house, Jean and her normally stoic husband, George, were in the throes of a fight. After our perilous journey, before we were even offered tea, Jean stormed out of the house while George escaped to his office. Giving up on her miserable family, Grandie retreated to bed leaving me alone with my gin-and-tonic-sodden mother. From her chair in the shadowed corner, her eyes glinted with malice. I knew what was coming. Soon I was sitting frozen on the couch, incapable of moving, while she threw verbal knives into me, her vicious words devastating what was left of my meager self-esteem. She snarled and spat her rage at me, her rage at everything— the husband who had betrayed her, her rotten childhood, her four selfish children who had allegedly abandoned her, the Christmases that would never be again. All of it was somehow *my* fault. With my schizophrenic mother, I always felt like a mountain climber, struggling to get to the top of a mountain, yearning to see for miles, to finally understand. To exhale. Now once again, I felt as if my lifeline had been shredded and I was flailing, like so many times before, falling to my spiritual death.

I tried feebly to move, to fight back, but I was lying at the bottom of a crevasse, broken and bleeding. The words had been said, the knives had been thrown. The blades had stabbed me where intended, then twisted to make sure they had gone deep. She was never happy until the damage was done.

When the verbal blows finally subsided and I could move again, I dragged myself off the couch and walked woodenly out of the room. As I cried myself to sleep that Christmas Eve, I couldn't shake the eerie feeling that the unending nightmare of my mother was somehow an echo of the ghost in my home. Before I finally succumbed to sleep, I vowed never to spend another Christmas with my mother. Never again.

One February night, two months later in my own home, I had gone to bed early, hoping to catch up on some sleep. But I tossed and turned in a bad dream, attempting to break free of a vague feeling of something—or somebody— trying to overpower me. Now someone was shaking me by my shoulders, an urgent voice invading my nightmare.

"Sam . . . Sam . . . Sam . . . ."

I struggled to fight him off but he held me in a vice-like grip. "Leave me alone," I sobbed. "Leave me al-o-o-ne." Then I came to.

I was sitting up in my bed, breathing hard, sick to my stomach. The bedside light was on, and Derek, clad in his tartan dressing gown, was sitting on the side of my bed.

"What are you doing here?" I asked.

"Are you all right?" Concern showed through his glasses.

I was embarrassed, not only because I wondered what Derek had heard but also because he was breaching the unspoken flat-mate rule: thou shalt not enter the bedroom of your flat mate when he/she is in bed. I pulled the covers up under my chin.

"Yes," I murmured, brushing my long, tousled hair out of my face. "Sorry. Did I wake you up?" His eyes were puffy and bleary with sleep.

"Yes, you did." Derek sat back now, something unsettled lurking behind his persistent gaze. "I thought somebody was trying to do you in." He smiled a little but a question still lingered.

Now my nightmare was replaying vividly in my mind. This wasn't the first time I'd experienced this nighttime horror. When I thought about it, the bad dreams were becoming a nightly occurrence. I just hadn't realized I was screaming out loud. And I wasn't ready to share the sickening images with Derek, or anyone. "I'm okay," I said, still trembling under the covers, hoping Derek would go back to his own bed. "Just a bad dream."

"Well, all right then, my dear," he said, "if you say so." He stood up, started toward the door, and then turned. "Sam?"

"Yes?"

"If you ever want to talk about it . . ."

"Talk about what?" The pit of my stomach felt suddenly leaden. *Did he know?*

"Your nightmares."

"Oh . . . no. It's nothing, really."

"All right," he said and left.

Even though Tom and I had split up, his friends continued to visit me. One evening, his best friend John dropped by while all three flat mates, Di, Derek, and I, were enjoying a rare dinner together. Tall and slim, with a shock of thick blonde hair, John was aware of his handsome looks—and he put them to good use. He usually entered a room in a whirlwind of energy, looking for fun. If none was happening, he would somehow create some drama.

We invited him to have a glass of wine with us. As soon as he sat down, I saw that look in Di's eyes that said, "And who are *you?*" I didn't even have time to introduce them. Sparks were flying, an easy flirtatious banter instantaneous between them. Derek and I adjourned to the couch, recognizing that a romance had just begun and that we were suddenly superfluous.

A little later, when John and Di had disappeared to the pub together and Derek and I were watching television, I noticed he was deep in thought.

"Penny for them," I said, smiling.

"Oh, I were just thinkin' . . . that you should get married."

"What?"

"I think it would be good for you, my dear."

"Even if I *did* want to get married, what do you expect me to do? Just pop down to Sainsbury's and pick a husband off the shelf?" I smiled wryly. "Maybe they're on sale this week."

"You know what I mean."

"No, I don't, Derek. Please tell me."

"Well," he said, sitting up and picking his words carefully, "it's like you've got this big wall 'round yer. And you're so independent. You scare men away."

"Well, that's good," I snapped. His words stung. I had witnessed the bitter ending to my parents' marriage and what a man and a woman can do to destroy each other after thirty years, not to mention the abuse of their children. "I don't want to get married, anyway." Since Tom's rejection, I had decided marriage was not in my cards.

"You say that, but you really do." He got up. "You can't fool me, Sam." Derek raised his arms high in a stretch and then moved toward the staircase. "Sweet dreams," he called over his shoulder.

After Derek had gone to bed, I decided to listen to music alone in the living room, putting off the time when I would have to face sleep, perchance to dream. Derek's words were still stinging as Simon and Garfunkel's gentle tune "I Am a Rock" echoed his comments. Maybe he was right. Maybe I did want to get married. I had never seen myself as being scary, though. I was the one who was scared—of being crazy like my mother or abusive like my father.

Finally exhausted, I must have dropped off. Then

I became conscious of somebody gently shaking my left shoulder as if to say, *Wake up and go to bed*.

I opened my eyes and glanced up, expecting to see Derek or Di. But nobody was there. And when I rose to turn off the record player, I stared at it, stunned. The little red power light was already extinguished.

The next night I was in bed and just dropping off to sleep when something moved in the darkness. Somebody was in my room! I couldn't see them in the shadows but I could feel them coming closer and closer to my bed. I wanted to scream but my body was paralyzed. I lay there helpless. Suddenly, something, some material was covering my face. I couldn't breathe. I struggled, twisting and squirming under the weight of the invisible force, fighting for life. Then just as suddenly the pressure was lifted. The thing was gone and I was sitting up in bed awake, sobbing and gasping for breath.

The landing light went on and there was a gentle tap-tap-tap on my bedroom door. Derek appeared, silhouetted in the lighted doorway.

"'Nother nightmare?"

I nodded, not looking up.

He came over, sat beside my hunched form on the bed, and listened to me cry. After a while he put a tentative, comforting hand on my bare shoulder. "I know it's none of my business, chuck, but I think you should go and talk to somebody 'bout these nightmares. I mean, it's not like they're goin' away, is it?"

"You mean a psychiatrist?" I snarled, echoes of my mother's sarcasm in my voice. *Crazy people go to see psychiatrists*.

"Well, somebody that can 'elp you. Maybe it's the job. Maybe you just need a bit of break, like. I don't know. But I will tell you something."

"What's that?" I turned to face Derek. His face was soft in the shadows.

"If you won't go and talk to a doctor, you'll 'ave ter talk to me 'cos I need me bloody sleep, too, you know."

I smiled then. "Okay, you're right."

But of course I didn't go for help.

In the spring of 1977, tired of hearing Di talk about all her wonderful trips, I finally took the plunge and applied to British Airways for a job as a stewardess. I knew BA's flights were ninety percent long haul with stopovers all over the world. To my complete surprise, I was hired. And that's how I met David.

Apparently it didn't happen very often—a passenger asking a stewardess out on a date. So when the jumbo lumbered into Heathrow Airport on its final descent from LA, and the tall, blond-haired passenger who had been flirting with me the whole flight—not so surreptitiously—suddenly asked if he could call me, I blushed profusely and stammered, "Yes." He gave me his card and told me his name was David Spencer. The phone rang three days later.

David was dynamic, a little shy, very intelligent, and lots of fun. His family owned a farm just ten miles away and they had founded an international sports business based in London. He opened up my world to a multitude of small surprises. Life was suddenly wonderful. I was in love.

Most of the marriage-minded girls I flew with were looking for tall, dark, handsome, and rich. But when I found out that David's family actually did have old money—lots of it—the information intimidated me. And the fact that he went hunting with lords and his friends lived in mansions while my friends and I lived in semi-detached houses and dilapidated cottages didn't help. Whenever we began to get close—maybe because of these differences in our status— some nameless monster in me would rise up snarling and scare him away. I don't know where the monster came from. I had no control over it. The monster did its job well. I wouldn't see David for weeks. Then I would apologize. We would reunite and begin the dance all over again. The closer we became and the happier I felt, the more ferocious the monster became, David's absences were longer, and my apologies more profuse.

My suitcase was so heavy. Dragging the burgundy Samsonite out of my car into the July mugginess after an exhausting sixteen-hour duty from Barbados was, I decided, the worst part of the whole trip. But I was happy to be home and looking forward to seeing David. I put my key in the lock, opened the front door, and jerked my luggage over the threshold.

"Anybody home?" I called into the silent entrance, closing the door behind me. From upstairs, I heard a click. Di's bedroom door was opening. I waited, expecting her warm, deep voice to call a greeting down the stairs. But there was just an odd stillness and then a crash. The door that had just opened slammed shut again, almost with a vengeance. I wondered if Di was angry about something. Then I remembered she was in Mauritius. And Derek was at work. There was no one in the house.

"If you buy paint, I'll paint me own room," Derek offered one Saturday morning a few weeks later when we were all home.

"Deal," I responded gratefully. "In fact, I just happen to have some sage green that you might like."

Apparently the color was manly enough for Derek

and he started preparing his room that morning. I was in the kitchen cleaning out the oven and Di was folding laundry in her bedroom when Derek came down to the kitchen. He had borrowed a white lab coat from work and it was now splattered with green paint. I put some newspaper on the kitchen stool so he could sit down and then joined him on the other one, offering him a mug of coffee.

He took a crinkled piece of paper out of one of his pockets.

"'Ere," he said, handing me an old brown and white photograph with white cracks running through it. "I found that when I were pulling out the old 'eater in me room." Those brutish brown storage heaters, full of bricks, would have to go when I could afford central heating, but for the time being they took the edge off the winter chill.

I studied the photograph of a young girl, her brown hair cascading down in thick waves over her shoulders, huge sad eyes looking out from a small pert face. "It's not mine," I told Derek. "It's old."

"Yeah, but it looks like you. When I first saw it, I thought it was you."

I flipped it over but there was no writing on the back. "I wonder who she is?" I guessed she was about fifteen. There was something desperate in those eyes as if she was reaching out to me from the photo. I put it on the counter, away from me.

"Probably someone who used to live 'ere," Derek suggested.

"Really, Watson?" I smiled at him. "Brilliant!"

In September, Di's sister Helen came to visit. On the Saturday night as I stood in the kitchen making a cup of tea to take to bed, both sisters came in the front door arguing. I knew they had been to John's for dinner. When they saw me, they both stopped and stared, embarrassed.

"What's the matter?" I asked. "Seen a ghost?"

"'Ow did you know?" Helen asked, peering at me.

Di put her handbag down and unbuttoned her jacket. "I don't know 'ow to tell you this, Sam, but we just 'ad a séance over at John's."

"So? What happened?" I was feeling that familiar unease in the pit of my stomach. "Anybody I know show up?" I teased, trying to lighten the eerie mood.

"Oh, it were nought really," Helen said dismissively, plugging in an already steaming kettle. I knew she was trying to spare my feelings. But Di always had to tell the whole truth—it was one of the reasons I liked her so much.

"We got hold of a spirit called Samantha. Yes, Samantha," she confirmed as my eyes widened, "and . . . well . . . but the message was for me."

"What did it say?"

"Leave."

"What do you mean? Leave. Leave where?"

"I don't know, chuck. It just spelt out L-E-A-V-E." Di shuddered at the memory.

"You don't think that was me psychically telling you to leave here, do you?" I inquired of Di seriously.

"No, no," she replied, hanging up her jacket and avoiding my eyes.

"I wouldn't put it past John to rig the whole thing so he gets to marry you," Helen said, giggling.

Di's expression lightened and she laughed then. "Aye, you're right, kiddo. 'E did 'ave 'is hand on that glass pretty tight, didn't 'e?"

"And if I wanted you to leave, which I don't," I said to Di, "I'd tell you to your face, not through some

28

hokey séance, wouldn't I?"

"Aye, you would, chuck." She walked over to the fridge. "Let's 'ave a glass o' wine, shall we?"

The next morning as I lay dozing in my bed, I could hear Di and Helen downstairs moving about the kitchen, the kettle being plugged in, and the sisters chatting while waiting for it to boil.

The happy sounds were interrupted by a great smash, the sound of china breaking on the floor. With Di around, and her penchant for clumsiness, my crockery supply had diminished greatly. *She must have dropped another plate or something,* I thought. When I joined them downstairs a few moments later, the pieces of a shattered mug lay strewn across the kitchen tiles. Di and Helen, in quilted, floral housecoats, were standing at the far end of the kitchen, clutching each other and staring at the mug. But the wreckage was over by the washer, ten feet away from where they huddled.

"I didn't do it!" Di snapped defensively. "I was down 'ere. It just flew off counter."

I believed her.

"Will you look at that!" Helen exclaimed, walking across the kitchen and crouching to gingerly pick up the pieces.

As she held out the jagged shards of crockery, both Di and I stared. It was Di's own mug, with DIANE embossed in gold script on black glaze. Now ragged strips of pottery lay in Helen's hand, each strip with a letter on it, as if someone with very sharp claws had methodically separated each character.

Soon after that, Di moved out.

For some reason, I was reluctant to find a replacement for Di. Maybe because I didn't know how to explain the ghost to a new renter.

A month passed before Di came to visit me at Weeping Willow. Her brown eyes shone as she stepped into the doorway. But she was bursting with exciting news. I was just about to pour tea into mugs for us when she splayed a tanned hand in my face, a dainty cluster of white diamonds glistening on her ring finger. She was beaming from ear to ear. "Look, chuck."

"When did this happen?" I asked as I carried the tray with tea and digestive biscuits into the living room.

"Last night." She giggled and sat down on the other end of the couch. "What do yer think?"

"Lovely. It's lovely." I hugged my mug of tea. "When's the happy day?"

"Next year, March 18th. Eee, I've got so much to *do*. And in five months." She beamed. "Flowers, music, invitations. And better not forget to call t' vicar." Di laughed, gulping her drink. I'd rarely seen her so illuminated from within. "Make sure you request that day off," she continued. "David's invited, too, of course. Maybe t' wedding will even give 'im a bit of a nudge, if you know what I mean, chuck." She smiled and winked.

I knew what she meant, all right. But David and I were not even ready to get off first base, let alone discussing marriage. Di's wedding would probably bring him out in a cold sweat.

Sleep didn't come easily that night or—I realized—any night for that matter. I wasn't sure when I had started dreading coming to my own bed. With Derek away on business again, I was acutely aware of my aloneness. As I tossed and turned in an exhausted attempt at slumber, it occurred to me that, when I was away and sleeping in hotels or at friends', I never had the nightmare. Why was that? Maybe, I surmised, it was something to do with the responsibility of owning the house or . . . but I wouldn't think about that now.

That night I dreamt about a wedding. David was holding out a ring on a silk cushion to me while my mother and the rest of my family were cheering and throwing flowers at me. Everyone was laughing and happy. Suddenly the scene vanished as someone or something crashed into my dream and lay on top of me, it's insidious, groping energy pawing at me. Suffocating, I tried to scream out loud but no sound came out of my mouth. Ferociously I fought whatever it was but I awoke struggling, thrashing at thin air. And as I cried in terror and helplessness, there was no Derek to comfort me. I was alone in the house.

Christmas came around again like a hundredth heartbeat, a dreaded reminder of everything that was missing in my life. David announced that he would be spending Christmas with his family and apparently that didn't include me, so over the three-day holiday I volunteered to do a long-haul flight.

On Christmas Eve, while waiting in the crew room for the rest of the LA flight crew, I pinned a card on the notice board, advertising for a new flat mate. Eve Connelly introduced herself to me as one of the crew, and we liked each other instantly. Once on board, as she was ripping tops off cardboard catering boxes in the still-cold galley, she told me she was planning to move away from home. That she would become Di's replacement didn't even warrant a discussion. But it wasn't until the whole crew was sitting in Los Angeles's Great American Food and Beverage Disaster Restaurant, enjoying steaks and the entertainment of singing waitresses that Eve talked about her boyfriend, Chris, a detective with Haddenham's police force. I didn't know then the strange role he would play in my life.

When I returned home, I asked Derek not to scare our new flat mate, Eve, with tales of the ghost. But she would soon find out—from the ghost itself.

Meanwhile my relationship with David was becoming ever more tempestuous. I didn't understand why I would suddenly rant at him, saying things I didn't mean. The monster inside was taking over—I was becoming like my mother with her vengeful, histrionic behavior, and David had begun to tire of my laments of remorse. One night in January we had yet another fight and once again he ended our relationship. This time I knew it was over.

The next day at home in my bedroom, I was kneeling on the floor surrounded by tapes and records, sorting through all David's gifts to me and placing them in a bag to be returned, when Eve came up the stairs.

"I heard you come in last night, you dirty stop-out." She stood in the open doorway, smiling that mischievous grin of hers.

"What do you mean?" I asked, a little preoccupied. I wanted to make sure David got everything back. It really was over this time.

"You must have been pretty drunk. I heard the front door slam and heard you stagger up the stairs."

I stared at Eve. *What was she talking about?*

"I even called out to you," she continued. "'What time do you call this then?' But you just ignored me, stumbled into your room and slammed the door."

Our eyes met. She saw my puzzlement and her grin faded. We stared at each other for a while. I debated whether to tell her about the ghost. Maybe *I* was the ghost?

Eve finally spoke. "You didn't come home late last night, did you?"

I hesitated. "No."

"Oh."

"David and I broke up for good last night. So I went over to Rosemary's and drank too much wine to drive, so I stayed at her place."

Eve's brain was struggling to compute the implications of the noises she had heard.

"Look—" I began.

"This place is haunted, isn't it?" Eve blurted.

"Well . . . ."

"It's okay. I can handle it." Her brown eyes bored into mine, needing the truth. "Just tell me."

"Let's put it like this." I sighed. "Some people who have lived here think it's haunted."

"I knew it." Eve clenched her fist and thrust it into the air as if she had just won something. "Do *you* think it's haunted?" she almost whispered as if the ghost might hear us.

"It's possible," I admitted grudgingly. In my ambivalence, I hadn't wanted to consider the ghost as something real. It scared me, sometimes gave me the creeps, made me nervous the odd time to stay alone in my own home, but until now it hadn't really interfered in my daily life. Or had it? Di had moved out because of it, and I had the feeling that something . . . big was going to happen soon. In the meantime, the nightmares were my secret horror.

I waited for Eve to tell me that she couldn't live here, that she would have to move, but she just beamed at me. "Well, that certainly makes life more interesting, doesn't it?"

I could have hugged her at that moment. Instead, I said, "Yes, it certainly does."

We both giggled.

Eve accepted our invisible flat mate but I soon noticed that many more doors slammed and more objects moved, apparently by themselves. However, I had the feeling that it wasn't Eve who was affecting the ghost's increased activity but her boyfriend, Chris.

One wintry night, as I returned home just after eleven, I could hear the television still on so I opened the door to the living room. Eve was sitting in the armchair as if she was frozen there. Her normally pale mass of freckles now stood out against her ashen face, and her big brown eyes were dilated with fright. She jumped as I entered.

"Sorry. Didn't mean to scare you." I smiled, but I noticed that the armchair was pushed back to the far corner of the living room as if she had been waiting for an attacker to come through the door. "Are you okay?" I asked.

She shook her head mutely. "Did you see it?" she asked.

I frowned. "See what?" I sat down on the couch and she came and joined me. "What's going on, Eve?" *Had someone died?*

She took a long breath before she spoke. "I was sitting here minding my own business . . ." The corners of her mouth curled up in a small smile. My shoulders sagged in relief. *No big disaster then.* " . . . when I heard this almighty great crash." Her eyes widened even more until they were like brown satellite dishes. "Then I heard a sound like *bonk, bonk, bonk,* as if something was coming down the stairs."

The previous week Derek had helped me rip out the old carpet on the upstairs landing, exposing the wooden floor so I could paint the landing and stairway walls.

"Then a final crash," Eve was saying. "So I got up to investigate, as one does, and there it was. Just lying there on the floor, unbroken."

"What?"

"The light bulb!" she exclaimed as if I should know what she was talking about.

"What light bulb?" The light bulb in my head wasn't illuminating.

"The one from the landing!" Eve waved an arm behind her. "You know, the one you couldn't unscrew."

She was right. I had struggled for a good half hour last week to extricate the light bulb that hung from the landing ceiling so I could remove the whole fixture, but it wouldn't budge. I had given up and finally thrown a protective cloth over the lampshade to shield it from stray paint flecks.

"Well!" Eve continued. "The light bulb just fell out of the socket from that ceiling and crashed to the wooden floor, rolled down those wooden stairs, and landed on the hallway boards . . . without breaking." She puffed indignantly. "Don't you think that's a little *odd*?"

"Downright scary," I agreed.

"It should be still there." She jumped up, her perky self again. "Wanna see it?"

We both stood at the bottom of the wooden staircase in silence, towering over the white light bulb lying still and miraculously whole on the oak floorboards. The bulbous, misty glass should have appeared harmless enough but something ominous seemed to emanate from its unbreakable fragility. For the life of me, I couldn't think what. Neither of us ventured to pick it up.

"Brrrr, it's so cold in this house," Eve said, suddenly shuddering as she skirted around the bulb and started up the stairs. "You should think about getting central heating put in."

"Funny you should say that," I told her as I followed, leaving the bulb where it lay. I would ask Derek to dispose of it later. "I have an appointment tomorrow with a man who installs just that."

Eve's boyfriend, Chris, appeared to be the quintessential English detective—well built, stocky, with a thick moustache and eyes that expressed a permanent cynicism. And, like many detectives who are constantly faced with the horrific side of life, he had a sick sense of humor. He would often shock Eve and me with stories of murders, rapes, and even the secret, gory details of the Yorkshire Ripper's heinous deeds. Eve obviously loved him and would cook an elaborate dinner for Chris almost every night she was home. I wasn't too happy about his constant presence. Not because I didn't like him. I did. But he really seemed to agitate the ghost. Door slamming was now a daily event. Was it because he was male, or was it his individual energy that offended the ghost in some way? Or was the ghost just trying to get someone's attention?

Meanwhile, Derek's work sometimes took him away all over the country, and even when he was home, he spent a lot of time at his new girlfriend's place. It surprised me how much I missed him. Now constantly imposing on Chris and Eve's romance, I was the piece of a jigsaw puzzle that didn't fit. Chris would frequently go around the house flicking off lights, turning down the electric heaters, and complaining under his breath, as if *he* were paying the bills. His behavior only accentuated even more the feeling that I was an unwelcome stranger in my own home. The sound of wedding bells for Chris and Eve, however, were now ringing loudly. Would it ever be my turn to get married? Or was I doomed to the role of perennial landlady?

A week later, the painting was finished and all the light fixtures reinstalled. After yet another evening of playing the third wheel, I retreated up the stairs to my bedroom to read.

I had turned off the main light in my room, snuggled into bed, and was reading by the glow of my bedside lamp. The landing light was still burning brightly outside my room when I heard the front door open downstairs. Eve and Chris were saying their goodnights in the hallway. Kiss. Kiss. Giggle. His voice. Her voice. Giggle. The front door opened and closed.

Then it happened.

My bedroom light came *on*. Simultaneously the landing light went *off*. Chris was playing tricks. He had to be. Although I knew he couldn't be downstairs *and* turn on my bedroom light upstairs.

I clambered out of bed, still staring at the offending light, and went to tell Chris I didn't think his joke was very funny.

But Eve was already at the top of the stairs.

"Was Chris playing with the lights?" I asked. My tone was accusatory.

"No, he's gone. And he didn't touch the lights," Eve responded, a hint of indignation in her voice.

"Well, Eve, my bedroom light just went on by itself," I exclaimed, "and the landing light went off!"

"How could that happen?" Eve pushed past me. "Must be something wrong with the switch," she said and started flicking the light on and off furiously as if that would fix the problem.

"Maybe it's the electrical circuit for all the lights," I offered lamely, sorry that I had snapped at Eve.

"Yeah. That's it."

"I'll ask Derek."

"Yes, ask Derek," she muttered, retreating to her own room, just as disturbed as I was.

Later that night I was awakened by the sound of an older woman's cackling laugh on the landing just outside my door.

The beginning of February, I attended a friend's birthday party. As I walked into the kitchen David was leaning against the counter. When he saw me—to my complete surprise—his eyes lit up. I was even more shocked when he came over and gave me a long hug. We talked. Before the end of the evening, we were back in our relationship. Now we were getting on wonderfully. Whatever had been causing the conflict between us seemed to have evaporated and we were finally getting closer. On Valentine's Day I received a vibrant array of flowers. I was happy. Everybody, it seemed, was happy. Except the ghost.

"It's getting worse, isn't it?" Eve's expressive brown eyes were apprehensive. We were sitting in the living room, munching on toasted tuna fish sandwiches.

"Yes," I agreed, "it is." We both stared into space.

"I've been thinking—" I started.

"No!" Eve jumped on my words, her huge eyes dilating with fear.

"An exorcist—"

"No. Please don't," she begged.

"Why?" I didn't understand Eve's panic.

"It'll make it worse." She was emphatic. "Remember the movie *The Exorcist*."

I contemplated Eve's frightened face. I had been too afraid to see that movie so maybe she knew something I didn't. "Okay, if you say so," I said, acquiescing. We sat in silence. "By the way, I asked

Derek about the lights."

"And?"

"They are all independently wired."

"Oh."

"What about you two?" one of the other guests at Di and John's wedding inquired, nudging our elbows. With the harmony in our relationship still so new and fragile, I had been afraid this would happen. Well-meaning friends goaded David, "Have you asked her yet? Wink, wink." I groaned inwardly, knowing it might send him over the edge.

He couldn't even wait till we were inside Weeping Willow that night before he uttered the words I dreaded. "Samantha," he began as we sat in his jeep, parked in the dark shadows of my driveway. When he used my full name, I knew it wasn't good news. "You're a great person, but . . . ," he muttered, studiously fondling the steering wheel.

"I wish I was dead." Despair suddenly washed over me, the words just tumbling out, surprising even me.

David groaned. "No, you don't."

"What do *you* know?" I cried, struggling with the jeep door. "You don't know anything about me." As I stumbled through the front door of the cottage, I realized that after a whole year of dating, David really *didn't* know anything about me—because he hadn't asked and I hadn't told him. And when I flung myself on my bed that night, sobbing, the suspicion crystallized in my mind that I was indeed cursed and would end up a miserable, lonely old woman, haunting my own home.

In retrospect, what happened then was inevitable, though at the time I didn't see it coming. The black hole was waiting for me. I tumbled right in and kept falling. The family legacy had finally caught up with me. I was crazy like my mother, or that's what I believed; was the reason I couldn't get out of bed, why my whole body was in excruciating pain, and when I caught a glimpse of my reflection in the mirror, why a gray corpse with dead eyes looked numbly back at me. When the phone rang, I would burst into tears. I prayed every night, bargaining with the deity not to make me wake up and face another day of hell. But he didn't listen.

After two weeks of sleeping most of the day and night, when I eventually crawled out of bed, Di and John came to visit. I saw concern, even fear in their eyes. They suggested walks in the fresh air as if that would simply heal my devastated soul. But the sound of their voices grated, their muffled words settling offensively like gobs of meaningless drivel in my ears. I wished they and everybody else would just go away and leave me alone. And even though Derek tried to tempt me with tenderly cooked meals and kept me quiet company in my silent terror, I just wanted to die. When the initial body pain dulled to a throbbing, dull ache, I was still exhausted but I could feel something shift. The dense fog began to lift.

When Derek tentatively suggested he could drive me to the doctor, I was grateful.

"Make sure you mention yer nightmares," Derek whispered as we sat in the waiting room.

I liked Dr. Fitzpatrick's cheery but no-nonsense style. He scrutinized me as I shuffled into his office and sank down into the black leather chair.

"Are you depressed, Samantha?" he asked straight away. Tears welled up in my eyes and I nodded, surprised at the realization. *Why was I depressed?*

"And are you crying a lot?" I burst out crying in response. "And how are you sleeping?" he continued.

I squirmed in my seat. "Not well," I muttered.

"What do you mean exactly?" he persisted.

"Well . . . sometimes I have these nightmares." I admitted, remembering Derek's instructions.

He was scribbling something on a pad. "Nightmares? They could be a symptom of the depression." Then he looked up. "What are the nightmares about?"

I sank further down in my chair, embarrassed.

The round-faced doctor stood, came around the desk and sat on the edge, facing me. "Samantha," he said very gently, "I'm going to make a suggestion to you. You are severely depressed and I think it would be a good idea in the short term if," he said, handing me a prescription, "you took some valium . . . . Just for the short term."

I exhaled a great sigh of relief. *You mean I'm just depressed and not schizo!* Depression made so much more sense.

"Personally," he continued, "I don't believe that valium will cure your blues because depression is often just a sign of suppressed anger and hurt."

Yes, my rages at David. Where did that anger come from?

"So I am going to suggest that you talk to Dr. Smythe."

Angela Smythe was the airline psychologist. An ex-flight attendant herself, she exuded a warm, gentle intelligence, and I trusted her.

"How does that sound, hmmm?" Doc was handling me like a china doll and I loved him for it.

I nodded submission. Derek was right. It was time to talk to someone who would truly understand.

On the way home, Derek seemed ecstatic that I had agreed to see the psychologist. "That calls for a celebration, my dear." He beamed from behind his glasses. "Are you up to goin' to the pub?"

"Just for one," I agreed, feeling as if a great weight had already been lifted from my weary shoulders. It was so good to know I was just angry and depressed and not schizophrenic like my mother.

We snuggled into our own private alcove. A garden in the throes of early summer was visible through the latticed window. Derek turned his wine glass around and around on the bumpy oak table. "I've got something to tell you, chuck," he announced finally.

My heart sank. *Another flat mate bites the dust,* I thought. I would miss Derek very, very much.

"I'm thinkin'—" he started.

"About getting married . . .?" I droned, although I couldn't remember Derek having talked about his girlfriend recently.

"Well, some day soon." He blushed, smiling at me. "But first, well, I'm thinkin' about buying me own place."

"Oh." It was my turn to play with my wine glass. "And *then* getting married?"

"We'll see." He pulled a half-smile, half-frown. "Time will tell."

"Are you and your girlfriend happy?" I was surprised how much it hurt just to ask that question.

"Who?" he asked, seeming genuinely surprised. "Oh, no. That's over. 'Bout two weeks ago now. Course, you wouldn't know. You've been a bit out of it, chuck."

Attempting to disguise my great relief, I asked lightly, "I'm so sorry. What happened?"

"Let's just say I realized there's only one girl for me." He took a sip of wine and stared out of the window. "And it weren't Sarah."

I waited for him to elaborate but Derek suddenly

stood, picked up both wine glasses, and headed for the bar.

Doc Fitzpatrick had told the airline that I needed at least a month off, and Angela and I started our first session. Very slowly I began to inch my way up out of that black hole towards the light. "Be patient," Angela warned. "It will take time."

During this period, Fred and Will, dusty-overalled workmen, arrived with the new radiators. They said they would need a week to install the central heating, including the time needed to consume copious cups of tea. Now I would be able to tell all my smug American friends, who believed the English were still cave-dwellers, that "Yes, in fact, I do have central heating in my home, thank you very much." Derek, Eve, and Chris were warned that there would be some disruption with two workmen in the house for a week, hammering and pulling up floorboards. The inconvenience would be worth it, I told them.

My words were more prophetic than any of us could have imagined.

When we are the recipients of terrible news, it's strange how every minute detail of the scene is branded into our memories like enlarged high-definition photographs.

On Wednesday, June 6, 1979. Derek was at work. Eve and I were relaxing in the living room. She was stretched out on the brown couch sipping a mug of coffee, browsing through a *Cosmopolitan* that a passenger had left on her aircraft. I was curled up in the armchair, ruminating on my latest session with Angela. A light gray spring mist hung over the narrow lane outside, our only view of the world.

Capital Radio was playing John Lennon's

"Imagine" while a muffled banging was coming from my bedroom. Will and Fred had already installed three of the six radiators, and I was looking forward to the temperature finally being warmer inside the house than outside.

Suddenly the banging stopped. There was a long silence followed by a confusion of sounds. Thumps, raised voices. Tools dropping. Swearing.

Eve looked up from her magazine and frowned at me. My stomach lurched. Something was terribly wrong. We got up slowly and moved over to the bottom of the wooden staircase. Our heads tilted towards the top of the stairs, waiting, listening.

"Bloody 'ell!" It was Will's voice. He sounded shocked.

"Don't touch anythin'." Pause. "We'll 'ave to tell 'er," Fred said. They were speaking quietly, almost reverently.

Eve and I exchanged wary glances. Silently we stood waiting, then, my mouth suddenly dry, I started woodenly up the stairs. Eve was right behind me. When I arrived on the landing and peered into my room from the doorway, Will was crouched, his back toward me. Fred was standing facing the door. Both men were staring down at something but when he noticed us, Fred glanced up quickly. Even through the white dust on his skin, I could see that his face was ashen, his eyes almost tragic.

"Don't—" Fred put his hand up as if stopping traffic. "You don't wanna come in 'ere, luv,"

Then Will turned. Was he on the verge of tears?

"What . . .?" I asked, advancing.

He stood up quickly to try to stop me. But it was too late. I was in my bedroom now. I could see into the gaping black hole in my bedroom floor by the closet. I could see everything now. The pieces of an ugly jigsaw puzzle slotted together in a quick flash and suddenly were gone again.

I fainted.

Ordinarily Mrs. Sykes was the kind of person who would pass through my world without stopping. We had nothing in common. Except Weeping Willow Cottage.

We were sitting in her front room in a small semi-detached in Bristol's outer suburbia. Eve had driven me there, not only because I was still an emotional mess but also because she was curious. Derek had made me promise to call him later while Chris, in his role as detective, had done what he did best—snoop. In fact, he had gone above and beyond in arranging this meeting between Mrs. Sykes and me. She had apparently been close-mouthed with the police and wouldn't entertain any reporters, but she had agreed to see me. Of course, Chris hadn't done this just out of concern for my sanity. I had the feeling that Mrs. Sykes was his Number One suspect, and he wanted to see what I would find out. But before we went to meet her—and for some reason he wouldn't divulge—Chris had been adamant that Eve and I use our surnames only. That's the deal, he had said. We agreed. Why not?

Eve and I were seated in two threadbare armchairs facing Mrs. Sykes who was slumped on a faded red couch. Wearing blue polyester pants and a woollen cardigan that had seen better days, she was staring past us out the bay window to the house opposite, a mirror image of her own home. In her hand, a green cup and saucer were shaking almost imperceptibly. Her husband, a large, untidy, unshaven man, sat by her side. His gentleness towards his wife contradicted his rough appearance.

"You okay, luv?" He put a thick-fingered hand on

her knee.

Mrs. Sykes pulled a face as if to say, *No, I'm not bloody all right but let's get it over with.*

"I'm sorry if this upsets you," I blurted, sickened by the feeling that I was responsible for having unearthed yet another horror, this second one emotional.

Mrs. Sykes snorted. "It always upsets me."

Her husband stood up. "Gotta get to work, luv." He bent and pecked her on the cheek. As he walked around our chairs, he glared at us. I was relieved when the door closed behind him.

Judging by her tightly permed gray-blonde hair and pallid skin, Mrs. Sykes was in her early fifties. She might have been pretty in her younger days, but a hardness had crept into her features, and her blue, flinty eyes betrayed an old hurt through the toughness. She let out a long sigh as she replaced her teacup on the chipped square coffee table and fumbled in her pocket for her cigarettes.

"Must have been a shock for you, dearie," she muttered, lighting up.

In some strange way, I felt as if my life had just begun last Wednesday, reborn as someone else. The terrible discovery seemed as if it had happened an eternity ago but the five long days had since been filled with questions, policemen, reporters but strangely enough, no nightmares. The police had removed Eve, Derek and me from the house as it was a crime scene. Not that I believed I could sleep in that cottage, especially that bedroom, ever again. Thankfully my friend Rosemary had welcomed me as a houseguest, while Derek was crashing with a friend until he was granted possession of his new house. Eve was tolerating life back at home with her parents.

Other ghastly nighttime dreams plagued me now. The macabre images hadn't left me alone since I first laid eyes on those gnarled, enmeshed bones, one tossed on top of the other like discarded trash, bits of faded, dusty fabric hanging from them. The female's skull, even without human eyes, lips, and teeth, was frozen in a long scream of terror as if begging for mercy. None had been given.

"Yes, it was a shock," I murmured.

Mrs. Sykes nodded, blowing smoke.

"The police believe that . . . they could be your parents?" Chris had told us they were still checking on dental matches.

"Oh, it's them all right, dearie." I thought I saw a smile on her lips.

Eve was staring at the woman. "How could you know? I mean . . . how could you be so sure?"

The woman didn't hesitate. "'Cause I know who did it."

Eve and I sat back in our chairs, waiting. Mrs. Sykes took another drag of her cigarette then ground the end into an ashtray already swimming with ash and lipstick-coated butts. Her rough hands turned the red and white cigarette packet in her lap over and over. The crackling cellophane and the ticking of a clock above the fireplace were the only sounds in the stale room.

"She did it," she stated with finality.

"She . . .?"

"My sister!" Mrs. Sykes snapped as if I should have known. "She killed the old man and woman. Those two skeletons were my . . . so-called mother and father."

Eve's voice softened as she asked, "Why? Why did she kill them?"

"'Cause they were bastards, that's why," she

snarled at Eve, her eyes glinting with hatred. Mrs. Sykes groped for another cigarette, her hands shaking as the flame touched the tip. "Bastards!" she repeated, exhaling a cloud of smoke.

A light trembling was taking over my body. What did this woman's parents do to evoke such a violent act? And in my house! I remembered—couldn't forget—the dented skull of the man, struck with an axe in his sleep, they said. Had it been him "breathing" in my bedroom closet? The woman's skeleton was distorted, broken. She had been hacked to death. I shuddered.

"Mrs. Sykes, I really don't want to pry but the reason we're here is because we need to understand what happened. Things . . . in the cottage . . . ."

She eyed us suspiciously for a moment as if we might be posing as reporters trying to worm the story out of her. But then she leaned forward. "So you really wanna know, do yer?"

I nodded slowly.

Mrs. Sykes pulled herself wearily up from the couch and walked towards the window, her shoulders hunched.

"I dunno who was worse," she told the window, crossing her arms, "the old man or her." She spat the last word out bitterly. "He started with me when I was eleven." There was a long hopeless sigh. "I tried to protect my sister from the old man but the bitch encouraged 'im." Her head was shaking as if she still couldn't believe it. "Crazy old slag!"

I gulped and shrugged at the same time, embarrassed. A small sound like a groan came out of Eve's mouth. "Couldn't you tell anyone?" Eve asked finally.

"Ha!" Mrs. Sykes turned to glare at Eve, then

moved towards us, pulling the tattered cardigan wide open, unfastening the top two buttons of her blouse. Small round scars, pink and shiny, littered the freckled skin above her breasts.

"Cigarette burns." She covered herself up again quickly. "That's why, dearie. If we so much as looked at 'er sideways, we'd get the cigarettes or the belt . . . or 'im." Eve and I exchanged shocked expressions. Mrs. Sykes returned to the window, her back to us again.

Part of me wanted to get out of there and not see the pictures that her words created in my mind, but some other force kept me pinned to my seat.

"I was the lucky one," she continued. "I got out of there when I was fifteen. Couldn't stand it. If I'd stayed, it would 'ave been me that killed 'em." Then, as if to herself, she said, "I wanted to take 'er with me. She was eleven . . . when I left."

"How old was your sister when she . . . did it?" I mumbled the question.

"Eighteen." None of us spoke for a long time. "I know what you're thinking," she sighed. "Why didn't she just leave, get the hell out o' there?"

Actually, I was wondering how an eighteen-year-old girl could overwhelm two people with an axe and then hide the mutilated, bloodied bodies under the bedroom floor all by herself.

"Wasn't that easy to get away, not for 'er. When you're in it, you forget you 'ave a choice." She was still talking to the window. "The old man wouldn't let 'er out of his sight. Dirty old bugger." Then she spun around. "You know 'ow it is." She shrugged, a sad, guilty smile on her face. "I told 'er when I got enough money for the both of us, I would go back for 'er."

Mrs. Sykes returned to the couch, adding another

stub to the ashtray's collection. Slumping down into the cushions, defeated, she said, "But by the time that 'appened, it was too late."

"Because of your parents, you mean?" I persisted.

"No." She fidgeted with the cigarette packet again. "My sister was dead."

"Oh, no. I'm so sorry," I offered lamely.

"How . . . ?" Eve probed.

"Suicide."

"My god . . . ." *This poor woman.*

"Because she had killed your parents?" Eve wasn't letting up.

"No." Suddenly her eyes glistened with tears. "Because those bastards wouldn't leave 'er alone, not even when they was dead. They 'aunted her." Mrs. Sykes' stony eyes found mine and held them. "Made 'er crazy, they did."

I took a large gulp of cold tea.

The older woman took out yet another cigarette and sucked on it as if it would give her breath. "We couldn't sell the place, see. Not then. Might 'ave raised some awkward questions."

"What about friends and neighbors? Weren't they suspicious when your parents disappeared?" I suddenly wondered if Eve had been primed by Chris to make "certain enquiries."

"No." She coughed. "The old man 'ad retired from 'is job in Nottingham and they'd just moved into that 'ouse when it 'appened. So nobody knew 'em. Not that they 'ad any friends anyway. My sister just told people that 'er folks 'ad gone abroad for a few years."

How convenient.

"Yer know," she pointed a stubby, nicotine-stained finger at me, "you look a little bit like 'er. She was very pretty. Too bad for 'er."

Eve stared at me. The old brown and white photo that Derek had found sat in my handbag but I made no move to take it out. I thought about my rage towards my own mother and father, often wishing they would just disappear and never taunt me again. But I had never considered murder.

"See, my sister talked about this young lad," Mrs. Sykes continued. "Kevin was 'is name. Sounds like she was in love with this young feller. 'E lived just up from 'er, she said, in one of them other cottages. When 'e didn't even say hello to 'er one day on the street, seems like it sent 'er into a real tizzy. Said 'e didn't care. No one ever would, she said."

I knew how that felt, being rejected. We sat in silence for a long time. The clock on the mantelpiece ticked relentlessly. In my mind, I was trying to superimpose Mrs. Sykes' tragic story over the ghostly occurrences, but some piece of the jigsaw was missing.

"Do you know how she . . .?" It was a gruesome question but I had to know.

"Killed 'em?" Mrs. Sykes picked up her teacup but it was empty so she replaced it on the table. "The old man went for 'is booze snooze, as we called it, every afternoon." She snorted, remembering. "My sister waited till Ma went out shopping and 'e was lying snoring away on the bed. Then she took 'is axe and smashed 'is brains in while he slept." I visualized the man lying on *my* bed in *my* bedroom and shivered. "'E didn't make a sound, she said, just the crunch of bone and gristle. Said she wanted to chop off 'is you-know-whats but decided there would be too much blood." A small smirk crept onto Mrs. Sykes' lips as if a bit more blood wouldn't have stopped *her*. "She waited in the bedroom closet for the old woman to come back. Waited two hours with the old man dead and bleedin' on the bed," she said as if her sister's patience was to be applauded.

Eve was transfixed by the older woman's story. I wanted to throw up.

"When Ma came back and saw 'im lying on the bed, blood everywhere, she didn't even 'ave time to scream or see what was comin'. My sister let 'er 'ave it. Told me she couldn't stop hacking at her even after the old woman was long dead. There was so much 'ate in her, she said." Mrs. Sykes took another drag. "I think she detested the old woman the most."

"Didn't anyone smell the bodies rotting under the floorboards?" Eve asked. *My friend would make a good detective herself,* I thought.

"She sprinkled 'em with lime. Gets rid of the smell, dearie," she responded as if giving us a gardening tip.

"How do you know all this?" Eve probed.

Mrs. Sykes reached into her trouser pocket, pulling out a piece of paper, folded into four, the corners curling up as if it had been read many, many times.

"She sent me this." She held the letter up. "I got it the day after she died." She caressed the paper. "Said she was going mad. Couldn't stand living in that 'ouse with . . . them."

Their ghosts?

"How long was it after . . . ?" Eve didn't have to finish. Mrs. Sykes expected each question as if she had been waiting many years for this interrogation.

"Seven years." The older woman shook her head. "Just twenty-five, she was. We was goin' to declare them missing an' sell that 'ouse. She was nearly 'ome free. If only she could 'ave waited a little longer . . . but the snorin', the bad dreams, doors slammin' an' such were makin' 'er loony." She pulled her cardigan around her tightly as if for protection. "After she died, I sold that 'ouse lickety split."

I studied the tea leaves at the bottom of my cup as if they would hold the answer to my question. *Why had that house picked me as a conduit to uncover its tragic history?* No answer came, just that familiar disturbed gnawing feeling that somewhere deep inside me I did know but I was refusing to see.

"It was when she found out," Mrs. Sykes was saying, "that this Kevin 'ad married some other girl. That's what finally sent 'er over the edge."

A long tip of gray ash dangled from the end of her cigarette but she didn't move. "She tried to hang 'erself from the light fixture on the landing but either it didn't work or she fell." There were no tears from Mrs. Sykes. I suspected she was done crying a long time ago. "It was me that found 'er at the bottom of the stairs with a broken neck."

Eve turned to me, eyes wide. I could tell what she was thinking. *The light bulb. Bonk, bonk, bonk.*

The ash finally fell into Mrs. Sykes' lap and she let it sit there. The woman was spent. Her shoulders sagged now.

"Mrs. Sykes, I'm terribly sorry for . . . ." What should I say? For the cruelty of her mother and father, the loss of her sister, or finding the bones of her slain parents under my bedroom floor, forcing her to relive all of this pain.

She waved a hand. "It's all right, dearie." She stood up with a weariness that would probably never go away. The interview was done. As she ushered us towards the door, she sighed, "It's over now, isn't it?"

Is it? I wondered about the ghosts, the nightmares. Were they gone?

As she opened the front door, she said, "And maybe now Samantha can rest in peace."

Eve and I stopped and turned. "Who?" we asked simultaneously.

"My sister."

"Is this her?" I asked, fumbling in my handbag for the aged photograph.

Mrs. Sykes studied the pretty face, grimaced, and nodded. "Yeah, that's Samantha, all right. Where did you find that?"

Of course, it was Derek who finally connected all the dots for me. Later that evening, he pulled up in front of Rosemary's house.

"Is it okay if we just go to the Plough?" he suggested. As I climbed into his Renault, he threw a concerned glance at me. I was still stunned and pale from the day's revelations.

"Fine." I shrugged. Although the pub produced excellent fresh homemade delights, I didn't know if I could eat.

As we drove in silence through the gold-tinged Buckinghamshire countryside, I was still sorting out the jigsaw pieces of the puzzle. Derek finally broke the silence. "You don't 'ave ter talk about it, you know, Not if . . . ." he said softly.

"No, I do. It's just that . . . it's all so horrible, I don't know where to start."

"The beginnin' seems like as good a place to me." Derek grinned at me and I instantly felt lighter.

By the time the car pulled up in front of the Tudor-style pub, I was still relating the whole ghastly business of the two victimized girls, the physical and sexual abuse, and the murders. Derek didn't move after he switched off the engine but just sat there and listened. When I was spent, he whistled through his teeth. "Bloody 'ell!"

I still couldn't bring myself to admit that the axe murderess and I shared the same name, not just yet. "I think we need that drink." Derek opened my door for me. "C'mon, my dear."

In the darkened pub, he led me to a low soft couch by the fireplace. Midweek the establishment was relatively quiet, and I was glad. Derek brought two glasses of wine over and we sank back into the comfort of the floral sofa, sipping our drinks in silence and staring into the fire.

"It doesn't make sense," Derek said after a while.

"What?"

"Well, why did the ghost pick you, chuck? I mean to buy that house, to be the one to unearth those bones. It were all because of you."

"Because we shared the same name." I blurted, staring into Derek's puzzled face. "Her name was Samantha."

"Bloody 'ell!" he exclaimed once more, his eyes huge.

We sat in silence again, the fire crackling as the bartender added logs to the dying flames.

Derek sat up suddenly. "Yeah, but there's something else . ."

Instinctively, I knew I didn't want to hear any more, but Derek was concentrating on the fire as if the answers were in the flames.

"When did your nightmares begin?" he asked.

"About six months after I moved in . . . but I think . . . ." Suddenly I knew where Derek's mind was going.

55

"About the same time the snorin' stopped? Right?"

"Yes, but . . . ."

"Maybe they weren't nightmares, chuck." He squeezed my hand urgently but tenderly.

I heard myself take a short, sharp breath and something came crashing down all around me. "What do you mean?" For the second time that day, thick bile rose in my throat.

As Derek moved closer to me on the couch and took both my hands in his, I was shaking all over. "You don't want me to say it, do yer?"

As I looked into his eyes, I saw that he knew! Oh my God, Derek knew what I hadn't even wanted to consider, what Dr. Smythe had urged me to admit—that for the last two and a half years I had been raped by a ghost.

"Oh God . . . ." I collapsed then, covering my face with both hands, allowing my head to rest on Derek's shoulder. "Oh God." The full horror of my invisible sexual predator—Samantha's monstrous father buried just six feet from my bed and violating me in the night—spilled out of me in long, deep, violent shudders.

Derek put his arms around me and pulled me to him as I sobbed and sobbed, oblivious to the curious stares of the bartender. With each shudder and Derek's warmth, I felt as if I was releasing that repulsive energy from me, that it was leaving my body, and that it would no longer have any hold over me. I was being cleansed. Everything was suddenly clear. I was me again.

When at last I sat up and attempted to wipe the streaked mascara from my face, Derek offered me his clean handkerchief.

I'm sorry," he said, laying a warm hand on my

back. "It's over now, Sam. You won't ever 'ave those . . . visitations again."

"God, I hope not," I said, still attempting to regain my dignity and push my unkempt hair back into place. It was like being told I wasn't nuts all over again. Sweet, sweet Derek.

"The nightmares only 'appened in the cottage, didn't they? So they belong to the cottage, not you. And I think you've laid those ghosts to rest now." He put the wine glass in my hand. "You're not thinkin' 'bout moving back in, are you?"

"I don't know what I'm going to do," I moaned.

Derek covered my left hand lying dormant in my lap. "I 'ave an idea, Sam," he said. "But you may want to think about it," he added shyly.

"What's that, Derek?" I smiled at him then. Even in the midst of all this, he could still make me smile.

He took a deep breath. "Well, I thought you might like to come and live with me, my dear."

"You mean in your new place?" I grinned at his earnest face.

"Aye."

"You mean, as your flat mate?" I smiled, teasing him.

"Well, we'll see." His coyness was irresistible.

"And what shall we do about my haunted cottage?"

"Oh," Derek waved a hand and grinned mischievously, "you can sell that to some American who 'as to 'ave central 'eatin'." He grinned. "Then you could charge double for the ghosts."

And for the first time in a very long time, I heard myself laugh out loud.

3

SUMMER DREAM

Diane relished the quiet after the pandemonium. She loved her two daughters dearly but was always grateful when her husband, Mike, offered to take them out on the boat fishing. She watched from the patio of her parents' expansive summer home as the three of them cautiously descended the rocky path to the dock below. She smiled as she watched Lisa, her chubby seven-year-old, push her older sister Jeannie into the small dinghy. They owned a larger speedboat but Mike and the girls chose the grey Zodiac for their fishing expeditions. As sisters went, they were reasonably good friends. Lisa preferred her father's company to her sister's, a partiality her mother thought unusual for such a young girl. Maybe it was because Lisa was such an old soul. *So much uncanny knowing in that little girl,* Diane thought. *It's almost challenging. She certainly doesn't get her wisdom from me.*

The dark green water was calm, and an array of boats bobbed and buzzed in and out of the inlet. Diane sighed contentedly. She would make the most of her quiet time.

The sun was high in the pale blue August sky but an early afternoon haze lay indolently on the horizon. Diane stretched out on the old familiar blue and white chaise longue. *This chair is like my body,* she thought wryly, *starting to sag in the middle.* What had her naturopath told her? Buddhists believe that until the age of forty, we live for the physical aspects of life, and after that our purpose is to acquire wisdom. *At thirty-eight, the physical was definitely on its way out,* she thought, *but I'm not sure if the wisdom is anywhere in sight.*

Recently she had begun to feel a need to deepen her spirituality. Compared to Lisa who exuded the wisdom of a little Buddha, Diane knew she was just at the beginning of her journey. Often her daughter opened her mouth and jewels of mature insight poured forth, leaving Diane aghast and wondering if there hadn't been a mix-up at the hospital. Was this little girl really her daughter? But the intense brown eyes and high cheekbones, almost a clone of her father's features, allayed any doubts as to her heritage. Maybe that's why Lisa and Mike were so close. They were reflections of each other.

Diane also wanted to be closer to Lisa. Maybe then she wouldn't feel so excluded from Lisa and Mike's connection. But that wasn't the only reason for her desire to dig deeper. The uneasiness was something she just could not place.

Her sudden interest in spiritual matters wasn't only in response to a new emptiness she was feeling. Surely there had to be more. More of what, she didn't know. Just more. Was she losing her grip on her marriage? She hoped not though the closeness she and Mike had previously enjoyed was strained. Now it seemed they were floating farther and farther away from each other.

After lathering herself from head to toe in #15 Hawaiian Tropic while trying not to take inventory of her numerous body flaws, she lay back and allowed the warmth of the sun to seep into her weary muscles. With two children, a husband, a large home, and her own work as a court reporter, she had to admit that relaxation wasn't the strongest word in her vocabulary. "I wish time would stand still so I could catch up," she had complained out loud one day to which Lisa had piped up, "But, Mummy, time doesn't really exist. It's just space, and there's lots of that."

"Eleanor! Eleanor!" Her father's gravelly voice called from upstairs. Though Diane could come to her parents' retreat whenever she wanted, they all spent at least one week a year together. It was tradition. Unfortunately, this week her father had contracted a nasty flu virus and he was still convalescing in his bedroom. Diane heard footsteps as her mother scurried halfway up the spiral wooden staircase that rose out of the living room.

"What is it, dear?" her mother called up.

"How about some tea?" came her father's muffled answer.

A few minutes later, Eleanor suddenly appeared between the sliding glass doors of the living room, one foot out on the patio. "I'm taking tea up to your father," she announced. "Would you like one, dear?"

"Yes, that would be lovely," Diane responded, sitting up and propping herself on one elbow. She reached for *The Course in Miracles* lying open on the white plastic table. Maybe she would read the book in peace and finally understand its concepts. But as she stared at the page—her own mind brimming with too many thoughts—the words conveyed no meaning. They were just black ink on white paper.

She settled back, allowing the book to lie open on her stomach. As she closed her eyes, she was aware of the faint chatter from the television inside the house and the lapping of water against the rocks below. The occasional squawk of seagulls reminded her of a carefree childhood when she had come to this same summer house with her parents and older sister. Just like Jeannie and Lisa, Diane and her sister had spent hours scrambling over the rocks, engrossed in the search for crabs or buried treasure until their father would beckon them to go out on the boat fishing. Happy days.

Now, she was always on the run. She didn't enjoy having these sour feelings, especially toward Mike and, she suddenly realized, toward her own daughter. Whatever it was, something . . . something big had changed between her and her husband. Even when the passion of their first married days had waned, they had settled into a loving friendship, good partners working side by side. Even that harmony had evaporated. Every time they fought about something small, the discussion escalated into an argument as if . . .? As if what? As if he didn't need her? Or she didn't trust him. *Did she trust him?* Yes, she trusted Mike. Not only was he a good provider but he was so loving with their daughters, especially Lisa.

As Eleanor reappeared, white mug of tea in hand, Diane placed the book back on the table. "Thanks, Mum. I'm going to have a snooze, I think," she told her mother, squinting at her through the sunshine. "Will you be okay?"

"Oh, yes, dear." She chuckled. "There's an old Fred Astaire movie I want to watch. I may even have a little nap myself." As Eleanor was about to fade into the darkened living room, she turned and laughing, said, "Rest in peace."

Diane melted back into the chair, sipping on the hot steaming liquid, her mind drifting back to Mike. *How do you get that feeling back?* she questioned. *Was it possible?* Maybe this week at the cottage they would revitalize some romantic feelings. She laid her head back.

The warmth of the sun was soothing and soon she drifted into a deep sleep.

Suddenly she jerked in the chair. She didn't know what had awakened her. How long had she been asleep? The hands on her watch told her it was almost three o'clock but the hands weren't moving. She shook the watch. Nothing. *It must be at least four-thirty,* she thought. They would be back soon. She listened. Everything was peaceful. In fact, it was silent. She sat up, straining her ears to hear the television, but there was only quiet. *Maybe Mum decided to go and have a nap after all.* But even the ever-present lapping waves on the rocks below had ceased. *That's strange,* she mused. The silence was almost heavy.

Slowly, she pulled her legs over the side of the chair and tried to stand. But her body didn't want to move, as if a strong magnet were keeping her pinned down. She struggled against the heaviness and with every ounce of strength finally pushed herself to a standing position. Once erect, the muscles in her body felt like dead weight. It occurred to her that maybe she had succumbed to her father's flu.

She surveyed the scene from the patio. Something struck her as strange about the image, like one of those contests where you have to spot the deliberate mistake. At first she couldn't pinpoint what was so *odd.*

Everything was so . . . still. The breeze that had been wafting across her body as she fell asleep had been replaced with a stifling thickness. She stepped carefully over to the chipped railing that surrounded the patio. Her eyes searched the hillside below covered in sturdy evergreen undergrowth. She squinted at the old dock and the murky green water of the inlet. When she had last looked, the harbor had been a hive of activity. Now it was a still life with not a person in sight.

Panic rose like bile in her throat. She turned and ran into the house, nearly tripping over one of her daughter's rubber thong sandals. In the cool of the living room, images were still flickering mutely on the television screen. Eleanor was not there.

Diane darted up the stairs. Normally when in the house, she was careful to cover her bikini-clad body, but now all she wanted was the familiar comforting sight of people . . . a person . . . anyone.

The solid oak doors of her Mum and Dad's room were closed. *They must both be sleeping,* Diane assumed, her ear against one of the doors. Carefully, she turned the brass doorknob and peeked into the yellow-walled room. She stopped, puzzled. The bed was neatly made. No traces of her parents' recent presence lingered. She threw the door wide and strode across to the ensuite bathroom.

She stared unbelievingly at the white bathroom countertop, sterile and empty of her mother's cosmetics, creams and her father's toiletry bag.

"Where *are* they?" Diane demanded of the bedroom walls as if they could break the awful silence. Her father was so sick, why would he go out? Of course, maybe her mother had finally taken him to the doctor or maybe they had even decided to return home. She would find a note on the kitchen counter. They always advised Diane and Mike of their movements. She ran out of the room and back down the stairs.

There was no note.

But something else lay on the tiled kitchen island. Diane didn't recognize the object but somehow she knew it was meant for her. Tentatively she picked up the chain and cradled the silver heart-shaped locket in her right hand. The piece was eerily familiar, but Diane knew she had never seen it before. She held her breath and slowly undid the delicate, laced clip that held it shut. The locket flipped open almost by itself. She inhaled quickly. On the right side was a photo of Mike, a little greyer, thinner, older, but with a woman. Diane took a moment to realize the woman wasn't her. She was Diane's age, had dark hair like Diane, and brown eyes. But this woman was definitely not her.

What she saw in the left side picture took her breath away. Two girls, Lisa and Jeannie, *her* two girls, but maybe five years older than now beamed at her from the locket. Between them was a very young boy. He had the eyes of this stranger posing as Mike's wife. *Had she, Diane, died and she didn't know it?*

A deep sob escaped her and echoed around the vacant house. She wanted to throw the locket away or smash it to bits on the kitchen counter but she just slammed her clenched fist on the tiled surface. How cruel that her family was being taken away from her. She didn't deserve to lose them.

Or did she?

Pull yourself together, Diane. She clutched the locket, evil as it was, in her right palm. What was he trying to do to her? Make her go insane?

She wandered, stunned, back out onto the patio, her head spinning with images that made no sense. What was happening? Where was everybody? Where were all the boats? Was everyone conspiring to play an elaborate, scary joke on her? Maybe she *had* died and someone had forgotten to tell her.

Then she remembered her children. *Ohmigod, where are they?* With only images of the girls' faces in her mind, she ran blindly down the path and, barefoot, clambered over the rocks, praying aloud as she went that she would see them in the Zodiac coming back, her husband steering from the stern.

But as she ran down the dock, its familiar bounce under her feet, she knew with a chilling certainty that they wouldn't be there. She was alone.

Diane stood on the wet boards, struggling to keep calm, to not let panic take hold. She swiveled around, scrutinizing the coastal waters. An archipelago of evergreen-covered hills surrounded her; white summer cottages nestled in the trees overlooking the water. Everything was ominously tranquil. No human movements disturbed the still life. Just one boat bobbed almost imperceptibly on the water. Old Nelson's clinker-built, battered fishing vessel was moored in its usual resting place, uncharacteristically serene on the island opposite. A much thicker crust of barnacles clung to its bottom than she remembered.

"Where are you?" she screamed at the top of her voice. She knew her cry was a feeble attempt to defy the quiet that was becoming heavier and heavier. But the thick silence threatened to crush and swallow her. Her voice only echoed around the stillness of the empty inlet. *Someone* must be in one of the houses. "Maybe I am going insane and I don't know it?" she muttered. "I know. The Stephens!" she cried, desperation in her voice. "The Stephens will be home."

She turned and ran up the dock then up the path, oblivious to the pain and cuts caused by rough rocks on her bare feet and her ever-increasing shortness of breath. Joan and Albert Stephens had lived next door ever since Diane could remember. They were very good friends of her parents and considered themselves extended family. Now in their early eighties, they spent their time puttering around their well-manicured and colorful garden.

"They have to be there." she repeated to herself, almost breathless. "They were home this morning." She hesitated to go through her own house, which was now dark and empty and . . . menacing. Instead she stumbled into the scraggly undergrowth along their neighbor's fence unaware of the multitude of thin bloody scratches now criss-crossing her bare shins.

She called over into their property. "Joan! Albert! " Diane yelled, hearing the hysteria in her own voice. She didn't know what she would do if they weren't home. Her other closest neighbors were miles away. "Jo-a-n!" she cried again. She expected her white-haired neighbor to pop her head up from one of the flowerbeds, trowel in hand, "Yes, dear?" But no reply came. No movement in the house either. "Well, maybe they're having an early dinner," Diane told herself and climbed gingerly over the fence, trying not to crush the delicate flowers. Though the familiarity of their sweet scent would normally have comforted her, when she stood directly above the deep colored roses, the intense perfume was sickening. She suppressed the wave of nausea that threatened to overtake her. Diane also noticed that the customary host of butterflies and bees that swarmed the masses of sweat peas that adorned their back fence was now absent. And the roses were growing wilder.

As she walked around to the front of the quaint cottage, Diane expected to see the familiar lace curtains at the wooden door and a butterfly mobile hanging in the kitchen window. But something was different. *What was it?* The curtains were now blue and no mobile dangled anywhere in sight.

Diane sensed the same lack of life that pervaded her parent's summer home, as if the whole world were filled with a suffocating heaviness. At the wooden front door, she took the cumbersome brass doorknocker in hand and rapped twice. The noise reverberated around the quiet garden.

No one came to the door.

Their blue Lincoln was also absent from the driveway.

On the side of the house, she peeked through the kitchen window. Pots sat on an unlit stove, fresh green vegetables lay half-prepared on a chopping board. An apron was slung over a kitchen chair. Although the scene reminded her of a painting, eerily frozen in time, something about the picture also struck Diane as unfamiliar, chaotic, as if the inhabitants had left suddenly and in a state of panic.

She knew that their bedroom was on the other side of the house. *Maybe one of them had taken ill?* she thought. She needed to reassure herself that she wasn't going crazy. She carried on around the side of the cottage to the back. At first, she couldn't see into the bedroom because thick blue curtains obscured her vision. Then she saw that the bed was made but the usual display of lace-covered pillows had been replaced with large blue and white striped satin cushions. *Perhaps the older couple had redecorated and vacated?* But just yesterday she had waved to them across the fence. They would have told her if they had had plans to leave.

Diane sank to the ground and put her head in her hands. Suddenly aware of her scratched, half-naked body, she sobbed. Where *was* everyone? Had they all been spirited away except her? And why was everything somehow different? Had there been some kind of invasion from outer space, or maybe they had heard terrible news and all left without her? What if she were alone for the rest of her life?

As she lifted her head, she saw her neighbor's vista of the inlet. She searched the horizon again.

Oh Mike. An overwhelming ache for her husband surged through her. He had always been there for her, she realized, during the crises in their fourteen years of marriage. Ever the rock, he would silently put his strong arms around her and hold her when she needed comforting, sometimes even before she was aware that she sought reassurance. She depended on him to know her, not to have to explain things to him. He was a good man. Whatever this thing was that had come between them had to be resolved. Was she the problem? Tears rolled freely down her cheeks.

Of course, it was remorse. How many times had she snapped at him impatiently because he was uncommunicative or because he had scattered his oily tools on the kitchen counter or left his socks on the bedroom floor? Or because he had taken Lisa's side in arguments.

Lisa. Was she jealous of Lisa? With horror, she realized the recent gulf between them had been aggravated by his apparent favoritism toward their younger daughter. "How could I have been so awful? I'll make it up to him . . . and to Lisa," she said out loud, the words sounding odd in the silence. "That's if I ever see him and the girls again."

Suddenly terribly weary and with an overwhelming urge to sleep, she got to her feet and retraced her steps to her parent's house. Once through the gate and the thick undergrowth, all she wanted to do was lie down again and sleep in her own bed. But she was too tired to climb those stairs. She would just rest on the chaise longue for a while. She pulled a light blanket over her bloodied legs and feet. This mystery could all be figured out later but now she just had to sleep. She was so, so tired.

"Mummy, Mummy, wake up." Lisa's voice sounded close.

Diane slowly opened her eyes. Her daughter was shaking her by the shoulder, her rosy cheeks illuminated with excitement. Jeannie was standing behind Lisa, equally pleased with herself. Disoriented, Diane tried to remember . . . . Something had happened this afternoon . . . or was it before, a long time ago. Then it all came back in a rush: the terrible silence, everyone disappearing, the boats, the terror of being all alone.

"Oh, thank god, you're all right!" Diane exclaimed, pulling Lisa to her. "Where's Daddy?"

Jeannie looked on, mystified by her mother's sudden, fierce affection.

"He's taking care of the boat," Lisa responded, as if her mother should have known that.

It must have all been a bad dream, Diane thought. *Of course, it was just a dream.*

"Mummy, look what we caught." Lisa proudly held up the smelly bucket for her mother to see. "I got the first fishes and they're bigger than Jeannie's."

Diane raised herself and peeked inside. She saw four dark brown things with corrugated fins and blank staring eyes, three of them lying inert, one of them still thrashing spasmodically, fighting for the last breath of life. *How awful to be the last one alive,* she thought.

"Very good." Diane tried to sound enthusiastic but the sight of a poor creature in the final throes of death was the one aspect of fishing that had always disturbed her. Nature could be cruel, she thought. Did people die when fate threw them a hook or was there something within that drew them to their own demise?

Mike appeared at the top of the path, his lithe movements contradicting his large frame. He was smiling to himself as he took in the scene of his two daughters showing off their catches to their mother.

"Mike!" Diane called happily to him, as if she hadn't seen him in years. She sat up and opened her arms. "I'm so glad you're back." Surprised, her husband came over and squatted beside by her chaise.

"Are you okay?" he asked, holding her shoulders and searching her eyes.

"I'm fine . . . now. I just had a really horrible dream, that's all." Diane moved over and invited her husband to sit beside her. "Please," she turned to Mike as he sat down. "Just hold me." As Mike placed an arm around his wife's shoulders, Diane leaned in and buried her head against his wide chest, his familiar smell comforting her.

"What was the dream about?" he inquired, gently stroking her hair.

She noticed Lisa hovering, listening. "I'll tell you later." She looked up into Mike's concerned blue eyes. "I know I haven't told you in a while but I do love you, Mike . . . very much."

"I know," he said quietly and pulled her to him again.

"Can we have pizza for dinner, Mummy?" Jeannie exclaimed, breaking the spell.

"No. I want to eat my fish," Lisa chimed in.

"I've already made pizza, you two," Diane told them. "We'll freeze the fish. Now go run a bath and get changed out of those smelly clothes."

The girls obediently entered the house, arguing about who had caught the biggest fish.

Diane started to sit up. "You stay put," Mike said,

pulling himself up. "It's only three-thirty. The girls can watch a movie for a while. "

"What?" Diane exclaimed. "But I thought . . . . How long were you gone?"

"Not long. Your daughter insisted we come back early." He smiled. "Lisa said she had a bad feeling about Mummy being alone. Don't know what I'm going to do with that psychic child of yours," he muttered, shaking his head. He picked up the bucket. The last fish, she noticed, was still twitching, almost imperceptibly now.

Mike smiled down at Diane. "I'd better get those corpses taken care of before they start to stink," he said. "Okay?"

Diane smiled. "Yes, that would be good."

After her husband had disappeared into the darkness of the living room, Diane lay back on the chair, struggling to make sense of her afternoon nightmare. What was it that Lisa had said once about dreams? Oh, yes. "Mummy, I think dreams are the real bits and everything else is just pretend." *I wonder if that includes nightmares.*

Just as she was about to make a move to get up, Lisa appeared in the frame of the patio door.

"Are you okay, Mum?" the little girl asked.

Diane wanted to avoid her daughter's piercing gaze but she reminded herself Lisa was just a little girl. "Yes, sweetie . . . I just had a bad dream . . . but I'm okay now."

"What was the dream about?"

"Oh . . ." How could she explain it to her seven-year-old?

"I had a feeling that you were all alone," Lisa offered.

"You and your feelings." Diane smiled at her

youngest. "I think I'll go down to the dock for a while," she said, starting to lift the blanket that was covering the lower half of her body. An old childhood habit of sitting on the pier boards and dangling her feet in the cool green waters had always been something she did when she needed to think. "Do you want to come with me, Lisa-loo?"

"I think I should," Lisa responded, sounding more like Diane's mother than her child.

As Diane pulled the blanket back and swung her legs over onto the deck, something metallic fell out of the folds onto the wooden plank. Lisa asked calmly, "What happened to your legs, Mum?"

Diane glanced down, first at her legs and then at the locket lying open by her foot. Her knees, ankles, and feet were covered in a mass of tiny red scratches, and two pictures stared up at her, threatening, daring, challenging.

"Ohmigod!" Searching for solidity in her world, Diane clasped the corroded frame of the chaise longue. Was the dream real? Which was which? *Reality or dream? Dream or reality?* She glanced up at her daughter standing there in the doorway, a knowing look in her eyes.

"Did they show you?" Lisa asked, not sounding like a child—her daughter—at all.

"Show me what?" Diane's heart was thumping in her chest.

"The In-Between."

In between? "I . . . what do you mean, Lisa honey?" Her daughter's eyes became distant, darkening almost to black.

Diane shivered.

"The In-Between World is where we show you your possible futures," Lisa responded, her voice sonorous, echoing.

Deep inside Diane, a vague but newly familiar trembling began.

"It's what will happen," her daughter continued in that eerie voice, her eyes now a soulless jet black, "if you don't do what we want."

4

DEADHEADERS

"Tell us a story!" It was a familiar request when I put Julie and Markus to bed. All three of us were squidged on Julie's narrow four-poster, lying in the almost-dark with just the light from the hallway casting shadows onto the bedroom walls. While I affectionately called Julie and Markus my "adopted children," they were officially the children of my house-mate, Stephen.

I was still grieving after the death of my fiancée one year previously. Just days after proposing, Peter had died very suddenly. Heart attack. Gone, just like that. A genetic weakness, the autopsy had revealed. Nothing could have, would have, saved him as it was one of those untraceable conditions. With Peter went my dream of a family, children, and all the other plans we had made for a new life together. Now my biological clock had ceased to tick and I had no desire to entertain another relationship. Ten months after his passing, I had moved to another community where I was a complete unknown. With my flight attendant days long behind me, I was now making my living from an online consultancy business and had the luxury of living anywhere with internet access.

Not knowing a soul in this country village—which is the way I had wanted it—I had bought an old, remote three-bedroom cottage. My new home sat hidden in a dense copse of silver birch trees and was only accessible by a winding unpaved driveway, which gave me the privacy I craved. Resenting other people's happiness, I did not encourage curious neighbors to visit asking painful questions. As Greta Garbo used to intone, "I vont to be alo-o-o-ne." And I vonted the same thing.

But after two months of arranging then rearranging the furniture, I began to feel like a ghost rattling around in my own home. Maybe, I thought, I should rent out one or two vacant rooms. The thought, however, of placing an ad in the paper and having potentially weird strangers show up at my door was something I couldn't face. So I resigned myself to living with the ever-palpable silence.

It was Tuesday. A thick early morning mist lay over the fields in front of my home. My coffee had gone cold at my computer desk. While on my way to the kitchen to top it off with hotter liquid, I heard a tentative knock at the door. I stopped, put the mug down on the kitchen counter, and listened. Another knock, firmer this time.

Maybe it was the guy from the tree-topping service I had spoken to last week. Even now in early summer, the winds howled around the house some nights and the taller, weaker trees leaned precariously close to the roof. *Darn!* Hadn't I asked him to call first? As I opened the door, my stomach churned with a mixture of excitement and fear and I didn't know why.

The forty-something man smiled back at me shyly. He was flanked by two children, a girl and a boy. Both under ten, I guessed. Though the children were clean and well dressed and the father was elegant, they all emanated a feeling of . . . what was it . . . being lost? Then both children beamed up at me. Instantly I felt a sense of both empathy and déjà-vu, as if I had been waiting for them to show up.

"Can I help you?" I asked the man, sure that they

were simply looking for directions.

"Well, I heard that you might be renting rooms?"

"Oh . . . er . . . you did?" I couldn't remember mentioning the thought out loud to anyone. How had he heard? "Well . . . er . . . ." I was stalling for time, trying to make a decision. Then glancing down at the children, I heard words coming out of my mouth as if spoken by someone else. "Yes, I am actually. Would you like to see them?"

As if remotely programmed, I stepped back, allowing the small troupe to enter my sanctuary. I turned and led the way to the back of the cottage, indicating through the open doors the two vacant bedrooms. The beds were made up and furniture arranged, I realized, as if the rooms had been waiting for this particular family to arrive.

Stephen told me his story. We soon discovered that we shared a commonality. A year ago, the whole family was involved in a bad car accident. He was driving. The children had been fighting in the back seat and Stephen had been distracted, just for a moment. His wife had died. Since then, they had apparently been staying with the children's grandparents on the other side of the country. But now Stephen wanted to begin again in a new place where nobody knew their background and there were no memories. I understood.

We easily meshed into a family unit. Anyone could see that Stephen was still suffering from not just the trauma but also the self-recriminations of causing the loss of his children's mother. The children clung to me, an accidental surrogate mother, strangely shunning any outside contact even with other children, putting off the thought that they would, after summer was over, have to go to school. And in my way, I clung to them, a respite from the constant pain of unfulfilled dreams. We were unwitting consolers of our individual grieving. Yes, we all enjoyed our collective isolation from the intrusions and pain of the outside world.

Now three weeks later, we had lapsed into a nightly ritual of bedtime stories.

"What kind of story do you want?" I asked. "A tale from my flying days, a scary story, or the adventures of my childhood?"

"Mmmm . . . flying," ten-year-old Julie decided.

"No, scary," Marcus, her younger brother, chipped in, just taking his thumb out of his mouth long enough to speak and then sucking on it furiously again.

With the loss he had already endured in his seven short years, I was beginning to despair of his ever giving up thumb-sucking. Gloves, hot mustard, and his father's constant reprimand, "Thumb!" weren't working.

"How about scary *and* flying?" I suggested. Anything to avoid an argument.

"Okay," Julie and Markus responded in unison, getting more comfortable. As they trampled over me to find a cozy spot, totally oblivious to my sensitive body parts, they giggled in anticipation.

"Ow! That hurts." I grimaced as Julie stepped on my ankle and finally nestled into my side.

"Sorry," she apologized, not sorry at all.

This is a true story of a deadheader, I started.

"What's a deadheader?" Markus asked, burrowing his head into my lap.

"Well, when I was a flight attendant, deadheaders were airline crew members who had worked their maximum number of hours so they had to fly home as passengers, either on an empty aircraft or on another passenger flight. But this story is about a completely different kind of deadheader."

They both nodded. I wasn't sure they understood but I continued anyway.

This particular flight was headed from London to New York, which is about a five to seven-hour flight, depending on the winds.

"Were you on this flight?" Julie always needed to know if I was actually there.

"No, this happened to a friend of a friend of mine."

"Oh." Markus sounded a little disappointed.

"What was her name?" Julie wanted to know.

"Rosemary."

Satisfied, she snuggled down again.

"Now, where was I? Oh, yes. *They were on a DC-10, which holds three hundred and fifty passengers plus ten to twelve cabin crew. It was about two hours into the flight. Dinner had just been served, and the stewards and stewardesses were pouring tea and coffee in the cabin. Suddenly they heard a piercing shriek from the rear galley. The only person back there was Rosemary, who was making the hot beverages. "Aaagh, aaagh!" she screamed again and then broke into hysterical sobs.*

Julie and Markus sat up, eyes wide. The thumb-sucking was even louder.

In the last few rows of seats heads swiveled around with worried faces, alarmed to see the stewardess collapsed against one of the toilet doors at the back of the plane.

The steward who was serving coffee in the rear cabin rushed back to the galley.

"She's probably just seen next month's roster," he joked reassuringly with passengers as he went to the rear. "What on earth's the matter, dearie?" he asked the

distraught young woman as he set the coffeepot down on the metal counter. "Calm down. You're scaring the passengers half to death."

Simon—that was the steward's name—glanced around the rear of the aircraft. He couldn't see anything or anybody that could cause her to be so upset. But Rosemary was sobbing and shaking uncontrollably.

"Sssh," Simon hissed. "It's all right. Come and sit down." He guided Rosemary to the closest jump seat where she crumpled in a heap. Her usually serene expression had transformed into one of terror, and she was trembling violently.

Airline crew are not allowed to drink alcohol while on duty or eight hours before flying, but the steward decided this crew member needed a drink fast to soothe her nerves. He poured a generous shot of brandy into a plastic cup of black coffee and handed it to her.

Rosemary, still pale and trembling, took a couple of gulps of the burning liquid. After a few minutes, her shaking subsided and she became more composed. While she sat there clutching the warm cup, Simon took both the tea and coffee pots and hurried up and down the rear cabin. Once he had served all passengers their first after-dinner beverage, he returned to the jump seat and knelt down beside her.

"Now, can you tell me what happened?"

"This man," Rosemary gulped, starting to shake again. "I . . . I was making the coffee and I felt this really icy cold draft come over me." She paused, shivered, and stared at the door, remembering. "I thought for a moment that one of the rear doors had come open somehow. I know . . . that's impossible . . . but . . . . So I turned around. And what I saw was . . ." she faltered, squeezing the still warm plastic cup between her hands.

"Yes? Yes? What did you see?" the steward urged. "Second coffees, remember? The crowd is getting ugly out there."

"This . . . this . . . man was in a . . . gray suit, and I watched as he just walked . . ." Rosemary exhaled a shaky breath, "he just walked up to the door and . . . then . . . disappeared. He just disappeared through the fuselage, right through the door!" Her eyes were huge with fright.

Simon didn't know what to say. "What did he look like?" he asked, humoring her slightly, wondering if she had been flying too long. Or not long enough.

"He was tall, six-two maybe, slim, very slim. He was wearing an expensive gray suit, short gray hair, about fifty-five, somewhere in there. He looked quite . . . distinguished."

"Mmm, I see." Simon considered his options. He couldn't argue with her, and he wasn't quite sure what to believe. He didn't know if he even believed in ghosts, if that is what Rosemary had seen. He had flown with her several times, and she had never seemed like the neurotic type. Had she just suddenly gone nuts or had she really seen an apparition?

"Why don't you just stay here, sweetie. I'll take care of second coffees," he offered.

"No, no," Rosemary clutched his arm. "I . . . I don't want to be back here alone again. Let me do the coffees. Please."

"Now, why do you think she wanted to be out in the cabin?" I asked Julie and Markus.

"'Cause she was scared," Julie exclaimed. "I would be, too!"

Just then the steward had a better idea. "Do you want me to ask the IFD if you can swap with one of the girls up front? Maybe Number Seven or Eight?"

"Changing positions isn't allowed, Simon,"
Rosemary reminded him.

"Why not?" Markus, ever-the-inquisitive, asked.

"Well, each member of the cabin crew has a
numbered position and is responsible in case of an
emergency for those specific passengers in those areas.
You're not supposed to change positions mid-flight."

"And what's an IFD?" Julie interrupted.

"IFD stands for in-flight director. She's the chief
stewardess or the boss on each flight. Everyone has to
listen to her, kind of like you have to listen to me when I
give the orders. Right?

"Yeah, right." Julie chuckled.

"Go *o-o-n.*" As always, Markus was impatient
with interruptions.

Simon told Rosemary, "Don't worry. 'Scuse the
pun but the IFD's not a stiff. Better just tell her you're
nauseous back here. She'll understand."

So thanks to Simon, for the rest of the flight,
Rosemary was permitted to help with serving in the
middle cabin.

Once a plane has landed and come to a full stop,
the stewardesses' job is to assist the passengers with
getting their coats and luggage down from the overhead
bins. The stewardesses, who are usually very tired at the
end of a long flight, are happy to help because then the
passengers get off the plane lickety-split and the
stewardesses can get home and into their beds sooner.

"Did you used to get tired?" Markus asked
sympathetically.

"I was so tired, Markus, that I propped my eyes
open with teaspoons."

Markus considered the image and giggled.

The first-class cabin, which is at the front of the plane, is separated from the rear cabins by the forward galley and a curtain. Passengers normally exit through Two Door Left in this galley area. Rosemary pulled back the curtain to allow first class occupants to deplane before passengers from the two rear cabins surged forward. After a small group of businessmen and a well-dressed couple had said their "thank yous" and "goodbyes," Rosemary noticed a man slumped in one of the first-class seats, his head lolling to one side, sleeping.

The IFD, who was standing at Two Door Left called across the aisle to Rosemary, "Go and wake that man, will you?"

As Rosemary approached the passenger from behind, something about the gray head struck her as familiar. When she came around and saw the man from the front, lying slouched in his seat, she gasped.

"Oh-mi-god! Oh-mi-god! That's him! That's him!" She backed away, holding her hand over her mouth, her eyes wide in disbelief and confusion.

"Who? Who's him?" Jane, the tall, freckled stewardess standing on the other side of the cabin, asked.

"The m-man," Rosemary stuttered. "The man who walked through the back of the plane!"

"What are you talking about?" Jane smiled, thinking Rosemary had gone quite mad. "He's just sleeping, silly."

Impatient, Jane leaned over the wide seats and started to shake the passenger by the shoulder. "Sir, sir, we've landed." He didn't move. "Time to wake up. Wakie, wakie." He still didn't move.

"He's dead," Rosemary blurted.

Jane, the smile gone from her face now, put two fingers on his neck to feel for a pulse. Almost instantly, she recoiled. "Good lord!" As she started to undo his tie, she told Rosemary, "Tell the IFD we need an ambulance! Quickly!"

"It's too late," Rosemary murmured. "He died three hours ago."

"How did he die?" Markus asked, uncurling from his fetal position.

"Heart attack," I responded.

"Why did he walk out the back of the plane?" Julie sounded sad.

"Because it was closest to heaven?" Markus offered. "Like Mum went through the roof of the car when she died."

Hearing Markus refer to the accident, I gulped back a wave of sadness. Had he seen his mother's spirit separate from her physical body or was he talking about seeing her being physically catapulted from the car? He had been just six years old when it happened. I couldn't and wouldn't ask him for clarification. Not now.

"Did the others believe Rosemary then? That she'd seen a ghost?" Julie questioned. I got up and offered my back to Markus to give him a piggyback to his own bed. It was another part of our nightly ritual. He climbed on.

"Some did, some didn't," I responded as I deposited Markus onto his Superman quilt and tucked him in. "It helps if you believe in ghosts. Then you can usually see them."

As I leaned over to kiss Julie on the forehead and arrange the flowery duvet up around her chin, she chuckled.

"You believe in ghosts, don't you?" Julie was smiling a strange smile.

Markus muttered, "Yeah, Julie, of course she

does. It's the same with us. Some people can see us and some can't."

"What do you mean?" I stood up, staring at Markus. His voice had sounded eerily different, almost adult. I shivered as a cool draft suddenly enveloped me.

A noise behind me made me turn. Stephen was standing just inside the doorway. After my storytelling, he always came in to kiss the children goodnight. His tall frame was silhouetted by the lighted landing behind him, the outline of his body blurry, almost *misty*.

His voice was disembodied and his whole being seemed to be fading as he said, "There's something I have to tell you."

The room was chilly now, as if a fine hazy fog of cold air had blown into the house and settled on everything. When the air cleared and the temperature rose again, the beds were made and the room was empty almost as if they had never been there at all.

5

INTO THE VALLEY OF DEATH

"Pull over," my brother Ben instructed.

"Why?" I asked as I yanked the steering wheel towards the narrow grass curb.

I was taking my turn driving the blue Thunderbird we had rented in Los Angeles to tour California and Nevada.

Illuminated in the beam of our headlights, the words "YOU ARE NOW ENTERING DEATH VALLEY" loomed out of the night. Tiled in yellow on a black and white jagged background, the letters stood out like lightning, as if warning those entering this place to travel at their own risk. I shuddered.

"I want to take a photo!" Ben said, leaping out of the car. "Get up on the sign and I'll take a shot."

When I opened the door and stepped out into the blackness a suffocating wall of heat took my breath away. I turned to look back at Joanna, my older sister, in the back of the car. Her head lolled against the window. She was fast asleep. Obediently I waded through the brittle undergrowth and climbed onto the ledge at the back of the rectangular sign. Draping myself over the words "DEATH VALLEY," I opened my mouth and eyes as if frozen in a long horrific scream. Ben chuckled and the white flash briefly blinded me.

"Watch out for the rattlesnakes!" he called over his shoulder as he made his way back to the car, he in his closed leather shoes, me in open-toed sandals.

"Rattlesnakes?" I cried, running to catch up with

him. "There are rattlesnakes here?"

"Probably."

The memory of Ben poring over the map in Los Angeles where he had planned our route flashed before me. He had muttered something about going through Death Valley. On the map the long strip of mottled brown with the thin red line snaking through the area appeared innocent enough, but the name conjured up images I didn't want to entertain. "Only on one condition," I had said, "as long as we go through during the day." But today Ben and Joanna had wanted to linger in Las Vegas, and now here we were just getting to Death Valley at nine o'clock at night.

"Joanna will just love you for that," I cautioned as Ben poised the camera in front of the back window. Another bright flash of light and still my sister did not stir.

"She looks so innocent. And this picture might be her only souvenir of Death Valley," he commented.

I climbed back into the driver's seat, wondering why we were the only car on the road. There must be others who had to travel this route.

Although the atmosphere outside was laden with heat, air conditioning blasted a cool breeze into the large car. The only sound now was the purring of the engine as it sped along the narrow road and the light snoring coming from the back seat.

I marveled at my sister. We were so different. I tended to meet unpleasant situations head on while Joanna demonstrated a knack of merely tuning out. Still, the three of us shared an unlikely closeness.

"How long is Death Valley?" I asked my brother, keeping my eyes fixed on the grey tarmac ahead that seemed to stretch into eternity.

"Oh, I dunno. Long. It'll take us three or four hours to get through it probably."

"Don't you think we should turn around and fill up on petrol before we go any further?" I asked, wondering about the needle that hovered just below the half empty mark.

"Nah, don't worry." He waved a hand. "There'll be plenty of gas stations along the way."

Ben had lived in Canada for five years so I generally deferred to his knowledge of North America and its facilities. But I also knew my brother, the artful procrastinator.

This trip was the first family holiday we had taken together since childhood. Ben had flown down from Vancouver to Los Angeles and Joanna and I had traveled from England. All of us were in transition. One night about six months ago Joanna had up and left her husband after nine years of incompatibility; she had wanted children while he preferred to work and play golf. My own two-year relationship had come to a grinding halt when I had mentioned the Big M word. And Ben? Well, he was just in between girlfriends. A two-week holiday in California would be good for all of us . . . or so I thought.

We drove on in silence. Still there were no other cars to be seen. No gas stations either. Ahead, all that was visible was the ten foot patch of gray tarmac immediately in front of the car illuminated by the yellow beam of our headlights. Surrounding us was a heavy blackness punctuated by even blacker patches where bushes contrasted against silvery sand.

Weary of concentrating on the narrow road, I asked my brother, "Do you want to drive?"

"Sure," he responded, his face lighting up, always happy to retrieve control from a woman driver. Not that he considered me to be a bad driver—for a woman.

I pulled over to a graveled, sloping hard shoulder and we opened our doors simultaneously. After the cool interior of the car, the hot, thick air hit us like a furnace. I stood for a moment staring into that dark oppressive clamminess. What was that sound? Was it the sagebrush rustling in the breeze or was it voices whispering?

"C'mon," Ben's voice behind me made me jump. I hurried around to the other side of the car, snuggling into the safety of the passenger seat quickly closing the door. Suddenly cold, I pulled my denim jacket around me.

Ben climbed in behind the steering wheel and pushed the seat back to adjust to his long legs and six foot frame. I sensed his relief at being able to focus on the driving. As he pulled back onto the road again, I turned to look at Joanna. Her body was curled away from the window. How I wished I could go to sleep like that and wake up in the normalcy of daylight and civilization. This was going to be a long, long night.

"Ben, do you know why it's called Death Valley?"

"Well," he began, relishing his position of chief storyteller, "back in the old days, there was a big fight between the cowboys and the Indians and about two hundred of the Indians were massacred. People say that their ghosts still ride across the road in front of oncoming cars, causing people to swerve and crash."

I visualized a herd of ethereal horses suddenly rearing in our headlights, their ghostly riders staring soullessly, relishing their imminent revenge. Then Ben grinned at me.

"You're joking, aren't you?"

He nodded smugly.

We hadn't gone much further when Ben gasped, staring at something caught in the beams.

"You're not going to get me this time," I said, resisting the temptation to follow his gaze.

"No, Carla, look at those!" He sounded scared.

I sat up. Immediately in front of us, long blackened skid marks ran for twenty feet and then veered off into the ditch. The tread marks were fresh as if a car had just . . . . Then we saw it—a long, dark-colored sedan, lying on its side in the ditch. As we passed the eerily still vehicle, Ben shifted nervously in his seat.

"Do you think there was anybody . . .?"

"Nah, that happened a while ago," he assured me as he sped on.

My seat reclined easily when I pulled on the lever, but sleep wouldn't come. I studied my brother's green-tinged profile, the lights from the dashboard accentuating a slight strain in his eyes and cheek muscles, his lips forming a tight line. Was he nervous or just tired?

He spoke, breaking the monotony of the droning car. "Did you know that some people drive in here and are never seen again?"

"How come?"

"Abducted by UFO's apparently."

He knew that the UFO topic always fascinated and scared me.

"Really?" I tried to sound nonchalant.

"Yeah. The first signs are when the radio starts to crackle then the engine dies and finally the lights go out. Or people drive through here and they lose a day or two of time."

"Perhaps the aliens will give us some petrol."

He laughed and I relaxed slightly, laying my head back against the seat. *Please let me sleep. If I just close my eyes* . . . .

The roaring came suddenly and loudly. I sat up and screamed. Where was I? What was that noise? Then I remembered we were still driving through Death Valley. My window was wide open and the radio was making a horrible crackling noise.

"Why's the radio doing that?"

Ben was laughing.

"That's not funny!"

"Sorry."

"And don't open my window again!"

Ben obviously didn't want me to sleep, didn't want to be the only one awake, so I settled back, resigned to staying conscious.

Maybe it was an illusion that we were actually moving. As we drove on and on, with total darkness all around, we could have driven off the edge of the earth into a black hole, forever lost in our own twilight zone. Joanna's snoring and the purring of the car were merely part of the illusion to make us think we were still in the same dimension.

I'm losing it and it's not even midnight, I thought. "What are we going to do about petrol, Ben?"

"Don't worry, there'll be a gas station soon," he replied, an edge in his voice as he glanced out of his side window into the void.

"How much do we have now?" I asked.

"Under a quarter of a tank."

The interior of the car was still cool. "Have you turned off the air conditioning?" Ben gave me one of his of-course-don't-be-stupid looks.

"Maybe this is one of those cars that runs for miles on E?" I suggested hopefully.

"You mean reserve?" Ben always needed to name

things. "Maybe."

Our headlights continued to cut through the endless blackness while the gas gauge crept closer to empty. According to the clock on the dash, it was exactly midnight. I peered through the window. Nothing, nothing, nothing.

"Look! Look!" Ben exclaimed, pointing, finally waking Joanna from her innocent slumber.

"What?" Joanna responded drowsily. She sat up, poking her head between the front seats, squinting, trying to see something out of the window.

"Lights." Ben indicated straight ahead. "Over there."

We couldn't miss them now. What a relief to see those yellow orbs. And more lights appeared in a cluster as we rounded the first bend leading into a town.

"Thank God," I muttered. Civilization again, people, and hopefully a twenty-four-hour gas station.

"Where are we?" Joanna asked.

"Somewhere in Death Valley," I replied. "I didn't see a name for this place. Did you, Ben?"

He didn't respond but slowed the car as we pulled towards the lights. An assortment of vehicles was parked haphazardly in the center of the community. Groups of people were walking aimlessly, staring as if magnetically drawn to something in front of them. *Odd. And so many people out and about this time of night*. The slightly robotic way in which they were walking reminded me of the movie *The Stepford Wives*, a film about a town of men who murdered their spouses so they could turn them into female robots who could then cater to their every whim. I shuddered. The surreal feeling reminded me of a Dali painting. "This is Dali-ville," I muttered.

Most of the lights appeared to be coming from the

outside of a circular brown brick building, a large windowless fortress perched on a hill projecting skywards out of a scattering of houses or business buildings. *What's a tower like that doing in the middle of a desert? Maybe it's a prison. Or just the local restaurant?* Whatever it was, the fortress seemed to be the center of the community as clusters of people were moving woodenly up the narrow ramp that wrapped itself up and around the solid impenetrable walls.

Ben spotted two men and a woman talking together at the base of the hill. We pulled up closer. Our presence seemed to disturb them, almost as if we had interrupted their secret meeting. And when my window whirred down so Ben could speak to them, the group split up. One man and the woman moved away in opposing directions, leaving the other man staring at us coldly.

"Excuse me," Ben inquired, leaning towards the window, "could you tell us where we could buy some gas?

The man dressed in dark overalls was wiping his oily hands on an old frayed rag. He glared down at me, unsmiling, as if all his problems were my fault.

"There's a town called Fortnum, forty miles down the road," he snarled. "You'll find a gas station there that's open all night." Then something behind me caught his attention. I realized he was staring at Joanna, as if fascinated by her. As he gave Ben further instructions, I could see a garage to the right behind him where several mechanics were working on a car up on a hoist. Even taking into account extreme daytime heat, why were they working so late at night? The whole place felt surreal, like one of those dreams where none of the pieces fit together.

As if reading my mind, Joanna leaned forward

and asked the man, "Excuse me, but what about over there? Don't they have any petrol?" She inclined her head towards the lighted workshop.

The man just peered at Joanna in an unfathomable, creepy stare then turned to walk away. Ben called out, "Thank you," to his departing back before the electric window hummed to a close.

'They're not very friendly, are they?" Joanna exclaimed indignantly. She expected all strangers to be automatically welcoming, one of her many charming but naive qualities.

I shuddered in response. "Let's go and get some petrol."

We pulled away slowly from Dali-ville and drove on. Joanna resumed her fetal position on the back seat and slept again while I stayed alert to watch for Fortnum.

The road was brighter now, lit up intermittently by small clusters of houses. Every time we saw some lights, Ben slowed the car. But we never saw a sign announcing Fortnum nor a gas station, even a closed one. And comforted by the yellow lights, the normalcy of the houses, I felt myself drifting and then finally lapsing into unconsciousness.

A man was pulling up his sweater and showing me his mechanical innards. "All the gas stations have been sent to Saturn," he said, laughing. But it wasn't a human laugh. And he was the same man we had spoken to in Dali-ville.

"Carla! Carla!" I opened my eyes. Ben was pulling over. *What a weird dream.*

"What's up? Did we get petrol?"

"Not quite," Ben replied resignedly.

"Oh, no!" I squinted through the window into the night. We were back in the desert again. No more comforting lights. Now instead of darkness, a full moon lit up the desert, giving it an eerier silvery light. The road here meandered through some small hills, and Ben had stopped our car on the wide shoulder of a ridge overlooking gullies and sand. A strong wind was blowing, whining as if complaining about our presence. The clumps of bushes could be discerned clearly now, black patches against almost white sand, their black-tentacled branches swaying jerkily in the wind, taunting us as if they too resented our invasion of their land.

"I couldn't find Fortnum," Ben apologized. "I thought we had better pull over. We don't want to conk out right in the middle of the road. It could be dangerous."

"Do you mean that we are going to have to sleep in the car?" I asked, horrified.

"Yep." Ben sounded flippant but I could tell he didn't relish the idea either. It didn't make much difference to Joanna who was still in the Land of Nod. I wondered if that girl would ever regain consciousness.

"I better get blankets out of the trunk," Ben said.

"Please don't get out of the car, Ben!" I pleaded, remembering the story of a young traveler who stepped out of his camper one windy night in France. He intended to secure the luggage on the roof. The sleepy girlfriend awakened from her slumber thinking she heard scratching noises above her. She didn't realize until the morning when the police were banging at the door that the scratching had been the frantic clawing of her boyfriend's nails on the camper roof while a lunatic with an ax decapitated him. Even though I knew it was probably just an urban myth, the very idea terrified me.

"It's okay," he reassured me gently, smiling at my paranoia. Ben opened the driver's side door, pulled himself out of the car and onto the narrow road. I held my breath as he went to the back of the car. The trunk hood went up. I couldn't see him but I heard fumbling noises for a long time before the trunk hood slammed shut. The driver's door opened and Ben climbed back into the car with three blankets. The doors clicked as he pressed the lock.

"Let's get some sleep," he suggested blithely, handing me a blanket, throwing a cover tenderly over Joanna and then snuggling down as if we were at home in our own beds.

I slept lightly, the awareness of where we were never far from consciousness.

Ben stirred and I opened my eyes. "Look at that!" he whispered, pointing forward into the dark. I followed his gaze, peering into the distance. A small round yellow orb of light shimmered on the black horizon. As we watched, the light expanded, ballooning into the darkness until it cast shadows onto the surrounding hills.

We sat transfixed by this light as it grew and grew. Suddenly the ball of light transformed into two smaller lights, throwing beams up into the sky, as if searching.   Then both beams were redirected downwards, scanning in our direction.

Oh My God! It's a UFO!

Ben exhaled "It's just a car."

I also breathed out, my fears of alien abduction at least temporarily silenced.

Now I could see the vehicle driving through a gully in the distance, the headlights wending their way towards us, the only car we had seen on the road that night.

"Why don't we stop them and ask for help?" I urged Ben.

"No," he murmured, more to himself than to me. "We could get into even more trouble." In England there were few, if any, guns in those days. The culture and the crime rate were very different from the United States. Perhaps he was right. The car passed without slowing.

With a mixture of relief and disappointment, I pulled the lever and let my seat fall back. With heavy eyelids, I finally dozed.

Tap, tap, tap. The noise was coming from my side at the back of the car. "Aagh! What's that?" I shook Ben's arm and he stirred.

He listened for a while. "Don't worry. It's just the wind blowing the bushes against the back of the car."

"Oh." I knew he was right but it sounded like a ghost wanting to come inside. Just as I closed my eyes, the tapping started again, taunting me as if to say, "I'm not going to let you sleep."

The engine turning over awakened me. Ben was starting the car. Thank God. It was daylight. The yellow sand dunes and sage brush stretched into the distance and now I could see the narrow road winding through a canyon up ahead. The desert looked harmless enough in the early light but something ominous still hung in the air.

"What time is it?" I asked sleepily, relieved that I was still alive after a night in Death Valley and promising myself I would never come here again.

"Ten past five."

The sage bushes made me think of aliens watching us. I still wanted to get out of there.

Ben pulled onto the road. The comforting sight of a distant snowcapped range glistening in the morning sun promised an end to this nightmare. The mountains and civilization, though, were still a very long way away.

"How much further before we're out of the valley, do you think?" I asked.

Ben shrugged. "If we can find gas, about two hours."

I glanced over my shoulder to see if Joanna was still sleeping. Then turning again, I blinked my eyes, not sure of what I was seeing.

I forced myself to control the panic that was clawing at my throat. "Stop the car!"

"What?" he asked, puzzled as he jerked the car to the right and braked.

"Ben?" I wanted him to confirm that I wasn't insane.

And then following my gaze, he saw for himself. "What the hell . . .?" And looking at me, "Where the hell . . .?"

The blanket that Ben had thrown over Joanna the night before lay flat and crumpled on the back seat. There was no Joanna.

"Turn back," I urged, attempting to stay calm. "Maybe she just went for a walk to stretch her legs. . . Or go to the loo," I suggested, not believing my own words. Although Joanna had a penchant for taking off on her own—no matter time or place—there was something ominous about the blanket as if it was trying to give us a message.

The tires squealed on the paved road as Ben swerved and turned the car around to retrace our route. "Jesus Christ!" he spluttered.

"Slow down," I urged him, scanning the sandy dunes. Maybe Joanna was behind a bush. Why hadn't we heard her get out of the car? Neither Ben nor I had slept deeply. Joanna had already proven to be a liability on this trip when she had taken off by herself early one morning in LA. She explained later that she had walked to Venice Beach for a coffee with this "very interesting man" who on further discussion turned out to be a street person and drug addict. He had even shown her his needle-ravaged arms.

"This is where we were, isn't it?" Ben screeched to a halt on the familiar bend and jumped out of the car. I opened my door. Already the air was heavy with warmth. I inspected the desert that went on and on. An early morning haze just sat atop the landscape. All I could see was sand and bushes, bushes and sand. No Joanna. Now the breeze had stilled, the bushes appeared almost hushed, as if keeping a secret.

Ben stood, one foot still in the car, squinting in the early morning light. "J-o-ann-a! J-o-ann-a!" he bellowed. His voice went limp in the thick air. I joined in, calling her name. Still the bushes remained unmoving. And still no sign of Joanna.

"What are we going to do, Ben?" I cried tearfully.

"Let's think about this logically," he said, sitting back in the driver's seat. "Where could she be?"

"Maybe she went to see if she could find some petrol?" I ventured, clutching at straws.

"In the middle of the night? I don't think so."

"Who knows with Joanna? She has her own logic."

"Got that right." Ben's shoulders slumped as he leaned over the steering wheel, thinking. "Well, we know there's no gas back there so maybe she went towards the mountains."

"She couldn't have been . . . taken . . . could she?"

"Carla, the doors were locked," he reassured me. "We would have heard something . . . I'm sure." Only he didn't sound so sure.

"Listen, we have to get gas anyway." Ben was trying to keep the panic out of his voice for my sake but I knew he was terrified that we had lost our sister. "Maybe she's up ahead. If we don't see her on the way, we'll find some gas and then we'll go back and look for her. Okay?"

As Ben turned the car around again on the winding road, I studied the sandy expanse once more but it felt empty, empty of Joanna.

Once we were through the gullies, the unpaved gravel road stretched before us in a straight line toward the mountains. No sign of my sister. No sign of any towns. *The vultures may have us all for breakfast yet,* I thought. Our family would never know what happened to us.

"Isn't that a road sign there?" I pointed to a square blue marker up ahead. The sign read *Darwin – 5 km.* There was a picture of a small airplane under the words.

"If they have an airport, they must have gas," Ben reasoned.

We turned left into the wide gravel entrance. A huge wooden frame structure straddled the road, reminding me of old western movies where each town had a welcoming gateway. A thick wooden plank hung from the center of the frame, barely attached by a couple of rusty nails at one end. I cranked my head sideways to read it. *WELCOME TO DARWIN* swung back and forth, creaking in a non-existent wind.

We drove past the sign and stared in silence.

One straight road cut a line down between shabby prefabricated shacks sitting atop the sand as if dropped there. Some of their windows were smashed, jagged edges jutting into the desert air while other windows were haphazardly boarded up as if the locals had to leave town in a hurry. Alongside them sat vast winged-tipped cars, the pale pink and blue of the fifties contrasted with blotches of rust. The tires were flat and weeds sprouted through their bumpers. As we crept along, a skeletal cat slunk under the first car, the only sign of life.

"This is a ghost town!" I cried, disturbed by what I saw. "Let's get out of here."

"We can't." Ben tightened his grip on the steering wheel. The car sputtered and then slowed. "We're out of gas."

He slipped the car into neutral and let it roll down the slight incline, coming to a halt about ten yards before the end of the straight road.

"Well, here we are," he muttered, slumping back in his seat, defeated.

"And here we'll stay." I took in our surroundings. *The last person in this town probably left fifty years ago.* "Do you think we're ever going to get the hell out of here?"

"Of course we will, Carla. Come on, let's go look around." I followed him out of the car, grateful for his optimism, even if it did sound hollow. The dead-end road petered out in a pile of dumped trash; broken bottles, dented, rusty beer cans, old tires and bits of wood. On either side of the debris, beginnings of paved road went nowhere except into sand and dried grass.

On the right corner off the main street sat an abandoned post office. Wide yellow boards covered the window. Painted in thick red letters the word: *CLOSED* stared back at us.

To the left, on the other side of the dump, was the local gas station. Ben and I walked closer. Leaning against the single, rusted, old-fashioned pump was part of a battered, splintered white door, splashed with the same chaotic red lettering: *SORRY NO GAS· BE BACK IN MAY.*

"But Ben . . . it's only the fifth of March!"

"I know."

"What are we going to do now?"

He was still staring at the single pump. "How do we know they meant this May?" he muttered.

"Oh God!"

Visions of dying of thirst and being pecked to death by vultures fuelled my burgeoning terror. I took a deep breath.

We turned and looked back up the road. We were invaders in a still life.

"Where the hell is Joanna?" I cried out loud as if the town knew the answer. But my cry was sucked into some invisible silent vortex.

"The only thing we can do is wait for a while and see if anyone comes out. It's still early, just seven-thirty." Ben reminded me. I silently scoffed at the likelihood of any humans existing in this godforsaken heat hole.

We returned to the car. Ben lay back in his seat, closing his eyes.

"How can you sleep in this place? It's too creepy!"

But he was already unconscious. I tried to do the same but I was haunted by images of Joanna being dead or tortured or crawling on her hands and knees through the lonely desert, crying out for us to save her. I sat up, vigilantly watching the houses. Nobody could possibly survive in this place, could they?

I don't know how long I had been sleeping when

a movement awakened me. "Look, there's a man, there's a man!" I screamed as if males were an extinct species.

Ben bolted upright, following my gaze out of the back window. A figure had appeared out of a cabin on the left, slightly behind the Thunderbird. I expected Ben to leap out of the car and ask the man for some gas so we could get out of there. But he didn't. He just sat there.

"Well, go on," I urged.

"Just a minute." Ben adjusted the rearview mirror so he could scrutinize the reflection of the stranger.

Apparently satisfied, my brother finally pulled himself out of the car and walked across the road. Barely breathing, I followed. The man was in his early fifties, stocky and clad in an oil-stained red and black shirt and equally oil-smeared jeans. A dark thick stubble covered his square chin.

"Howdy." The greeting was subdued as if he had been expecting us and we were late. He watched the two of us approach with a glint of amusement in his eyes.

"Excuse me," Ben inquired in his best British accent, "could you possibly tell us where the nearest gas station might be located?"

"Way-ill, let me see now." The man rubbed his whiskered chin. "'Bout eighty miles on da-own the road."

"Oh." Ben appeared flummoxed.

"You folks all out o' gas, are ya?" I felt the man was trying to suppress a grin.

"Yes," Ben confessed.

"Way-ill, let's see na, I just maight have some roun' back."

He ambled up a short path and disappeared into his ramshackle house. Ben and I exchanged wry grins of hope.

"Ask him if he's seen Joanna," I whispered as we

returned to the car.

Ben nodded. "I will. I will. But don't rush me, okay?" His eyes searched the apparently uninhabited gold rush settlement. "How does he live here?" Then he added, "Doesn't look like anyone else does."

"Maybe he's an escaped convict," I ventured.

The man reappeared holding a dented red can. "Way-ill, I got 'bout four gallins I can let ya have," he offered as he strolled over to the car. "Just siphon it in," he said, handing Ben the can with a short, dirty green hose attached.

Ben took the hose reluctantly, stared at it, tentatively sucked on it, then started to choke. The man grabbed it from him, shaking his head. Expertly he inhaled on the hose and then inserted it into the fuel tank.

"Do you get a lot of people through here that have run out of gas?" I inquired, feeling a little more relaxed. At least the vultures would have to go hungry for the time being. Now we just had to find our sister.

"All the tay-ime," the man drawled, sounding weary of being pestered by strangers. "Where you folks all from?" he inquired, still filling the gas tank.

"England," I supplied. "I expect you don't get too many English people through here?"

"Yais," he said dryly. "I git all khy-ens comin' through here."

"Have you seen our sister?" Ben blurted. The question sounded ridiculous out here in this vast expanse but the man didn't smile. "You see, we slept on the road last night and she . . . well . . . we woke up this morning and she wasn't in the car. She's about five feet four inches tall, brown hair, big brown eyes . . . ."

Something in the man's eyes flickered. Slowly, deliberately, he screwed the cap back on the fuel tank and wiped his hands on his dirty jeans.

"Have you seen her?" Ben insisted.

"Ah reckon you know why it's called Death Valley, don't yer?" he asked, peering into Ben's eyes.

I held my breath. Ben didn't move.

The man stepped up closer to my brother until he was almost breathing on his face, his beady brown eyes peering into Ben's. "Qua-ite a few people d-i-e-d out thay-er."

Then he pulled back, staring off into the distance as though remembering them all. Turning his stare on me, he added, "Sometaimes they just up an' disappear."

"Oh my God." I slumped against the car.

"Please . . . do you know where we can find our sister, Mr . . . ?" Ben urged, attempting to keep the impatience out of his voice.

"Darwin's ma naime." *Just like the town*, I thought.

I cleared my throat. "So what do you mean exactly, Mr. Darwin, a-a-about people disappearing?"

"Sometay-imes," his eyes bored into mine, "they don't bring 'em back."

"Listen," Ben pulled a twenty-dollar bill out of his pocket and offered it to Mr. Darwin but he waved the money away impatiently as if he had no use for the green paper. "We really have to go and find my sister. Thank you very much for the gas." He took my arm. "C'mon, Carla."

"Who? Who is *they*?" I persisted with the strange Mr. Darwin while Ben yanked my arm towards the passenger side. "Please just tell us so we can go and find her."

"Just go back whay-er you came from," he pronounced as if in a trance. "Go back to the town with no name." His attention was suddenly caught by something over my shoulder as if his name was being called.

"No name? Which town?"

"That's whay-er they all disappear," he continued in the trance, still focused on a spot in the distance. "In the town with no name. Hottest goddam place on the planet."

"Come *on*, Carla." I finally surrendered to Ben's urging and left the man standing there, entranced by the same invisible force.

As the motor hummed to life and Ben turned the car to drive back up the road, I put the window down and called to Mr. Darwin. He was still standing, staring into space, where we had left him. "Thank you, thank you so much. . . ." I called. "Oh my God . . . Ben, look!"

The man was fading, getting paler and paler as if his cells were rapidly disintegrating, disappearing in front of our eyes. The only evidence of his former existence was a red gas can stark against the sandy drabness, the ramshackle house and the deathly quiet.

The car lurched forward as Ben put his foot on the gas and sped up the dusty road, the abandoned shacks seeming even ghostlier now. As we raced through the dilapidated wooden archway and hit the paved road, the tires screeched in protest as we turned back the way we had come.

"What the hell was *that*?" Ben whispered as though someone was in the back seat listening to us.

"I . . . I don't know," I stammered, shaking. "My God, what about the gas?" I leaned over to look at the fuel gauge. "Do we really have some or is that going to suddenly disappear too?" But the needle remained steady just below the F mark. How could four gallons fill this tank? He must have been a ghost. But then could ghosts manifest fuel?

After we had re-entered the winding part of the road and were almost at our sleeping spot of the previous night, Ben slowed down.

"It's as if he was de-materializing like Scottie in *Startrek*," I muttered, still stunned.

As we wove our way through the gullies, Ben, I noticed, was pale in the early morning light. "Well, if we are going to listen to his advice," he surmised, "I read somewhere that Death Valley is like a bowl so the hottest place on the goddam planet would probably be in the center, wherever that is. The town with no name . . . . Were there any towns that we drove through that didn't have a name?"

"There may have been lots after we left Dali-ville but I slept some of that stretch."

"That's it!" he exclaimed. "Dali-ville! Remember we didn't see a name and it's about in the center of the desert. And it was very strange."

"You mean we have to go all the way back *there*?" My mouth suddenly went dry. Ben and I exchanged grimaces.

"We have no choice," he said, affirming my thoughts.

Maybe it wouldn't be so creepy now it was daylight. And we had to find Joanna. "I'm going to watch for her along the way," I insisted, fixing my eyes on the barren landscape. The road was starting to straighten out now, the sun rising higher in the sky creating a shimmering haze in the near distance.

"How long will it take us to get to Dali-ville?"

Ben shrugged. "About an hour at this rate." We were still crawling along, hoping and praying that Joanna would magically appear on the side of the road. "We should get there between nine and ten," he estimated, peering at the dashboard clock.

As we got closer to the strange town, the man's words echoed in my mind. *Quay-ite a few just up an' disappeared . . . sometay-imes they don't come back . . . .*

Ben's lips were pulled together in that telltale tight line, his whole body tense.

"Shouldn't we be seeing the houses we saw last night, the lights . . . the towns?" I wondered aloud.

"I don't know, Carla!" he snapped.

We drove the next few miles in silence.

"There it is!" Ben sat up in his seat, leaning forward as if that would help him see better. The familiar sight of the fortress—or whatever that strange building was—loomed ahead, arising out of the desert like the monolithic Ayres Rock.

Ben drove very slowly down the street and pulled up exactly where we had stopped the night before, in front of the fortress. But we had seen buildings lining the center square and there were none there now, just sand. And where was the garage? All that was left of this town was the round, windowless tower.

"Am I going crazy, Ben?"

"If you are, I am, too," he muttered as he turned off the engine.

"Now what?" I asked.

"There's only one place left to go and look." Ben nodded towards the fortress shimmering in the heat, even more ominous in the daylight. "Up there."

"Oh God . . . ."

We opened our doors and climbed slowly out of the car. The air was just as oppressive as the previous night. The click of the car doors locking sounded surprisingly loud in the thick atmosphere. Ben went ahead of me as we started up the stone ramp that wound its way up and around the building, where only last night we had witnessed entranced humans climbing up and up and going inside. At least the gravel beneath our feet appeared normal.

"Can you hear that?" I exclaimed. My breath was coming short and fast as I leaned against the dark brick wall.

"What?"

"That . . . high pitched humming?" I panted, short of breath.

"No." He was frowning at me. "Carla?"

"I'm okay. I'm okay." As suddenly as it had come, the humming stopped and I could breathe again. "Let's keep going."

Ben took my hand and almost pulled me up the stone ramp, up, up and around.

"There must be a door here somewhere." He brushed the vast expanse of wall with his hand but there was no opening. "Where did they all go in?"

"I don't see anything," I said, looking for hidden entrances. We walked up and up the ever-steepening path. We were almost at the top, when Ben— slightly ahead of me—stopped.

"But . . . how?" I asked, dumbfounded as I came up behind him. There were tears in his eyes as he pointed forward.

The stone ramp tapered off and disappeared into the concrete.

He slumped down on the rough stone gravel, his back against the wall. "I was so sure she'd be here," he said.

Helpless, I sat down beside him and put my hand

on his arm. His head was buried in his hands.

"Where is she? Where *is* she?" he demanded between his fingers.

I scanned the empty square down below and the desert that went on and on and on.

"Ben . . . ?" I started tremulously. "We need to get help."

"It's no use. She's gone." He shook his head. "She's just gone, I know it." He raised his face and the tears were glistening on his stubbled cheeks. "She's gone."

"No. No. She's here somewhere. That man said . . . ."

"That man was a ghost, Carla, or an alien or something. I don't know but he wasn't real."

His despair was catching. I had to defend my fragile hope. "Ben," I urged, "we'll go to a police station. They'll send out a search party."

"Hah!" He waved an arm at the expansive desert vista. "From where, Carla? It'll take us hours to get to the nearest place. She could be long dead by then . . . if she isn't already."

"C'mon, Ben, we can't stay here." I pulled at his arm. "Let's at least keep looking."

He got up, brushed the tears from his cheeks and let me lean on his arm as we cautiously descended the ramp. The air was lighter at the bottom. I could breathe more easily despite the intensifying heat and my heart thumping in my chest.

As we moved towards the car, Ben was slightly ahead of me. He stopped so abruptly that I stumbled into him.

"What is it?" I asked from behind.

He didn't speak but pointed at the pale blue

Thunderbird sitting there in the hot sun. At first, I didn't understand. Then I saw it. In the shadows of the car's back seat, a dark, formless shape was shifting from side to side.

"Who is it?" I whispered.

"Or . . . what is it?" Ben stepped gingerly towards the car.

The rear window hummed down.

"C'mon, let's get out of here," a female voice called from the interior shadows of the car. "It's creepy." Then Joanna poked her head out of the car window. "Where have you two been anyway?"

6

KNOCKING

"Ms. Blankenship?"

"Yes," Charlotte sighed, recognizing the thin voice on the phone as that of the arrogant young man in Crewing.

"David at Jet Air Crewing here. We would like you to do a Munich, departing at thirteen hundred hours, Flight number JA 5278. Can you confirm you'll be there?"

"Munich!" *The same destination as Annie*, she thought.

David's enquiry wasn't really a question but an order. The challenge lingered in the phone line. Charlotte knew he was expecting a fight. And she *did* want to argue, even to plead, but she knew it was useless. As a senior Crewing member, he had heard too many excuses. He was all out of compassion.

"I'll be there," she confirmed despondently. "Thirteen hundred, did you say?"

"Thank you, Ms. Blankenship." David sounded relieved at her acquiescence.

She glanced up at Annie's flowered clock on the kitchen wall. Ten minutes to ten. Today would be Charlotte's first day back on duty. *It'll be good for me*, she told herself as she sat down in front of her make-up mirror.

The house was so quiet since Annie was gone. Being with people again would be healthy, Charlotte thought. Even though her flat mate had worked for another airline and the two young women were like ships in the night with varying schedules, they hadn't only shared accommodation for six months, they had also become good friends. Until the incident.

Charlotte didn't want to think about searching for another flat-mate now. Although she loved the roomy neo-Georgian house just twenty minutes from her base at London's Gatwick Airport, the house would never be the same, especially with Peter, their handsome next door neighbor and pilot also gone. His absence only accentuated the void.

When the ritual was done, the war paint complete, she studied her reflection. Thick blonde hair piled into a small knot on top of her head, high cheekbones, a too-small mouth, a dullness in the usually clear blue eyes. *Not the look of a harlot*, she thought ironically. The angst hadn't faded in Charlotte's time off. Her face looked thinner now, drawn, and she had lost a few pounds, which wasn't a bad thing on her small frame. *I have to go back sometime,* she told herself. *The sooner the better.*

As Charlotte donned her white blouse and navy uniform, appraising her own slimmer reflection in the bedroom mirror, she remembered Annie standing behind her once saying, "You know, I can't live without Peter. I can't and I won't." Her manic expression had concerned Charlotte and she remembered shivering.

Annie flew for the same small airline as Peter, which meant that for good or for bad they saw each other frequently. While Annie clung to the hope that one day Peter would come to his senses and realize that she was the one for him, the gregarious and charming pilot continued to be an incorrigible flirt. When Charlotte oh-so-tactfully pointed out to her friend that perhaps the man of her dreams wasn't quite ready for commitment, Annie only became defensive and accused Charlotte of wanting Peter for herself.

"Do you really think that I have a *choice* about loving him?" Annie had retorted shrilly. '

While her friend's complex mixture of emotional fragility and obsessive determination worried her, Charlotte also had to ask herself if that was true. Had she wanted Peter?

Perhaps it was a good thing that the twenty-minute drive to the airport along winding country roads was instilled into Charlotte's pre-flight routine. She drove almost on auto-pilot, most of her mental faculties focused on the nightmare of Annie. The scene from that last night played over and over in her head—as if by repeating what had happened—she might be able to create a different outcome. But the awful ending was still the same.

Annie and Charlotte had been home together that early evening. Peter had invited himself over for dinner, bringing as always a litany of funny flying stories and his own recipe for an exotic cocktail. All three had downed his variation of rum punch and lots of laughter had ensued. By the time dinner was over, inhibitions were loosened. When Annie popped upstairs to go to the loo, Charlotte began to clear the dishes from the table. Suddenly she had felt Peter behind her, sliding his arms around her waist. She had turned her face toward him to rebuke him, but he used that moment to plant his lips firmly on hers. Slightly inebriated and shocked that she enjoyed the feeling of Peter's arms around her, Charlotte had taken too long to react. A noise in the hallway made her come to her senses and she had opened her eyes. To her horror, she had seen Annie standing in the kitchen doorway, staring at the two of them in their cozy embrace.

Charlotte would never forget the complete devastation on Annie's face. She, not Peter, had been the recipient of Annie's glaring accusation of betrayal. When her flat mate had turned and run upstairs crying, Charlotte had pushed Peter away with an "Oh no! Now look what you've done!" Flinging open the kitchen door, she had snapped at him, "You better go home. *Now!*" Then she had run up the stairs after Annie.

But her distraught friend had already locked herself in her room. Through the door, Charlotte listened helplessly to Annie's desolate sobs, and somehow she knew that Annie was spiraling downward into a dark abyss, so deep no one would be able to reach her.

Charlotte pleaded, "Annie! Let me in. Let me in. I didn't want to. It just happened . . . It wasn't my fault . . . ."

The next morning Annie had left early for her morning flight leaving Charlotte no time to make peace with her wounded flat-mate.

The crew room where the in-flight staff assembled before and after flights hadn't changed in the two weeks Charlotte had absented herself. No luxuries here, just a brick-walled, concrete-floored square chamber barely painted an insipid yellow. The large, abused wooden table still sat in the middle of the stark room, its only adornment an offensively overfilled ashtray of lipstick-coated butts. A scratched formica-topped surface was attached to the wall in the left corner with a black telephone on it, the hot line to Operations and Crewing.

A crew of inbound stewardesses blew in through the airside door as if propelled out of a wind tunnel. Their make-up was smeared, their previously perfectly preened hair now hung down in wispy tendrils. In contrast, the outbound crews, Charlotte observed, appeared as if they had just emerged from a beauty salon.

Charlotte recognized her friend Teri Coulsdon sitting against the far wall, on one of the low red plastic chairs. She was relieved to see Teri's cheery, familiar face.

"Hello, Charlie." Teri waved, a smile then a trace of concern flitted across her face.

Charlotte made her way through the other stewardesses and sat down next to Teri. "Are you on the Munich?"

"Yes, I am. Aren't we lucky?" Teri peered directly into Charlotte's face. "Don't take this the wrong way but you don't look so good. Are you sure it's not too soon for you to be back flying?"

Charlotte sighed. *No, I'm not sure*, she thought. "I'll be okay," she murmured and realized she was trembling. "I have to get back to it sometime, don't I?"

"Well, yes. But . . . you poor thing. It's bad enough that Annie died on that flight, but the pilot—was it Peter?—was your next door neighbor, wasn't he? Weren't you all good friends?"

Charlotte barely nodded. To compound her grief, she had not been able to tell Teri or any living soul of the ugly truth about that last night.

"And why did Crewing put you on a Munich on your first flight back?" Teri added. "Bastards!"

With her long brunette hair pulled up under her hat and her large brown guileless eyes, Teri's innocent-little-girl look often belied her mischievous nature. "Don't you worry," Teri patted her colleague on the arm. "They'll get what they deserve."

Charlotte squirmed at her words. "I'll be okay,"

she repeated as if convincing herself. The sleepless nights when she tossed and turned, the absence of Annie and the pain of that last evening pulled at her raw emotions. Even before her duty had begun, she felt exhausted. *Please God, let me just get through this flight.*

"And sorry, there's more bad news." Teri contorted her cherubic, freckled face into a fake expression of horror. "Polly Parrot's our Number One!"

Joan Ferguson was not so affectionately named Polly Parrot by her colleagues, not only for her huge hooked nose but also for her unfortunately high-pitched voice. Her clipped instructions to her crew often sounded like a parrot. But Charlotte didn't really care about Joan. Instead, she glanced around the crew room at the other young women and wondered if the crash was still on *their* minds. *Was it courage or denial that allowed us to keep working on aircraft,* she wondered, *especially after a crash?*

"They still don't know what caused it, do they?" she heard one stewardess whisper, standing by the mailboxes glancing over—not very surreptitiously—at Charlotte. Crews talked and news travelled fast in the airline. *She knew,* Charlotte thought, *but what did she know?* "I mean, planes don't normally just suddenly spiral down from thirty-five thousand feet, do they?"

"Maybe it was sabotage?" the other stewardess offered. "They recovered the black box, you know, and there's a rumor that someone went nuts on the flight," she added as they exited the crew room door, just as Joan Ferguson came through it.

The diminutive woman strutted directly over to the black phone in the corner. As she spoke with Operations, Teri and Charlotte stood, donning their gloves and gathering up their crew bags. Joan delegated flight

116

positions to Teri and Charlotte; Teri would fly in number two position and operate the galley while Charlotte would work in the cabin as number three with Joan.

Transport arrived at the airside door and took them out to the aircraft waiting in the drizzle on the tarmac. Once on board, Teri went to work at the front of the plane preparing the galley while Charlotte checked emergency equipment throughout the cabin and dressed the toilets at the rear with the prerequisite tissues, hand towels and soaps. She was glad to be back in the routine, trying not to think about how Annie would have gone through a similar pattern just before she died. As she mindlessly completed her tasks, she reflected on how many air crews believe "it" is never going to happen to them. But this fated flight had taken off from their home base, Gatwick, and so the tragedy had struck much closer to home.

Had it been sabotage? Airlines were subject to constant terrorist threats so the crash could have been caused by a bomb. Or a technical malfunction. She did not want to imagine Annie's or Peter's last moments. But once the Civil Aviation Authority released their report, compulsory reading for each crew member, Charlotte would know those gruesome details. *Don't think about that now.*

As Charlotte put finishing touches to the cabin, a mix of eighty-nine German and English passengers filtered onto the plane. Clutching packages and oversized bags, they squeezed into their assigned seats.

Once passengers were settled, Charlotte and Teri performed the usual pre-take-off rituals; safety demonstration of oxygen masks and life jackets, passenger seat belt check and "cabin secure" notification to the flight deck crew. After a brief taxi, the two-engine plane was positioned for take off and hurled down the runway and up into the air. *Here we go*, Charlotte thought.

On the forward jump seat, as the plane steeply ascended, Teri recounted her latest humorous fiascos with Crewing to Charlotte, taking both their minds off their anxieties, temporarily at least.

Once aloft, Charlotte braced herself for what was to come. She knew that during the one-and-three-quarter-hour flight from Gatwick to Munich, the plane would go through approximately twenty minutes of mild air turbulence over the Alps.

As she waited in the galley—while Teri filled another coffee pot for the second beverage service—she tried not to think of Annie's and Peter's last moments. When the plane began to gently quiver, Charlotte wasn't sure whether it was her own body trembling or the aircraft. She glanced back into the cabin and through the oval windows she caught a glimpse of the mountains far below. *This must be the spot where Annie's plane crashed.* She shuddered. *Down there somewhere amongst those cold, snow-capped peaks. Don't think about it; just don't think about it.*

Charlotte took the now-full coffee pot and walked carefully towards the rear. She forced herself *not* to glance out of the windows and see down into that abyss. At the last row of seats, she stood for a moment and adjusted her grip on the hot, stainless steel container. A young German couple and an elderly woman seated on the port side held out their small plastic cups in the direction of Charlotte's pot. She was poised to pour the hot liquid into the receptacles. A fleeting movement in her peripheral vision made her look up. She glanced at the rear door window. Something was on the outside of the plane.

Startled she turned toward the rear door and glared at it transfixed. Her hand holding the coffee pot trembled, slightly spilling the hot liquid. She tilted her head to one side and frowned. Then her puzzlement dissolved into an expression of wide-eyed horror. She and the pot began to shake violently, coffee dribbling onto the carpet. Whimpering unintelligibly at first, she gradually became louder and clearer.

"No! No! No! Ohmigod, no-o-o-o!" she wailed.

Passengers watched confused as the terrified stewardess kept her glare on the rear door. The woman sitting in the aisle seat had instantly paled. She craned her head around the back of her seat to try and see what Charlotte was seeing. *"Meine Gute!"* she exclaimed. *"Was ist los, Fraulein?* Are vee going to crash?"

"N-o-o-o!" Charlotte shrieked in the direction of the door. She dropped the coffeepot at her feet and clamped a hand over each ear as if she were subject to some unbearably high-pitched whine that only she could hear. She turned and ran up the aisle toward the galley and cockpit, pushing past an astounded Joan who was collecting used meal trays.

While hot coffee gushed out of the abandoned pot onto the carpet, the last few rows of passengers stared at Charlotte's retreating back then gaped back at the rear door, wondering if they should panic.

Charlotte tore through the curtain into the galley and fell onto the jump seat, hands still clenched tightly against her head and her face contorted in agony. She was gasping for breath.

Teri was crouched on the galley floor attempting to shove messy plastic meal trays back into their stowage. With the steady drone of the aircraft, she hadn't heard

Charlotte's screams. Now she paused in her struggle and gazed up at Charlotte, puzzled.

"What's the matter?" Even in the subdued light of the galley, she could see that her friend was ashen . . . and crying. Teri scrambled to her feet and came to kneel in front of her colleague, trying to read her distraught expression. Charlotte had buried her face in her hands and just shook her head. Teri pulled the curtain back and peered down the cabin. Joan was talking to passengers at the rear of the plane, a stack of meal trays in one arm, a coffeepot in the other hand. Nothing obviously disturbing. She closed the curtain again. "For god's sake, tell me what happened!"

Charlotte grabbed Teri's bare arms, clinging to her to as if to make sure she was real. She raised her face. Blue mascara streaked down her pale cheeks and the question in her eyes was frenzied. Suddenly she stood, pushing Teri away as if needing room to breathe. The galley curtain billowed inwards and Joan burst into the narrow space.

"What on earth was that little performance all about?" she snapped at Charlotte, thrusting her load of used meal trays at Teri and slamming the coffee pot down on the metal surface. "I've just spent the last five minutes trying to convince those poor passengers they aren't in mortal danger!" With her back against the curtain, Joan intertwined her arms tightly across her chest, her small mouth receding even further into her pointed chin. The angrier she got, the more she resembled a parrot.

As if afraid of being pecked to death by Joan, Charlotte backed up against the flimsy flight deck door. "It was *her*!" she murmured between snatched breaths.

Teri softened her voice in an attempt to calm her friend. "Who, Charlotte? Who was her?"

Charlotte stared at the galley curtain as if facing something horrifying through the blue fabric. Teri pulled the curtain back and peered into the cabin again. Some passengers were heading toward the toilets at the rear of the plane. Joan snatched the material from Teri and pulled it back into place.

"Did one of the passengers upset you?" Joan asked, sighing as she struggled for patience.

Charlotte shook her head. Tentatively, she raised a shaking arm and, as if no curtain separated the three women from the rest of the plane, she pointed straight down the cabin "It was . . . Annie," she rasped.

"Annie!" Teri exclaimed, "But that's—"

"Who's Annie?" Joan snapped.

"You know . . . the plane," Charlotte began slowly, struggling for breath, ". . . the plane that crashed two weeks ago?"

"The Air Court flight that crashed into the mountains," Teri reminded Joan.

"These mountains . . ." Charlotte's eyes were pleading with Joan to remember.

"Oh." Joan shuddered visibly. "Of course, I remember, Charlotte," she continued, in a much softer tone. "But what's that got to do with—?"

The curtain moved again. They all glanced up. A thin, older man stood there almost apologetically.

"Can I get a glass o' water, luv?" he asked Joan, who was standing closest to him.

"Yes, certainly." She offered her unsmiling smile. "We'll bring it right down." She almost pushed the man back into the cabin as she yanked the curtain tight against the bulkhead. "Go on," she ordered Charlotte.

"My friend," Charlotte whispered, "my friend . . . my flat-mate, Annie, was one of the stewardesses on that flight." Her voice quivered as tears silently rolled down her cheeks.

"I'm sorry . . . but I still don't see—," Joan's impatience was creeping back into her voice now.

Teri studied her friend's distraught features. She understood her grief, but why was Charlotte so terrorized?

"Christ! We don't have all day!" Joan suddenly snapped as she filled a clear plastic cup with murky urn water. "I suppose *I'll* have to take this myself." She disappeared into the cabin, muttering something under her breath about loony cabin crew. Charlotte crumpled onto the jump seat again.

"Don't take any notice of her," Teri told her. "We're all a bit on edge. Just tell me . . ."

"I was down the back." Charlotte spoke softly, staring up at Teri. "At first I thought I heard a banging on the rear port door. Of course, I thought . . . . And then the noise turned into something else. It sounded like finger nails scratching on the metal . . . clawing at the door and then I heard . . . loud knocking, *really* loud, on the outside window! So when I turned to look . . . ." Charlotte shuddered. "I saw . . . Annie's face . . . staring at me! From the outside, Teri! How could that be? Her face! Oh, god, her face. "

Charlotte stood again. The jump seat flipped shut. She grabbed Teri's hands as if holding on to her for dear life.

"That's not all. I heard Annie's voice. She sounded so . . ." Charlotte paused, searching for words to fit the images, ". . . wretched. It *was* her voice. I *know* her voice."

Teri shivered.

"The worst of it was . . ." Charlotte now spoke in

a raspy whisper, "They were *my* words. My god. Do you think *she* could have caused it?"

"Caused what?" Teri trembled as she saw Charlotte's facial features change, as if her friend was beginning to disappear, to spiral down into some dark abyss from which there was no return.

Scared, Teri asked, "For God's sake, Charlotte, what did she say?"

The deep, hollow voice was not Charlotte's, as the words came not from her but emanated from the space around her filling the whole galley. "'Let me in. Let me in. I didn't want to. It just happened . . . . It wasn't my fault . . . .'"

7

SOUL MATES

"You'll need something warmer than that!" Rhea exclaimed in her mild Australian accent as she hurried up the path towards me, snuggled against the evening chill inside a bulging purple jacket. She was eyeing the flimsy mauve fabric of my "psychic" outfit.

That's the trouble with being psychic. People think you know every detail about the future, especially your own. But it's not true.

Rhea was the other psychic hired to work alongside me that cold night. I had never met her but instantly warmed to her outgoing intelligence. "They told me—after I had left—that we would be going up Whistler inside the gondola," I explained, "and not Blackcomb on the open chair lifts."

Rhea foraged in her enormous leather shoulder bag and, like bringing a rabbit out of a hat, magically produced a black scarf and matching fuzzy pillbox hat. "Here."

"Thanks." I put them on, grateful for the extra warmth.

It was the fifteenth of June and the evening was drizzly, surprisingly chilly and gray. I had been hired along with Rhea to provide palm readings for a conference group. The original venue was to have been the restaurant at the top of Whistler Mountain, but a call to my cell after I set out had advised me that the group would instead be dining at the Rendezvous, two-thirds of the way up "the other mountain." So at six-fifteen we were standing, as instructed, at the base of Blackcomb.

I detest chair lifts even in the best of weather. It's a wonder that I ever allow myself to be transported up a mountain by what I deem to be a dangerously flimsy contraption. Coming down alone is the worst. Absolute terror takes over when sometimes the descending chair lift stops and sways back and forth, back and forth. The reality of dangling in space with only a thin cord hooked onto a slim cable by an open metal grip—the difference between life and death—only fuels my phobia. And when young mischief-makers on the same lift occasionally decide to bounce up and down, that grip can easily become dislodged—with fatal consequences. The sickening panic causes my hands to sweat on the cold metal bars, and I am overwhelmed by a frightening urge to lift up the bar and leap lemming-like into the void.

On this June night, standing unprotected from the heavy drizzle, Rhea and I waited for the other "entertainers" at the cedar ticket booth. The mountain was covered by early evening mist, but our liaison, Beth was smiling cheerfully as she approached. Walking by her side was a young man dressed completely in black.

Beth, like so many others in Whistler, was a no-make-up, long-hair-tied-back-in-a-ponytail, Gore-Tex-jacketed kind of a girl. Her clear blue eyes danced nervously as though ticking off a thousand details on her mental list.

She smiled as she introduced the black-clad young man. "This is Greg, our magician." The twenty-five-ish, slight, blond man was white-faced. Was he ill? His eyes were dull as if all the magic in his life had been decimated long ago. The silver earring in his left ear appeared cheap against his clammy-looking skin, the black pants and jacket only accentuated his pallor. As I

125

shook his limp hand, I felt something missing in Greg's energy. And then it hit me. Maybe, like me, he was terrified of chair lifts.

Blackcomb Mountain was closed to skiers at this time of year though open for special events at the restaurant. As we moved along the rubber mat to get on the lift, a solitary "liftie" in a grey and black uniform emerged from the hut to ensure our safe boarding.

The heavy, black, four-seater chair jerked around and whisked the four of us up and away from the base station. Rhea, her rosy cheeks glowing, chatted happily as we climbed higher and higher through the floating mist and away from the now shrinking outlay of Whistler village behind us. The plexiglas cover kept the rain but not the cold from seeping into our bones. Rhea continued to share her theories on why we were psychic while Greg and Beth made light conversation. Greg's monotone voice made me wonder at the irony of this almost-lifeless being practicing magic. We always teach what we most need to learn, I remembered. Or maybe his subdued energy was a sign of   *his* fear of heights.

The lower brown and gray slopes of the mountain appeared oddly naked without their usual covering of snow. I scanned for bears that could often be seen lumbering across the slopes at this time of year. Though I knew that the blackened tree stumps could sometimes be mistaken, from a distance, for a yearling in the early evening dusk, there were no bears tonight; just a mist that floated and swirled around the covered chair, enclosing us in our own microcosmic world.

"Who's the group?" I turned to ask Beth.

"Security Insurance. Three hundred of them from across the country," she responded.   "Seven to nine o'clock. Okay?"

I imagined a multitude of excited people crowding around, pinning us in our chairs for two hours while one after the other, expectant, apprehensive and even cynical, they waited for a tiny glimpse into their future.

By now we were riding above deep, rutted old snow and I felt a yearning to ski again. The top of the Wizard Chair loomed ahead. The station consisted of a small hut and a ramp sheltered by a blue corrugated overhanging canopy. Another lone figure waited to make sure we alighted without incident.

"Bar up!" Beth called, warning us to move hands and feet off the metal foot rest.

The cover clanked as it slid up and over our heads. Then we lifted the safety bar high and back. There was now nothing between our chair and hard stony ground thirty feet below. Suddenly feeling vulnerable, like being naked in a crowd, I jerked back involuntarily and clung to the metal back rest.

"Are you all right?" Rhea inquired, a trace of a smile on her face.

"I *hate* heights," I admitted.

Rhea nodded her understanding as we reached the black rubber mat-covered off-ramp. We climbed from the seat and crunched our way along a short gravel path towards the base of the Solar Coaster Chair, our next station for the second and last stage of the journey up to the Rendezvous Restaurant. I peered to the left where brown slopes criss-crossing down towards the village were lined with scrawny fir trees, ghostly through the low cloud. I shivered as the mountain mist permeated my clothes and clung to my skin.

"So how come they changed venues?" Rhea leaned forward to ask Beth as the chair lurched upwards and out of the station.

"Oh, something weird at the last moment with the gondola. I don't really know." Then she waved an arm dismissively and rolled her eyes. "It's crazy having it up here."

A sudden chill wind on my back only emphasized her point. "Let's make sure we ride down together," I suggested to Rhea, trying to sound nonchalant. "I'll buy you a glass of wine afterwards."

"You're on." She beamed.

We finally arrived mid-mountain and alit onto the path. On a sunny day the expansive restaurant afforded a vista of snow-capped mountains that seemed to stretch into forever. During the day, the interior would be filled with hundreds of rosy-cheeked, brightly clad skiers. Tonight we were enclosed in a large damp nebulous mist. Now rows and rows of tables were covered in white linen adorned with sparkling wine glasses stuffed with bleached-white napkins. Four uniformed musicians were setting up in the back of the restaurant, their black suits silhouetted against the large mist-covered windows.

Beth pointed to a spot near the entrance where, she said, Rhea and I could set up our "psychic tables." She directed Greg to perform his magic on the other side of the foyer and, with a "See ya later" tossed over her shoulder, she disappeared into the back of the restaurant.

I covered my table with a rich blue sequined cloth, added a single rose in a blue vase, laid out my palmistry books, business cards, a small clock and a box of tissues—just in case.

Soon men and women began to spill into the warm restaurant, shedding jackets and hats and—like dogs out of water—shaking themselves free of the cold. I had taken out my lavender scented candle and lighted it, a sign that I was open for business, when a tall, slim man in his fifties with friendly blue eyes and a full head of thick gray hair sat down at my table.

"I've never done this before." He grinned, opening his generously wide palms for me to read.

"Well then, it's time." I smiled. "Hmmm. Looks like between the ages of twelve and fifteen you had some life and death experiences."

The man's grin faded.

"You're still protecting yourself and hanging on very tight as if that situation still exists."

He peered more closely at his own palms, trying to see what I was seeing.

"I understand that you needed a survival instinct then but you need to let it go now. If you live in fear, your health will suffer." I smiled. "So chill out, relax and be healthy."

In a husky, quivering voice he thanked me and got up, vacating the chair for an elegant redhead.

While I took a quick sip of water, I noticed that Greg, clad now in black cape and top hat, was in the throes of his first magic tricks. A flash of multicolored scarves swirled into view. But I could not see exactly what he was doing with them as a woman with a mane of brittle, dark blonde hair was obscuring my view. From her body language, she seemed fascinated either by Greg or his magic as she was standing directly in front of him, transfixed. Was he casting a magic spell over her?

Like Greg, she appeared wan, her body sagging as if laboring under some great weight. Something about the scene bothered me, something . . . *eerie*. But I couldn't place it. Then the woman shocked me when she quickly turned around and looked straight into my eyes as if she had been reading my thoughts. She smiled weakly at me and then, as if magnetically compelled by this stranger, she turned back to gaze at Greg.

The redhead laid out her palms expectantly.

"Looks like you're going on a trip . . . ," I started. And so it went on, one five-minute reading after the other; mothers anxious to know how their children would fare, men apprehensive about careers, women eager for relationships, men stunned at hidden truths. Numerous messages from deceased relatives and friends emerged. Long suppressed emotions were unleashed, providing a need for the Kleenex.

I had to bellow above the band to be heard and now my throat was aching. I glanced at my clock. Quarter to nine. Only fifteen minutes to go, but the line-up was still six deep and a dozen more people were standing around, waiting. I stood up.

"Excuse me," I shouted to get their attention. Faces turned towards me surprised. "I can only do three more readings and then my time is up."

As I expected, they just stared at me, crestfallen, though some pulled faces of resignation and moved away. Suddenly a man with an official-looking badge emerged out of the crowd and approached my table. Apparently he represented the Security Insurance group. "If you read those people, we'll make sure you are both paid for an extra hour." He grinned, his glasses glinting in the light.

I glanced over at Rhea. A few people were standing around her table, including Greg, his work done now. My throat was aching, my stomach gnawing with hunger. I hated to see this handful of people so disappointed.

"Okay," I agreed, "but I need to check with my colleague and the organizer."

As I stepped up to Rhea's table, Greg was just shuffling the tarot cards. *She must be giving him a freebie,* I thought. He was irritated by the interruption but Rhea glowed when I asked her if she wanted to stay longer. "Too right," she nodded enthusiastically. "I'll have to make this quick then," she told the disappointed Greg.

Beth emerged from the crowd. "Another hour? Sure," she confirmed. "I'm leaving now. Maybe see you at the Chateau later?"

The crowd was thinning out, the waitresses clearing away and the darkness outside was casting shadows into the restaurant. I was relieved Rhea wanted to stay.

For the last reading of the night, a blonde woman sat down and I recognized her as the person who had studied Greg so intently. Sitting across the table from her in the dimmer light, I was shocked at her smooth, deathly-white skin. The invisible burden she carried was wearing her out, her brown eyes dull as if deeply depressed. Early fifties, I guessed, but her hair hanging down in straw-like clumps and the bags under her eyes could mean she was even older.

I asked every client the same question. "What's your name and your age, please?"

"Shelley," she muttered as if even the effort of moving her lips was painful. "Forty-two."

Wow. Something is wearing her out, I thought. Taking her frail hands in mine, I examined the complex network of lines. Her palms felt clammy.

"Oh my God!" I exclaimed, feeling the energy being sucked out of her as if a vampire was paying her nightly visits. "Something happened to you about twenty years ago." It was not a question.

Shelley nodded, her eyes glistening with tears.

"A huge loss . . . as if someone died," I continued. "A man . . . I get the initial K. Kar . . . . Something like that."

"Kyle," Shelley offered breathlessly.

"He was your soul mate . . . . Were you engaged to be married?"

The tears flowed freely now. I passed her the box of tissues. She could only nod.

A gust of cold air blew around my back, making me shiver. I turned and saw that a number of people, including Greg, were standing with the door ajar, preparing to leave. I waved at Greg, hoping he would get the hint to close the door. Instead, he gazed from Shelley to me then gave me a cold, hard stare. I had the creepy feeling for a moment that I didn't exist, that he was mesmerized by something *through* me. I shivered again. When I turned back to Shelley, she appeared confused.

"O-o-oh, someone's walking over my grave!" I said, smiling while attempting to lighten the mood before inspecting her palms again. "Did Kyle love the mountains? Skiing? And was he a bit of a daredevil?"

Shelley smiled, a faraway look in her eyes. "Yes. He worked on this mountain for a season . . . before the . . . before he died."

"You poor thing!" I felt her pain, after all these years still an open wound. "You know, it's almost as if . . ." I picked my words carefully. "As if you don't like being here . . . in this life. Only half of your energy is here and the other half is with him in spirit, on the other side. Have you been very ill?"

"Yes."

"Was it fibromyalgia, something like that?"

"Yes, it comes and goes. How did you . . . ?"

A five-minute reading with this woman was not enough to explain what I was seeing and feeling but this sliver of time was all I had. "Shelley, you have to decide . . ," I urged her.

"Decide what?"

"Whether you want to live or die."

She shifted uncomfortably in her seat. "I want to live." She mustered a little indignation in her voice, but even that diminutive burst of energy drained her.

"Yes," I insisted, "but something is pulling you over to the other side, and your work here isn't done yet."

I waited for a response but she just stared at her palms, frowning.

"Do you understand?" I squeezed her hands. "This is a matter of life or . . ."

"Could it be him? . . . I mean, pulling me?" she asked.

I considered the concept. I had never heard of a spirit from the other side being able to pull someone toward death.

"It's possible," I said, "but you do have the power to resist. And you are not resisting. That's why you're ill. It's simple but not necessarily easy. You have to commit to either this world or the next." I clasped her hands, trying to give her some of my own strength. "Decide to live!"

She frowned at her palms again as if a movie of her life was playing and she was trying to understand each scene. The weariness of it all was etched into her face. "What can I do?" she asked finally.

"If you allow yourself to succumb to him in the spirit world and you die before your time, you will only have to come back and do this life all over again. It's up to you."

The five minutes was up. I ended the reading by gently placing her hands together.

Shelley stared, stunned for a moment and then pulled herself laboriously out of the chair. "Thank you."

"Shelley!" I called as she was turning away. She blinked back at me, her white cheeks wet with tears. "Here, take my card. Please . . . call me if you still need . . . ."

She wrapped her long slim fingers around the peach card as if it was a lifeline. I watched her as she moved woodenly towards the door where, to my surprise, Greg was still standing, waiting for her. As if in a trance, he opened the door for her and they left together.

"That was fun!" Rhea exclaimed as we trudged to the chairlift. We were almost the last to leave. A handful of wait staff and other skeleton crew were staying behind to do the final clean up.

"Yes, hard work though." I couldn't get Shelley out of my mind, wondering if my reading had been of any use to her. I was also vaguely troubled by her fascination with Greg. Something was missing from both of their psyches.

Wearily, I sank down onto the chair lift next to Rhea, tossing my bag onto the seat beside me. "The day after one of these gigs, I feel as if I've drunk three bottles of wine and smoked five packs of cigarettes. And I don't even smoke."

"Maybe you should," Rhea chuckled.

The mist was even thicker now and the dark night air was much colder. I wasn't going to enjoy the descent but at least I had Rhea for company.

"Hey, is that you, Rhea?" Behind us an Australian voice came out of the shadows. The vague outline of a man standing by the chair moved forward. The liftie was stocky, his face half-hidden by a baseball cap.

"Ritchie?" Rhea cried gleefully and jumped off the seat. "I've gotta talk to my friend here," she explained to me. The chair jolted forward. "Meet you at the bottom," she called as I found myself alone in the swirling fog, dangling thirty feet above the ground. "We'll go for that glass of wine!" Her words trailed off into the mist.

In the dark it was hard to gauge how far down the ground was, and the fog made the ride even more disorienting. Now I felt I was flying aimlessly through space. Trembling, I reached up and grabbed the safety bar, pulling it down in front of me. Clunk. And now the cover. *I'll be all right,* I told myself, *now the hood is down.* The mist and darkness obscured the reality that there was four thousand feet between me and terra firma, and the safety of the village.

I sat back in the chair. *I'm okay. I'm okay,* I intoned. The only noises were raindrops on the cover, a gentle whirring sound and a *click-click* as the chair lift bumped and swayed past each tower. When the quiet became unbearable, I began to sing "Amazing Grace." My pathetic croaking sounded eerie in the cold night air but the words always soothed my raw nerves.

My knees, shins and ankles were hanging below the shield, exposed to the elements. Cold was creeping up my body; the thin material of my pants was not enough to keep me dry and warm. Thank God, though, for Rhea's scarf and hat.

When about fifteen minutes had elapsed, I guessed the next station would soon appear out of the mist. I peered out through the murky plastic. Would I be able to see through the swirling fog to get off in time or would I miss it and end up being carried all the way back up the mountain? Peering downward, several small yellow lights, edges blurred, emerged out of the fog. Were those the station lights? I must be still thirty feet above ground. *God, how I hate chair lifts.*

Suddenly the chair stopped. It lurched forward and back, back and forward, my stomach swaying in time with the sickening motion. *Stop swinging*, I told the chair and then prayed to God, not that far above me, for the chair to get moving. My mind instantly went to one winter's day on Whistler when three passenger-laden chair lifts had become mysteriously detached from the cable and crashed forty feet into the snow. Some of the occupants died, some survived but with serious injuries. Mustn't think about that. The handles of my bag were making imprints in my palms. If my clients could see me now, they wouldn't have to be psychic to read my fear.

A metallic grinding noise broke the silence and the mechanism moved forward again. I exhaled. How much longer could it be before I reached mid-station? Each *click-click-click* seemed hauntingly loud in the stillness of this outer space.

The lights grew larger. *Thank God!* The bottom of the Solar Coaster was only a hundred yards further down. I clutched my bag in anticipation of disembarking.

Another grinding noise. *Oh no.* The chair was stopping again.

Had I imagined it or had a shadow moved in front of the cover? Now a large dark shape floated outside the chairlift hood. I jerked back. What could it be, thirty feet above the ground? The amorphous thing loomed larger. *Thud* against the plastic. I screamed. What the . . . ? Another *thud* and the plastic cover sprang up and over the seat. Cold mist stung my face. I yelped as the bar in front was lifted by some invisible force, ripping it from my firm grip. There was nothing between me and a huge black void. I fumbled for then clung to the cold metal bars at the side and back of the chair.

My God, what could this thing be? What was it going to do to me? And where was it now? I waited. Nothing. I dared not even flinch.

The station lights were in my line of sight. *Oh so close*. Maybe if I jumped? Broken bones might be less painful than sitting here terrorized and frozen.

As if reading my thoughts, the chair jerked forward, downward and then abruptly stopped again, swaying. At the same time, the warm yellow lights of the station that had cast shadows across the mountain went out. In the black void, I imagined cold invisible hands clutching at me as the night closed in.

"Now you know how it feels." The echoing male voice was right next to me. But nobody was sitting there! I squirmed back into the corner, whimpering.

The chair started to swing again, gently at first and then more forcefully as if being pushed from behind like a swing.

"Stop!" I pleaded with the entity. My fingers froze in claws on the metal bars. "Ple-e-e-ase stop!"

"I know you can hear me," he jeered in my ear.

"Yes, I c-can hear you. Just stop the chair, please." My voice sounded pathetic.

The pushing ceased and the chair gradually settled into a mild rocking motion. I exhaled.

"Who are you? What do you want?" I inquired of the void around me.

"I want you to know how it feels." His breath was suddenly in my left ear now. A slightly rancid, acidic odor made me grimace. Sour milk.

The chair began to shudder, vibrating and rocking

me from side to side.

Was he trying to make me fall? I was hanging on for dear life, "How *what* feels?" I yelled, through rattling teeth. He was behind the chair now, his breath on the back of my neck. "To be alone, afraid. And in the dark."

Yes, I was terrified. In the dark. And alone. Rhea was up there somewhere on the chair lift or still talking to Ritchie. No one could help me now.

"Why me?" I sobbed, ashamed of my own fear. "What do you want from me?" Was I going to die here?

"Sh-e-ll-ey, Sh-ell-ey, Sh-ell-ey!" The voice moaned as if in terrible, terrible pain, filling the night air all around. *Oh God! The last reading*! The pieces suddenly slotted into place.

"Kyle?" How was this spirit able to manifest a physical voice? And then I remembered. Like a vampire, he was living off Shelley's physical energy. He was right in front of me now, his shadow emitting a biting cold as if he had just walked out of a freezer.

"Decide to live!" he jeered in my face, eerily mimicking my own words. That sour milk breath again.

"But Shelley deserves to live, she needs to live," I shouted defiantly.

A high-pitched screeching began.

"Oh God . . ." I cried and then a blast of cold air came at me, the force of his energy ripping the hat and scarf from my head and carrying them off somewhere into the night. The freezing air was shocking as it infiltrated my scalp and my thin clothing.

Was he going to kill me? Or would they just find me in the morning frozen, the color of my skin matching my mauve outfit. An image of rescuers unhooking my permanently clawed hands from the bars came unbidden to mind.

"I don't want to die," I sobbed. "I don't want to die."

"I don't want to die, I don't want to die." At first I thought he was mocking my fear but then somehow I knew that he had screamed those very words as his body succumbed to death all those years ago.

Think, Natasha, think! If this spirit feels my fear, he could keep sucking me down into his own personal hell. But dealing with stuck entities was not my forte. I usually left the darker forces to exorcists who were confident in dealing with intense dramas and evil beings. But now there was no choice. I had to do something. The first thing to do when encountering a ghost is to remind the troubled spirit that it *is* dead.

"Kyle, you are stuck between two worlds," I began soothingly, "the physical world where Shelley is and the spirit world where you are meant to be. I know you miss her but to find peace in the spirit world, you must let go of Shelley. Let her live out her life."

The force flew by me again, not quite so violently this time. The chair rocked slightly.

"No-o-o-o . . . His voice was breaking up now like a crackling radio "Greg . . . ."

Greg? What had Greg, the magician got to do with any of this? Now I was really confused. Maybe he's becoming disoriented. I persisted with my amateurish exorcism.

"Kyle, your fear of never being with Shelley again is keeping you stuck here alone and in the dark. When it is her time, she will come to you. You are soul mates and soul mates are eternally connected. You know that, don't you?" I urged, tossing the words out into the darkness.

"Your angels can come and take you home to the

light now, if you allow them to. For your own peace, let your spirit guides and angels guide you home. In heaven, you will never be alone or in the dark again. There are loved ones waiting for you there." I searched the blackness for some sign that he had heard me. "Do you feel them?"

No sound came out of the void but I sensed a shift in the atmosphere. The mist started to clear.

"Kyle? Kyle?"

More silence. I exhaled. Perhaps all his spirit needed was to be heard and reassured.

The grinding noise of the chair lift starting up again sounded deafening in the quiet night. The mountain contours were once again visible as the light shone from the canopy below. The chair was gliding slowly down toward mid-station and solid ground.

"Go in peace, Kyle!" I threw the words up at the heavens where I was now surprised to see stars.

"Natasha?" Rhea, her cheeks flushed with the cold, jumped off the chair at mid-station. "You didn't have to wait for me. Are you okay?"

"Yes, just frozen," I responded, still trembling from head to foot. I would tell her later when I was well away from this place why I was too terrified to get on the next chairlift alone.

"Here, you might want to put these on," she said, her hand outstretched, holding the black hat and scarf.

"But how did you . . .?" I could only stare.

"Oh, it was the strangest thing. I'm sitting there, minding my own business, when the chair stopped. I raised the cover trying to see what the hell was going on and the hat and the scarf just flew into my lap."

"Yes, it's been a strange night," I agreed, as we sat down on the next lift and it moved forward and downwards.

Now that the mist had completely vanished, we could see a comforting blanket of orange lights over the village below. With the hat and scarf, the slightly warmer temperatures and a real live person by my side, I gradually stopped shaking.

"Beth and a couple of stray guests are meeting us for a drink at the Chateau. Still wanna come?" Rhea asked.

"Yes." More than ever, I needed a hot toddy.

"Greg told me he might join us," she added.

"Tell me, Rhea, what did you see for Greg when you read him?" I inquired as the Wizard whirred us down to the bottom. I was still trying to make the jigsaw fit. "He doesn't look well."

"Oh, I didn't really have time to read him properly but something's definitely . . . weird!" she exclaimed. "Have you ever heard of soul retrieval?"

Rhea lifted the bar up and we jumped off into the lighted village. Even the pungent smell of horse manure from the paddock at the base was strangely reassuring, especially after the sour milk odor that I would forever associate with Kyle's ghost.

"Soul retrieval? What do you mean?" Still stiff with cold, I tried to keep up with Rhea's long-legged stride while also struggling to revitalize my frozen brain cells.

"Well, I've only seen it a couple of times," she began, "but it's when an aspect of our soul gets stuck in a past life due to a sudden traumatic death. The reincarnated spirit often appears to be only half present in this life because, understandably, a large part of their spirit is still out there somewhere in the ether. And those lost souls are often pining for, or feel guilty about, their soul mates. I've seen some really sad cases."

Fragments of disjointed information were starting to merge together somewhere in the back of my foggy mind, something to do with Shelley, Kyle and Greg and the other-worldly events of the evening. If only my synapses would fire, it would all click into place. And I wondered how after twenty-five years of readings, I had never encountered this phenomenon. "So how do you bring the two parts of the soul together?"

"The deceased spirit has to be willing to forgive and let go of what happened in the former life so they can move forward and become one with the new spirit in this life."

"But how do they do that?"

"C'mon, I'll tell you over a hot toddy," Rhea said as we reached the hotel. "You look like you could use one."

The Mallard Bar extended most of the length of the rear of the Chateau Hotel. The muted greens and reds of the Queen Anne chairs, the comfy couches and dimmed lighting were warm, cozy and reassuringly familiar. The bar hummed with locals, tourists and convention guests. Although my gig seemed like an eternity ago, I had only just met some of them on the mountain less than two hours previously. Almost immediately the warmth melted away some of the tension and chill in my bones. I began to feel a sense of safety again.

Beth waved at us from the far corner. Her group was huddled around a low square table. I recognized two male guests I had read earlier from Security Insurance and the company representative who had requested we stay longer. In the same cluster, a young man and an older woman were ensconced on the couch, chatting animatedly to each other, oblivious to their surroundings and our arrival. They seemed familiar but I couldn't quite place them. As we approached, the couple stood up preparing to leave.

"My God!" Rhea exclaimed. She was staring at the young man who was helping the woman on with her coat. Rhea's mouth was open and her stare, I thought, was bordering on rude. "Look at Greg!" She pointed at the blond man, the tell-tale earring in his left ear.

Like Rhea, I could only gape. Greg's face now had a healthy glow, his previously pasty features almost unrecognizable. His eyes were alive and there was dynamism in his energy. The pretty woman standing beside him, who I now recognized as Shelley, was obviously in love with him.

She beamed at me, her eyes dancing with joy. The former aura of death had transformed into a sparkling vibrancy. For a split second, an image of the young Shelley, her hair thick and shiny, cheeks flushed from skiing superimposed itself on her face as if the spirit of that young woman was alive in her again.

"Good to meet you all." Greg nodded at us. He smiled lovingly at Shelley. Taking her hand, they turned to leave.

"Shelley." I touched her lightly on the arm. She turned toward me. A vague recognition registered in her expression as if we had met years ago instead of just forty-five minutes previously.

"I'm sorry to have to ask you this question, but I have to know." I lowered my voice so that only she could hear. "How did Kyle die?"

She appeared stunned for a moment, and I could see traces of the old hurt flitting across her face.

Greg, with a protective arm around Shelley,

leaned forward conspiratorially and whispered in my ear, "He fell."

"Fell?"

"Yes. He bounced the chair lift and he fell," he said in hushed tones, a faint smell of sour milk on his breath.

8

CARMEL FOG

The couple crossed the road in silence. At the top of the beach they paused in the shade of a cypress tree to absorb the tableau of sun, sea and sand, the ocean still shimmering under a late afternoon cloudless blue sky.

"Carmel," she breathed.

"Yes." Gary nodded.

Tourists were beginning to work their way back up the soft sandy hill to their cars. While it was the end of their beach day, it was just the beginning for Cheryl and Gary.

The only shade was offered by a few limbs of the indigenous and sporadic cypress trees at the top of the hill. Then the beach rolled down into a flat strand before it met the ocean. Slimy long brown sea pods were strewn close to the water's edge, but in this beautiful setting, even the Carmel seaweed was somehow inoffensive.

Gary exhaled. "Wow! Look at that ocean!" he muttered almost to himself. His weekend hobby as a scuba-diving instructor always kept him close to or in the water.

"It's all yours," Cheryl said removing her sandals and scrunching her toes into the fine, granular sand. "You won't catch me in the Pacific!" A beach hadn't felt this good since they had been in Barbados on their honeymoon. Their other life. A second honeymoon would be asking too much but maybe this trip could be a healing for what they had both been through.

"Where do you want to sit?" Gary asked,

automatically taking the heavy blue and yellow beach bag from his wife's shoulder. Cheryl shivered. She felt a cool bite in the breeze that wafted gently across her freckled face. A long bank of fog had appeared, and was sitting just above the horizon, creating a narrow black shadow on the ocean. As if waiting for something, she thought. She shook her head to dismiss the shadowy notion. This is a healing time, she reminded herself. Think good thoughts.

There was something else missing from the beach, she thought. Oh, yes. Of course. There were very few children. Good. No painful reminders of excited toddlers building sandcastles with their mums and dads. There were all kinds of dogs, though, lots of them.

"How about over there?" Gary pointed to a spot farther down the hill, to the left just below a patch of green ice plant. "The hill might offer us some shelter."

"From what?" She smiled. "Gale force winds?"

"You never know. Nature can change very fast," he muttered, removing his brown leather sandals from his long feet and wading through the soft sand down the hill ahead of her.

Once Cheryl had unfurled their colorful queen-sized towel, or "the tablecloth" as her husband referred to it, she organized book, sunglasses, suntan lotion. Then she sat, taking in the other people on the beach. Who came to Carmel? By the variety of languages she heard passing—French, Italian, Spanish, Japanese, German and others she didn't recognize—people of all kinds.

Gary emptied his pockets onto the towel and stripped off his outer shorts and shirt and lay down next to Cheryl. He stretched out his long body, carefully placed his sunglasses beside him and, drinking up the heat of the sun, closed his eyes. "Ah, heaven," he said.

Cheryl surveyed the scene, letting her mind wander. Judging by the number and the noise of the motorcycles they had seen pouring into town, there must be a biker's convention blasting through the elegant serenity of Carmel. As it was the middle of July, the couple's first priority had been to find overnight lodging. Cheryl had visualized staying in one of the cottage, ivy-covered inns or even the more exclusive L'Auberge Carmel, but they were all full. Still, they had by some miracle found a vacancy at an affordable but comfortable chain hotel. As Gary traveled for his work as an engineer, he had commented somewhat cynically that even this normally generic hotel had been "caramelized." Voluminous and glorious coral red bougainvillea adorned the parking lot walls. The hotel pool deck was also lined with luxuriant baskets bursting with blossoming red, pink, purple, white and yellow petunias.

As they dumped their suitcases in their room Gary had suggested wearily, "Let's put up the posters after the beach, honey. We can check in with the police later, too. Okay?"

"Sure." Even though she hadn't driven at all, Cheryl was exhausted from the trip. The ever-constant rollercoaster of hope—thinking she saw her son's cherubic face in a park, a restaurant, a store, followed by the inescapable crushing grief—had sapped her energy.

When they had requested a fan to relieve the stuffiness of the room, the front desk agent informed them, "The weather is unseasonably hot,"—as if the intense summer heat was his doing. "That's why there are fireplaces in the rooms but no fans," he had added, shrugging apologetically. "Be warned. Our infamous fog might be denser, too."

Though their room wasn't the best—ground floor,

darkened by the necessity of drawn curtains for privacy and smaller than they were used to—room 33 still offered all the amenities they would need for one night: a comfy bed, clean bathroom, wide-screen television, gas fireplace and fridge to keep their champagne cold. Despite Cheryl's protestations, Gary had insisted on bringing the bottle of Veuve Cliquot. "It's for when we find him," he had said. Cheryl both loved and hated Gary's abiding optimism.

As they had driven down the main street to the beach, the photographer in Cheryl feasted on the natural luminescence all around them. It wasn't only the vivid gorgeous floral displays which gave Carmel its charm. The quaint country cottages reminded her of her native Devon in England. The lack of traffic lights, the non-existent billboards and the conspicuous absence of MacDonald's or other food chains also charmed Cheryl. Their friends were right. Carmel was a piece of heaven. "The whole town reminds me of a chocolate box," her husband had commented.

Gary had parked their Toyota truck at the top of beach at the end of Ocean Avenue. It was the only dirty, dust-smeared vehicle among the other pristine high-end sedans—Jaguar convertibles, Accuras and BMWs. Yes, we are definitely in Carmel, thought Cheryl. Paradise is expensive. Good thing we're just passing through.

Their drive down from Kamloops in Canada had taken four days. Not bad considering they had stopped in quite a few towns to put up more posters of their son—ignoring the advice of police, to expand their search.

When family and friends had urged them to get away, both Gary and Cheryl had agreed that they would get in the car and "just drive south and see where we end up." There had been no rush to get to southern California.

When their friends had strongly suggested Carmel for a good healing spot, the small seaside town had been one of the "must-sees" on their list. And now here they were.

Cheryl glanced over at her husband. "I thought you couldn't wait to get in the water?"

"I will," Gary responded, still relishing the waning warmth of the sun. "Just going to relax for a while first. That was a lot of driving today."

"Wow, look at that fog now." Cheryl gently touched her husband's arm. "It's coming right in. And so fast."

"Something to do with the heat inland," Gary murmured groggily, his eyes still shut, "which draws in the moisture from the ocean."

"What are those thin lines of brown stuff out there?"

"Seaweed," he murmured.

"Yuck. So if you were swimming out there, could you get tangled up in it?"

"Trust you to think of a disaster." His words were low and slurred now.

"Are you going to sleep?" she demanded, a little disappointed.

"Might," came the even quieter response.

Cheryl picked up her camera. Through the tiny window in her digital, she scanned the scene from left to right. The beach—click. The famous Pebbles Golf Course above the beach on the right—click. She trained the camera on the end of the peninsula peppered with a variety of very large and expensive properties—click. The fog was still sitting at the water's edge. If I didn't know any better, Cheryl thought, the sea beyond the mist could have disappeared and no one would be any the wiser—click. People were walking singly, like automatons, into the ocean and disappearing into the fog as if walking off the edge of the earth into another dimension. Spooky, Cheryl thought. Click.

She brought the camera round to her left and saw how the beach stretched around in a long curve—click. Sprawling homes and cottages lined the top of the slope. There must be a road up there that follows the beach—click. Later, when Gary woke up, she might drag him along the beach to drool over the million-dollar—or more likely twenty-million-dollar—waterfront homes. Maybe they could buy one? Right. And I'll get pregnant again, too, she thought.

She glanced at her husband. His head had dropped to the side and she could hear his light snore. His short, dark, curly hair was beginning to tinge with grey at his temples. He was a handsome man, she thought. With her five-foot-five tall, slender build and short blonde hair, people said they made a cute couple. But she hadn't felt cute in a long time. Initially, they had blamed each other for their son's abduction. What a horrible time! Gary had been such a naturally good father, Cheryl thought. If only she could become pregnant again. While they could never, ever replace their three-year-old, perhaps another child would alleviate some of their agony. Or would anything ever be all right again? One thing this experience had taught them was that they had to get through it together.

She pointed her camera at Gary. He appeared more peaceful than he had in so long. She liked the image of him sleeping in the sunlight. Click.

"What is it?" He sat up, quickly, jittery.

"Nothing, honey. It's okay. I was just taking a photo."

"Oh." He squinted at the beach, now emptier of

people. Cheryl glanced at her watch. 4:44 p.m.

"Well, it's now or never," he said, standing up. "I think I'll go in."

"You don't have to," she said, somehow wishing he wouldn't. She didn't like that fog. As she watched him unfold his long limbs and extend to his full six foot two inches, she added, "Watch out for the sharks."

"Okay, Miss Worry-Wart. And the seaweed. Anything else?" He grinned down at her. Cheryl was shocked when her husband suddenly leaned down and kissed her on the lips. "I'd give my life to be able to bring him back to you, you know."

Cheryl could only nod. Tears threatened to break loose.

He was studying her face. "I love you and I always will," he added, peering into her eyes for a moment as if to make sure that she understood.

"Me, too." Her voice almost choked on the words. Maybe one day she would be able to actually *feel* that love again.

She watched him lope down the beach, his feet causing loose sand to fly, his shoulders slightly hunched. He didn't hesitate as he walked straight into the shallow calm waters and was swallowed up into the fog.

Cheryl reached for her book and lay back on the towel. She wondered if she and Gary would ever feel happiness again. She was a different person now and so was he. Who wouldn't be? When there's a tragedy, especially involving a child, it's not just one person who goes missing or dies. So many more are dragged into the void with them, she thought.

She and Gary were both trying hard, too hard, to regain some semblance of   sanity. Their conversations were strained with forced joviality, as if trying to show each other how strong they were. The polite edginess of their relationship—unspoken thoughts of guilt and blame—just added to her weariness.

As if the word *weariness* had suddenly made her tired, Cheryl put her book down beside her and closed her eyes . . . .

Drifting in and out of consciousness, she was aware of her own restlessness, tossing and turning. She pulled her sweater around her middle and turned on her side. *"Mommy, Mommy." Scenes of her son flashed before her, calling out to her and as always, the dream never allowing her to reach him. But then the dream changed. Suddenly Gary emerged out of the mist and was holding the child in his arms. He handed Cheryl her three-year-old son, her baby. Finally, she could hold him, feel his little fingers on her skin, kiss him. Oh, my baby!*

On some level, Cheryl knew the breeze was getting colder but her eyes felt heavy and refused to open. She should wake but she didn't want to leave this feeling. Whole again, she was in the center of her family, embracing her child and her happy husband.

Then something jolted her out of her other-world. Cheryl's eyes flew open. She was lying on her side in a fetal position, her sweater pulled over her midriff. From this point of view she could see the yellow and blue toweling, white sand, and through a light mist, crashing white surf. Where was she? Oh yes, Carmel. That's right; Gary was swimming . . . and her son. . . was still missing. But something had changed. She sat up. *Brrrr.* It was really cold. The fog was swirling all around. Through thick and thin mist she could catch glimpses of the beach, the ocean, the peninsula. She yanked her sweater up around her shoulders and squinted through the murkiness, searching the beach from left to right.

Where was everybody? Except for one lone figure attached to a dog by a leash further down the long, curved sweep of sand, the rest of the beach was completely deserted. The scene was eerily silent. How long had she been asleep? And where was Gary?

She turned and saw his shorts, crumpled t-shirt, sunglasses, suntan lotion. Their cell phone and car keys were still sitting on the towel where he had left them. Like clues to a puzzle, she thought, not sure why those words popped into her head. Where was he? She stood and scanned the water. The sun was lower in the sky now and like a roll of carpet the fog had begun to curl back on itself. Still, the grey-blue ocean was barely visible. Cheryl squinted but couldn't see anyone in the water. Gary was nowhere in sight. He must have gone for a walk, she thought, her old paranoia threatening to give birth to itself again. She studied his pile of personal belongings. But something was missing? His wallet! Then he must have gone somewhere. She exhaled. That's what happened. He came out of the water, saw me sleeping and decided to go for a walk and took his wallet. Yes, that's it.

Something wasn't right, though. God, how she hated this feeling! It brought it all back again, the nightmare, the terrible panic, the sick clenching of her stomach, the not-knowing. Dear God, please don't take my husband, too! I couldn't bear it.

Cheryl stood up and turned towards the top of the beach, peering up the hill. Her eyes searched the trees. Maybe he's back at the car?

She glanced at her watch then. My God, it was 6:20 pm! No wonder the beach was empty now. But why hadn't Gary awakened her? And, after all they'd been through, wouldn't he leave her a note? They had discussed the torture of not knowing what was happening, what the imagination did. It was crazy-making. But she mustn't panic. He was always telling her to think the best until the worst had been proven, even about their son. There was still hope.

Well, I'm not just going to sit here and wait. That's what the police had told her to do before. "That's all you can do," they had instructed her when every fiber in her being wanted to run through the streets of the suburban neighborhood, screaming her son's name and searching every corner of every home. Sitting still with her thoughts had been agonizing.

She picked up their cell, the keys, his sunglasses and her camera and shoved them into her purse. In one deft movement, she scooped her husband's clothes into the large beach bag while grabbing the towel and throwing it over her shoulder. Something black fell out of the towel. Cheryl frowned and glanced down. It was Gary's wallet. Oh no! He wouldn't go for a walk without his wallet.

The lone figure walking the dog was now all the way down at the other end of the beach. Cheryl was well and truly alone. "Don't panic, don't panic," she told herself as she started up the hill. "It's okay. He's at the car." The familiar terrors were already rising like a phoenix from her ashes.

While scanning the parking lot and still hoping and praying for Gary to appear, she cursed the weight of the beach bag and the soft white sand that impeded her progress. Without his clothes, he can't have gone far, she reasoned, but it gave her little comfort.

Cheryl stopped and swiveled towards the ocean. The ever-metamorphosing fog had now suddenly lifted. Like glass, the water was calm and blue and serene . . .

and beckoning her. Why hadn't it occurred to her? The water! Oh my God, he could have drowned out there. But he was such a good swimmer. The water is calm. Are there currents? Rip-tides? She had been joking about sharks but were they really out there? Did he get caught in that seaweed? Ohmigod! Or that fog. *Don't be silly!* The ever-so-practical voice of her long-deceased mother chided her. *Pull yourself together.*

Cheryl stood, her feet sunk in white sand, completely alone, her heavy bag weighing on her shoulder, just staring at the ocean. Tears of helplessness spilled freely then.

Get a grip, Cheryl. First go to the car. He's probably there. She turned again and fought against the heavy weight of the sand and the steep incline. God, it was taking forever!

When she reached the crest of the hill, their dust-covered jeep sat alone in the shadows, undisturbed in the once-full parking area. As she approached, her fragile hope evaporated. She already knew Gary wasn't there. And hadn't been there. She went straight to the rear, unlocked the truck, and lifted the heavy door. No, everything was as they had left it. Or was it? Something was missing. The posters of Nathan? She shook her head and unloaded the beach bag and towel.

What now? Cheryl turned around and searched the parking spots, the washrooms. The washroom! Of course, that would make sense. She scurried towards the beige-stone building at the corner of the beach.

"Gary! Gary!" she called from outside the *Men's* entrance, praying that no other males would suddenly appear. But the sound of her voice reverberated in the empty space.

Should she call someone? 911? What if he

suddenly appeared after a walk? She would feel like a hysterical fool.

The ocean. Maybe he went back in for another swim? As she picked her way along the top of the beach between rocks and sand, Cheryl became aware of a trembling. God, she thought, when I find him, I'm going to let him have it for putting me through this.

Why was there no one to ask, "Have you seen my husband?" Wasn't it the height of the season? Some would be eating dinner, of course, or napping or shopping. And there had been plenty of people in the ocean. She had seen them walking into the fog. Surely, someone would have seen if he'd been in trouble.

Now unencumbered by bags, she flung her sandals loose and ran down the hill. She slipped and slid down through the loose granules until her feet found the firm wet flat. The large brown seaweed pods and limbs made designs in the damper, darker sand but she crunched over them, oblivious to their slippery feel and popping sounds.

The seemingly innocuous ocean was tranquil. She scanned the shimmering surface for a black, curly covered head moving out there. But there was nothing. Nobody. Just strands of seaweed now amassed in long brown lines on the horizon. The fog had rolled back even further and was once again just sitting on the skyline, still waiting for something, she thought. Cheryl suddenly felt that she was being watched.

"Is everything all right, dear?" It was a woman's voice coming from behind.

Cheryl swiveled around.

The woman was wearing a pink shirt and navy slacks. Her full head of long silver hair was scooped back into a thick braid. Cheryl recognized her as the figure she had previously seen walking her sheep dog up the beach.

"No . . . I mean . . . I don't know." Cheryl was so grateful to have someone to talk to. This older lady exuded grandmotherly compassion.

"My husband, Gary . . . he went for a swim two hours ago." Cheryl gasped. Speaking the words out loud made the nightmare a reality . . . again. "I-I fell asleep you see and . . . I just woke up and now I can't find him." A loud sob burst out of her. The woman's dog began licking her sand-covered feet. Grateful for the momentary distraction, Cheryl leaned over and stroked the dog's soft fur.

"Oh, dear." The woman's eyes fixed on the ocean. "Not again," she murmured.

What did she mean? Cheryl wondered, but too many erratic thoughts were tumbling through her head. She stood up. "I don't know what to do," she said, her tears coming easily. "I can't think . . ." She was aware of sounding unhinged. She told herself to pull it together, to sound sane. "So I thought perhaps he had just gone for a walk."

"Well, maybe that's exactly what's happened." The woman's eyes were highly alert, Cheryl noticed.

"But Gary wouldn't normally go without his shorts and T-shirt." Cheryl waved an arm behind her towards their spot, the gesture full of hopelessness.

The woman reached out and put a wrinkled but elegant hand on Cheryl's arm. "I'm Sophie Baumgartner." Cheryl couldn't help but notice the flash of several diamond rings. "Do you have a cell phone, dear? Maybe he called you?"

Of course! The cell. Cheryl groped in her purse for her phone.

She flipped it open and hit number one for

voicemail, then waited while it went through the roaming process. Her heart thumped in her chest. "You have one new voice message," the woman's automated drone reported. Hope soared. Cheryl punched in her password.

"Cheryl."

"It's Gary!" she turned to Sophie. Then the static cut in and was so grating she could not distinguish the words. The crackling noise became even louder, uglier, until it was deafening and his voice was just a plea underscoring the scratchy noise. The line went dead.

"What time did he call?" Sophie asked.

Cheryl hit the menu for more details. "4:47 pm!" She frowned. "But that's impossible," she muttered.

"From which number?"

Cheryl checked the details again. "Blocked ID."

Sophie sighed. "He must be alive then."

"No, it can't be. At 4:47 he was just going down to the water."

Sophie nodded as if understanding something that she was not going to share with Cheryl. "We should call the police . . . just in case," Sophie said ever-so-soothingly. "I'm sure your husband has gone for a walk like you say . . . but just in case." The woman yanked on her leash pulling her dog away from Cheryl's feet and held her other hand out for the phone.

"Yes, yes, of course." Cheryl felt so relieved that Sophie was taking charge, that someone knew what to do. As she handed the black shiny device to the older female, a memory flashed from just a few hours ago of Gary talking on the cell. *Ohmigod!* She prayed, *Not again. Please God, not again.*

The woman dialed and then handed the phone back to Cheryl. "Speak to Sergeant Boyle. He'll know what to do."

While it rang and rang, Cheryl studied the ocean. The water was calm, masses of brown seaweed sat still on the surface. The fog had completely disappeared now. The sun was high and bright in the early evening light. The perfect scene didn't seem right—as if everything were normal. But it wasn't. Some ominous secret lay just beneath the calm.

"Hello, Sergeant Boyle. Hello. My name is Cheryl Menet. I'm down on Carmel Beach and my husband, Gary went into the ocean and . . .." Cheryl knew the words were tumbling too fast out of her mouth.

"Oh? . . . . I should have called 911? But this lady on the beach said I should talk to you . . . ." Cheryl glanced at Sophie who was standing as if frozen and searching the horizon. "Well . . . my husband went for a swim two hours ago and . . ."

The sergeant's deep voice was official but compassionate. Unlike the policeman she had dealt with before, who had treated her with ice-cold cynicism—as if she could possibly have hurt her own son.

She listened while Sergeant Boyle spoke.

"It was 4:44 pm," she responded to his first question. "I remember looking at my watch," she explained. At his next question, she faltered. "Er . . . no, he hasn't called me." The message at 4.47 must have been an old one, she reasoned.

While Cheryl heard Sergeant Boyle issue directives to other emergency services on another line, she scrutinized the waves once again, praying, hoping that Gary would rise up out of the waves, wipe the salty water from his eyes and come running towards her. The mild trembling in her limbs was evolving into sporadic spasms of shivering.

Suddenly Sergeant Boyle was back on the line

talking to her.

"Mrs. Menet? I've just dispatched the Coast Guard, a chopper and a lifeboat crew to go and look for your husband. Are you sure he's in the ocean?"

"No . . . no. I'm not." Cheryl felt so stupid. "The last time I saw him he was going in for a swim but . . . I fell asleep . . . and I thought . . . maybe . . . "

"Okay. Is he a good swimmer?"

"Yes," Cheryl stated definitively. "He loves the water. He teaches scuba-diving."

"Uh-huh. Does he like to swim far out?"

Cheryl continued to answer the questions that Sergeant Boyle threw at her, but when he asked her about his physical details, she broke down. Talking about his body, his hair, his face made it all so real. "No, he's in good health," she managed, when asked about the possibility of a heart attack. *Although he had been under a lot of stress in the last nine months,* she wanted to say but held back. Then she would have to tell the whole story and she couldn't do that, not now. As if reading her thoughts, his next question made her gasp. "Is there a chance he could have disappeared . . . deliberately?"

"Do you mean . . . suicide?"

"That or he just wants to make it look as if he's disappeared?" Then softening he added, "Sorry to have to ask these questions but it will help us with the search."

Cheryl paused. Here we go, she thought. The ugly interrogation begins. "No," she replied a little too quickly. Could he? Would he? *No, no, no.* But how many times had *she* thought of just taking all those sleeping pills. Anything to end the excruciating pain. And what had Gary said just before he went in the ocean? *I would die to be able to give you back your son.* Oh, Gary.

"Ma'am, do you have a photograph of him?" the

officer was asking.

Before she could reply, the wail of sirens pierced the early evening stillness. Louder and closer now, Cheryl's stomach lurched remembering the last time.

"Mrs. Menet? . . . Are you there? Do you have a photo of your husband?"

"Oh, yes," she answered finally, her voice wavering. "It's on my digital. I took it just before he . . ." She couldn't speak.

"That's okay, ma'am. That's good for now. Just wait there. We'll be right down."

In the distance, another familiar sound started up. A chopper. Now numbness was setting in, earlier this time. Cheryl remembered how this went. The different stages of shock: first fear, then disbelief, followed by denial and then trembling and the agony of acceptance, or if she was lucky, no feeling at all. This was the pattern. Now she was an expert, she thought with dread.

Sophie and Cheryl stood side by side, scanning the water. The large mess of soft yellow curls that was Sophie's pet companion just sat by Cheryl's feet, also staring out at the water, as if searching, too. A strange noise emanated from the dog's throat and Cheryl realized it was his version of a growl. She followed the dog's intense gaze and saw that the animal was focused on something—or please God, Cheryl thought, someone— out there in the water. But when she squinted into the gathering dusk, searching for even a speck, there was nothing in the grey-blue mass.

The emergency services arrived quickly and all hell broke loose. Frenetic activity; men's voices giving instructions, shouting, reciting drills, the whoop-whoop- whoop of a helicopter overhead and the ugly shrill of sirens ruptured the former stillness. Cheryl was vaguely aware of instant warmth as a blanket was placed around her shoulders. And then a man in a navy uniform was standing in front of her.

"Mrs. Menet?" He thrust out a large, beefy hand. In this dual reality, the man's lips were moving, mouthing words but she couldn't distinguish the sounds because of the loud buzzing of multiple voices in her head. She heard Gary, then her mother, her son, her friends all talking at once but above all their garbled words, her own voice was silently screaming, *This isn't really happening*. Gary's voice urged her to be strong. She suppressed an urge to laugh. This was all so surreal. Cheryl wondered if this was how it would feel to take acid.

"Mrs. Menet?" the man repeated. Suddenly her fog cleared and she snapped back into the present reality.

"I'm Sergeant Boyle," the man was saying. "We spoke on the phone. As you can see, we'll do an extensive search for your husband. Have you any more information you can give us?"

Everything about Sergeant Boyle was big, Cheryl noticed. His size was not just his more-muscle-than-fat body type. His bushy salt and pepper moustache suited his powerful energy. His brown eyes weren't unkind but at the same time, there was a don't-mess-with-me air about him.

"No . . . ," she responded shaking her head, and then froze when a stretcher appeared to her left on the sand. Paramedics were preparing, she knew, for the worst. Men in wet suits with flippers on their feet plunged into the ocean, ropes trailing out behind them, like a strange species of sea animals.

She became aware of an arm around her waist, a supporting, gentle touch. Comforting. It was Sophie.

"Can I see that photo of your husband?" the Sergeant persisted.

"Oh yes. Yes." Cheryl groped in her bag locating the familiar smoothness of her digital camera. With shaking hands, she fumbled with the buttons, clicking back. Wasn't the photo she took of Gary almost the last one? But it wasn't there! There were the shots of the ocean covered in fog, Pebbles Golf Course, the peninsula. But no Gary. She clicked through each one again with no results.

"That's so strange!" The panic in Cheryl was rising up again. "I- I don't understand." She clutched her stomach as if she felt the urge to vomit but she suppressed rising bile. "It's not there. I know, I *know* I took it."

"Can I take a look?" Sergeant Boyle held out a hand. He knew how to handle the camera. There were definitely no pictures of Gary, just people on the beach. He would keep the camera though, just in case. Cheryl gulped as she felt the policeman's scrutinizing stare as if to say, *does this hysterical woman even have a husband?*

Cheryl pleaded with him, "Please . . ."

"You must have another photograph, dear? Passport, driver's license. Perhaps in your purse? The car? Your hotel?" Sophie whispered in her ear.

"Oh, yes, of course." Cheryl exhaled. She told the officer, "There's a photo in the car—my other bag."

"Okay," Sergeant Boyle also seemed relieved. "We'll let these guys do their job." He waved an arm at the melee of rescuers on the beach. "Officer Densen," he said turning to a young uniformed man behind him, "why don't you take Mrs. Menet to her car to get the photo of her husband and then bring her to the station. We'll check the hotel again. What room number did you say?"

"Thirty three," Cheryl answered woodenly, thinking about the peace that they should now be enjoying in that room instead of this horror. Then he added pointedly, "Once you've got the photo, you'll need to give Officer Densen your car keys."

"Why?" Cheryl frowned. But she already knew the answer. She was potentially the evil perpetrator of some horrible crime—in the eyes of the police—now having also murdered her husband. Their vehicle would be torn apart, again, now a possible crime scene. Evidence. "Yes, of course."

The two officers then turned, just out of Cheryl's earshot to consult with one another. "I'll meet you back at the hotel, dear." Sophie told Cheryl. "Come on, Nate," she added, tugging on the dog's leash.

As if the older woman had punched Cheryl in the stomach, she stopped and glared at her. "What . . .?" she asked Sophie, frowning. Cheryl's freckled face was contorted in agony. *"What did you say?"* she hissed, glaring at Sophie.

"Nate." Sophie looked surprised, "My dog's name."

Would it ever end—the whole nightmare, the last one that wasn't over and now this? As if a tidal wave had surged up from the ocean floor and thundered down on her, Cheryl's knees buckled and she sank down to the wet sand.

Though she was aware of all the men and some women around—paramedics, coast guards, police who were witness to her breakdown—she couldn't stop the gut-wrenching sobs that came from the depths of her being, from her womb. Cheryl collapsed, her legs curled under her. She rocked back and forth, clutching her stomach, crying "My baby! My baby!" Why was God doing this to her again? *Why? Why? Why?*

Some of the men stepped back, awkward, silent and puzzled. The older woman stood close, frozen, letting Cheryl unleash her anguish. Her sobs finally subsided and when she was finally spent, she felt a gentle touch on her left shoulder.

Sophie helped her to her feet. "I'm *so* sorry," she muttered in Cheryl's ear, stroking her tousled blonde hair. Cheryl realized that somehow Sophie understood her pain.

"How embarrassing," Cheryl whispered as young Officer Densen shyly approached. She wiped her face, attempting to regain a semblance of dignity and glanced around at the other people in uniform. They had quickly resumed their work. Sergeant Boyle, she noticed, had taken a step back, but he was still observing her very, very closely.

"Nothing embarrassing about the grief of losing a baby," Sophie said matter of factly.

"Officer Densen, take Mrs. Menet up to her vehicle to get her things and then bring her and her car keys back to the station."

Cheryl addressed the sergeant, "But shouldn't we wait here . . . in case?"

"Let them do their job," the young officer responded softly. She knew what he really meant. It was better if she wasn't here when they pulled Gary's limp corpse from the water.

But the ocean still tugged at her. She turned once more and stared hopelessly at the horizon. The frenetic activity had quietened. The chopper and the other searchers were farther down the beach now. Cheryl whispered to herself, "Gary, where *are* you?"

Her soft words hung in the stillness of the

encroaching sunset. The only movement in that scene, apart from a distant splashing of a diver, was a seagull that swooped down, picked up something from the surface of the water in its beak and swooped away. Back down on the beach, Sophie's dog growled again as if he had something against the bird or the ocean.

"We need to get that photo, Mrs. Menet," Officer Densen urged. Cheryl allowed herself to be led away from the scene and up the hill by the young policeman.

"You can tell me the story of your baby later," Sophie called out after her.

As she climbed to the top of the beach, she wished the grandmotherly woman would come with her, but the policemen were ignoring Sophie. Who was she anyway? Cheryl guessed that the once-beautiful silver-haired lady was a local, rich widow. With another stab of pain, it occurred to her that she might be a widow now, too.

"That's our jeep." Cheryl pointed to the travel-worn vehicle, strangely still as if abandoned a long time ago. She walked woodenly to the car and unlocked the trunk. While the officer watched, she groped underneath the blanket for her other purse where she knew she kept one of the few precious photos of Gary, herself and Nate. Once the door was slammed shut, the officer held out his hands for the keys.

"Over here." He led the way to the black patrol car, its yellow lights still blinking, and helped her into the front seat.

As they drove up Ocean Avenue, she refused to entertain the idea that Gary had drowned. *Just doesn't feel true*, she thought. But then again, she had refused to accept that Nate would not reappear either. Even after nine months, a part of her maintained that her son was still alive. She could *feel* him. Most of the time, she still held out hope for his return. Did she have any choice? The pitying, condescending looks from her friends were hurtful. She knew what they were thinking, *When is she going to accept that he's gone?*

"Do you intend to go back to the Inn-By-The-Sea?" the young man asked as the car glided up the main street.

Cheryl nodded. Where else could she go?

"We have an officer posted outside the door just in case he goes back there."

But Gary, Cheryl knew, would never have walked from the beach to the hotel without his clothes or his wallet. But what if he'd been taken . . . somewhere else?

As they entered the station reception area, Cheryl was struck with how everything in Carmel—as if by decree—was small and quaint, including the police station. The officer ushered Cheryl into an enclosed glass and wood-walled office and left her alone, perched on the edge of a less-than-comfortable wooden chair. Sergeant Boyle's words still reverberated in her brain, *disappear deliberately*? Although Gary experienced his own version of pain after losing Nate, he wouldn't commit suicide, would he?

Cheryl shook the thought away. No, no, no. She knew Gary. He wouldn't do that to her.

Sergeant Boyle's bulky physique suddenly loomed just behind the fluted glass of the door before he entered the office.

"Coffee?" he offered as if caffeine would soften the blow he knew he was about to deliver.

Cheryl shook her head. "Is there any . . .?"

He sighed as if weary of the same old scenario— imparting bad news. He laid his meaty arms on the desk in a gesture of defeat. "We're doing everything we can . . . two boats, a chopper, scuba divers. In a way, that's good news." He shrugged, hoping she would get his drift. "Do you have that photograph, Mrs. Menet?"

"Oh, of course," Cheryl responded. With trembling hands, she foraged in her purse.

"They'll stay out until dark, another hour and a half . . .," he informed her as he pulled out forms from his desk, "and then . . . . May I?" Sergeant Boyle leaned over the desk and deftly removed the photo from Cheryl's grasp and studied it. A small grunt escaped his lips.

"What is it?"

Sergeant Boyle was frowning.

"It's over a year old," she explained. "It's the only one I have here . . .." Her voice wavered but she held it together, "so please, I really need it back."

"We'll take good care of it," he said, still frowning. "Where is your son, Mrs. Menet?"

Cheryl had known the question would come. She knew she would have to answer. But even now, forming the words in her mind was still excruciatingly painful. She cleared her throat. "Er . . . we don't know . . . he went missing . . . nine months ago. He was taken . . . while we were shopping." Her voice cracked. "He's still missing." She put her head in both hands and shook her head, attempting to erase this nightmare.

Finally, she raised her head and saw that Sergeant Boyle was still studying the small photo of the young couple and blonde-haired, blue-eyed boy. Why was he scrutinizing it so intently? What was he thinking? Was there something about Gary? What was it? Maybe something about Nate? Had he perhaps seen a bulletin from Canada in the missing children files? But there were so many children who went missing. Would he remember

Nate even if he had seen his photo before?

Hope fluttered for a second and then Cheryl instantly suppressed it. Sergeant Boyle was making notes. Cheryl wondered if the veteran officer was beginning to suspect her, this young woman whose family disappeared on her. Or was it just her own paranoia?

"What *is* it?" she asked again.

As if her voice pulled the sergeant out of a trance, he sat up and focused his eyes on her. "Not sure. Probably nothing."

But Cheryl knew it was far from *nothing*.

"So you and your husband's prints are already in the Canadian system?" he asked in a neutral tone.

She nodded, remembering the devastation of being incriminated in her own son's disappearance. "We've been putting up posters everywhere," she added, although she realized that's not what the officer was asking.

Sergeant Boyle's voice was softer when he spoke. "Was there anyone suspicious on the beach today? Anyone that you recognized or did anyone approach you that seemed a little strange?"

Cheryl shook her head. "No, we had only just arrived."

"When did you say your son . . . disappeared?" Sergeant Boyle was making notes. "He was three when it happened?"

"Three years, two months."

"Where?"

"The Quick Mart, a supermarket just outside of Kamloops, British Columbia."
Cheryl repeated the same words she had recited a thousand times. "We were shopping. Nate just disappeared at the grocery store. Gary thought I had him.

169

I thought he had him. It happened so quickly. So quickly!"

"Your husband? Was he on any drugs?"

"No!" Gary on drugs was laughable. He was one of the straightest people she knew—solid, reliable—until he disappeared into an ocean.

"So you and your husband have been under a lot of stress since your son disappeared?" Sergeant Boyle probed.

Cheryl knew exactly where he was going with his line of questioning. And she was ready for him. "No, there aren't any other women, although I wouldn't blame him if there were. And no, he doesn't take drugs, not even sleeping pills, which I have taken by the way. I suppose you want to confiscate those. And no, he is not involved in any crime—white collar, gambling, embezzlement, child trading, drug dealing or otherwise. He doesn't have Aids or any other deadly disease. No, I didn't kill him and stash the body in the car. And no, he didn't commit suicide, although I have definitely felt like killing myself many times especially after being treated like a criminal by the police." Cheryl exhaled, still glaring at the large man.

Sergeant Boyle sat back in his chair, laying his chunky hands one over the other. He merely listened, observing her.

"Anything else?" she challenged. "Because if there isn't, you can take a photocopy of that picture you have in your hands and I want the original back before I leave."

Still maintaining an inscrutable expression, the sergeant said quietly, "I'm very sorry that you have had to go through this, Mrs. Menet. I'll be right back."

With that, he pulled his bulk from his seat and left

Cheryl sitting in the chair that felt more uncompromising by the minute. *Probably another tactic to get people to talk*, she thought. Maybe she shouldn't have spoken to the sergeant like that but it felt good to get angry. Her therapist had said, don't get sad, get mad. They had treated her and Gary like criminals instead of victims. How could they? Parents had rights, too.

From behind the glass of the sergeant's office, she could see the blurred shapes of the two policemen standing there, their voices muted so no words could be distinguished. Their body language, however, communicated something intense. What were they discussing?

Finally the sergeant reentered the office.

"Do you have any friends here in Carmel?" he asked, friendlier now. "Is there someone you could call?"

Cheryl couldn't bring herself to call any of her friends or relatives and tell them she had lost Gary. What would they think? She would wait until . . . later.

"The lady down at the beach. She's meeting me back at the hotel."

"Which lady is that?" Sergeant Boyle asked, taking his pen and preparing to write something.

"Oh . . . I just blanked on her name." Cheryl rubbed her forehead as if it would bring it back. "You know, the older woman who was down there."

The sergeant searched Cheryl's face, some question on his mind that he didn't verbalize. He pulled his bulk out of his chair and stood up. "Okay, you can go now," he said as he handed Cheryl her treasured photo. She took it, grateful for the only proof that she once had a husband and a child.

"And there's my direct line." He extended his hand, offering her a business card. "Call me if he . . . if you remember any more details." As she took the card, and to her complete surprise, the sergeant covered her small hand in his large grip. "I apologize if I offended you, Mrs. Menet, but there are a lot of crazies out there. Sometimes it's hard to tell who's real and who's . . . make-believe."

Cheryl just nodded, noting that his hand was surprisingly warm and comforting. "We'll be in touch," he added, showing her the way out. Why had his attitude shifted? What did that mean? "Officer Densen will drive you back to your hotel."

The thought of returning to an empty, sterile hotel room was already filling her with a familiar dread. This trip should have been a healing experience and now it was turning into an ever-deepening nightmare. *Please God, let Sophie be at the hotel.*

"What were you and Sergeant Boyle talking about?" Cheryl asked the younger officer as they drove the three blocks. "Your boss seemed more interested in the picture of my missing son than my husband."

"I'm sorry but—," he started.

"You're not at liberty to say," Cheryl finished for him.

He sighed, relenting. "He thinks that *maybe* they are connected . . ."

"How do you mean?"

"He won't tell me either but I think he's got a hunch," he confessed as Cheryl was climbing out of the car. "Do you want me to come in with you, Mrs. Menet? Check the room . . .?"

"No. Thank you."

"Try and get some rest," he said as he signaled for the police sentry to get in the patrol car. Then Officer Densen, the guard and his black car were gone.

"Any news?" Sophie was standing right behind her, her dog Nate by her ankles.

Cheryl jumped. "I didn't hear you . . ."

"I'm sorry. I try not to scare people." Sophie smiled. "Was Sergeant Boyle kind to you?"

"He's not sure if I murdered my son *and* my husband now."

"I know." Sophie was still standing close to Cheryl's left shoulder.

Even though the policeman had been watching the hotel door, for Cheryl hope was conflicting with possibility. Maybe someone else had brought him back to the hotel? Maybe he had hit his head on a rock and got amnesia? God, maybe he had even met another woman and come back for a roll in the hay? She wouldn't have blamed him. She had been so terribly miserable to live with. But none of it was possible. The sentry had already checked the room.

Cheryl withdrew the plastic key card from its slot and the green light flashed in the door lock. Her heart was pounding in her chest. The dog was whimpering and scratching at the door as if he sensed a presence within.

A huge "pop" exploded from inside the room.

"Oh, Thank God. He's here!" she said out loud. A long, deep growl came from the dog.

As Cheryl pushed the door wide, she called into the shadows. "Gary? Gary?" But what she saw made her frown.

No one was in the room. The bed was made and undisturbed. The bathroom door was ajar.

She rushed in and over to the sound of the "pop," on top of the fridge in the far corner, closely followed by Sophie and her dog.

"Look!" Cheryl cried, pointing.

The bottle of champagne that she and Gary had bought and stashed *inside* the fridge was sitting in a bucket of ice *on top* of the fridge. The champagne now spewed forth and was falling in foamy rivulets down the green neck of the bottle. Cheryl could still feel the just-opened-effervescence touching her cheeks.

"How could that possibly happen?" Cheryl demanded of Sophie, her voice rising. "If the metal brace and cork had blown off and was sitting somewhere on the carpet, I could rationalize that it had been shaken in transit and exploded by itself. But . . . see! The foil, wire and cork are neatly lying there on the tray."

The pitch of Cheryl's voice was escalating as her hysteria threatened to break through. She stared at the still bubbling champagne that had been poured into two champagne glasses, taunting her. "Only a live being could have done that," she argued, as if Sophie's silence implied her contradiction. "But who? Or what? Gary *must* be here."

Cheryl strode over to the closet and yanked the mirrored sliding doors open. "Gary? This is not funny." Then Cheryl realized voices were coming from somewhere. The television? Cheryl went to the closed oak doors of the television cabinet and threw them open. But the large screen was black. "How can that be? It's off!" she exclaimed. The voices, wherever they were coming from, dwindled to a furious whispering and then gradually ceased. A hush settled over the room.

Preferring the sound of human voices, Cheryl leaned in and hit the TV power button. A rerun of *Murder She Wrote* was playing. She turned up the volume and closed the doors on the unit, muffling the dialogue.

The older woman stood still as Cheryl whirled

around again and searched the room with her eyes. "Gary, where *are* you?" But apart from the Angela Lansbury's familiar intonations coming from the television cabinet, there was still an unearthly hush.

Cheryl walked toward the bathroom. She pushed the door wide and threw back the shower curtain. The gleaming white bathtub was empty.

"Maybe room service got their orders mixed up," Sophie suggested, "and opened the wrong bottle of champagne?"

"But, Sophie, that's crazy!" Cheryl hissed. "We just heard it pop. That bottle was opened while we stood outside that door." She stared at the vignette the scene suggested, the cruel irony of the story that might have been. The champagne was meant to celebrate finding Nate but now Gary had disappeared. She finally broke down, collapsing on the bed, her hands covering her face in spasms of sobbing.

She had worked so hard since the loss of Nathan to get a sense of solidity back in her life. And now someone—or something—was playing a horrible, sadistic joke on her. Why? To push her right off the edge again—and for good this time?

Sophie sat down by Cheryl in her fetal position on the edge of the bed. "Why don't I run you a nice hot bath, dear?" Sophie was already going towards the bright white bathroom. "And then I'll go and get us some hot food."

Cheryl sat up and grabbed a tissue from the nightstand. Through her emotional fog, Cheryl thought Sophie's reaction strange. But maybe like her, the room was giving the older woman the creeps. And the way Sophie's dog was cocking his head to one side as if listening intently to someone speaking to him from the bed was also eerie.

"How about some homemade soup, hmmm?" Sophie offered, emerging from the bathroom, with the sound of water gushing into a bathtub and the scent of freesias floating into the room.

"I'm not hungry . . . ." Cheryl said dabbing at her eyes. "And . . . " *I don't want to be alone in this room.*

"Let's turn the TV off," Sophie suggested, reaching into the cabinet and silencing the voices. "I don't think you should listen to the news. It can be heartbreaking." As she put a leash on Nate, Sophie said, "And why don't you enjoy that champagne with your bath?"

Ugh! Cheryl thought. She would choke on the champagne. As the older woman was about to close the door, Cheryl stood up. "I don't want you to leave, Sophie. I don't need anything . . . please . . . stay."

"I'll be back soon." She smiled knowingly at Cheryl. "I'll bring you some sleeping pills too. So you can have a nice deep sleep."

After Sophie was gone, Cheryl walked woodenly into the brightly lit bathroom and contemplated the bath filled with foamy bubbles. If only she could just climb in and let the warm water and sweet smell take her to another reality. But she wouldn't relax in this room. Instead, she turned off both taps, splashed some cold water on her face at the sink, and sank her face into the soft hand towel. She returned to the bedroom and paced around the large bed in the claustrophobically small, dimly lit space.

What a nightmare! Would it ever end? *Gary, where are you?* Should she call someone? Her friends would think that she was cursed . . . or guilty . . . or insane. She herself couldn't believe how her loved ones were being stolen from her. Finally, she sat on the edge of the bed and lay back, her mind still racing with different horrific scenarios.

She was drifting somewhere between fragments of movies when a noise brought her back to full consciousness. Cheryl listened. There were voices in the room again. She knew that Sophie had switched off the television but still a man's and a child's voice were coming from behind the television doors. They were familiar, laughing voices. Gary? Nate?

Cheryl clambered off the bed and walked gingerly over to the unit. She took a deep breath and yanked the wooden doors wide open. She moaned and fell back on the bed.

There was Gary beaming at her from the television screen. Gary in the back garden pushing Nate down the small bright yellow plastic slide they had given him for his third birthday. Cheryl, her back to the camera, was standing at the bottom of the slide, arms wide, ready to embrace her son. Little Nate was sitting at the top, giggling, ready to plunge down the slide into his mother's arms.

How? How did that old video get into this TV? She had refused to watch it since Nate had disappeared. The video was hidden at home, she thought. Gary must be playing this awful trick on her. Had he gone missing so that he could torture her like this? Or was it someone else? But why and to what end?

"No-o-o-o!" Cheryl screamed, "No-o-o-o!" her pain too big to hold inside. She didn't care if the neighboring hotel guests had her arrested.

There was a knock at the door. *Gary?* She rushed to the door. "Oh. It's you," she said as she pulled the door open.

Sophie was clutching a brown bag that smelled of

177

warm chicken soup. She marched into the room and began unloading steaming food onto the small coffee table. "Chicken noodle, warm bread, sleeping pills," she said, as she laid them out. "Was that you making that noise? What's the matter?" she asked, eyeing the younger woman's fraught expression.

Cheryl pointed to the television but it was a blank quiet screen again. "What's happening to me, Sophie?" she whimpered. "I think I'm going mad."

The older woman came and sat next to Cheryl on the bed. "The mind can play terrible tricks on you when you're in grief." Sophie snapped her thumb and finger with a surprisingly loud click and said, "But the fog can lift, just like that. Come on. You need to eat."

"Maybe I'm just remembering," Cheryl muttered, still staring at the silent screen now reflecting a black, shiny distortion of her and the hotel room.

"Come on." Sophie urged. "Have some soup."

"No, I'm sorry. I can't . . . ," Cheryl muttered. "I think I'll just lie down," she said as she got under the covers. Before she could protest and tell Sophie that she didn't want sleeping pills, the little pink drugs were in one hand and a glass of water in the other. "All right, dear. I know. You need rest. Lots and lots of rest."

"Will you stay with me?"

"Until you fall asleep, dear," she said as she pulled the covers over Cheryl's shoulders. "And if you need to call me in the night, call any time. I don't sleep much. Any time."

"Sophie, how does anyone ever get over losing a child and a husband?" Cheryl muttered, exhaustion giving way to sleep.

"Oh, they don't, dear." With wrinkled hands, the older woman patted her hair. "Get some rest now."

But Cheryl was already drifting into unconsciousness.

She's running after Nathan. She can see his blonde curls. She is so close, his chubby legs, running away, always just out of reach. Then Gary grabs her from behind around the waist and pulls her to him. He is stroking her back, her arms, his hands moving up to her breasts as he kisses the nape of her neck. His caresses melt all the tension she is holding onto. He is touching her legs, her inner thighs, moving up, probing. She feels his warmth and physical strength all over and in her body now. Both bodies are moving in sync, gently at first, filled with so much tenderness, and then with more urgency. There is a purpose to this, more than just making love and being together. They need to bring a child into their world.

A shiny silver bell appears dangling from a pale pink ribbon and jangles in her ear. Gary's voice is whispering, Wake up! Wake up!

The ringing won't stop. The disturbance is distant and close at the same time. Now it's louder and coming nearer. The urgency of the ringing is taking over their rhythm.

Cheryl jolts awake. Where am I? The ringing is on her right. Of course, Carmel, the hotel room, Gary is missing. The phone! Groggily, she reaches out and grabs the receiver. Ohmigod. Maybe someone found Gary.

"Hello?"

That static sound again. There is a voice amongst the crackle, a male voice. "Who is this?" Cheryl is wide awake now. She sits up.

"I've got Nate."

"What did you say? Gary? Who is this? Speak up, I can't hear you."

More static.

"Gary? Gary! Is that you?"

"I've got Nate," the voice says again, fainter this time.

"Please . . .," Cheryl pleads. "Who . . .?"

Click. The dialing tone drones in her ear. She continues to hold the receiver, hoping that someone will return to communicate with her. But there is just silence.

Was she dreaming? Was that Gary? Someone has Nate? Or was it the person who is determined to drive her insane? She should call someone. But who?

Cheryl leaned over and peered at the bright red numbers on the clock radio. My God! 5:55 . . . the triple numbers again! It was too early to call Sophie, even though she had offered.

Maybe she should call Sergeant Boyle? Why not? She didn't mind disturbing *his* sleep. That was his job, she rationalized. She dialed his number. His deep tones recited the usual message on the answering machine and then added, "If this is an emergency, please call 911."

Was a strange phone call an emergency?

She couldn't go back to sleep now. That dream with Gary had been so . . . real. Cheryl threw back the covers. She needed a coffee.

While the coffee machine made gurgling noises, she climbed into jeans and a sweater. Even with that familiar noise, the hotel room emanated an eerie silence. If she put on the television, what pictures would show up on the screen this time? As she tentatively hit the remote, Cheryl never imagined she would be so relieved to hear the thick Slavic accent of Ivana Trump on the shopping channel.

But she couldn't remain in the room. Nothing would be open in Carmel at this time but staying alone in this tight space with her thoughts and the threat of another other-dimensional experience was not an option.

She opened the hotel door onto a paved parking lot. The air was cool and fresh. Maybe she should walk down to the beach. God help her if she saw Gary's body washed up on the sand. But at least if she was alone when she found him, she would be able to grieve in private. Something she hadn't been able to do with Nate. His abduction had been such a horrendously public affair.

Clasping a small cup of pungent hotel coffee, she stepped out into the early morning. The temperature was cool on Cheryl's face and the early morning silence was peaceful. No one was around. Good.

She walked the ten blocks down Ocean Avenue towards the beach —past the jewelry and fashion shops, art galleries and realty offices that were so still the buildings themselves appeared to be sleeping. But as she approached the bottom of the street and the parking area with its diagonal slots still empty of cars and saw the beige stone of the washrooms tucked under some trees, she faltered. What if she went down to the beach and *did* see Gary's body lying there? She glanced to her left and saw a street lined with more flower-adorned houses. Maybe that was a better option.

She had only gone one block when she realized this street joined with the road above the esplanade. The beach was just below to the right but fog had rolled in again; the distant sound of waves lapping on the shore was the only proof that the ocean was nearby. Now the sun was rising in a hazy yellow glow through the mist. Perhaps later the fog would clear and blue sky would appear, Cheryl surmised. Up here, for the time being, above the fog, she could be alone with her thoughts. Maybe she could even think clearly.

Scenic Drive meandered around the cove, clinging to the curve of the cliff. On the other side of the street, Cheryl noted the assortment of houses and cottages. Where she walked, the sandy sidewalk was lined with a protective wooden railing. Beyond the fence, the cliff fell away to the beach and a sprawling green carpet of ice plant blended into the fog.

Yellow warning signs were posted periodically along the top of the cliff path. *Wading, Swimming, Dangerous Riptides, Sudden Changes and Currents.* Why hadn't she and Gary seen those warnings yesterday? *Oh, Gary. Where are you?* Lying at the bottom of that ocean, cold and alone? She couldn't bear the thought. At least with Nathan, she could imagine that whoever had taken him had badly wanted a child. They could . . . would be loving him. Or so she chose to believe. That's how she stayed sane. Of course, there were much darker, more horrific reasons why Nathan might have been taken. She didn't want to think about those possibilities now.

Wooden steps leading down to the beach were situated at one hundred yard intervals, but the stairs just disappeared into the fog. On a whim, Cheryl decided to go down the next stairway. As she approached, something colorful to her right caught her eye. A steel bucket filled with a vibrantly fresh display of pink and yellow daises was clamped to the top railing. When Cheryl came closer, she saw on the ground beneath the bucket an arrangement of stones and shells with writing on them. Oh God. Cheryl realized, this vignette was a memorial. She stopped to read.

To Robert and David. Taken too young. We miss you. We'll always remember you.

Cheryl recognized the raw words of fresh grief, reminding her of the plethora of flowers and heartfelt messages that had appeared on their doorstep when news broke of Nate's disappearance. As if he had died.

What had happened to Robert and David? How long ago had they been taken? How old were they? What was their relationship—friends, brothers, father and son, like Gary and Nate? Had they also been taken by the ocean? Would there be another bucket alongside for Gary? Cheryl wanted to find the mother of those two men and talk to her. So they could comfort one another.

As she started down, Cheryl thought about disappearing into the fog, too. What exactly did she have to lose? Clutching her runners in one hand and hanging onto the rough railing with the other, she descended the wooden stairs tentatively, feeling each step with her bare feet. Soon she was completely enveloped in fog.

Soft cold sand through her toes let her know she was on the beach but the limited visibility only allowed her to see three or four feet ahead. She could hear the surf lapping gently on the shore about twenty feet in front of her. If she walked toward the sound of waves, Cheryl reasoned, and then right—back in the direction she had come—she would eventually arrive at the spot she and Gary had chosen yesterday. Who knows what she would find in that soft nothingness?

The day was still dawning. Probably little chance of bumping into other early morning walkers, she thought. Her heart pounding, she walked toward the sound of waves landing on the beach. Overhead—or was it to her left—Cheryl heard seagulls squawking. The fog was disorienting, making illusions of sounds and distances, warping reality. Time and space seemed to expand and shrink.

Is that what happened to Gary yesterday? Did he get completely disoriented? He was tired from all that driving, Cheryl remembered with a guilty pang. Even though he's an expert scuba diver, had he overestimated his strength? Neither of us noticed the warning signs but Gary is aware of the different moods of water.

A cool breeze coming from the ocean wrapped itself around her shoulders. She shivered. The lapping was suddenly loud and the sand beneath her bare feet was flatter, wetter. She must be close to the water's edge. Sooner than expected, she felt cold water licking at her feet. The soft, thick fog enveloping her was disorienting.

She turned to her right and followed the sound and feel of the waves. *This way, I can't get lost,* she thought. *And the regular lapping was meditative.*

There were so many, many questions, just like before. "Don't try and figure it out," her husband had said when Nathan disappeared. "You'll go crazy. Just deal with the facts."

But what were the facts?

Gary had gone into this ocean for a swim at 4:44. He may have somehow called her at 4:47. Or not. But this morning at 5:55 a.m, he had managed to call her on their cell. The photo of Gary had been deleted or had disappeared from her camera. The champagne had popped by itself. An excerpt of their home video had somehow found its way into their hotel room and shown up on television. The dream last night of them making love had been so vivid. And now there was heaviness in her womb. *As if another soul already inhabited her body.* Cheryl had felt this way when she was pregnant with Nate. But that's impossible, she thought. It was just a dream. Or was it? So *who* had called and wakened her?

There were no facts. Just the unexplainable. Someone or something was trying to torture her.

Maybe the sergeant was right. The disappearances

of Gary and Nate were connected. But how? Where *was* her baby? Somewhere alive, safe and loved, or dead, discarded like a piece of garbage? Cheryl would never be able to forget the blatantly cruel comments that some people, even unthinking friends, had thrown at them, their words landing like a swarm of knives in their raw, ripped-out hearts. Then they had to shield themselves from the unspoken accusations in the hardened, disbelieving eyes of the police, not to mention the media's outrageous distortions of the truth.

The rhythmic lapping of the small waves was almost hypnotic. When Cheryl looked back toward the cliff, the fog swirled so she could catch intermittent glimpses of green-covered cliffs, houses, stairs. Then they vanished and she was once again cloaked within the fog. Now as she walked, Cheryl was only aware of not stepping into the cold sea lapping on one side and avoiding the brown, slimy strands of seaweed and their pods on the other. She prayed that her feet wouldn't meet with the bloated bulk of her husband's corpse. Sickened, she thrust the thought away.

How she missed Gary. Despite his own pain, he had been her rock. Maybe he wasn't even in the ocean? But men don't get abducted. Or do they? Not by humans anyway. The fog. It had something to do with the fog. What had Gary said before he went in the ocean? I'll do anything to bring Nate back to you?

Sometimes the fog seemed lighter and then just as suddenly it became denser again. It was easy to lose track of time within it. She didn't know how long she had been walking but she must, she figured, be close to the end of the beach. Now the mist wafted around her in puffs. As Cheryl looked up and through a swirl of fog, she thought she recognized the shadowy slope of green where she and

Gary had lain yesterday. Maybe if she sat there again, she would remember something.

Once on the steeper incline, she saw the familiar dark clump of green ice plant dotted with delicate pink flowers springing up in large profusions out of the soft sand. Yes, she was sure this was their spot. Cheryl sat down. The dampness seeped into her bones, her very soul. Exactly how she felt on the inside, she thought. As without, so within.

A blanket of fog wrapped itself around her. She was alone, a lost soul with just her pain for company. Repressed sorrow flooded her being. Grief came in great spasms. For the first time in nine months, Cheryl allowed herself to cry and scream and sob, venting her rage into the silence, not caring whether her despair would be heard or dissipate into the fog. There was probably no one to hear her anyway. She allowed the numbness to melt, her feelings to come to life again, to feel the exquisite agony of it all. No one had understood her loss, not even Gary.

Then it suddenly occurred to her that Sophie had understood. How? Her compassion had to be from someone who knew this pain.

"Cheryl! Cheryl!" A voice came from somewhere in front of her. Sophie emerged out of the fog followed by her dog. "I thought you might be here," she said. "I couldn't sleep, Sophie. I thought if I came down . . ."

"Yes." Sophie sat next to her and the dog snuggled in between them. "What *did* you think you would find if you came down here, Cheryl?"

"I dunno . . . maybe . . . ."

"You would find Gary dead or alive?"

Cheryl nodded. "Maybe."

"Facing your fear is the first step."

"To what?" Cheryl asked.

"Moving forward. Don't stay stuck, Cheryl."

"Sophie, what happened to you . . .?"

"You have to get out of your own way." Sophie was staring straight ahead at something.

"I don't understand."

"If you focus on your fears, dear," Sophie said, patting Cheryl's hand, "eventually they will come true."

They sat in silence in the fog.

"Sophie, thank you for . . . I don't know what I would have done if you hadn't been here."

Sophie put a hand again over Cheryl's. The coldness of her touch shocked the younger woman and made her shiver. "It's what I do now," Sophie muttered.

"What do you mean?"

"Living in fear will eventually kill you. Trust me, I know," she added.

"What happened to you, Sophie?"

"You must be tired. Just lie back and sleep now."

Cheryl *was* exhausted, spent not just from crying but fearful thoughts, nights, days and months of them. Sophie was right. Fear was killing her. "What's going to become of me?" she asked the older woman, as she lay back on the surprisingly warm sand. "I'm all alone now."

"You're never alone, dear, even when you think you are. No one ever dies. Everything is just an illusion."

Cheryl's eyelids were getting heavier.

"You need to sleep. I'll stay here with you . . . until you wake up."

As Cheryl drifted into unconsciousness, she was sure that Sophie had tenderly laid a warm blanket over her, a blanket so warm that it felt as if it was made of love.

"Mommy! Mommy!" The old dream again. Cheryl thrashed and turned from one side to another to escape the pain of her son's voice. She would have to wake up and feel the stab in her heart, that pain of loss again. Nate was gone, gone, gone. Why did her mind keep torturing her like this?

But like the volume on a radio, Nate's cries were getting louder, more urgent. Intermingled with *Mommy, Mommy*, she heard Gary's voice calling, *Cheryl! Cheryl!* Gary? She opened her eyes but the brightness of the sun made her squint. *Where am I? Where was the fog? Where was Sophie?*

Restless, she turned over. She saw the sand, the ice plant, the edge of her blanket and then she peered at the scene ahead of her down the beach. Cheryl sat up quickly. She could only see bright white light so she focused on the voices coming from that direction. She squinted again. Was she awake or asleep? Or dead?

Then she blinked, not believing what she was seeing. *It must be a dream, a mirage,* Cheryl thought. She instantly leapt to her feet. A savage cry escaped from her belly. She rushed down the hill to the flat beach, sand flying as her feet barely touched the embankment and then raced along the still soft but flatter incline.

"Cher-y-l! Cher-y-l!" She heard his voice now and knew this wasn't a dream. It couldn't be. Just a hundred yards away now, Cheryl could see Gary running toward her. "Gary! You're alive!" she yelled to no-one in particular and laughed. He was back! Somehow, from somewhere he was back. But he was clutching something to him. From this distance, he appeared to be holding a small child, a boy. *Could it be? Could it be Nate?* Both frantic and happy thoughts collided in Cheryl's mind as she ran. Even though she was physically panting with the exertion of running in heavy sand, she was aware of emotionally holding her breath.

As Cheryl came closer and closer, she was vaguely aware of two other figures behind Gary. They seemed to be trying to chase him, or to keep up with him. The first was a man in uniform; a police officer who was somehow familiar. Behind him was a heavy, middle-aged woman, her shoes clutched in one hand, her purse flying from the other shoulder. She was also running, or trying to but she was hampered by her office attire—a snug suit. Normally, Cheryl's brain would have tried to make sense of this scene but the only piece her chaotic mind focused on was the little boy being jostled in Gary's grasp.

"Oh God! It must be him. It must be him," she cried out as she sobbed and rushed closer and closer, cursing the sand for hindering her speed. Breathless, Gary was slowing, only yards away now. As the space narrowed between husband and wife, Gary shouted, "Cheryl, I've got him. I've got Nate!" Loosed somewhat from his father's tight grip, the little boy turned towards her, stretching out his arm, calling "Mommy, Mommy." The four-year-old blonde-haired boy was oh-so-familiar but different. His blue sweater and dark pants were slightly grubby and his blond hair now browner, longer and scruffier than she remembered but he looked so much like Nate. And this little boy was reaching out one of his chubby little hands for her and calling her Mommy.

"Ohmigod! Nate!" A primal, agonized sob and hysterical laughter simultaneously came out of Cheryl's mouth. Her knees wanted to buckle but she had to keep going. The little boy's hand, bouncing with his father's frenzied gait, was clutching the air as if he couldn't wait to hold her. Only feet away, she could now see the mixed joy and anguish in Gary—and recognize her baby.

"Mommy, Mommy!" Nate reached out to Cheryl, just as he had in a million dreams. Cheryl was afraid to lean forward and touch him in case he evaporated into thin air again. Had it all been a nightmare? What had Sophie said? Everything is just an illusion. And then a veil lifted and she knew he was real.

Nate leaned toward his mother, thrusting both arms at her now, wanting to be in her embrace.

"Nate! Nate! Nate!" Cheryl threw her arms around her son and husband. All three collapsed into a group hug in the sand. She pulled him from her husband and wrapped him tightly in her arms, feeling his little body against hers, burying her face in his neck, smelling his little-boy smell, kissing his hair, and sobbing.

Gary enveloped mother and child in his arms, crying and laughing. Cheryl reached up and kissed Gary on his cheek. So many questions were rattling around in Cheryl's brain but all she could do was lose herself in this fantastic joy which for so long had been eclipsed by nothing but pain. Cheryl could only let the laughing and sobbing erupt out of her as she stroked the tousled head of her baby. He had grown, and changed but this was definitely her Nate.

Nate cried and clung to his mother, his little hands clutching her long strands of hair just like he did when he was a baby. Finally, Cheryl held him from her so she could see him, check his face and hands and feet to make sure he still had all his body parts. His blonde hair was browner, longer and untrimmed and his chubby face had thinned but he seemed to be unharmed, physically at least. The growth in him caused a pang of pain as Cheryl realized how much of his formative time she had missed. But he was back now. He was back and safe! Thank you, God.

"Mommy, where were you?" Nate cried. "Why did you go away?"

Cheryl gulped. *Oh God*. She realized that Nate believed *they* had abandoned *him*. In his world, he had no idea of the nightmare they had been through, the sleepless nights and the ever-constant rollercoaster of hope and despair. The eternal search. How would she be able to explain to her little boy the agony of having him stolen from them? She glanced up at Gary, a silent question in her eyes. *And where have you been?*

"We lost you, Nate," Gary answered. "And we looked and looked . . .. "

Tears flowed down Cheryl's cheeks but she tried to regain her composure for Nate's sake. The poor child must be so traumatized and confused.

"I think we should let Mummy and Daddy explain that to you later, Nate. The woman's voice was soft, compassionate but still breathless when she spoke to Nate and included his parents. Cheryl had been so wrapped up in her own emotions, she had not noticed the police officer and the woman waiting patiently behind Gary. "Mrs. Menet, I am Annette Wilson," she continued, "I'm a social worker in Carmel. I think we should have a conversation with both you and your husband before you talk to Nate. This is Sergeant Boyle," she said, pointing to the heavy officer behind her who was still panting. "I know he wants to talk to you both."

Nate nestled his head against his mother's shoulder as if ready for a nap. Cheryl beamed up at Gary.

"Where . . . where did you find him and where were *you?*" Cheryl demanded of Gary, her anger colliding with joy. So many questions raced through her mind, she could barely muster her thoughts. Her heart felt as if it was bursting out of her chest with happiness when only what seemed like moments ago she had been in a black hole of despair.

"Honey, you were totally dead to the world so I took the posters out of the car and walked up to the police station . . .."

Dead to the world! Police station? Cheryl tried to make it fit.

"But why didn't you call or leave me a note . . . ?" Cheryl wanted to demand but Gary was inclining his head to the bulky man standing patiently behind, the police officer who up to this point had been studying the emotional reunion. Cheryl could still only see his dark shape against the glare of the late evening sun.

". . . and Sergeant Boyle instantly recognized Nate from the poster," Gary was saying as if he himself had only been gone a couple of hours. "But why don't you tell the story, Sergeant?"

"How do yer do, ma'am?" The bulky man in uniform inclined his head toward Cheryl. She was clutching Nate to her, burying her nose in his neck, remembering the smell of him, and leaning against Gary but she observed the policeman with interest. Though he was still in shadow something about the man's voice was familiar, Cheryl thought.

"We had an anonymous call from an elderly lady a few nights back reporting somebody screaming in the neighborhood," the sergeant began. "When we got there, no one was screaming. But we interviewed the woman who lived in the house and we saw the little boy. I just knew something wasn't right about that set-up but I couldn't place it until your husband showed me the poster of your missing son." He paused, choosing his words carefully. "Turns out the woman who took your boy lost her own three-year old in a car accident a few years back.

192

She just wouldn't accept that he had died. So I guess she went lookin' for him. All the way hell up in Canada apparently. The good news is he's probably been well taken care of. Loved you might say."

Loved. Cheryl breathed a sigh of relief. She knew the circumstances could have been so much worse. There were still many, many questions, of course, but they could be answered later.

"How can we ever thank you, Sergeant Boyle?"

Cheryl asked, still not able to shake the feeling that she had met him somewhere before.

"I sure am happy to be able to be a part of this story," he commented, "a happy one for a change."

Thank you, so, so much," she said, one arm clutching Nate to her left hip and then stepping forward to offer her hand. The sergeant responded by giving her a firm, beefy handshake. Then she was able to see the man's face. Cheryl inhaled sharply.

"This is Sergeant Boyle," Gary was saying.

"I'm sorry you had to go through this," he said, still holding her hand, his large eyes peering deep into hers.

"Sergeant Boyle!" Cheryl exclaimed.

"Er . . . have we met, ma'am?"

"Didn't we . . . er . . . Sophie . . . I . . . ." Cheryl still couldn't decipher what was dream, nightmare or reality but she liked this illusion more. "Oh . . . er . . . maybe I confused you with someone else?"

"My wife has psychic moments." Gary beamed proudly down at Cheryl, and hugged both her and Nate to him.

"Well . . . I hate to break up the party," Sergeant Boyle tentatively began, "but Annette here and I need to get you all back to the station so we can go through some procedures with you folks. Annette, I'll see you back there?" The social worker nodded.

Before she turned and plodded back through the sand, she advised the parents, "We need to debrief so just be careful what you say in front of Nate right now."

Cheryl nodded, still basking in the heaven of holding her little boy tightly to her.

"You can go up that way." Sergeant Boyle pointed to a set of wooden stairs a little farther down the beach. "Mr. Menet, if you give me the keys, I'll bring your vehicle around."

Cheryl remembered the pain of handing over her keys to a uniformed officer in her dream. But had it been a dream? A smiling Gary gave the bunch of keys to Sergeant Boyle who turned and made his way up the beach, picking his way between straggling sunbathers who were making the most of the early evening sunshine.

While Nate stayed snuggled into the familiarity of his mother's warmth, Gary and Cheryl just clung to each other in gratitude and joy. "The nightmare is really over now, honey," Gary murmured into Cheryl's ear. "Just like a bad dream, that's all."

"We should go," Cheryl murmured huskily, pulling back. "The sergeant will be waiting and we still have to pick up our stuff."

Back down the beach, in one deft movement, Gary scooped their paraphernalia into their bag, and threw the towel over his shoulder. With Cheryl clutching a sleepy Nate to her, and Gary supporting them both, the three of them worked their way through the sand and climbed the wooden stairs, the same wooden steps it seemed to Cheryl that she had just descended earlier.

Their dusty Jeep was sitting waiting at the top of the staircase on Scenic Drive. Sergeant Boyle stayed in the driver's seat with the engine running while Cheryl carefully positioned herself, still clinging to Nate, in the back seat. Gary was just about to climb in to the passenger seat when he stopped and walked over to the fence. "Look, honey. I saw this earlier." He was pointing to a steel bucket on the railing containing a fresh array of flowers. "It's really sad."

Oblivious to the chaotic thoughts racing through Cheryl's brain, Gary asked, "Sergeant Boyle, do you know who died? It doesn't say what their relationship was, just two males."

The policeman sighed. "Father and son. They drowned in the ocean during an especially bad bout of fog."

Gary groaned. "Poor family!"

"Yes, it actually happened twenty-five years ago. Weird thing is flowers are always fresh but no one ever sees them being replaced. Local rumor has it that the wife and mother died of a broken heart. Sophie Baumgartner, her name was. When it's really foggy here, people say her ghost and the ghost of her dog are seen roaming the beach looking for them. And because she can't find them, she takes others into the fog with her."

"Do you believe that?" Gary asked.

He shook his head. "There are a lot of crazies out there." Sergeant Boyle stared in the rearview mirror and caught Cheryl's eyes. "Sometimes it's hard to know who's real and who's make believe, eh, Mrs. Menet?"

Gary turned and peered into Cheryl's eyes. "Hey honey, are you okay?"

As Cheryl stared numbly at her husband, she felt a familiar stirring in her womb.

9

CLOSING TIME

It was twenty minutes past ten at night when the Citroen pulled up in a back street of Rheims.

"*Voilà l'auberge*," our driver announced, pointing to a large house set back from the narrow, cobbled street. The Youth Hostel Directory had confirmed that, though it was still early for the summer season, the accommodation in Rheims would be open. With its weatherworn brick and trailing ivy adorning the large wooden front door, the house— or what we could see of it in the dusk through an eight-foot, wrought-iron fence—resembled an old country home. Three storeys high, the front of the building was punctuated by large square windows on each floor.

This was only the second night of our trio's hitchhiking adventure. I was nineteen. My two girlfriends, Julie and Hilary, and I had decided that we would leave our respective jobs in England and, as the Americans say, "do" Europe. Julie, a small, lean redhead with clear blue eyes, and Hilary, her physical opposite, tall, large-boned, with long brown hair, had traveled a similar route the year before. I was the rookie.

After we had extricated ourselves and bulbous backpacks from the cramped tiny auto, our *chauffeur* left us standing on the wide sidewalk looking up at the hostel. To our relief, the ground floor windows streamed yellow light onto the small front lawn, a sign the hostel was not yet closed for the night. We shouldered our backpacks and walked single file down the precariously uneven flag stone path through the garden to the front door and stepped into the shadowy entranceway. Facing us was another door. Above it hung a sign, *Bureau*. A small handwritten notice on the door read, *"Fermé entre le 9 et le 11 Juin."* Some other words were scribbled underneath in a cramped freehand.

"What does it say?" Julie asked.

"Closed between the 9th and the 11th of June. Or is it the 17th?"

"What's the date today?" Julie asked

"The thirteenth," Hilary responded drily. "They should be here."

I peered more closely at the messy writing. "I can't read the rest."

Tapping once more on the office door elicited no response.

Julie turned to her right. "Looks open to me," she said. She slowly pushed the door wide, revealing a high-ceilinged, brightly lit games room. A green ping-pong table took up most of the space. Two worn, rubber-backed paddles, one at each end of the ping-pong table, were tossed down on the smooth green surface as if the players had recently abandoned a game. From the sculpted cornices and ornate woodwork on the sweeping staircase curving up the opposite wall it was likely that this elegant building had once been a French nobleman's mansion. Now with the ivory-colored walls marked and chipped, it appeared shabby, uncared for. On the wall, beneath the staircase, a variety of mens' and womens' coats bulged from a rack underneath the staircase next to another small foyer and door.

"Hello-o-o," Hilary called out. "Hello-o-o-o!" An eerie stillness was our response.

"Maybe they've all gone to bed," I suggested

hopefully, although I was beginning to get a creepy feeling about the place.

"I'm going to look in that room," Hilary-the-Brave announced and she went across to the door on the far side of the ping-pong table. In silence Julie and I waited and waited and waited, our eyes fixed on the door through which our friend had gone. Finally she reappeared, shrugging her sturdy shoulders. We both exhaled audibly.

"It's a lounge of sorts," Hilary reported. The lights are on and there are things lying about, but nobody's there."

"Let's go and look around." Julie took the lead, and like lambs Hilary and I followed.

Two glass double doors toward the back of the hostel led from the games room into a large square kitchen. From the light cast from behind us, the shadowy room was quiet but still emanated a warmth as if people had been here cooking within the last few hours. The metallic surfaces were clear and shiny, all the clean dishes were stacked in their open shelves and the utensils had been put away in their jars.

"They must all be in bed." Hilary's voice behind me sounded as if she were trying to convince herself.

"There's only one way to find out." Julie led the way again.

We turned from the kitchen back into the games room and toward the wide staircase. The click of the light switch as Julie flicked it on sounded very loud in the silence of the big old house. We started up the wooden stairs. They creaked under our weight and I realized I was holding my breath.

At the top was a square landing. To our right another staircase spiraled upwards into a black void. We stepped into the center of the space. There were two single, painted doors, one in the end wall, facing us, the other set into the wall on our left. The far door bore a yellow-tinged sign that read "*Privé*." Julie walked over to it and tried the door handle. She turned back toward us. "Locked," she said, not surprised.

The door on our left was slightly ajar. A match-stick figure with a mass of long frizzy hair was scratched into the flaking yellow paint. Something about the electrified-hairdo gave the figure an air of madness.

"Must be the girls' dormitory," Julie whispered as she gently pushed on the door. I expected a creak but instead the door made a strange shooshing sound. A thick, cold cloak of air swirled around me and then passed through me. I shivered. By the light from the landing, we could see sleeping bags strewn on the six or seven rows of two-tiered bunk beds. Backpacks, similar to ours but half-emptied, were sitting at the end of each bunk. Pairs of walking shoes were parked under the narrow beds. But there were no occupants. Where were they?

"Can you hear that?" Julie was straining to listen. "Sounds like lots of people whispering."

Whatever the sound was, it got louder and louder until the whispering filled the whole dormitory. Quickly we backed into the landing to get away from the deafening noise. Finally it stopped. Silence fell over the landing like a soft blanket.

"What the heck was that?" Hilary demanded, as if Julie or I would know the answer.

"I don't like this!" I exclaimed, feeling that we were not alone but being watched by a thousand pair of invisible eyes.

"Look!" Julie pointed to the expanse behind us.

On the bland, yellow-painted landing wall, somebody had taken a knife or some other sharp implement and scratched the shaky figure of a matchstick man. But while the image was innocent enough, there was something frightening about the way the figure's hair stood on end and about the otherworldly symbols unsteadily carved around him—as if the person who had scratched those drawings had been in a state of great panic. Or insane.

"I think we should leave now," I urged, moving toward the top of the stairs afraid that Julie might want to solve the mystery, even if it meant risking her life.

"Let's search the next floor," she said, almost gleefully, pointing towards the spiral staircase leading to what might be an attic.

I groaned inwardly.

Julie flicked on the light switch on the right wall, and Hilary followed her upwards. I tagged behind, too scared to stay alone on that eerie first landing.

Balancing our heavy backpacks, we tiptoed up the ever-narrowing circular staircase. *Maybe people were hiding under the beds in the girls' dormitory,* I thought, *playing a trick on us.* But no, the space had felt empty of physical bodies . . . and that whispering . . .?

"It's like the *Mary Celeste*," Hilary whispered, barely disturbing the thick silence.

I vaguely remembered the story of a boat called the *Mary Celeste* found floating off the Azores. Everything appeared to be in order, but not one person was found on board. Like here, no sign of a struggle or mishap was evident. Theories were put forth as to what could have happened to the captain, his family and crew on that ship, but no bodies were ever found and the mystery had never been indisputably solved.

Something touched my ear. I let out a cry and

brushed at it. "Must have been a fly," I whispered loudly to the others and fought an overwhelming urge to turn and flee from this place.

The upper landing was similar to the first, though smaller and more claustrophobic. On the only door, another stick man had been etched into the fading yellow paint but this one had shorter, less frenzied hair. This time we did not cross the threshold into the dormitory but just pushed the door wide and peered into the shadows. A similar scene met us: a dormitory in darkness, sleeping bags, backpacks, shoes, people's personal belongings lying around on beds, but still no sign of life.

The pale yellow walls of the upper landing boasted more graffiti that made me shudder.

"Hello-o-o, hello-o-o. Anybody here?" Julie's words ricocheted off the walls. I felt the invisible eyes laughing, mocking.

"Maybe they've all gone out somewhere," Hilary ventured unconvincingly.

"It's so strange." Julie frowned, studying the creepy wall drawings.

"What are we going to do?" Hilary asked. I wanted to know, too, but I couldn't think in this place, as if a multitude of voices were all talking at once inside my head. "Let's go downstairs," I suggested.

We moved slowly down the spiral staircase to the first landing. Nothing had changed. The door was still open to the girls' dormitory. The air was still stagnant . . . but with what? Huddling closer together, we moved down the next set of stairs to the ground floor then crept back through the games room and gathered in the dark entranceway.

"Well," Julie, ever the pragmatist, summarized the situation, "we have three choices. We could stay here, keep hitchhiking, or," she said, brightening, "we could go to the local police station and ask if we could sleep in a cell for the night." The previous year Hilary and Julie had spent a night in a Spanish prison cell when they couldn't find an open hostel.

"That sounds like the best idea," Hilary responded.

"Yes." I breathed. "I definitely don't want to stay here."

Julie nodded, her eyes searching the room, letting them rest for a moment on the coats covering the opposite wall. Then together we moved out the front door, down the path, and out through the wrought-iron gate. There Julie turned and stared back at the place. We followed her gaze. All three floors were brightly lit. We had neglected to turn off the lights. "That is *so* weird," Julie muttered.

Just as the words came out of her mouth, the whole building was suddenly shrouded in blackness.

"Aagh!" we all shrieked in unison as we realized that every light had been simultaneously snuffed out and someone *or something* must have pulled the building's master switch, perhaps as a warning to us.

"Let's get out of here." I tugged at Julie's sleeve, pleading "C'mon, let's go!" afraid that she might choose to go back and investigate.

The three of us wandered down the narrow cobblestone street, not knowing where we were going. On either side, the tall, terraced houses were shrouded in darkness. On the corner, we found some youths standing around talking.

"Ask them about the hostel," Hilary urged, pushing me toward them.

"*Pardon.*" I hoped I wouldn't offend them with

my corny French pronunciation. *"Qu'est-ce qu'il y a avec l'auberge de jeunesse?"* What's going on at the hostel?

A tall young man with a thick shock of black hair was just demonstrating a dance to his friend, but I seemed to have made myself understood because he shrugged. *"Je ne sais pas. Pourquoi?"*

"Est-ce qu'il y a un phantom là?" Is it haunted? I asked.

"Je vais voir," the young man said and disappeared, running up the street.

While we waited for his return, I asked the other boys the way to the nearest police station. The youngest one gestured in the direction from where we had just come. Then they wanted to know what we were doing on the streets of Rheims at eleven o'clock at night and why we needed *"le gendarmerie."*

As I struggled to tell them, the tall lanky boy returned, running. *"C'est rien,"* he explained, shrugging again. The French shrug a lot, I noticed. "All the lights are on."

"They're on?" I repeated, making sure that I had understood his French correctly.

"Oui, oui."

"But they all were turned off when we left."

Another shrug and we were dismissed. Following their instructions to the police station, we walked back up the street. But as we passed the dreaded hostel, we stood in disbelief as we saw that the lights were now *off* and the building was again in darkness.

"It's like one of those Alfred Hitchcock stories where everything starts out so innocently," Julie muttered in her best disembodied-voice imitation, "and then something suddenly turns very bad."

I shuddered. I did not want to be scared out of my English skin on the second night of our adventure. We turned the corner and walked past a brightly lit café just closing for the night. Ahead was the edge of the French countryside and blackness.

"They don't believe in wasting electricity around here, do they?" Hilary joked.

A sudden movement in front of us startled me. Somebody stepped out of the shadows. We all stopped. "Can I 'elp you?" A tall, slim, bearded man approached. From what I could see of his face, I guessed he was in his mid-twenties.

Julie, unfazed, explained, "We're looking for the police station."

"Ees somesing wrong?" In the dim light, I detected his amusement. I felt a little irritated by the mocking curves at the corners of his mouth.

"We can't stay in the youth hostel," Julie explained, "so we were going to ask if we could sleep at the police station."

"Ha!" The man laughed out loud. I was really annoyed now.

"Ach, you Eengleesh, you are so naïve!" he exclaimed, raising both hands in the air in a hopeless gesture. "Maybe you can do zat in England but in France, *non*." Without hesitating, he added, "You must come and stay wiz us. My fiancée *et moi*. "My name is Jean and we live just over zair." The man gestured behind us to some point off in the black night. Then he crossed the street, expecting us to follow. Before I could open my mouth to protest, Julie and Hilary began trailing along behind him as if in a trance.

"Don't you think this is a little suspicious?" I muttered in Julie's ear. "I mean, we just came from the hostel and suddenly a man appears like magic and offers us accommodation."

"People offer hospitality all the time in Europe. It's better than sleeping in a cell, isn't it?" Julie dismissed my fears. "You're being paranoid."

I turned to Hilary. "Don't *you* think it's a bit weird how he just appeared like that?"

"Stop worrying!" Hilary hissed. "He's fine."

Before we had left England, the three of us had made an agreement about two things—money and intuition. With money, we agreed that we were all totally responsible for sticking to our own budgets. There would be absolutely no borrowing. And with intuition, we had said that if any one of us had a "bad feeling" about getting into a car or any other situation, we would all listen to that person and respond accordingly. Julie and Hilary had obviously forgotten *that* part of the conversation.

I peered ahead into the darkness. The man was moving silently, his outline just visible in the shadows. He turned around, beckoning. "*Venez*, come."

He suddenly veered off to the right. Was this his home? We followed him through the blackness toward the back of a tall building. He was hard to see in the darkness but we heard the clanking as he started up a narrow, winding metal staircase. I followed behind Hilary and wondered, as we climbed up and up and up what was awaiting us.

Suddenly a yellow beam flooded the staircase and I realized that he had opened the door to a small brightly lit apartment. Just one large room, the space was divided into two sections with a basic kitchen on the right and a double bed on the other side. In the far corner, in the sloped ceiling beyond the bed, a lacy, cream linen wedding dress hung from one of the bare beams.

A slim, dark-haired woman in her early twenties stood by the sink. Maybe they had just finished dinner as she was polishing a large platter. She frowned when she saw the three of us laden with our bulky backpacks trailing in behind Jean. He muttered something to her that I couldn't catch. Perhaps an explanation of what he was doing with these three forlorn travelers?

She responded in rapid-fire French and then turned to us and smiling stiffly, she pointed to a space on the floor. "Yooo can sleep 'ere," she said a little offhandedly. Maybe her manner was just the French way, cool. Softening a little, she added, "My name is Monique." Pulling her man to her possessively, she announced, "An' you know zis is my fiancé, Jean. We are getting married ze day after tomorrow."

"Congratulations!" we all chirped together. If we had known them better, we would have done the French thing and kissed them on both cheeks, but we just stood there. "I'm Jo and these are my friends, Hilary and Julie," I offered, feeling more comfortable.

"Can I take a photo of the happy couple?" Julie asked, searching for her camera as Hilary and I started to unravel our sleeping bags.

"Non! NON!" Monique waved her arms in front of her face, extremely upset. *"Pas de photo!"* she cried.

Julie lowered her camera. "I'm so sorry, Monique. I didn't mean to upset you."

"Ça fait rien. It's nossing." Monique recovered quickly but still seemed disturbed.

"Why don't we all 'ave a glass of wine, hein?" Jean suggested, opening a cupboard above the sink.

"Do you know what is going on at the hostel?" Hilary inquired casually, sliding into her sleeping bag then wriggling out of her jeans.

"*Pourquoi?*" Monique was frosty again as she pulled back the covers on their bed.

"Well, it looked like it's being used as a hostel, but nobody was there," Hilary continued.

Our sleeping bags were now lined up like soldiers on the kitchen floor. I was about to snuggle down into my fuzzy bed when Jean leaned over and passed a glass of rich red wine to me. As I sat up, he peered deep into my eyes and smiled an intense, warm smile. My fingers brushed his as I took the glass. I was taken aback somewhat by his flirtatiousness but more by the coldness of his touch.

"*Je ne sais pas.*" Jean shrugged as he also passed wine to Hilary. "No idea. We 'ave not been zair in a long time."

As the three of us sat in our sleeping bags and Jean and Monique lounged on their bed, all of us sipping red wine, we exchanged brief life histories. Monique, I noticed, couldn't take her eyes off Jean. She obviously adored him.

"I am so sorree zat we can't show you Rheims," Jean apologized, "but I 'ave to be at a meeting earlee." Placing his arm around Monique's shoulders, he added, "Mais ma cherie will take you to zee auto route." He glanced at Monique seeking agreement. "Hein?"

She nodded, giving him a strange distant smile. *What was it about Monique that bothered me?*

"From zair," he continued, "you can continue your journeee."

"Actually, don't worry about us, Monique," I piped up. "We'd like to get up before dawn. Make an early start, you know."

I felt the other two glaring at me for not taking

up the offer of a lift.

"As you weesh," the French girl said and shrugged. Then, to our surprise, she proceeded to the kitchen where she pulled down her jeans and sat over the sink. It took us a few stunned minutes to realize that she was, in fact, peeing. We lay on the floor in our sleeping bags, trying not to look or listen. When she was done, Jean came over to the sink and did the same thing.

Once they were in bed, we all chatted a little more. They seemed to be a very down-to-earth couple after all, I told myself, and, finally relaxing I fell asleep.

The next morning we were awakened by the sounds of Jean moving around, getting ready to leave. In the early dawn, we grunted a *"Bonjour"* and thanked him for his hospitality. I felt ashamed that I had had such bad thoughts about them. I wondered if he had sensed my apprehension. Now that it was morning and daylight poured into the attic apartment, my paranoia was funny, really. He was such a nice young man, and his girlfriend was just, well, very French.

After Jean had done the sink thing again, kissed his fiancée, and left, we arose and slowly got dressed. Being British, I decided there was no way I would pee in the sink. "Monique, where is the closest toilet, please."

Slightly amused, she responded, "Sthrough zaire," pointing to another door recessed in the kitchen that I hadn't noticed the night before. "Downstairs on ze ground floor, two flights of stairs, at ze front of ze building." She smiled wryly at my British prudishness. I didn't care.

"Me first," I said and rushed for the door, toothbrush and toothpaste in hand.

The door creaked open. I followed Monique's directions, to the right along the lighted, wooden-floored corridor and then left down the stairs. She had said I would find a door at the bottom and then I should continue down one more flight of stairs to the bathroom on the ground floor.

The building was old and smelled a little damp. All the walls were painted the same bland yellow. *Must be in fashion,* I thought. How did this couple survive having to hike a mile every time they needed a bathroom? I supposed that was why the sink was multi-purpose.

The staircase was narrow, dark and steep, but with the brightness from the upper landing I could see the door at the bottom. I grasped the handle and turned it. The door was stuck. I turned the handle again and again. Finally it loosened, suddenly giving way and opening wide. My god, it was dark. I grappled in the darkness along the wall to find the light switch.

When I first saw the landing in the light, the scene was vaguely familiar. Then it became surreal, like a nightmarish recurring dream, as I recognized the graffiti on the right wall and the stick woman on the dormitory door, still standing ajar. I was back in the hostel!

I turned to look at the door I had just come through and there was the yellowed sign with the word "*Privé*" on it, the door that had been locked last night. *This must be the front of the hostel. Jean must have led us in through the back of the building. But why had they lied when we had asked them?* The question disturbed me.

Now once again I could feel the invisible eyes watching, watching. And had the door to the dormitory just opened wider? Then, as if an echo of my jumbled thoughts had reverberated around the landing, a busy *shooshing* sound started, like a large group of people standing in a cluster, all whispering at once, though not one word could be distinguished. The sound came toward me from the dormitory, like a large cloud closing in, getting louder and louder. I turned to go back through the door and rush up the stairs. But the handle did not turn and the door was firmly shut! I knew I hadn't closed it. I grabbed at the handle and pulled, yanking and yanking, but it wouldn't open. Oh god. I glanced behind me. Just empty space. The whispering was deafening now, like a swarm of bees swirling all around me. I banged on the door and yanked at the same time. "Hilary! Julie! Help!" I yelled. But I knew that my friends couldn't hear. They may as well have been in Siberia.

Then just as if somebody on the stairs was holding the handle tight and had suddenly let go, the door abruptly flew open outwards. I fell back, landing on the cold wooden floor with a thud. My toothbrush and toothpaste flew across the landing. The whispering ceased. Through the open door, I expected to see someone standing at the bottom of the stairs. Only a dimly lit staircase gaped back at me. I scrambled to my feet, grabbing my paraphernalia and ran up the steps two at a time. Panting, I rushed along the corridor and back to the apartment.

When I burst in, just Hilary and Julie were in the room, happily chatting and packing up their sleeping bags. Innocents.

"What happened to you?" Julie laughed at my disheveled appearance. "Seen a ghost?" I'm glad she thought it was funny. She wouldn't soon.

"Where's Monique?" I asked, breathing hard, scouring the apartment with my eyes.

"She's just gone out to get something," Hilary said, pointing to the door we had entered through the previous night. "Why?" She was frowning as she started to pick up on my panic.

"Do you know where we are?" I was aware I was shouting. "This is the back of the hostel!"

"No. We—" Julie began and then, puzzled, asked, "How—?"

"I just found myself by the girls' dormitory! Remember the whispering?"

They both stared at me.

"The whispering?" they repeated in unison, trying to absorb the implication of my words.

"Yes! We have to get out of here!" My voice was rasping. "I don't know what's going on, but we have to go. Now!"

Finally they understood. And this time they didn't question my judgment. Hurriedly we scooped up our belongings and stuffed them into our packs.

"Which way out?" Hilary asked, breathing hard as she got to her feet, her backpack not even fastened.

"If we go down the back of the building, we could bump into Monique," I reasoned.

"Through the hostel," Hilary whispered. I led the way this time.

We tiptoed along the corridor, aware of the groaning floorboards. Looking back at the apartment, we couldn't hear any sounds. Monique must still be out. Thank god. The narrow staircase was harder to negotiate now we were carrying our bulky packs. The door at the bottom of the stairs was closed again, but the handle turned easily this time. I exhaled.

Julie and Hilary inhaled sharply as they stepped onto the landing as if they hadn't quite believed me until they saw the hostel again for themselves.

"C'mon." I waved them forward, feeling braver now my friends were right behind me. The landing wasn't quite as spooky in the growing daylight. And there was no whispering now. A hushed silence prevailed.

All we had to do was get down the curved staircase and we were nearly out of this awful place.

"What's that noise?" Julie asked from behind me.

We all stopped, steadying ourselves on the banister. An unrecognizable metal-on-metal scraping sound reached us from below the stairs. I frowned as I looked back at the others, questioning what to do. But Hilary motioned with her head to continue down. This was our only escape.

The three of us clustered at the bottom of the stairs, glancing around the games room. The paddles still lay on the table, the coats hung on the rack just as they had the night before but bathed now in pre-dawn shadows. I moved to go around the ping-pong table. Julie and Hilary followed. We were almost out of the door.

Something moved quickly from the shadows. Monique! She took her position, blocking the doorway. Her dark brown eyes were now wide, deranged, her almost-black hair loose and unkempt. We stood very still.

From behind me, Julie whispered in my ear. "She's got a knife!"

A large black-handled kitchen knife was gripped in Monique's right hand. Judging by the maniacal expression on her face, she intended to use it.

"Monique," I started in a soothing voice, "we were just—"

"Ne me mentez pas!" She spat out the words, moving towards me, forcing Julie and Hilary also into retreat. The three of us were backing into the kitchen. "Don't lie to meeee. I know what you arre doing," Monique hissed.

"What is she talking about?" Julie asked,

shedding her backpack.

"You . . . you . . . ," Monique pointed at me accusingly, brandishing the shiny steel blade in my face, "are not going to take 'im away from me!"

The three of us stepped back and back, transfixed by this crazy woman. Paralyzed, we cowered against the kitchen counter. Monique came to a halt right in front of me, the pointed knife almost touching my T-shirt. On either side of me, Hilary and Julie inhaled sharply.

"What are you—?" Before I had time to finish, Monique threw her head back. As if she were communicating with some dark force above the ceiling, she let out an unearthly howl, raising the knife high above her head, shaking it ferociously, and wailing at the force. Then with eyes as cold as steel, she glared at me again, unfathomable rage burning in her eyes. She brought the knife down, down. Neither Hilary nor Julie could do anything. I was going to die.

Monique howled again. I saw how the knife glinted in the light. I heard a scream. I think it was me. Everything went black.

A radiant white glow was bathing my face in warmth. Where was I? *Oh, yes, I remember now. Monique had stabbed me.* I was surprised that I wasn't feeling anything. No pain. *I must be dead. And of course, nothing hurts when you are dead. This is probably heaven.*

I opened my eyes. The light was streaming in through a large window. Then I saw the distraught faces of Hilary and Julie hovering above me. Why were they staring at me like that? Their mouths were moving but I couldn't distinguish the sounds. Were they dead too? The ornate ceiling was above. I must be floating out of my body. Or was I on the floor? But something was hurting, sticking into my back. The knife?

"Am I dead?" I finally asked my friends.

They both cried out. Julie grabbed my hand and came closer, peering into my face. Tears were trickling down her pale cheeks.

I must be dead. People don't survive a knife in the heart like that. I was afraid to look down, to see blood coursing out of my heart. But I felt fine.

"Oh, thank God," Hilary answered. "You're okay. I . . . I mean, no . . . you're not dead, Jo." she stammered. "Oh, god, I'm so sorry, I couldn't—"!

"C'mon," Julie urged. "Let's get the hell out of here. We can talk about it outside."

With a friend on either side, I was pulled to my feet slowly, legs like jelly, eyes searching the room again, expecting a howling Monique to leap out.

Still shaking, with Julie and Hilary supporting me, we moved back through the shadowy games room toward the front door. I peered down at where I had been stabbed. There was no blood, no knife, no wound. Nothing. My backpack is what had caused the temporary discomfort.

We walked out of the building and didn't dare look back.

The early morning sunshine felt so good on our pale faces. Once out of the grounds, as if on auto-pilot, we turned towards the corner where the teenagers had gathered the night before.

As we walked, still in shock, Julie asked in a small voice. "Jo, are you okay?"

"I think so. I'm not sure." My head felt very light. I touched the slight bump on the back of my skull where I had hit the floor.

"Where did Monique go?" I asked, glancing over

my shoulder.

"She disappeared," Julie responded.

"Disappeared?" Nothing made sense. "How?"

"I . . . we'll tell you," Julie breathed, "but when we sit down," she added. "To heck with the expense. Let's treat ourselves to a real French breakfast."

The teenagers were on the corner again. They waved but we ignored them and carried on, away from them and that terrible place.

The smell of freshly baked croissants drew us toward a small street-side café on the opposite corner of that quiet intersection. The sight of ordinary people coming and going was comforting. A few patrons were seated outside, some of them older men who habitually frequent cafés for hours over one large cup of coffee. They were clustered in the fresh air watching the world go by. We chose one of the round tables away from them and set our packs down. Over a breakfast of heavenly warm, crusty croissants served with a huge *tasse* of fresh French coffee, and with the warm sun on our faces, a sense of normality gradually drew us back into the real world.

"So what the heck happened back there?" I finally asked. Julie and Hilary stared at me still stunned. "I don't know." Julie answered, her face pale.

"God, it was awful." Hilary stirred her large cup of coffee. "She just went at you with the knife." She shuddered. "Then when the sunlight streamed in through the window, she . . . just . . . faded like a . . . . We thought you were dead, Jo."

"I'm sorry," Hilary said again. "I mean for not listening . . . . You said there was something strange about them."

"Me, too," Julie added, embarrassed.

215

Something strange was right.

Julie stared down into her café au lait as if the foam might give her an answer.

I shrugged a French shrug. With the daily machinations of morning life moving all around us, I began to feel a cloud lifting as if awakening from a bad dream.

Julie sat back and tilted her face up to the warmth of the sun. She squinted at me. "Why did she pick on you, though?"

"I don't know." So many questions unanswered. "And how could she just disappear like that . . . I mean, are you trying to tell me—?"

"Zat she was a ghost?" The rasping voice from behind startled us all. We turned to see who had been listening in on our conversation.

When we sat down, we hadn't noticed the older man with a thick mustache, huge potbelly, and soulful blue eyes sitting at the next table. A bucket-sized coffee cup sat in front of him. His large black hat cast shadows across his face and the long black coat over a white shirt open at the collar appeared to be out-dated.

He coughed a deep gurgling cough. *"Pardon, mesdemoiselles."* He smiled disarmingly, dabbing his mouth with a large white handkerchief and inclining his head in a barely perceptible nod. "You must excuse me for being a little *impoli*, but I could not 'elp over'earing your conversation. I am assooming zat," he pointed to our backpacks lying on the ground, "you stayed in ze hostel last night. On *Rue Calibe?*"

None of us said a word. He moved his chair closer to our table. He folded the handkerchief carefully and stuffed it into his pocket.

"I 'ope you did not have a bad experience?"

"What do you mean?" Julie glared at him suspiciously.

"Strange zings 'ave 'appened zair at zis time of year." He shook his head. "Zey should 'ave a longer closing time. Close eet for ze 'ole month, not just a few days."

"Why?" Julie asked.

The man leaned forward conspiratorially and whispered, "Ze 'ostel, it ees, 'ow you say, *haunté*." He stifled another cough.

"Haunted?" I offered.

"*Oui, oui, exactement*." He sat back in his chair and glanced around the café to see who was listening. Everyone seemed engrossed in their own conversations.

"By a woman?" I suggested.

"Ah, *pauvre!* 'Ave you seen 'er?" The handkerchief came out again. He coughed into it. Before he put it away, I noticed small red spots against the white cotton. Something about his eyes reminded me of someone.

"I was killed by her," I snapped. "Can you tell us what on earth is happening there?" I didn't mean to be rude to the poor man, but the shock was wearing off now and I was in reaction. And his eyes bothered me. What *was* it about his eyes?

"Oh, I am so sorry zat you experience zis . . . zis *tragédie*." He barely touched my hand, a cold touch. "You see, about twenty-five years ago ze young woman, Monique, was engaged to be married to Jean. While zey were students, zey took care of ze 'ostel and lived in ze apartment above. Zey were so 'appee togezzer." The man looked away, saddened as if he had known them personally. "*Et puis*," he raised his hands in a shrug, "somessing 'appened."

We all leaned forward.

"Everybodee knew zat Monique was very . . . *comment dit-on en anglais?* . . . possessive. Ooh-la-la." He shook his stubby fingers as if he had just touched something hot. "Zen, one day, three girls, Eengleesh, came to ze 'ostel, but it was full. So Jean, her boyfriend, invited them to stay in zair apartment. Monique was very *jalouse* and thought that Jean was, 'ow you say, making eyes at ze blonde one. Or zat is what Monique believed." The man stared hard at my blonde hair. "Monique could not bear eet. She loved 'eem so much, *vous comprenez*, so she gets ze beeggest knife from zair apartment and treecked ze girl to come downstairs to ze kitchen."

I noticed that Julie shivered despite the warmth of the sun.

"Aach, ze Eengleesh, zey are so naive!" He raised his hands in a hopeless gesture.

Goosebumps rippled down my arms. His words and body language were somehow familiar but shock was still clouding my brain.

"Zen Monique stabs and stabs ze little girl!" The man demonstrated the crime, punching the air with his clenched fist. The image made me shudder. *"La pauvre!"* he exclaimed. His large frame shook as he coughed more ferociously and tried to catch his breath. Then he sat back in his chair. The stained handkerchief came out again and he wiped his mouth.

"Are you okay?" I asked.

"Oui, merci. It ees nossing. An old wound."

"Did Monique go to jail?" Hilary wanted to know.

"Ah, *non*," he shook his head. "It ees much worse." He leaned over again.

"Zen Monique must 'ave gone *totalement folle*,

completely mad, for she ran through ze 'ostel screaming and attackeeng all ze girls wiz 'er beeg knife. Most of zem ran for zer lives but many of zem were stabbed in zer beds. *Quelle horreure!*

"What about Jean?" It was Julie's question.

"Ah, Jean!" He paused, staring away to some other place, some other time. "Monique was tryeeng to 'ide ze bodies in ze cellar under ze stairs when Jean returned and saw ze terrible *carnage*. Of course, 'e told 'er, I must go to ze police but 'e promised to take ze blame. 'E felt so guilty, *vous comprenez? Naturellement,* she could not stand to live wizout 'er lover so she stabbed 'eem also in zee lungs." He banged his chest, indicating where the knife had probably gone in. "And zen she stabbed 'erself in ze 'eart."

None of us spoke.

"Ah, mon Dieu, it was . . . terrible, terrible." The man shook his head as if it had just happened yesterday. "*Et maintenant*, now zair are many ghosts."

I suddenly remembered Jean. Of course, he must have been a ghost, too! So that's why Monique was so upset by the camera! If they didn't exist, they might not show up on film?

"Did Jean die?" I don't know why I asked the question. The man was silent for a few moments and then gazed at me with his piercing blue eyes. "*Non.*" He paused. "Not then."

"What happened to him?" I felt as if it hurt this man to speak of Jean.

He paused, reaching for breath. "Monique, you know, punctured 'is lung when she stabbed 'eem—"

Our waiter came and cleared away our small white plates. "Encore un café?" he asked us, interrupting the older man.

"Non, merci." I responded quickly, anxious for the waiter to go away and to hear the rest of the story.

"—and Jean," the older man continued, " 'e survived but 'e was never the same."

"That's so awful! Why don't they close the hostel altogether?" I asked incredulously.

"Oh, fuff." He shrugged and put his handkerchief back in his pocket. "Zey close eet for a few days because it only 'appens at certain times with certain people. An 'zey want to keep it *un grand secret*, not to scare *les touristes, vous comprenez?*" He pulled his great weight out of the white chair and stood over us.

"And what are those certain times and certain people?" Hilary asked, looking up at him, shading her eyes from the bright sun.

He glanced around at all our faces. "Onlee if Eengleesh girls come just before ze anniversary of ze wedding date . . . and when one of zem is blonde."

Both Hilary and Julie stared at me.

"Et puis, it is time for me to go." The man said and turned. "*Bonjour.*" We watched as he wended his way between the tables and out onto the street. He stood with a group of school children waiting to cross the now busy intersection, going in the direction from which we had just come.

Our waiter appeared at that moment with our bill. "Who was that man?" I asked him. *Vous connaissez cet homme?*

"*Quel homme?*" Which man? The waiter asked, staring at me blankly.

"The one that was just talking to us. Over there," I said, turning and pointing to the crosswalk. But when I looked, only school children were still standing there, waiting for the light.

10

CHARLIE ECHO

BEGINNING OR ENDING?

"It's your mother," Emily's Aunt Renee began without any introduction. "I'm at Berrington hospital." She paused. "The news isn't good."

Emily's grip on the clunky black telephone receiver tightened. She stared out of her second-floor maisonette window at the line of cherry trees blossoming below. This would be a day to remember, April 15, 1975. In the late sunny afternoon, light grey clouds now threatened rain. And maybe the black cloud that darkened her life might soon dissipate.

"She's gone?" Emily asked, holding her breath.

"Not exactly—she's had a stroke. And there are other complications," she added. "The doctors don't think she has very long."

Emily sank into the high-backed chair she kept in the corner by her telephone table. Like so many times as a teenager when the brick-hard hands of her mother had slapped her cheek, leaving it smarting, she now flinched from a similar blow. Would she die soon, or out of sheer stubbornness, linger for months—or worse—would she need personal care?

"Do you want me to come?" she offered dreading the two-hour drive in her aging MG convertible from her home near Gatwick Airport to where her mother lived in Buckinghamshire. She would have to miss dinner and it was traffic hour.

"That's your choice, dear. Helen isn't able to talk, of course."

That's perfect, Emily thought wryly.

"But I think it would be a good idea . . . for your own sake," Renee continued. "I know hospitals remind you of your brother."

There was a pause as Emily remembered the doctors' futile attempts to save Derek. Although it was almost four years since that time, the images were still fresh and raw. But Emily *did* want to end it, to say goodbye to her mother—officially.

"Well, tomorrow is my last day of airline training. But I think they are just handing out our wings and certificates—"

"Oh, that's right. I forgot to ask. How is that going?"

"Good," she responded distractedly. "Maybe I should come up now." A quick glance at her watch told her it was already close to five o'clock. "I could be there around seven . . . Will you still be there?" Even with her mother in a quasi-unconscious state, Emily dreaded being alone with her.

"I'll wait till you get here," her aunt assured her.

Emily glanced around her spacious living room expecting to feel different. Everything was the same—the beige shag carpet, the brown furnishings, the hushed silence. She picked up the phone again and began dialing. "Suzi?"

"Hello, Emily." Even though the two young women had only recently met during airline training, they had become fast friends.

"I . . . my mother . . ." her voice quivered. She was surprised at her own emotion. "My mother's had a stroke and it doesn't look good. I have to go . . . . Could you please ring the office and tell them I won't be in tomorrow. But I will be back for my first flight on Sunday."

"Are you sure?" Suzi's sympathetic tone made Emily uncomfortable. "You might want to—."

From what little Emily knew of her friend's background, she did know that Suzi came from a normal, loving family and would probably not understand Emily's lack of grief.

"No, I'll be back." Then she added more softly, "Thank you, Suzi. I'll tell you all about my infamous family later."

"Oh, I love scandals," Suzi remarked.

"Well, we've got lots of those."

Two hours later, bracing herself against bad memories, Emily pulled into the small parking lot of Berrington Country Hospital. A stout matron in a well-starched uniform smiled maternally at Emily and directed her to the last room on the left. Through the fluted glass of the door, she could see the blurred shape of her dying mother propped up by copious starched-white pillows. There was a shadowy outline of a person sitting in a chair by her bed reading. She inhaled and pushed the door open.

Renee glanced up from her magazine.

Considering her 62 years, Emily's aunt was surprisingly svelte even though she had never done a day of exercise in her life and her soon-to-be-removed cataracts bothered her. Emily also marveled at her familial loyalty. Despite the lack of closeness between Renee and her sister—Helen—Renee was still at her sister's deathbed. Her aunt was the only family member who reminded Emily that there had been good times, and the only one who had ever spoken openly of her mother's "dark side." For that validation, Emily was eternally grateful.

Renee put her forefinger over her lips and pointed to the door, indicating that they should talk outside. As her aunt gently pulled the door closed behind them, she whispered, "She might still be able to hear."

Emily nodded, understanding but wondering why she should care. After her parents' rancorous divorce and Derek's death, she had tried to encourage her mother to get on with a new life. But Emily's words were only met with derisive sneers and below-the-belt insults. Her inability to save her mother combined with the relentless vitriolic phone calls had left Emily powerlessly raging for days and was probably the root cause of her recurring suffocating nightmares.

Emily glanced back through the fluted glass at the distorted shape of her mother lying in bed. "How long do the doctors think . . . ?"

Renee followed her gaze and shrugged. "Could be any time. I think she's been holding on for you to come."

Why? Emily wondered.

Before they went back into the strangely echoing room, Renee put a hand on her niece's arm. "I know Helen's put you through a lot, dear, but still . . . be kind."

"I wasn't the perpetrator, Renee."

"I understand. But you don't know—."

"And I don't want to know." Emily had not meant to snap at her aunt. She added more softly, "Let's just get this over and done with." She opened the door and went back in.

She stood at the bedside and surveyed the shrunken figure. Her mother's eyes were closed, eyeballs sunk into the hollows of their sockets. Even in this enforced sleep, her small mouth was tight as if she was holding onto her bitterness. It occurred to Emily that after putting her through hell, she had still hoped her mother would recover her old, healthy self so they could maybe have a loving mother-daughter relationship. But now that hope was forever gone.

Emily was surprised how loudly her heart thumped in her chest as she mustered the words she wanted to say. She took a breath. "I hope you'll be happier where you're going than you were here," she finally pronounced, her voice breaking. She was afraid that her malevolent mother might suddenly sit up, wild eyes open, fangs bared and lash out with those brick-hard hands again. But she just lay there. Rasping, labored breathing reverberated from deep within her emaciated body, making her sound like the monster she had become—to Emily anyway.

What does one say to a dying mother? "Wherever you are going, go in peace." *And please don't haunt me any more*, Emily added silently, relieved at the thought of no more harassing midnight phone calls. The shrunken woman in her floral gown in the bed did not move or even flinch.

"Anything else?" Renee had stepped forward and put an arm around her niece's waist. "This might be your last . . ."

Emily did a fast rewind of her family life— happier, carefree childhood days followed by the nightmare that just went on and on. "You were a good mother . . . in the beginning . . . ." She stared hard and long at the woman who had caused her so much pain. "I'm done," she whispered finally.

"We'll go then." Renee guided her towards the door.

Emily paused, suddenly feeling a pang of . . . what? Remorse? Guilt? Pity? She turned once more towards her mother. "Maybe we shouldn't leave her alone."

"There's nothing more to be done," Renee assured her tenderly. "The nurses will take care of her."

"Yes, of course." She paused. "Goodbye, mother." Emily searched her mother's face for micro signs of acknowledgment but there were none. "Goodbye."

As the two women walked down the shiny linoleum-floored corridor towards the lift, Renee reminded her, "Her cottage will have to be sorted, her paperwork prepared for the solicitors. Marsten & Marsten, I think. They're executors of the will." She stopped. "Here. You'll need this."

Emily surveyed the large brown key before taking it from her aunt's palm.

"I'd help you, Emily dear," Renee was saying as she continued down the hall, "but this is the weekend I get my first cataract done. So when can you . . .?"

Emily suddenly realized that she was all alone. Even though she had felt that way for many years, she was now officially an orphan. After Derek's death, her father had simply disappeared somewhere abroad. She didn't know if he was alive or dead. She had not had any contact with her mother in five years or stepped inside her mother's home. But dealing with the estate was her responsibility now—with the assistance of some starchy stranger, her mother's grumpy old solicitor. And the thought of being in her mother's house, the Old Chapel Cottage, made her shudder.

She stared vacantly at the opposite yellowed shiny wall. "Maybe I should just go there tonight and stay. *Get it over and done with.* My friend told the airline I wouldn't be in tomorrow."

"Oh, I wish I could help." Renee sighed. "I've been waiting so long for this operation and my eyes are getting worse. I don't want to . . . ."

"Of course."

Emily had acquired a survivor's strength. She would cope because she had to. "That's okay. Thanks for being here today, Renee. I know it's not easy."

Her aunt nodded, holding back tears. "No, none of it's been easy."

"Yes. I'll go to the Old Chapel Cottage tonight," Emily repeated preparing herself for the daunting task. "We should tell the matron to call me there if there are any changes?"

Renee nodded. "I'll do it now. I need to go to the loo, anyway."

Her aunt disappeared around the corner while Emily stood and absorbed her shock. Renee returned five minutes later. "So you begin flying soon?" she asked, cheerily.

Emily nodded. So many thoughts were tumbling around in her head.

"Won't you miss your old nine-to-five job?"

"As executive assistant?" Emily pulled a face. "No. It's time for a new challenge."

Aunt and niece continued toward the lift. "You're so brave becoming a stewardess!" Renee smiled, suddenly brightening and beaming proudly at her. "I don't even want to get on an airplane let alone fly on them everyday for work."

Sleeping in my mother's house is much scarier, Emily thought. "I'm not sure I want to work on planes either," she retorted, only half-joking.

As they entered the lift and descended to the ground floor, Renee asked, "What do you mean?"

"Oh, didn't you know? I'm scared of flying, too," she confessed. "But I'll get over it and I have to do something drastic to get my life in gear. If flying for an international airline doesn't liven things up, nothing will." She laughed. "And isn't it better to be scared than to feel dead?"

"I think you're quite mad," Renee responded, grinning, as she stepped out of the lift. "I'd rather be bored to death and have my feet on the ground."

"Well, *you* know how I inherited my madness. But for some strange reason," Emily mused, "I feel as if I have no choice."

At ten past eight, Emily walked up the path to the Old Chapel Cottage. The narrow country lane was shrouded in darkness. Large black shapes of unruly rhododendron bushes massed against the white cottage walls swayed in the light wind and threatened to hide the door. She dug in her pocket for the key.

She groped for the light switch inside the small vestibule. In the dim light, she was shocked to see a walker sitting in the corner of the hallway. Had her mother been *that* frail? Emily found it hard to imagine her bullying parent—that force of nature—as a fragile older woman. All that alcohol and anger had obviously sapped her life force prematurely.

Although her mother's home was surprisingly clean, a slightly musty smell permeated the dark kitchen. Her mother must have had a charwoman to take care of the place. Housework never had been her favorite occupation.

After making herself a cup of tea and raiding the fridge for a slice of cheese and an apple, she inspected the rest of the tiny cottage. Large eighteenth-century chapel windows made the white-walled, long, narrow living room bright. Her mother's bedroom, off to the right, had probably been the chapel's apse. Emily imagined the small congregation in the old days sitting in perhaps ten rows of wooden pews listening to the vicar orating from a pulpit on the end wall, where the wood-burning fireplace now sat empty of warmth.

She expected to identify some furnishings from her childhood home but all she recognized was the cherry wood bureau which sat innocuously in the corner. Apparently her mother had made a new beginning—in some ways at least.

"Where shall I start?" she said aloud, standing in the center of the living room. The bureau beckoned her. *Sort the papers first,* the voice in her head urged. She knew that those drawers would be full of personal information, and her mother had always been so secretive. Emily was not comfortable with her role as invader of that privacy.

Suddenly a wave of fatigue enveloped her. "I'll do it tomorrow," she told the walls. Collecting her overnight bag from the kitchen, she went into her mother's bedroom. Pleasantly surprised by the dainty Laura Ashley furnishings, she plunked her bag on the single bed and began to shed her clothes.

Her sweater was just about over her head when a loud click made her jump. She stopped and listened. *Is that a key in the front door?* Now she could hear noises, as if someone were shuffling around in the kitchen. *Who can it be?* Emily quickly pulled her sweater back on, carefully opened the bedroom door and walked toward the kitchen. The noises stopped. Tentatively, she pushed the kitchen door wide. The tiny space was empty. Aware that she was holding her breath, she walked through the kitchen to the hallway and the shadowy vestibule. No one. The walker sat in the same place and the front door was closed.

Hmmm? Was it Mother's spirit? Maybe she had just died. She shuddered. Perhaps she should call the hospital and get an update.

"Hello? Matron speaking."

Emily instantly felt comforted by the maternal voice. "It's Emily Carson. I just wondered if my mother . . . Helen Carson . . . how is she . . .?"

"She appears to be sleeping very peacefully."

Oh. She's still alive! "How long . . . do you think?"

"Not long now," the matron responded softly. "We'll call you when . . . there's any change."

"Thank you." Emily hung up. Maybe her mother's spirit had already left her body and she had come home. She shuddered not relishing the prospect of sharing the cottage with her mother's ghost. *Who else can I call?*

"Sorry, Suzi." Emily offered when she heard her friend's sleepy voice. "I was hoping you'd still be awake."

"Hmm. That's okay, darlin'. " There was a pause while presumably Suzi sat up in bed. "I didn't think I was so tired but all that mental work hurts my brain. Thank God my first flight isn't till Monday. Are you okay? How's your Mum doing?"

Emily smiled wryly at the idea of calling her mother "Mum," as if she were a warm, cuddly person. "Not good. They don't think she'll last much longer."

"Oh, I'm sorry."

"It's okay." In Emily's mind, her real mother had

died a long time ago so she was surprised at the wave of sadness that suddenly overtook her. "My mother . . . ." she began, not sure how much and what to reveal to her new friend. No one understood, especially people with sane parents. And even *she* couldn't explain her mother's schizophrenic personality. "Did you tell the airline?"

"Oh yes." Suzi suddenly remembered. "They said it wasn't a problem just as long as you are there for your first flight or to call them as soon as possible if you won't be." There was a pause. "But if you need to stay—."

"I'll be home tomorrow, most likely."

"What about your mother?"

"I've said my goodbyes. There's nothing more to be done."

"All right." Suzi paused. "Maybe we should meet at the pub for lunch on Saturday then? You'll probably need a drink."

"Yes, that would be great."

After she hung up, she turned back into the living room. She noticed a small TV perched in the corner on a round antique table. She decided to flick off the light and just switch on the television. She sat on the settee, then wearily lay back, covering herself in her mother's quilt.

There was a droning noise. Emily opened her eyes. Although the room was dark, a strange light was coming from the corner. Where was she? Oh yes, on the settee in her mother's cottage. That horrible noise and that bright white light was emanating from the television she had left on.

She pushed back the quilt, stood up and fumbled her way toward the noise, groping for the on/off button. There was a click and the screen went black. Silence. But before she could turn around, she saw a reflection of something move in the black shiny screen. Someone was behind her! She froze. She wanted to turn around but she did not dare. A pale blurry outline of a human being was standing right behind her. She recognized that shape. It was her mother.

The spectral vision was coming toward her.

Emily inhaled.

Everything went black.

IT'S NOT OVER YET

Sunlight was streaming into the room. Emily opened her eyes, frowned and sat up.

The single bed covered in the Laura Ashley quilt and matching curtains was not familiar. Where am I? she wondered. Oh yes, mother's bedroom! How did I get here? Something had happened the previous night. Something scary. Was it a dream or did her mother really come to haunt her? But she wasn't dead . . . yet! Or maybe she was. Despite the warmth of the bed, Emily shuddered.

That droning noise was coming from the television again. But I switched it off, Emily remembered. She pushed back the covers. As she put her legs over the side of the bed, she saw that she was wearing her nightdress. And when she placed her feet on the carpet, her slippers had been placed by the bed as if someone had lovingly put them there ready for her to slip into. Her overnight bag had been laid on the chair in the corner, her clothes from yesterday in a neat pile. She didn't know whether to be comforted by the thought of an angel coming in the night to take care of her or to be scared of her mother's ghost pretending to be motherly. Much of the kindness her mother had shown in life had been manipulative. No, Emily decided, I must have been sleepwalking. I probably came to the bedroom, tidied up and got ready for bed. Yes, that's what had happened. The apparition must have been some kind of dream.

The matron would have called if her mother had died in the night so she must still be alive, Emily reasoned. "Please . . . don't haunt me," she asked out loud again as she entered the living room. Silencing the TV again, she quickly turned away from the shiny screen and headed to the kitchen. She must get on with the tasks to be done and forget about ghosts.

After filling the kettle and finding some not-so-fresh bread for toast, she decided she would finish the paperwork by one o'clock at the latest, and be home by three. Then the rest of Friday and most of Saturday she could spend preparing for her flight on early Sunday morning. Emily wanted her uniform to be pristine, her emergency drills to be fresh in her mind and to make sure that her crew bag contained the correct in-flight kit before she met with Suzi. As she sat at the highly polished dining room table to eat her toast, a surge of excitement bubbled up as she thought about her new career, upcoming travelling adventures and new friends.

She sat down at the desk to begin the work at hand. The gold-plated antique clock on the wall read ten minutes past seven. After the intensity of the last six weeks' training, Emily did not relish dealing with more paperwork. But it had to be done. With trepidation, she turned the tiny key in the lock and lowered the bureau flap, musing how this was a nice, tidy way to temporarily hide all one's sins. *And family secrets* came the old voice in her head. For a moment she imagined her mother standing behind her, unhappy but powerless at her daughter's interference.

233

Emily placed her cup of tea on the now-flat surface. In front of her, wooden slots contained various sized envelopes. She discovered that the paperwork was surprisingly well organized in individual file folders. "Thank you, mother," she said aloud. She paused to take a sip of tea as she pulled out a yellow file. The label read, *Donations.*

She frowned. Maybe I shouldn't be surprised, she thought ruefully. That heart-warming profile of generosity didn't fit the woman *she* had known as her nasty-to-her-but-charming-to-others mother. She knew that Helen wasn't without compassion—just that for years, her mother had shown none for her own children. She opened the envelope and pulled out the contents, flicking through the receipts. My god, my mother gave to . . . a Home for Single Mothers? But she had always been so scathingly judgmental about girls who got pregnant out of wedlock. None of this made sense. She pulled out other files, diaries, bits of newspaper clippings and decided she could peruse those later.

The next package she laid her hands on was sealed. The white A4 envelope was old, slightly grubby around the edges as if it had been handled many times. Something special? A photograph? She flipped it over. "*Do Not Open Until After My Death*" was scrawled across the front in her mother's flowing script. She fingered the envelope. Now what?

Open it! Open it! the voice urged. But Emily hesitated. Although her mother was almost gone, did she want to know what was inside?

Time for another cup of tea. She took the envelope into the kitchen and, as if it contained a bomb, she laid it carefully on the counter. While waiting for the kettle to boil, she stared at the envelope. A loud ringing noise close by made her jump. The old-style black phone sat tucked in the corner on the kitchen counter. She inhaled sharply. Was it the hospital, Suzi, or her mother's friends wanting updates? Tentatively she picked up the receiver and put it to her ear.

"Hello." Emily said.

"Miss Carson?"

Emily didn't recognize the young woman's voice.

"I'm Nurse Wilson at Berrington . . . "

"Oh . . . Is she . . . ?"

"Gone. Yes, I'm very sorry. Just half an hour ago, at twenty to eight."

Emily glanced up at the kitchen clock above the fridge then exhaled a long sigh, surprised at her own sense of relief. It was over.

"We will also be notifying your mother's sister, Renee Cooper," the nurse was saying.

"Okay . . . Thank you," Emily said absently and hung up. As she stood in the shadowy kitchen absorbing the fact that her mother was actually deceased, the phone rang again.

"It's Renee."

"Have you—?"

"Yes." There was a long pause. "She looked quite peaceful apparently." Renee's voice quivered.

"I'm glad." Emily exhaled a long sigh. Maybe now she and Renee could find some peace for themselves. But from the kitchen counter, the white envelope stared back at her, as if to say, *it's not over yet.*

"What time is your operation?" Emily asked, suddenly remembering that her aunt might already be at East Croydon Hospital.

"Oh, not until eleven. But I have to be there soon to prepare. How are you getting on, dear?" Renee asked harried, her tone almost weary. "Did you sleep all right?"

Emily decided not to tell her aunt about the ghostly visitation dream just yet. "Not too bad. I'm just working my way through the paperwork. It's . . . interesting."

"What have you found?" Renee's voice tightened. "Oh dear, I . . . I should have warned you . . . ."

Warned me of what? Emily put a hand through her short thick hair. "Well, I've got something here that says, *Do Not Open Until After My Death.*" She heard a sharp gasp on the other end. "Do you know what that is, Renee?"

"Oh, dear." Renee sighed. "You haven't opened it yet, have you?"

"No. . . . . Why? Do you know what's in it?"

"Maybe you should leave that for the solicitors."

"Okay," Emily agreed, happy to delegate potentially bad news. "By the way, I need their number."

"Oh, yes." Renee sounded relieved to have changed the subject. "Just a minute."

Emily heard a rustle of papers and pictured her aunt sitting at her desk in her East Croydon home.

"Their names are Marsten and Marsten in Croydon, father and son. Their number is 01 273 4545. I spoke with Mr. Marsten Junior this morning, just before I heard. He's expecting your call."

"What about the cottage and the furnishings?"

"The Lions Club is coming to take everything. Help yourself to whatever you want. When you're done, just leave the key under the blue rock beside the front door. The solicitor will deal with the landlord."

"About the envelope—" Emily started.

The front door-knocker rapped smartly twice.

"Damn," Emily hissed. "Somebody's here."

"I have to get ready now anyway." Renee was shuffling more papers. "But before you go, I have to tell you that your mother doesn't want a funeral. She donated her body to medical science. The hospital will take care of her."

Thank God for that. Emily hated the thought of cremation or worse still, burial. It reminded her too much of her recurring suffocating nightmare. And not having a funeral to arrange was a relief. "Good luck with your operation!" she called out as she hung up.

When Emily opened the chapel front door, she frowned. In the early morning sunshine a bedraggled, wizened old woman, stood on the doorstep clutching a basket of flowers. Emily knew from long ago visits to her mother's cottage that gypsies sometimes came by to sell things. But they were not usually so early.

The woman beamed up at Emily. "'Ello, dearie."

Emily glanced down at her offerings. An array of daffodils and other spring flowers hung limply over the side of her basket. She looked up again. The older woman's eyes were boring into her own.

"I'm sorry, I don't have any change," Emily said quickly, anxious to be away from her invasive gaze. "Otherwise, I would—"

"Oh, dear. You've 'ad a lot o' loss, you 'ave, I can see." The woman held up a small bunch of bluebells. "'Ere, take these. An' never you mind, it's goin' to get betta now."

Emily was simultaneously astounded and unnerved by the woman's uncanny knowing. Dazed, she put her hand out and took the limp flowers.

"Not everyfin' is as it seems, though, is it?" she added as though Emily knew what she was talking about.

"What?"

"Oh, I know. You're tired, ain't yer? But once it all comes clean, you'll find a lot o' love, dearie. An' that's what you want, ain't it?"

"I . . . I'm sorry, I have to go." Emily handed the flowers back to the gypsy and closed the door gently but firmly in her face.

MR. MARSTEN

Back at the desk, she found herself staring at papers with numbers on them but she couldn't absorb any information. A whistling sound from the kitchen pulled her out of her daze. She realized she must have automatically put the kettle on for tea and got up to stop the sound. Just get the work done and think about all this later, she reprimanded herself.

Emily sat once more at the bureau. She sorted bills and personal papers into their respective piles and placed them in separate plastic Tesco bags—one for the solicitor, the other bag's contents for her to peruse later. But the unopened envelope—though still on the kitchen counter—was foremost in her mind. What horrible secret was inside? She wouldn't open it, she decided. She would take Renee's advice and give it to the solicitor. Let him deal with all the repercussions of her mother's unhappy life.

Oh! The solicitor! She reached for the phone.

"Er. . . Mr. Marsten? This is Emily Carson. I— "

"Hello," he said as if he already knew who she was and was happy to hear from her. The strong, male voice on the other end was surprisingly young. "I've been expecting your call."

Emily felt herself blush. His warm, dynamic energy took her breath away. "Hello."

"I'm sorry to hear about your mother," he offered. "She was my father's client. Unfortunately he's out of commission for a while so I've taken over his files temporarily."

"Oh? Is your father all right?" Emily didn't know why she asked. It was none of her business.

"Oh yes, thank you. Just some recurring health issues. He's bedridden for a while." There was silence on the line. "It might take me a few days to get up to speed with your mother's file." He paused again and added, "My father spoke very highly of your mother."

"That's nice." Emily gave her automatic response to the continual accolades for her mother and Helen, two different people inhabiting the same body.

Mr. Marsten paused. Did he sense her cynicism?

"I understand that you need all her paperwork," she continued in her back-to-business voice, "which I'm in the process of sorting. I'll leave the key for the Lions Club. Is there anything else you need me to do?" Emily realized she must sound callous. And why did she care what he thought?

"No, not for the time being anyway. Unless you want to take any of her—"

"No possessions. Just photos," Emily responded a little too crisply. "You're in East Croydon, I believe? I begin my new job on Sunday so I'll have to put the papers in the post. Registered, of course."

"Yes, that should be fine." He cleared his throat before he asked, "Can I ring you when I'm more conversant with her file?"

"Yes, of course."

"And there may be another issue I need to speak with you about."

"Oh? Like what?" Emily realized she sounded

239

combative.

"Well," he countered calmly, "nothing urgent I don't think. But strangely enough, your name came up in reference to one of *my* clients. I'm not sure exactly if there's a connection . . . ." There was a smile in his voice as he added, "You know how it is. Families are always complicated."

"Are they?" she wondered aloud. "And I thought it was just my family that was loony."

He let out a long sigh. "No, believe me, Miss Carson, most families are very complex."

So it's not just mine? Emily exhaled and found herself relaxing her grip on the phone.

"Will it be convenient to ring you tomorrow?" he asked. "Your aunt gave me your home number."

"Solicitors work on Saturdays?"

"Not usually but I have a lot of reading to do."

"Well, I hope *you* find it entertaining. And yes, I'll be heading home this afternoon so I'll be back in Horsham tomorrow."

"Splendid." He finally sounded like the old-world solicitor she had expected.

"Splendid," she repeated, grinning, and hung up, not knowing whether to be intrigued to meet Mr. Marsten or afraid of how he might impact her life.

In one of the slots, Emily found her mother's address book. She perused the pages and recognized the names of her mother's closest friends, some of whom Emily remembered from childhood. She would have to phone them, of course. She dreaded having to do this, remembering how they cherished and praised her mother, calling her "wonderful." No doubt they judged Emily for abandoning her, especially after Derek's death. But her friends of thirty years, it seemed, did not know the whole story of Helen.

To Emily's relief, they were conciliatory, expressing their sadness at their own loss—and not critical of Emily. She asked each one which possessions they would like as mementos and made a list for the Lions Club what to leave and who to contact. The friends, she sensed, were dying to question Emily about her estranged relationship with her mother, but thankfully they had the good sense not to.

Finally, at ten past twelve, she put the last of the files in the solicitor's bag and placed some family albums and other personal papers in the other.

On her way out through the kitchen, she collected the now-ominous-to-her white envelope, debated for a moment in which bag it belonged—solicitor's or personal—and finally placed it in her handbag. Closing the chapel door behind her, she slid the key under the blue rock, walked up the garden path and didn't look back.

THE GRAVEYARD

Emily slumped into the driver's seat of her car, fingering her ignition key. The white and blue Tesco bags bursting with documents lay on the passenger seat. Her mother was really dead. For many years she had yearned for the freedom her mother's permanent absence would give her but she did not feel quite free yet. A dark cloud lingered as if there was still something . . . or *someone* she had forgotten. Emily shook her head as if to rid herself of the shadowy thought and switched on the ignition.

While the car hummed to life, she made a quick decision and pulled out into the narrow lane. Instead of heading left for the motorway, she turned right down the main street. Driving past village shops, she felt the warmth of the spring sunshine through the car windows and was uplifted to see that the fields and hedgerows which rose above and behind the clustered houses were beginning to turn a lush green. She exhaled as if to blow away the tension of the previous day and night.

Bethany Baptist Church still sat perched on a grassy mound on the village outskirts. As Emily parked in front of the wooden gate, she saw that the white stone edifice was surrounded by headstones—some new and white—others grey and crumbling. As Emily picked her way through the untended graves, she felt a pang of guilt about how she had neglected her own family. But hey, she was here now, she reminded herself.

Derek's grave lay at the back of the churchyard toward the bottom of the mound in the half-shelter of a large elm. At the moment it was bathed in sunshine. Emily stood before the black granite slab. The engraving was simply marked. *DEREK J. CARSON DIED 1971.* She frowned as she saw that a small arrangement of daffodils had been lovingly placed on the grave. The flowers were fresh. Who would have done that? she wondered. Maybe Renee had come by the other day after being at the hospital. Yes, her aunt had been so devastated by Derek's death. It must have been her.

As children, brother and sister had been close but her older brother had left home at seventeen and only phoned his sister once a year after that. She had missed him. Despite his changeable moods, they shared the same wry sense of humor—and a family history.

Emily hunkered down on the grass in front of the grave. After giving the cemetery a quick glance to make sure no one could hear, she spoke aloud. "Well, Derek, you probably already know Mother has died. This morning. Yes, she's finally gone and I really, really hope she rests in peace. If you see her, tell her I hope she's happier now."

The gravestone stared silently back at her.

"You know, I am still really pissed off with you." Though Emily's voice cracked with emotion, she realized how good it felt to express her truth out loud as if her brother was really listening. "Not only did you leave me without saying goodbye, but you also left me alone with the monster mother. I became the dart board for even more of her misery after you . . . left. Now I am officially an orphan." Emily paused. A spike of grief surfaced for the loss of her family and tears rolled freely down her cheeks.

When Emily's left leg began to cramp, she shifted and sat on the ground, curling her legs to one side and supporting herself with one arm. "Why do you think she hated us so much?" she asked Derek. "It's almost as if she was punishing us for being born. And Dad was so mean to you. I understand why you told . . . stories . . . to make your life sound better than it was. I would have done the same thing." Tears edged out of the corners of her eyes. Emily looked up through the leaves of the elm tree, its branches shifting over her head, giving her intermittent shade from the sun. "But don't worry," she continued, wiping her cheek. "Mother won't be joining you here. I think she's haunting *me* already and she's only been gone a few hours." Emily glanced around. Still no one in sight. "You know what I think, Derek? For some reason, I think she was afraid of me in some way." She tugged absently on clumps of grass between his grave and the next. "Maybe 'cause I'm a bit, you know, psychic and I can see things. But why should that have bothered her?"

At the top of the mound, an older couple appeared around the side of the church, clutching a bouquet of multicolored flowers and moving towards a grave to the far right. Maybe because she had seen this kind of grief in her own family, Emily guessed that it was their deceased child they were visiting. The tragedy in their body language was easy to interpret.

"But you know I didn't see her for the last four or five years," Emily continued. "Not since you . . . . It was her or me. I decided to save myself," she said her voice breaking. "But Thank God for Aunt Renee. She's been my only friend—."

She was startled by a large black crow which swooped and landed on Derek's headstone. The big bird shuffled from claw to claw, squawking loudly as if trying to get Emily's attention. She watched fascinated as the crow's beady brown eyes focused on a something just above her, cocking its head to one side, as if communicating with someone behind her. Suddenly uncomfortable, Emily stood up. Apparently interrupted, the crow flew up into the elm.

"Well, Derek, I'm sorry I haven't been to see you more but maybe now that Mother is gone, I can come here to talk to you again." Emily brushed the grass and dust from her jeans. "Actually, I feel a bit better talking to you. I miss you, Dustbin." Emily smiled at the bitter-sweet memory of giving her brother his nickname because of his bottomless capacity for eating any and all leftover food.

"Bye for now." She leaned forward and affectionately touched the top of her brother's headstone.

Driving through the Buckinghamshire countryside Emily only half listened to the news on Radio

Four. Queen Elizabeth was visiting Samoa and Fiji. Maybe I'll fly there some day, Emily thought. It sounds so exotic. Two IRA bombers had been sentenced. Emily was relieved that she wasn't living in London any more, having survived numerous bomb scares and too-close-for-comfort explosions.

While barreling down the M4 motorway, Fleetwood Mac's new song "Chain" was belting out of the car radio. *Now here you go again, you say, you want your freedom. Well, who I am I to keep you down?* The lyrics could have been her mother's guilt-laden farewell. And yes, I do want freedom and love, Emily thought. Why not? She hoped the gypsy was right. What had she said? *Once it all comes clean, you'll find love.* Something like that.

By the time she reached the winding Sussex country lanes that would bring her home, she was reaching for earlier happier childhood memories. There had been picnics full of laughter, Christmases where her parents had smiled indulgently as she and Derek ripped wrappings off presents, lively family dinners with friends and neighbors. And then something had gone terribly wrong—as if a bomb had dropped on their happy clan. Was her father's affair the only reason her mother became so embittered? Could the breakdown of their family have caused Derek to end his life? No. There must have been something more, something deeper, something worse. But what?

As Emily parked in front of her three-bedroom townhouse in Horsham, she shook these unsolved mysteries from her head. She remembered that on Sunday, there was a whole new adventure waiting for her. She decided that she would release the past and enjoy her new life. Yes. It would be a new beginning. Maybe she would even meet Mr. Wonderful, get married and create a new warm and loving family of her own. But why then could she not shake an impending sense of dread?

MEETINGS

I have to get out. I must not panic. If I just keep banging, someone will hear me. Oh God, I can't breathe and no one's around.

A distant ringing began to mix with the banging. Emily's eyes flew open and she sat up, gasping for breath. Oh, Thank God it was just the dream again. The phone was ringing. What time was it? Had she slept through till Sunday and missed her first flight? She reached out blindly and grabbed the white receiver from her bedside table. Once she opened her eyes, the bright red numbers on her radio alarm clock stared back at her. It was ten past ten.

"Miss Carson?"

"Yes."

Through Emily's sleepy fog, she realized it was the voice of the solicitor. "Mr. Marsten?"

"I'm sorry. I didn't mean to wake you on a Saturday morning."

"Oh. It's all right," she mumbled, pulling her legs over the side of the bed. "I have to get up."

"Would you like me to ring you later?"

"No . . . no . . . I'm sorry." Emily struggled to gather her thoughts. "Did you have time to read up on my mother's files?"

"Yes," he said hesitantly as if bracing himself to relay bad news.

"And?"

"I'll need to see you in person. But I also need to

confirm the date when you turn twenty-five, Miss Carson."

"What? . . . Why?"

"Your age is a stipulation of a document I have been instructed to give you."

He sounded more officious this morning, Emily thought. What had he found out? "Um . . ." Emily had to think. "Actually, I turn twenty-five in about two weeks, the twenty-eighth." In all the excitement of her new career and then the suddenness of her mother's death, she had completely forgotten about her upcoming birthday.

"Well, if you don't have any plans on or after your birthday," Mr. Marsten sounded friendlier now, "perhaps you could meet me at my office?"

Emily had already memorized her upcoming month's flight roster. "I'm off on the days after, the twenty-ninth and thirtieth."

"Why don't we say the twenty-ninth then at eleven o'clock?"

"Okay." Emily gulped, feeling mixed emotions of fear and excitement at meeting the dynamic Mr. Marsten and learning *what?*

"Splendid. I am located just opposite East Croydon station, the big blue building, third floor, number 301."

Having visited her grandparents and Renee's home in East Croydon frequently, Emily was familiar with the building. She quickly scribbled down the details on the pad and pen that lay on her bedside table, usually reserved for recording her dreams.

"If you could send the papers to that address as soon as possible, I can have everything ready for you to finalize," he added.

Now that he had read about her dramatic family

background, he probably wanted to get this case off his desk as soon as possible. "Okay." Emily felt herself smile.

"I look forward to meeting you, Miss Carson," he said, a question in his tone.

After he hung up, Emily remained sitting on the edge of her bed. Maybe Mr. Marsten's document contained the same information as that in the white envelope. But the white envelope wasn't addressed to Emily specifically. And there was no mention of her age. She got up to put on her dressing gown but before she reached her bedroom door, the phone rang again.

"Oh good, you're back." Suzi's lively voice was like music to Emily's ears. "How's your mother?"

"Er . . . she's gone. Yesterday morning."

"Oh dear. Are you okay?" Suzi paused, probably not sure what to say. "Do you still want ter meet at pub for 't drink, lass?" she asked imitating her favorite *Coronation Street* character.

"Aye, 'appen," Emily responded, getting in the spirit. "'Ow about 'alf past twelve at 'Alf Moon at Copthorne?"

"All right then, chuck. See you there."

As Emily finished applying her make-up in the bathroom mirror, she suddenly remembered Renee.

When her aunt picked up the phone, her voice was thick as she said, "Hello?"

Emily wasn't sure if it was a reaction to the anesthetic or grief for her sister. "I'm sorry, Renee. I should have offered to pick you up."

"Oh, that's all right, dear. I got a taxi."

"Can you see better already?"

"Well, the doctors are happy." Renee chuckled and Emily felt relieved." I look like Mata Hari with my dark sunglasses. I'm very mysterious, you know."

Aren't we all? Emily thought. "Renee?"

"Yes?"

"Is there anything you need to tell me before I see the solicitor?"

"When are you meeting with him?"

"In two weeks, the day after my birthday, at eleven."

Renee paused. "Why don't you come for tea, dear, after you've seen Mr. Marsten. And what would you like for a present?"

"No presents." *Just the truth would be nice*, she thought.

"Okay. Then we can have a good chat." But the way she said "chat" didn't sound light and breezy at all.

"Are you sure you're going to be okay to fly?" Suzi asked Emily as they settled into their wicker chairs on the pub's patio.

"Oh . . . yes. My family isn't like yours, Suzi." Emily smiled. "You know, loving."

"You poor thing." Maybe because Suzi was four years older than Emily and four inches taller, she treated her new friend like a much younger sister. "Then lunch is on me," she offered, brightening, "in honor of your mother, whoever she was *and* celebrating our exciting new flying careers." Suzi squeezed her slim shoulders together and flashed her mischievous grin. "Oooh, chuck, we're going to have so much fun."

"God, I hope so!" Emily clinked her white wine glass on Suzi's. She beamed at her friend and sat back in her chair, enjoying the warm sun on her face and exhaling the tensions of the last few days.

Other patrons were also soaking up the almost balmy sunshine on the small stone-flagged patio. In the busy Tudor-style pub, the young women knew that the famed ploughman's lunch would take a while to arrive, but Emily was happy to sit and relax with her friend.

Suzi asked suddenly, "Does anything scare you?"

Emily took a sip of wine "Just ghosts."

"Ghosts?" Suzi frowned. "I'm talking about flying."

"Oh, yes." Emily wasn't sure why she had mentioned ghosts. "Going down in a ball of fire scares the hell out of me but somehow I don't think that's my destiny."

Suzi glanced around and then back at Emily. "Speaking of destiny, I have a feeling that your whole life is going to change. You never know, you might even meet the man of your dreams."

The man of my dreams. Emily flashed on her nightmares and shuddered. "Why do you say that? Are you psychic or something, Suzi?"

"You're not the only one who can sense things, you know," her friend responded, smiling.

Emily squirmed in her seat at the reference to her psychic abilities, a gift she tried to ignore.

Leaning back in her chair and tilting her already tanned face up to the sun, Suzi asked, "Do you want to talk about your mother?"

Emily shrugged. Did she? What was there to say? "Well, my mother was . . . how do I explain her? . . . very unhappy and she kind of took it out on me and my brother."

"That's too bad," Suzi frowned.

"And now she's gone," Emily continued, "I thought all the drama would be over, but it seems there are all kinds of mysteries she's left behind. The solicitor has a document for me, whatever that means. And my mother also left an envelope only to be opened after her death."

Suzi leaned forward. "So have you opened it?"

"Not yet."

"How can you stand the suspense?"

"In my family, it's more dread than suspense."

"Maybe your mother was hoarding cash and it's a big fat inheritance?"

"The only thing I am likely to inherit is her insanity," Emily confessed.

"Do you want me to open it for you?" Suzi grinned, gleefully rubbing her hands together.

Emily grimaced. "My aunt's in on it too but she won't fess up to anything—at least not until I've seen Mr. Marsten."

"The solicitor? You little devil, do you have a thing for Mr. Marsten?"

Emily found herself trying to suppress a smile. "Why do you ask?"

"It's just the way you say his name."

Two plates laden with chunks of crisp, fresh baguette and an array of fresh cheeses garnished with homemade relishes were placed in front of them. Suzi picked up her napkin and spread it across her lap. While her friend took a bite of bread slathered in gooey blue-veined brie, Emily glanced around at the other patrons, twosomes and foursomes, and considered the solicitor she hadn't even met. "Ah, he's probably married with six children."

"Well, there's a lid for every pot, whoever and wherever they are." Suzi laughed. "But in the meantime, *we* are going to have fun."

"Amen to that, sister. Emily said, as she reached for the relish.

CHARLIE ECHO

The sight of the young woman standing in her full-length bedroom mirror was pleasing, almost shocking to Emily. During the strenuous airline training, Emily had shed her extra roundness. The dark navy uniform with red trim certainly accentuated her now-svelte figure. And the bowler hat that almost covered her blue eyes added an air of mystery, she thought.

At only four thirty a.m. it was dark outside. She was still drowsy but excited and afraid all at the same time. The churning in her stomach was probably a combination—her fear of flying, the anticipation of which trick the crew would play on the novice "hostie" and the anxiety of failing in her duties.

There was so much to remember from training— Emily had sat up the previous night making sure she knew her emergency drills for crashing and ditching, where the fire extinguishers were located, what types, how to operate them let alone all the details of the different oxygen masks and air systems, crash axes and flight deck protocols. Added to that were first aid procedures, bar and catering service routines. She had even drifted off to sleep reciting the aviation alphabet. *Alpha, Beta, Charlie* . . . . A flash of her mother sneering when Emily had told her years ago she wanted to be a flight attendant came to mind. "Air hostesses are just glorified waitresses," she had scoffed. What did she know how much was involved? But then her mother had consistently cast judgment on people and things. Maybe it made her feel superior.

Though Emily had wanted to fly international routes on the DC10, her talent for languages designated her to short-haul Comet and BAC 1-11 European flights. Still, working for Anglo Airlines had somehow felt fated. She couldn't explain it but she knew she had joined the right company.

The airport parking lot, despite a few amber lamps, was empty in the darkness of early morning. The only activity in the main airport terminal was cleaners swishing their large swirling, polishing brushes around the shiny, tiled floor. When Emily finally reached the mostly glass building outside the main terminal that housed the crew room, she saw uniformed cabin and flight deck crew pouring in—and out of—the two glass doors.

Inside, the crew room buzzed with a melee of chatting navy-clad young women. Some were clustered around a battered table, the only piece of furniture in the center of the room, bent over a large white sheet of paper. By the number of crew, there must be quite a few early morning flights, she thought. Then Emily realized from the disheveled appearances of some that a few of them must have just returned from night flights; hair strands were hanging down, scarves were slung loosely around necks, and white gloves were now soiled. Others were taking stacks of mail from the wooden alphabetized pigeon holes on the wall and flipping through them. The remainder of the mostly female group stood in small clusters, chatting. No one noticed Emily as she stepped, full of trepidation, into the room.

She knew she was supposed to check the sheet on the table for her flight information and then find her boss for the flight, the Number One. She tentatively peered over the shoulder of a blonde-haired girl. Destination code for Milan: MXP. Flight number: AA 5238. The name of her Number One: Doreen Cabot. Passenger load:

119. Aircraft type: Comet.

Good, Emily thought. Though the Comets were so old the rumor was that the airline had pulled them out of museums, Emily still warmed to their old grace and the fact that they had four engines, rather than only two like the BAC 1-11 or three like the DC10.

The blonde girl glanced up. "Are you on the Milan?" she asked.

"Er . . . yes. Flight 5238?"

"Please. Don't tell me—this is your first flight?"

"'Fraid so." Emily shrugged and wanted to shrivel into the ground.

"Great." The sarcasm in the young woman's voice was undisguised. In training their teachers had neglected to warn them how much the more senior members of the crew hated flying with "new girls."

"I'm Doreen Cabot, your Number One. Come over here."

Emily followed her to the corner of the room, where two other girls were huddled, as if on a rugby team. The first two young women were already engaged in a familiar chat.

"This is Emily," Doreen told them. "She's brand new," she said wearily, making it sound old already. "So Emily, you're number four. You'll be down the back with me. You two can decide between the other two positions."

"Galley!" the brunette said quickly.

"Guess that makes me Number three then, doesn't it?" The smaller red-head just shrugged. "By the way, I'm Maria," she told Emily in a gentle Irish brogue. "And this is Sherry."

Emily was already aware that newer girls flew in the most junior position as Number Four until they had acquired some experience. This meant they sat on the rear jump seat next to the Number One for take-off and landing and worked in the cabin partnering with the Number One. The senior hostess's responsibilities also included taking charge of the cabin, overseeing any emergencies, liaising with the flight deck, filling out all the flight reports, counting the contents of the duty-free bar and accounting for all monies collected in-flight. Number Twos worked the galley, organizing and preparing catering working with Number Three at the front of the cabin.

"I'll call for transport." Doreen said, moving over to the other side of the room and picking up a black handset on the wall. As someone from operations gave her information, she made notes in her spiral book. "Oh no," she moaned loudly. "Not Charlie Echo." She was referring to the aircraft. Emily now knew that all British plane registrations consisted of five letters that all began with G. The crews usually identified the aircraft by the last two of those five letters, using the aviation alphabet which in this case was CE or Charlie Echo. Doreen's displeasure could be heard above the noisy chatter and there was a low, collective and commiserative groan from other girls in the room.

"I hate that plane," Sherry muttered.

"Bloody hell!" Doreen exclaimed, from across the room. Something else that Ops was telling her that she didn't like.

"Take no notice of Doreen," Maria said in her gentle lilt. "Her bark's worse than her bite."

Emily smiled, grateful for Maria's friendliness.

"Well, guess what girls?" Doreen returned to the group as she put her notepad away. "Charlie Echo's tech already but we're going out anyway."

The two girls grimaced. "How long?" Sherry asked. "I have a party to get back for."

"Thirty minutes is what ops said. Air system."

"Charlie Echo's always got problems," Sherry told Emily, "which is why we hate it so much."

"Some people say it's haunted." Maria sounded like Boris Karloff about to tell an eerie story, "and the ghost is said to always come when there's a new girl on board."

"Is that so?" Emily had been warned of new girl tricks during training. *Maybe*, she thought, *this is their idea of a trick*. She wished they hadn't chosen ghosts as a theme. But she just smiled. "Well, that might be . . . er . . . exciting."

"Exciting!" Sherry scoffed. "It's a bloody drag. Something always goes wrong; fire bells go off, undercarriage doesn't come down. One time–."

"Transport!" someone called and suddenly half of the people in the room pulled everything together; jackets, hats, scarves, gloves, cabin bags. En masse, they moved towards the door of the crew room and out towards the glass doors at the back of the building, airside, and into the still cold morning.

The doors of the bus hissed open and the young women climbed in. As the transporter raced along the perimeter of the airport, yellow lights flashing, the driver's walkie-talkie crackled with instructions. Emily loved how the aircraft large and small sat like frozen birds on the grey tarmac. Behind them, a hazy pink sky silhouetted their gorgeous shapes while the yellow glow of a sunrise gently expanded, turning the backdrop into streaks of yellow and pink.

The dawn tranquility was suddenly shattered by the noise of taxiing aircraft, numerous buses shuttling bodies

back and forth like cattle, catering trucks adding their
toxic fumes to the mix, baggage-handler tugs swerving—
and losing precariously stacked suitcases—fuelling trucks
billowing fumes as they negotiated their way under the
wings of aircraft. As the airport came to life, Emily
decided this would be her favorite flight time. Early
morning.

The transport driver expertly pulled up to within
inches of the aircraft's forward steps. "There you are,
people," he said cheerily as the bus door whooshed open.
"Good old Charlie Echo."

Emily's stomach clenched. Here we go, she
thought. What am I doing? I'm terrified of flying, let
alone potentially haunted airplanes.

"The engineers aren't even here yet," Doreen
groaned.

"They're on their way, luv," the driver confirmed
after listening to some static messages on his airport
radio.

As the four young women ascended the steps,
their high heels clanking on the metal stairs, the staircase
rocked unsteadily from side to side. They ducked into the
forward galley.

"Brrrr! It's like a bloody freezer!" Sherry
complained. "We'll have to wait for the engineers to turn
on the GPU. I can't do anything until they get here," she
declared, plunking herself on a front row seat, and
rubbing her hands together.

"What's the GPU?" Emily didn't remember that
abbreviation from her training.

"Ground Power Unit," Maria obliged. "We need
ground power for the lights, ovens and heat."

"Emily and Maria, you can start doing the seat
pockets and check the emergency equipment." Doreen

instructed as she opened a brown manila envelope and withdrew her paperwork. Emily took the pile of clean brochures, sick bags and duty free lists that Maria handed her. It was so cold; she was happy to get moving.

"I'll start at the back," Maria said and disappeared to the rear of the aircraft while Emily began the job of tidying or replacing the contents of the passengers' seat pockets in the front rows. Sherry, despite her complaints, had disappeared into the galley to organize the catering supplies that had just arrived. Doreen was sitting on one of the front seats preparing her flight forms, peering at them in the dim morning light.

"Is it always this cold?" Emily asked Doreen, as she saw the white plumes of her own breath in the grey mist of the interior aircraft.

"Only on Charlie Echo," the senior stewardess said without looking up.

Emily had replenished only five rows of seat pockets when there was a clumping up the front steps. A tall young man in green overalls appeared at the entranceway between galley and cabin. He stood there for a few minutes, staring straight down the aircraft to the rear.

Good, Emily thought. *An engineer. Heat!* "Good morning," she said, smiling.

The man turned his head towards her. His eyes seemed vacant as he stared right through her.

She shivered.

Without a word, the man then walked straight down the aisle towards the back of the aircraft. Emily heard noises, as if he was fixing something.

"Oh, bloody hell!" It was Maria at the center over-wing exit.

"What is it?" Emily was working her way

towards the rear and was only a few rows away from Maria.

"The spring on this seat is broken and it won't stay upright." She sighed. "We'll need an engineer."

"Why don't you ask the engineer who just got on?" Emily suggested. "He's down the back." But even as she said the words, she realized that the scuffling noises had quietened.

Maria gave Emily a strange look.

"Which engineer? They haven't shown up yet."

"But . . . the man in the green overalls who just got on. Isn't he an engineer?"

"Trust me, darlin', they travel in packs and there's no one down the back."

"Maybe he got off at the rear," Emily suggested.

"Not unless he jumped twenty feet. There are no rear stairs."

"Oh." Emily glanced toward the back of the aircraft, a deep frown on her face. It was very, very still.

"Go take a look for yerself," Maria said, sensing that Emily didn't believe her. "This isn't a trick," she added, as if reading the new girl's mind.

Emily put down the brochures and strode down to the rear vestibule. She checked both toilets. The door to the rear hold was open. Emily peeked in. It was just a void of black space waiting for the baggage to arrive. Both rear passenger doors were tightly shut. There were no rear stairs and no engineer. Where did he go?

If it was a trick, how had they had managed to make a man disappear into thin air?

"You're right," she told Maria returning to the middle of the aircraft. "There's no one there. " She then heard men's voices coming from the galley. Several men in button-up green coveralls were standing at the front flirting with Sherry. Then they burst into the cabin, laughing and talking.

"Alright, luv?" one of them enquired of Emily. His coverall was different from that of the first engineer she had seen.

"Just cold," Emily responded, shivering now. "And it's my first flight."

"Oooh, you better watch 'em, darlin'," he said, smiling broadly and nodding his head toward the galley. "They'll try and get yer wiv a trick."

"I think they already did," Emily muttered.

"Roight then," he said, springing down the cabin followed by two more men in green. "Let's give you girls some 'eat."

Once the plane was aloft and the flight attendants began their service, Emily almost forgot that she was thirty-five thousand feet above the earth. She was just finishing serving second coffees to the passengers when Doreen told Emily that she had been summoned to the flight deck. A little tremulous, Emily put down her coffee pot on the shiny galley surface and stepped tentatively into the cockpit.

She noted that the flight engineer sat on the right. He seemed preoccupied with the panel of dials before him.

"You wanted to see me?" she called out to the captain and first officer over the noise of the aircraft engines. Their backs were to her. Their meal trays were cast aside on the floor between their seats, the food picked over but mostly eaten.

The first officer turned and thrust a white sick bag at Emily. It appeared to be full . . . and steaming. "Hi, Emily," he said, clutching his stomach as if he had just that moment finished throwing up. "Can you take this away, please?"

She grimaced and leaned forward to take it.

Suddenly Captain Wilson turned. "No, wait, Peter," he said, reaching out for the bag. "Give it to me. I love to eat the chunky bits."

There was a flash from her right. Disoriented, Emily realized that her shocked and disgusted expression had just been photographed by the engineer.

"Very funny!" Emily could not help laughing. "You got me!"

She was still grinning when she stepped back into the galley. Doreen was sipping on a coke. "If you can take a joke, Emily, you can handle this job," she said smiling. "You have now officially been initiated."

"But what about the disappearing engineer?" the new stewardess asked. "I thought that was the trick?"

Doreen frowned. "What disappearing engineer?"

NIGHTMARE OR . . . ?

On her fifth day of flying, Emily found herself yet again on the dreaded Charlie Echo. While she hadn't seen any more of the phantom engineer, the plane had predictably encountered a technical problem. On their two and a half-hour flight inbound from Trondheim, Norway, the Captain had told the Number One that a warning light was "red" on the flight deck alerting them to a pressurization problem with one of the holds. Either the flight deck's micro switch was faulty or the hold itself was not properly sealed. At 35,000 feet, with a not-quite-closed-pressurized hold, the aircraft could implode and everyone would perish. But instead of diverting to another airport and investigating, the Captain opted to simply take the plane down to 10,000 feet where they could safely depressurize—or so he informed the passengers. At the lower altitude, the flight time doubled.

When the aircraft finally began its descent into Gatwick four hours later, and after Emily had made her announcements in Norwegian from the rear of the plane, she found herself alone on the rear jump seat. She felt an icy chill pass through her, reminiscent of her first morning on the fridge-like aircraft. Perhaps, she thought, I am not really alone back here. She tried to shake off the idea that the ghost of Charlie Echo was trying to get her attention.

Arriving home exhausted at three-thirty in the morning, she was tempted to go straight to bed without removing make-up or setting her alarm. But the potential for her to sink into a coma-like sleep was strong, she thought, and Emily did *not* want to miss her Berlin flight the next day, especially with only twelve hours between duties, not including travelling to and from the airport and the hour and a half pre-flight check in. She set the alarm for ten the following day and finally spent, crawled into bed.

There are lots and lots of people. Blue sky. Some clouds. Flying free, so free. She's on Charlie Echo, walking towards the back of the plane. There is a banging coming from the rear hold. Doreen has told her to check out the noise. A wooden coffin precariously placed on top of the other baggage has tipped over during turbulence. The lid of the coffin is partially open, revealing a crack of darkness inside the wooden box. Through the dark crack, a man's white naked arm is sticking out, his hand large and grubby, his fingernails torn and dirty. Emily knows that she is the one who has to put the arm back in the coffin and set it upright again. She leans over to take the arm by the wrist but suddenly cold fingers, like icicles, dig into her flesh. The claw-like hand clamps onto her wrist with an iron grip. She screams and attempts to break free. But the hand pulls her closer and closer towards the black void inside the coffin. Emily is being sucked down deeper into the darkness. Inside the box, the space is black and cramped. It smells of kerosene. She is alone. Above her, the coffin lid snaps shut. Everything is black. She can't breathe! A man's voice in her ear says, "Don't panic." But she can't breathe. There is the distant murmur of voices. She cries out desperately for help but no one can hear her. Everything goes quiet. There is no air. She is going to die.

Emily jerked awake, sitting upright in bed, gasping for breath. The familiar oak tree outside her window helped calm her rapid breathing, its branches swaying gently against a blue sky in the early summer breeze. *The dream again!*

What time is it? Only 7:05 am. She was clammy with perspiration and still panting for breath. *It's okay. It's okay,* she told herself. *It was just a dream.* But the voice in her head questioned *Was it?*

She swung her legs over the side of the bed and reached for her housecoat. Downstairs she boiled a kettle for tea. Clutching the warm cup, she moved into the living room and curled up in a self-protective ball in her favourite armchair. She had just over two hours before she had to prepare for her flight. This dream had been the worst. In every dream she had been sucked into some kind of vortex, but the coffin was new. The books she had read on recurring nightmares told her that the dream was trying to wake her up to some kind of truth. She knew she needed help. But who could she talk to?

As Emily sat huddled in the chair, she remembered that the bag of photographs and other papers she had brought from her mother's house still sat untouched on her pine dresser in the corner. The grubby white envelope sat on top, also unopened. *Forget waiting for the solicitor*, the voice said. *It's time.*

Slowly Emily got up and walked over to the dresser. She picked up the envelope and returned to the chair. At this hour, outside noises of people going to work would have usually invaded her quiet suburban space, but now, as if the air itself was holding its breath, a sacred hush seemed to descend on the room. Slowly Emily tore the top off the envelope and pulled out just one sheet of lined paper covered in her mother's familiar elegant scrawl.

NOT TO BE OPENED
BEFORE MY DEATH
HELEN MARY CARSON

To Whom It May Concern:

Now that I am gone, I am writing this letter to inform you of some truths that I was not able to divulge while I was alive. And I want you all to know how I suffered and the sacrifices I made for the sake of this family. Those sacrifices were made in vain as in the end I was also betrayed. I wish now that I had followed my heart.

Oh God, what was she going to say? Emily gripped the paper even tighter.

Graves End, Granny and Granddad's house, was hit by the buzz bomb in 1944. We couldn't live there, of course, so Granny and I went to stay at Aunt Fiona's, Granny's sister in Buckinghamshire. There I met an American Air Force pilot, Charles Wright. We fell deeply in love, and I got pregnant with his child.

What! She sat up in her chair.

Not for one moment did I regret our short time together but I am sorry for the terrible pain it caused my baby, my children and me.

So she did know she hurt us. Emily remembered how she was always so dismissive of Derek and just plain nasty to her daughter.

Charles Junior was born May 1, 1945 while my own husband, John, was fighting in northern France. Of course, at that time, there was no other choice for me but to have Charles Junior adopted.

My God! I have a brother or at least a half-brother! Inside the shock, a sense of elation bubbled up. She was not alone.

So many of her memories now made sense. Emily had thought her mother's histrionic rants were about her husband's infidelities, the breakdown of her marriage and the guilt of Derek's suicide but giving up her son and losing her soul mate were obviously what had tortured her mother's soul. She had given up so much—only in the end to be betrayed by her husband.

A neighbor, Mrs. Patricia Baldwin, who lived two doors down from us in Buckinghamshire had lost her new-born in a bombing raid in London. When I told her of my dilemma, we made an agreement. She would unofficially adopt my son as her own.

Maybe I can find him, Emily thought.

The contract between us was that I would never try to claim him and she would never tell my secret to anyone, especially the baby. As far as I know, my husband, John never suspected me of this affair or the birth of this baby. But he was no innocent either.

A vague memory wrestled to surface in Emily's mind. She recalled when she was eleven years old with her family of four seated at the dinner table, she had often felt the spirit of a young teenage boy pacing around the table searching for his place. "Mummy, I always feel like someone's missing," Emily had piped up. "Shouldn't there be five of us?" How her mother must have wanted to silence her psychic child. Maybe that's why she had hated her daughter. "Don't be so ridiculous," her mother had hissed, glancing quickly at her husband. Emily remembered only feeling shamed.

I called the baby Charles Edward in memory of his father, but Patricia might have called him by a new name. If, after my death, anyone attempts to locate my son, there will be no official adoption records.

So his name might be Charles Edward Baldwin. Emily made a mental note.

Charles Wright, my soul mate and the father of my child did not survive the war, so please do not attempt to contact his family. Although I sent him a letter advising him of the birth of his son, I am not sure that he received it in time.

Emily sank back in her chair. How sad and tragic for everyone. She gazed at the window, struggling to mesh this new information with memories of her mother and her own childhood.

She cringed at another recollection. After the divorce, she had constantly reminded her mother, "You're so lucky to have had a good marriage for twenty years and two healthy children. You can do anything." But her sherry-ravaged mother could only stare blankly out of the window and sob endlessly about some pain Emily did not understand.

My love for Charles was not simply a diversion from the war. Charles was my true love. I have missed him every single day of my life. And I am so sorry for my son. I only wish I could have introduced him into the family as he had wanted.

What did she mean, "as he had wanted?" Who wanted? Had her half-brother wanted to be a part of their family? Maybe he knew us—or knew *of* us. Oh brother!

I have never stopped thinking about them both, Charles Senior and my baby. I wish I could say that the sacrifice had been worth it but it hasn't.

Gee. Thanks, Mum.

By the time you read this letter, I hope I will finally be at peace and that Charles and I will be reunited for eternity.

I hope so, for yours and my sake, Emily said aloud, shaking her head.

If you do meet my lost son — or when he finds you — please tell him that I am sorry for all that happened. I did not want to give him up or keep him excluded, but the rules of the time demanded that.

If this letter is read in error by my ex-husband, I am sorry that you had to find out this way but perhaps now you will understand. And you had your affair. I did my duty. And in the end, that is love too. Judge me as you will.

Helen Carson.

July 1969

The hush in her living room expanded into a loud buzzing, as if, Emily imagined, everyone's spirit involved in this drama were in the room, invisible yet whispering. She shook off the feeling of being surrounded by discontented souls.

So there it was. Emily had wanted to believe that her parent's marriage had been—during her childhood at least—happy, but now she knew even that wasn't true. All the time, every day, her mother had thought of her lover and not of Emily's father. Even so, she had gone on to give birth to one more child, Emily. Why did she bother? Perhaps the daughter was meant to compensate for her lost baby. But how many times had her mother screamed at her, "I wish I'd never had you!" As a consolation prize, I failed, Emily thought.

Then she recalled how her mother had constantly reiterated, "Don't get married" and "Whatever you do, don't get pregnant." As if that was the worst tragedy for a woman. This seemed an odd thing for a mother to say because, as far as Emily could tell, her mother was happily married and at the time, had enjoyed being a mother of two children. Emily had always wanted to ask her *why?*—but had never really wanted to hear her answer. Both her children would have been a constant reminder of what was lost. With such a tragic secret, no one stood a chance of happiness.

This letter must have been written in one of her darkest but more lucid moments. Still, Emily felt that a lot had *not* been said. *We know more by omission than inclusion*, the familiar voice in her head whispered.

Where was this boy now? How old would he be? Thirty? So many questions—and now her mother was gone—so few answers.

Maybe Renee would know more.

As she stood up to make the call, something fell from her lap onto the carpet. Puzzled, she leaned over and picked up a small object attached to a grubby string. It was some kind of metal tag with the initials "C. E." on it followed by the stem of another letter which she could not decipher. A sob came up involuntarily from her throat as she realized what it was. A dog tag! But it was cut in half. Had someone sent her lover's identification to her mother to let her know he was dead—or half of it anyway? Who had the other half?

That meant someone else knew about their affair.

Or her mother had cut it in half to erase the last name of her lover and protect his family. Who knew what the truth was?

She tenderly placed the letter and the tag back in the well-worn envelope. Without consulting her clock to check if it was too early, she picked up the phone. Still in a state of shock, Emily didn't waste any time on a preamble.

"Renee, did you know that I have a half-brother?"

A sharp intake of breath and a long silence at the other end gave Emily her answer.

"Why didn't you tell me?"

"Well, while your mother was still alive, it seemed best—."

"To keep the secret," Emily snapped, surprised at her own anger. "Are there more secrets that I need to know about?"

There was an even longer silence and Emily realized she had raised her voice to her aunt. "I'm sorry, Renee. It's just such a shock."

"Yes, dear. I'm sure."

"And I knew that Graves End was bombed but I didn't know Granny and Mother had gone to Buckinghamshire to live."

"Oh yes. With Granny's sister, Fiona. Their house was uninhabitable. It was a good thing your mother didn't want to get out of bed immediately when those bomb sirens went off. Derek was just a baby. Your grandfather was out on black-out duty. Granny was trying to get her up and get them both down to the bomb shelter in time. When they walked through the kitchen the buzz bombers were already over their street. They had just reached the summer house and they knew they wouldn't make it to the bomb shelter so they dove under that big old oak dining table in the summer house. They cowered there as a bomb landed square in the garden bomb shelter and took the back right off the house, including all the glass of the summer house. They were so lucky to be alive."

Emily remembered she and Derek had spent many happy days in that house with their grandparents, playing in the back garden and the infamous overgrown bomb shelter.

"It was after that," Renee added, "while your father was in northern France, that your mother had that baby."

"Where is he now? I mean . . . the boy."

"Listen, dear. I'm sorry but I have to go. Let's continue this when you come on your birthday." The line went dead.

Emily lay down the silent receiver. Her mind raced. Did her father know? Is that why he had an affair and then disappeared? Is that why he was so horrible to Derek? Maybe he believed Derek wasn't his son? So many questions pushed themselves to the front of her mind that she couldn't think straight. The shock was causing her to tremble somewhere deep inside. Briefly she considered—like her mother before her—having a sherry before noon. Then she remembered it was early morning still and she had to go to work.

As she pulled herself up the stairs, it occurred to her how her mother must have suffered. What also struck

Emily was that for a woman to lie her way through a twenty-year marriage and scream unrelenting accusations of "liar" and "betrayer" at her husband was a tad ironic.

She decided, while putting the finishing touches to her lipstick, that the only way to find the answers to all these questions would be to find her long-lost brother.

REALITY?

Cabin crew, Emily noticed, tended to be fatalistic or highly superstitious, maintaining that all bad things happened in threes; bad passengers, life-threatening emergencies and, of course, plane crashes. But even Emily thought it was too much of a coincidence, when she discovered that although this was just her sixth flight, she was flying on Charlie Echo for the third time. Even one of her co-workers had mentioned, "I think the ghost of Charlie Echo likes you. You always seem to be on that aircraft." Emily had the creepy feeling that the plane had indeed chosen her. And Sherry's dread-inducing words from her first flight echoed in her mind—"things always go wrong on that aircraft."

Berlin was a popular destination for the elderly and Saga was the tour operator. Unfortunately, the prerequisite of all Saga travellers was that they had to be 65 or older. The girls dreaded these flights for, of course, three reasons. Instead of the usual thirty minutes to load, it often took over an hour to get some of the more senior and disabled passengers seated and comfortable. Then in the event of an emergency, getting 119 not-so-fit people out of a burning aircraft in 90 seconds would be highly stressful and probably impossible. The third disadvantage was that the most senior of these travelers sometimes died either in-flight or at their destination from heart-failure or from other old-age ailments. Dead or alive, they had to be brought back to their native country. For the sake of efficiency more than sentiment, the corpses were often packaged unceremoniously in cheap transport coffins. On the manifest, they were affectionately listed as "stiffs."

When Emily arrived in the crew room and heard Hazel, her very officious number one, announce the three most dreaded flight scenarios, Charlie Echo, Saga and "inbound stiff," she knew that maybe Doreen had been wrong. Perhaps today was her initiation.

"Where do they put the coffin?" Emily asked Hazel as she sat next to her on the idling transport bus waiting for a Boeing 727 to cross the tarmac in front of them.

"Down the back. Rear hold," Hazel replied.

Rear hold! Emily gasped. *Ohmigod. My nightmare.* I mustn't think about it now. I have to keep it together.

"Because it's pressurized," Hazel added, as if that made everything okay.

Once Emily was into the routine of preparing the aircraft, welcoming passengers on board and serving them, the thought of a coffin in the rear of the plane on their inbound sector had drifted to the back of her mind. But halfway through their flight back to Gatwick—and because the plane had to descend to 10,000 feet as they flew over the east German flight corridor—the plane began a familiar trembling motion. "We have to sit down," Hazel told the other cabin crew as she emerged out of the flight deck. "Stow everything. It's going to get rough for a while."

When Hazel made the announcements in English instructing passengers to fasten their seat belts, Emily repeated them in German over the public address system.

Once passengers were belted in, she retreated to the rear of the aircraft to ensure that the bar boxes were secure in their stowages. It wasn't the first time she had experienced a little clear air turbulence—and if she hadn't just had her dream pre-flight, she would not have been worried. But the eerie similarity to the nightmare sequence and the turbulence at the lower altitude was making her nauseous. She sat down, planting her back firmly against the bulkhead and took some deep calming breaths.

A few minutes later, the plane rocked from side to side, up and down, the motion unpredictable and irregular. Although the cabin had been secured, they were shaken like sardines in a can. From the rear jump seat, Emily listened to Hazel, sitting next to her, as she communicated through her headset with the flight deck. After just ten minutes of turbulence, Hazel nodded, and then turned to Emily to signal that she could undo her seat belt and get back to work.

She gulped, remembering the nightmare and suspecting what might be coming next. As if to oblige her, an odd but regular knocking emanated from behind them. "What the hell is that noise?" Hazel frowned and stared at both toilets. "Check the loos, will you? It almost sounds like someone's stuck in there and panicking." She unlocked her seat, hung up the headset on the hook above her head and started up the cabin. "I've got to get to the flight deck."

Emily moved woodenly toward the back, past the stowed metal bar boxes. She stood between the port and the starboard toilet but she knew the knocking wasn't coming from either one. She stared at the sliding door of the rear hold. The knocking was more like a regular thud now, nothing urgent about it, just loud enough to get someone's attention. Hers. The hold was pressurized just like the cabin. *Keep Closed During Flight* was written in large red letters on a white sign on the sliding door. Emily supposed that this was to prevent the danger of loose low-flying baggage . . . or coffins being catapulted into the rear cabin during turbulence. The sliding door was the only thing separating her from her worst nightmare; a box with a dead body in it.

Slowly she put her hand on the metal handgrip and started to slide the door back. It caught in the groove caused by many years' accumulation of grime and dust. The door was wide open now. As if aware of her presence, the knocking stopped. Emily's eyes took a while to adjust to the darkness. Then she saw it. Something white in the black void.

"Bloody 'ell!" The voice came from behind her. The flight engineer was standing at her left shoulder, shining a torch into the dark. The white beam of light scanned the suitcases piled chaotically on top of each other and then the wooden coffin, its virgin wood appearing pale against the dark bags. It had tipped on its side. The lid was still closed. Emily exhaled.

"I think it's one of the vents that causes that banging. It's a refraction of sound." The engineer was rubbing his forehead. "Who knows on this aircraft? Charlie Echo makes its own noises."

Emily nodded, grateful for his presence.

"Nothing to worry about, love." The engineer closed the door for her, turned and strode back up the aisle towards the flight deck. But as she followed, she thought she heard the knocking again, as if someone was still tapping softly on the underside of the coffin lid, wanting to get out and calling to her. *Let me out. I can't breathe. Let me out. I can't breathe.* She was close on the heels of the engineer as he entered the galley and reported back to Hazel.

After the snack service and when they had cleared the cabin of the left-over meal trays, the three junior stewardesses assembled in the galley to eat before beginning their descent into Gatwick.

"He vos amazink!" Gudrun, the Number Two, spouted in her guttural German accent as she wiped the stainless steel coffee pots and stowed them.

"Who?" Hazel demanded. She had barged into the galley and into the conversation.

"Zis psychic I vent to see. He liffs in Brighton. "

"It's all poppycock!" Hazel blurted, and still clutching her paperwork, she carried on into the flight deck.

"What did he tell you?" Emily asked, intrigued sipping on a cup of tea.

"All kinds of ssings." Gudrun recited a list of names and events that this psychic had identified.

"Can I get his number?" *Maybe* Emily was thinking, *he could help me with my nightmares.* Something or somebody was trying to get her attention. "Do you think he could see me tomorrow?"

Gudrun shrugged, handing Emily a piece of paper with a number on it. *"Keine Ahnung.* No idea. You telephone him und see."

THE PSYCHIC

Two days later Emily stood at the white front door of a bungalow in one of Brighton's tree-lined suburbs. She had asked Suzi to come with her, but her friend was on a Munich flight. And maybe it was better for Emily to do this alone. The psychic, Henry, had informed her that he only had one opening at 4:30 pm if she wanted to come straight away. She did.

When the door opened, she wasn't exactly sure what she expected. Her only psychic experience had been with the gypsy. The man at the door was probably in his sixties with glasses perched on the end of his nose. A brown cardigan—that had seen better days—hung from his tall, thin frame and gave him a pervasively crumpled appearance. He looked more like a bookworm than a psychic, she thought. At the same time there was a direct but gentle energy in his eyes that she found comforting.

"Good afternoon, Emily." He stepped back and allowed her to enter the darkened, musty hallway "I'm Henry."

Sounds were emanating from the kitchen, which she surmised was the man's wife preparing dinner. She followed Henry into his office. The room was small and square. Two walls were hidden behind tall, oak bookcases bursting with papers, books and lots of dust. A heavy oak desk covered in an assortment of crystals, boxes of tarot cards, burned-down candles and more papers took up another wall. A mildly sickening smell of incense mixed with dust assaulted her nostrils. Though she had never seen a professional clairvoyant before, she hadn't anticipated his reading room to look so *ordinary.*

"Please." Henry waved a hand, indicating that she should sit in one of the fading armchairs in one corner while he allowed himself to sink into the other. He rested his arms—palms upwards—on his knees and let out a sigh, as if already weary.

"The way I work is to channel information," he told her. "I just need your first name and date of birth please."

Emily gave him her details. She sat back in the

chair and deliberately unclenched her hands.

"Are you ready?" he asked, leaning over to click on the tape recorder on the desk.

"Yes," she said breathlessly.

"Then I shall begin." Henry relaxed back into his chair and closed his eyes. He let out another huge breath as if his spirit had to leave his body to make room for the information he was about to receive.

Emily also closed her eyes.

"I see you alone," Henry started in a trance-like voice, "as if you are at sea. All around there are boats with people in them but you are still alone."

Emily shrugged, not knowing what he was talking about.

"You might feel that you are in shark-filled water," he continued. "One person . . . two beings are your friends, but you are not sure who . . . or what you can trust. There are many secrets below the surface. Below, below . . . . or is it bellow?"

She wanted to ask him to elaborate but he also seemed to be searching.

"You have them mixed up," he said, still with eyes closed but waving a long, slim finger in the air. "The person you are afraid of is not the one to fear. Someone from spirit is trying to reach you but you are not listening. There are many things to be uncovered. I see new energy around you and this is good. But always when there is a new energy, there has to be a death. Has there been a recent death?"

She inhaled. "Yes, my mother."

"She is now at peace but someone else isn't."

Derek, probably, she thought.

"There is a lot of sadness in you and someone around you is very, very sad. Perhaps angry."

My mother? Derek? she wondered. *The whole dang family?*

"The letter "C" means something. Are you afraid of death?"

Emily's eyes flew open. She hadn't really thought about it. She surveyed Henry's expression. He was still in a trance-like state. Was she going to die? "I have nightmares about claustrophobia, suffocating and the last one involved—"

"And you can also see spirits?"

"Yes." She didn't want to admit that even to herself but Emily knew she could see ghosts.

"In fact, you could be quite psychic if you believed."

"Actually, I do believe in ghosts."

"I mean believe in yourself." Henry took yet another long breath in and then finally let it go. "A spirit is trying to contact you. You can hear what he has to say but you have to acknowledge him somehow."

He? *Was* it the voice she always heard in her head? "How do I do that?"

"Just listen." Henry cupped his hand around his left ear. "His voice will sound like your own voice but it is his."

Was it that simple? she wondered.

"There have been many broken hearts but that is ending." Henry smiled suddenly. "Ah, good news for you soon. And understanding. Peace will come to all. Someone will come into your life who will protect you, who will love you. He has something to do with the law. I see the initial 'A'."

I wish I could believe that!

"There is an opportunity for you to receive some money."

Maybe all psychics say that, she thought.

Henry's eyes suddenly flew open as if startled out of a sleep. "Any questions?" he asked as he took a sip of water.

"I have this recurring dream . . ." Emily started, shifting in her seat.

"What is the dream about?" Henry seemed not to be paying attention to her as he reached over and fiddled with a dial on the tape recorder.

"Well, it changes but I usually wake up in a panic because I can't breathe."

"Are you anxious about anything in particular at the moment?"

"I recently started flying for a living but I've been having the nightmares for about four or five years now."

"Recurring dreams mean that your mind is trying to work out a fear, real or imagined. But I also have a feeling . . . you might be picking up on someone else's energy . . . "

"Who?"

"This person in spirit who is trying to reach you. There has also been a sudden death? "

"Yes, my brother . . . suicide."

"I'm sorry. How?"

"He hung himself."

"Well, it does feel like a brother energy. And the way he died . . . ." Henry put a bony hand over his own chest. "I feel a struggling for breath so that would make sense. He's trying to communicate. Be more open to him while you are awake so he doesn't have to come in your dreams."

Poor Derek. That would make sense that he was not at peace. After all, he didn't leave a note. Everyone had been left to guess. "How—"

There was a click as the tape came to its end.

"I'm sorry. That's the end of the session for today."

She handed over four crisp five pound notes but she wasn't sure if she had gained clarity or if she was even more confused. As if reading her thoughts, Henry added, "It may not be very clear to you now, but as the future unfolds you will understand." Emily wanted to believe him but as she took her cassette and left Henry's house, she wasn't sure about anything.

THE GHOST BELO-W

The next day, as Emily checked in for her Zurich flight, she collected her mail from her pigeon-hole slot in the crew room. One of the envelopes addressed to her was from the airline's training department. Puzzled, she opened it first. The memo confirmed the rumor that the airline had suddenly acquired five new DC10s. Consequently they needed more crews for the additional London Gatwick –LA flights as well as London-Luxembourg-Barbados routes. Because of her five languages—German, Spanish, French, Scandinavian and Italian—which were needed on these routes, the memo read, she was one of two hundred girls who had been chosen to train on the DC10. Emily cheered internally. Long haul! She could barely contain her excitement. The psychic had been right. This was good news!

The five-day emergency and cabin service training would commence Monday of the following week. Good, she thought. That won't interfere with my meeting with the solicitor and Renee. And maybe, it occurred to her, this was how she would break her Charlie Echo curse. Even the other cabin crew had noticed how much Emily always ended up on that Comet and how much more active the ghost of Charlie Echo was when she was on board. As someone had pointed out, "Just because you are paranoid doesn't mean you are not being followed."

A week later, after having completed her DC 10 training, Emily was rostered for her first long-haul flight. Check-in for the LA was at 1300 hours. Although the flight time was ten hours—or twelve if they had to drop in at Bangor, Maine, to refuel—actual hours on-duty would be around sixteen. Still, she thought, at least we get three days off in Los Angeles. Maybe she would see Hollywood, go to Disneyland, and see film stars or just suntan on the beaches under wafting California palm trees.

She prepared for her flight by spending the morning doing her nails, relaxing and reviewing her drills. Instead of the four cabin crew on the Comets, there were ten attendants on the bigger aircraft. That meant on the DC10 there were now twenty drills to memorize; ten for a ditching over water and ten for crashing on land. Each attendant had to know all drills in the event that one or more of the crew were incapacitated . . . or worse. The emergency equipment was also numerous, complex and varied. But the larger aircraft were newer than the Comets so an emergency on the DC10, she reasoned, was far less likely than on her nemesis, Charlie Echo.

When Emily checked in for her first long haul flight and heard the DC10's registration was BELO, her excited smile faded. Was it just a coincidence or was this what the psychic had referred to in his reading? And what he had said exactly about BELO? She would need to be on alert.

After the first three hours of the London-LA

service, Emily was the first crew member to go on meal break. She descended alone in the galley elevator that went down into the aircraft's belly. As she stepped into the long narrow space, the "galley slave" was standing waiting to get in. On her arm, she balanced a tray containing three hot beverages for the flight deck crew.

"Can you keep an eye on the first class meals in the starboard ovens?" she asked Emily as she stepped into the lift. "I'll be right back." There was a click, the mechanism clunked and then hummed as the elevator ascended.

Emily was alone in the galley.

She surveyed the rows of steel convection ovens on both sides mounted at chest height. Below the ovens were stowages for the bar and catering boxes, including the drinks and meal carts that the "hosties" hauled up and down the aisles.

The air was slightly misty. First signs of a decompression, Emily thought, but then dismissed the idea. She just wasn't used to this galley yet.

Before she took her hot meal out of the oven, she decided to check the passengers' food. She stood in front of the first steel oven. As she grabbed the handle, she felt a presence behind her. Had someone else come down? She turned quickly, and glanced over. To the left of the elevator was a sliding door which concealed a pressurized baggage hold sometimes used by sleepy crew. It was closed. The elevator was still upstairs. She was definitely alone.

The atmosphere suddenly chilled as if a door had been blown open and a draft of frozen air had wafted in. She shivered. *How can the galley feel like a freezer when all the ovens are on?*

In the shiny steel of the oven door she could see a

blurred reflection of herself and the grey metal boxes behind her. She slid the lever, pulled the oven door down, picked up one foil container, lifted the cover and inspected the steak dinner. *Hmm?* She wondered. *Probably needs another five minutes.* She resealed the container, pushed the meal back onto the oven shelf and raised the oven door, clicking it shut.

The shiny steel mirrored the space behind her. A movement there got her attention. She stopped breathing.

Not six inches from her face, on that metallic surface, she could see the reflection of a shape manifesting right behind her. A mass of green was forming into the body and face of a man. The whole specter gradually came into focus. Oh god! It was him. Oh no! Not again! The engineer from Charlie Echo was almost breathing down Emily's neck. She froze.

Afraid to look at the reflection of his face, she closed her eyes. "This isn't real. This isn't real," she intoned. But she could still hear his words in her head.

"There will be a problem with this aircraft, the voice said. *Fuel contamination. Before you take off again from Bangor, tell the engineer,"* she heard. *"Tell the engineer!"* he repeated more loudly, the echoing words filling her head.

Then the green shape slowly dissipated and the galley instantly became warm again. She leaned on the steel counter as her legs threatened to give way.

Clunk. The elevator door slammed upstairs and a minute later, relieved, Emily saw the door open as the "galley slave" returned, used coffee cups in hand.

"What's up?" she asked Emily who was still standing like a rock formation in front of the oven. "You look like you've seen a ghost."

Emily could only nod, still shocked, mind racing.

Ghost. Fuel contamination. She didn't know what to think. If he was the Charlie Echo ghost, why was he on this DC10—BELO? Had the spirit followed her from the Comet? That meant that the ghost was attached to *her* and not necessarily an aircraft. She shuddered. What should she do?

"Do you know if we are going to land in Bangor?" Emily asked her colleague.

"Yes, we are," she said as she pulled steaming meals from the oven and placed them on trays in a meal cart. "The engineer just told me. He was hoping we could make it, even with a full load, but with strong headwinds . . . we'll have to do a tech stop to refuel." She shrugged. "It's a drag but what can you do."

"Ohmigod." Emily said out loud, realizing that perhaps the ghost was right. "Do you know what fuel contamination means?" Emily asked.

"Yes. Why?"

"Just wondered. A . . . passenger was . . . asking about it."

"It means that something or someone polluted the fuel," she explained as she wheeled the cart to the elevator and pushed a button. "One time, one of the Comets, I think it was Charlie Echo, had it. They mixed fuel types by mistake and the aircraft was on its last engine just as it touched down back at Gatwick. It was a close call."

As Emily picked at her meal of semi-warm green beans and coagulated butter chicken, she was conscious of the ball of dread in her stomach. She put the meal down, not hungry. What should she do? If I tell the engineer that a ghost told me we are going to have fuel contamination, I will be taken off in a straightjacket. But if I don't tell him we might crash. I'm dammed if I do and dammed if I don't. What did Henry, the psychic tell her? *Someone close to you is trying to protect you.* But was the ghostly engineer protecting her or haunting her? Then she got an idea.

When it was time for the flight crew to get their next set of hot beverages, Emily offered to deliver them to the flight deck. But before she did, she wrote a few words on a blank passenger comment card and slipped it into her apron pocket.

A NIGHT IN LA

Emily could not stop shaking. She was in California for the very first time, eight hours behind UK time and she and the crew were on the transport bus from LAX to their hotel in Santa Monica. She should, she thought, be marveling at the cloudless blue sky, the tall, wafting palm trees and the oh-so-wide multi-laned highways with very the oh-so-wide cars.

Instead she could only think of her guardian ghost.

She wasn't sure whether her trembling was from the fear of seeing a ghost and having his warning come true or gratitude that, through her, he had potentially saved more than 380 lives today. A written message from an anonymous psychic passenger before landing had spooked the flight engineer. On take-off from Bangor, when the port engine began to sputter, he instantly recognized the symptoms of fuel contamination. He remembered Charlie Echo, when only one engine was quasi operational on landing and that engine had come perilously close to choking.

The flight crew immediately took the prescribed actions. The crisis meant they had to circle for twenty tense minutes while two out of three engines threatened to fail and while they dumped fuel so they could land once more in Bangor. In the cabin, the rehearsed crash drills became reality as the crew prepared passengers on the descent for a premeditated emergency landing. After they touched down safely, the passengers were even more unnerved when peering out of their windows, they saw a foamed tarmac and fire engines roaring down the runway after their aircraft. Despite being two hours late, in shock and a tad grumpy, all on board were still alive and well.

By the time the crew eventually arrived at the Santa Monica Inn in Los Angeles, they were exhausted. Still recovering from the adrenalin rush of their potentially near-death experience, even the non-drinkers of the crew were ready for an alcoholic beverage.

The flight attendants' usual routine after arrival at their down-route hotel was to unpack, shower, change and then head to the Captain's room to claim their flight pay. There they might imbibe a cocktail before going out for dinner. Those less energetic would, after collecting their money, retreat to their rooms and collapse into bed.

This evening, however, while the crew waited in the spacious hotel lobby to check in, the Captain made an announcement.

"Listen up, everyone. Another Anglo flight crew inbound from Bangor is already pouring cocktails in Room 565. I'm tired so if you ladies want your flight pay tonight, you should be in that room in ten minutes. If you don't come, you will have to wait till the return sector for your flight pay. Okay? Room 565 in ten."

Weary but motivated, the young women hurried to their designated rooms to shed their less-than-than-fresh-smelling-uniforms and quickly climb, unshowered, into their civvies.

As Emily entered the softly lit room 565, she saw clusters of jean-and-t-shirt-clad girls and a few members of the flight deck—all still in uniform but with stripes removed from their epaulettes. Some of the other already-buzzed Anglo crew were sitting on the edge of the bed engrossed in a lively discussion about the Bangor emergency landing. In one corner, her captain was doling out dollar bills, so she went over and collected her flight pay. Today, she felt, she had earned it.

With two crews in the room there was very little space to sit, so she found a spot on the floor and leaned against the bed. Across from her, relaxing in the armchair, she recognized Captain Wilson from her first Comet flight. He smiled warmly and asked, "Had any tasty chicken vegetable soup recently, Emily?"

She laughed and asked, "Are you on DC-10's now?"

"I'm being trained," he explained.

The room was a hubbub as both crews continued to discuss fuel contamination and other emergency stories. As Emily sipped on her rum and coke, allowing its smoothness to calm her still shaky nerves, she laid her head back against the softness of the bed and merely listened to the conversation. Would she ever be able to tell anyone about her spectral warning? As it was, the galley slave had wondered why she had asked about fuel contamination just before it happened. Emily had fessed up to sporadic psychic feelings but then asked her colleague not to advertise it.

As if picking up on her thoughts, the conversation turned to ghosts. "Well, it doesn't surprise me that it happened on BELO," one of the girls exclaimed.

"Why?" someone else asked.

"It's haunted."

Emily sat up and turned to listen. Suddenly everyone had a story about BELO and its ghosts.

"Just like Charlie Echo, isn't that right, Emily?" Captain Wilson was addressing her directly.

"That plane seems to haunt *me*. I'm always on that Comet." Despite the free tone of the conversation about the paranormal, Emily wasn't sure how much she should divulge in a room full of unknown colleagues about her own spooky experiences on Charlie Echo.

"Well, you do know the story of that ghost, don't you?" Captain Wilson asked, his eyes were focused just on her.

"Is this another one of your tricks?" She cocked her head to the side, and grinned.

He shook his head. "This was no joke."

"What happened?" Emily whispered.

A hush descended on the room as everyone turned to listen.

"That aircraft belonged to the RAF when I was flying for them. One day they planned to take it out on training maneuvers—circuits and bumps." Emily had seen planes at Gatwick landing and then immediately taking off again, practicing their drills for overshooting the runway. "The ground engineer had gone out to do his pre-flight checks on the aircraft." Captain Wilson continued as he caressed a tooth mug filled with scotch and ice. "He climbed into the port engine. But then for some reason, they had a change of plan and without going through the proper channels of communication, someone boarded up all the engines, not realizing that the poor chap was still inside." There was a collective groan from the room. "It was late on a Friday afternoon and mostly all personnel had gone home for the weekend."

Emily inhaled. "Oh no. What happened to him?"

"He died." The Captain picked up his drink and took a short slug, as if he had been somewhat responsible for this tragedy. "Suffocated. He probably could have survived the weekend if he hadn't panicked. But he did."

"How awful!" The dreams of suffocating came back to her, the terror of gasping for breath and not finding any oxygen. Something in her mind was nudging her, but pieces of a distant jigsaw puzzle refused to come together. Others in the room began hushed conversations. Captain Wilson was still looking at Emily.

"Do you happen to know his name?" she asked him. "The engineer?"

"Why would you want to know his name?" one of the girls beside her scoffed.

"Oh, I don't know," she responded a little defensively. "Perhaps when someone knows his name and acknowledges his death, he'll stop haunting the aircraft." She wasn't sure where that idea had come from but it made sense.

"Actually, I do remember his name," the ex-RAF Captain said quietly, as if for her ears only. "But only because of the aircraft registration."

"What do you mean?" She frowned.

"It's almost as if the aircraft was registered for a ghost called Charlie Echo," he said, glancing at others in the room.

Emily still wasn't following.

Captain Wilson took another slug of his scotch and said, "Charlie's Echo . . . his name was Charles Edward Baldwin."

THE SOLICITOR

Emily would have loved to procrastinate meeting

with the solicitor, but she knew she had to face whatever he had in store for her.

Mr. Marsten Junior was mostly everything Emily expected a solicitor to be; clad in the stereotypical navy pin-striped suit, courteous, formal. What she was *not* expecting him to be was tall, broad shouldered and exuding a disarming boyishness through laughing blue eyes. When he shook her hand and smiled directly at her, she felt immediately at home with him—and was grateful for the courage his warmth gave her.

"Come in, Miss Carson," he said cheerily, leading the way into his sun-filled office where the venetian blinds covered only some of the expansive windows.

Emily sat in the chair facing his paper-laden desk—and the wide view—while he relaxed his tall frame into his own chair with his back to the window. Through those windows, beyond and three floors below she could see the familiar white-bricked sprawling East Croydon railway station. Happy childhood memories of coming to that station to visit her beloved grandparents surfaced. But now the brown railway lines that stretched out like single unruly strands of hair without any seeming pattern appeared sinister. The solicitor shuffled some papers bringing her back to the present and the deed to be done.

"Let's first deal with your mother's estate, shall we? It appears to be very simple. Essentially there was very little . . . er . . . money left, and what she did leave, she has apparently bequeathed to a Home for Single Mothers and The Lions Club." Mr. Marsten was apologetic as he glanced up at Emily, searching for her reaction.

"No surprises there." She shrugged. "My mother and I didn't have a good relationship."

The solicitor's face relaxed. Emily realized he was probably used to clients becoming hysterical with grief, anger or indignation in this office. "I'll send you a detailed accounting of her monies when it's done."

"Thank you." *Now can we just get on with the other business,* she thought. Emily was intrigued but dreaded finding out who this "client" of the junior Mr. Marsten's was and why she had to be twenty-five to receive this document.

The solicitor took a deep breath and handed her a large manila envelope. "This is from my client . . . I mentioned . . . his name is Charles Edward Baldwin."

She gulped. Oh God!

As if in slow motion, she watched as he passed the envelope over the desk. She lifted her hand to accept it. "I'm not sure whether you are aware," he added more softly, "but Charles Baldwin is your . . . half-brother and . . ."

On the drive down she had wondered if this client could be her half-brother. And if he was, would it confirm that the Charles Baldwin who had died on Charlie Echo was indeed one and the same. Now she dreaded what he was about to impart.

Emily sat back. So she had been right. Marsten Junior's client was Charles Baldwin and Mr. Marsten Senior was her mother's solicitor. Father and son must have known of the link, but the man in front of her didn't seem to be connecting the dots.

As if he had read her mind, he said, "Strangely enough, it wasn't until I took over my father's files— including your mother's—that we discovered the family connection between your mother and my client, Mr. Baldwin. Different names, of course," he added as if it explained everything.

"Of course," Emily repeated. She supposed that solicitors were sworn to confidentiality about their clients, perhaps even in a family-run legal firm.

"However . . . I am to give this to you," the solicitor continued, exhaling, "after your twenty-fifth birthday. I'm afraid that my placing this letter in your possession now means that your half-brother is . . . has died."

"Oh . . . no." Emily slumped back in her chair, all hope of ever meeting him gone. And did this mean then that her half-brother Charles Baldwin was undeniably the ghost of Charlie Echo?

"I'm very sorry," he said, looking down. He obviously did not enjoy being the messenger.

Some birthday present, she thought.

She stared at the manila envelope.

"I'm sorry to have to ask you this but before you open it, I'll need you to sign here." He gently placed a form and a black pen on the desk in front of Emily. She gave the questions a cursory glance and then signed and dated the bottom, confirming receipt of the information.

"Splendid," he said cheerily in an attempt to lighten the mood, she supposed. "Why don't I go and scare up some coffee for us."

"Is the news that bad?" Emily smiled, but her stomach was doing flip-flops.

"Let's hope not." He stood and headed for the door.

She called after him, "Just black, no sugar, please."

The envelope was new. Maybe it was the solicitor's way of presenting horrible news in a brighter package. Slowly she pulled it open. Inside was another envelope. This one was white. Gingerly she extracted it, noticing how the edges were a little tattered. She laid the offending package on her lap, reluctant to touch it.

On the front was typed in bold print:

IN THE EVENT OF MY DEATH
THIS IS TO BE PERSONALLY DELIVERED TO MY
HALF-SISTER, EMILY CARSON ONLY ON OR
AFTER HER TWENTY-FIFTH BIRTHDAY.

Her fingers toyed with the gluey flap. She wished Mr. Marsten would come back. She hated uncovering secrets by herself. As if he had heard her, the office door opened and he stepped in, followed by his secretary, carrying a tray with two elegant cups of coffee. She placed one of the cups in front of Emily and gave the other to her boss. Then the secretary left the room, closing the door gently behind her. Emily leaned forward and took a sip, grateful for the hit of caffeine and for the delay. Both the solicitor's presence on the other side of the desk and the warm liquid gave her comfort.

Inside the white envelope were several sheets of yellowed bond paper. As she pulled them out, a small moan escaped her as she saw the tight, angular handwriting. It reminded her of Derek's script. And, she realized, this letter might be the only personal connection to her half-brother she would ever have.

At the top had been written the words, *In the event of my 'accidental' death.*

Why was 'accidental' in quotes? *Oh God.* Did he mean . . . murder? She didn't want to think about that. If her half-brother *was* that engineer on Charlie Echo, had he been tricked or forced to climb into that engine and then left to die? What a horrible death! Who would have done that and why?

To her surprise, her eyes suddenly clouded with tears and the words on the paper blurred.

She shook her head. "I can't," she admitted, glancing up at the solicitor who was pretending for the moment to be engrossed in some other paperwork.

"Would you like me to read it to you?" he enquired gently, proffering a hand.

"Yes, please." Emily exhaled and, shaking, passed the letter to him. She took the warm cup between her hands, took a sip and braced herself.

The solicitor began in his deep, calm voice.

"Let me introduce myself. My name is Charles Edward Baldwin (born Wright). I am your half-brother. Your mother, Helen Carson, gave birth to me in 1945 in Buckinghamshire after a love affair with my father (deceased) Charles Arthur Wright, a US Air Force pilot."

This much I know, thought Emily. But how did he find out?

"Emily, you will be the only one to know the truth so be careful."

How strange it was to have her half-brother address her by name as if he knew her. And what did he mean, "careful"?

"There are certain people in your family who may have tried to kill me. If you are

reading this, it means that I have probably died 'accidentally.' "

Emily put down her cup. "My God! Either he was paranoid or . . ." She didn't want to think of anyone in her family being a murderer. None of this made sense. "Mr. Marsten, as his executor, you must know how he . . .?"

"Better if we finish reading this first." He cleared his throat. "Shall I continue?"

"Yes."

"As your mother was already married, she gave me to a neighbor, Patricia Baldwin. Patricia's husband had also died in action and then her baby was killed in a London air raid. So when Patricia just showed up in the village one day in Buckinghamshire with "her" baby, no one knew any differently. There was no paperwork.

Patricia was an alcoholic. When I was twelve, she blurted out the truth; that her precious baby had died and I, "the bastard" had lived.

So Patricia was like her mother, a mean alcoholic. And she could not keep a secret, Emily thought.

"She hated me for not being her real

son. So I decided to find my real mother. I wanted a better life."

Mr. Marsten paused and glanced up at Emily. But her head was down, tears rolling down her cheeks. So much tragedy, she was thinking, for these two women, and how they had both inflicted their pain on their own innocent children. The solicitor leaned over the desk and offered her a box of tissues. Abashed, she took several and dabbed at her eyes.

"When I discovered that your mother had gone on to have another child—you— and that your father was now wealthy, I was angry. At 15, I was living in poverty with an embittered alcoholic foster mother. It wasn't right. I decided to do something about it.

I wrote to Helen and asked her if she would like to meet her boy. She told me to stay away. At first, I was devastated and then I got angry, very angry. Being a part of my real family turned into an obsession. It's all I wanted. To belong."

"Don't we all?" Emily muttered to herself.

"For years, I imagined you all having Christmases together, getting presents around the tree, eating dinner, laughing and *enjoying each other. I should have been a part of that but I was always on the outside, looking in."*

Emily remembered seeing the spirit of a young boy looking for his place at the dining room table. But when she had announced to her mother that Emily felt a member of their family was missing at meal times, her mother had shushed her and told her not to be "so ridiculous."

"So I wrote again. Still she refused to see me, saying 'it would be better for everyone if we just left things the way they were.' She said she had made a promise to Patricia. But it was more like she was afraid of someone in the family."

The solicitor struggled to keep his voice professional. He took a gulp of his coffee before continuing.

"So I stalked your family for years. I was even in your home for two days as an apprentice electrician when I was sixteen. Do you remember?"

Emily groaned inwardly, scanning her memory. She tried to recall workmen in her home but no memory came. How weird—and tragic that she had not known her half-brother was right there in the same house.

Mr. Marsten looked up "Do you want me to keep

going?" he queried, concern for his client evident in his eyes.

She pulled her jacket around her. "Let's get it over with."

"I admire your courage," he said with a wry smile.

"In those two days that my boss and I were in your home I saw how it was. I even felt sorry for Helen. She was so miserable— and so mean to you. Maybe that's why I feel closest to you. It was obvious your father was having an affair and Derek was unpredictable and angry. Even though I didn't trust any of them, except for you, they were my family and I still wanted them to know who I was. And that's why I am writing this. Even in death, I will want this.

She shivered.

"When I was about nineteen, Patricia went right downhill. She got sclerosis of the liver. It was a bad time. I had no way of earning a living and taking care of her. I begged Helen for some help. Then when Patricia died, there was no money to pay for

her funeral. Helen just kept warning me, for my own sake, to stay away. So I threatened to reveal her whole dirty secret to her rich, precious husband. Then her respectable family would disintegrate.

"We didn't need him for that," Emily said wearily. "We did it to ourselves."

"After Patricia died, I was all alone. Every few months, I wrote to Helen. I just wanted to talk to her but she always refused. Then when I was around twenty-four, I got a scary telephone call. It was a man's voice. Was it your father? Derek? Your Uncle George? A hired gun? He didn't bother to play nice. 'If you don't stop harassing Helen,' he threatened, 'I know where you work, Mr. RAF, and I can make your death look like an accident.'"

Emily's breath caught, and she put her hands to her face, covering her mouth. All the jigsaw pieces were coming together now. Charlie Echo *was* Charlie Baldwin, her half-brother! And someone in *her* family had murdered him! Had her mother known? Was she capable of organizing the death of her own son? Who else could it have been?

"You, Emily, were the only one who was kind to me when I came to the house, even though you didn't know who I was. I remember that. You were only eleven at the time and I wanted so badly to tell you I was your half-brother. But even I knew that would not have been fair to you. If we had been given a chance, I think we would have been close as brother and sister.

I am sharing this information only after our mother's death. She might be the threat or just another victim. If I live, I will find you.

I am sorry if this hurts you but I do want someone to know the truth about me. I want someone to know that if they carry out the threat, that my life was taken. You are that person.

You are my sole heir. My solicitor, Alistair Marsten Junior, as the executor of my will has been instructed to give you my effects. He will also keep any money in trust *for you until your twenty-fifth birthday.*

If I am being paranoid and this "accident" doesn't happen, then we will meet and have a good laugh and a long talk as brother and sister."

Mr. Marsten paused. "There are some effects that I have arranged to be delivered here next week. I can also confirm that there is a sum of money in trust for you."

I don't want any money, she thought. She would prefer to have a living brother, one who hadn't been murdered by one of her own. "Is that it?" she asked, and despite her trembling, she carefully placed her coffee cup on his desk.

"Not quite."

"This truth is setting me free. Perhaps it will set you free, too. And if there is an afterlife, I will do whatever I can to help you from the other side.

My God, Emily suddenly realized as she stared down at those single railway lines straying in all directions without any seeming order, *he is the ghost of Charlie Echo. And he certainly is helping me from the afterlife.*

"Just one more thing," Mr. Marsten added. "There's a . . . poem at the bottom you should read." He handed her the letter.

She read:

From: Broken Wing by Charles Wright

A man comes to the world

His wings to unfurl

And to fly

But if there is no giving

There is no living

Then nothing is left

But to die

With love,

Your half-brother,

Charles Edward Baldwin

Dated: July 4, 1969.

Emily dabbed at her eyes with her mascara-smudged tissue.

"Would you like some more coffee?" Mr. Marsten's offer was perhaps an excuse for him to leave the room, Emily thought, so she could have a few minutes to compose herself.

"No . . . well, actually . . . yes, thank you." But this time, he stayed seated and spoke into an intercom.

"Did you know any of this?" she demanded, leaning forward, her voice rising. For some reason, she felt angry at Mr. Marsten and she didn't know why.

"No." He shook his head as if to shake off the somber mood in the room. "I was in possession of this letter but I can assure you that I didn't have any knowledge of its contents. If I *had* been aware of a threat to someone's life, I would have been obligated to report it to the police. Mr. Baldwin simply gave me the instructions for this letter to be delivered to you on or after your twenty-fifth birthday—and after your mother's death. Of course, I didn't know—"

"Did you meet him?" she persisted, softening and relaxing back into her seat. She still hoped for more details.

"I'm sorry. Our communications were all done by phone and post. He seemed reluctant to come to the office."

He searched Emily's face. She was staring out of the window at the view of East Croydon station again. He waited for her to move or speak.

Finally she exhaled. "So you know how he—" she started.

There was a gentle tap on the office door and the secretary appeared coffee pot in hand. Sensing the tension in the room, she simply refilled the cups, nodded at her boss and left, closing the door as if it were made of glass.

"How did he die?" Emily had to confirm the details although, in her heart she already knew.

Mr. Marsten sat back in his chair and tightened his tie. "From what I understand, there was a miscommunication at his place of work. They—"

"Charles was a ground engineer at Aldershot, working for the RAF, wasn't he?" she challenged him. "And he was lured into and then trapped in an engine and left to suffocate."

It was the solicitor's turn to be shocked. "Yes, but his death was ruled accidental. How did you . . .?"

"His spirit has been haunting the aircraft I fly on. I've been having recurring nightmares for the last four years. In my nightmares I'm always gasping for breath in a confined space. In the last dream. . . ." Once Emily began to speak of these things she couldn't stop. ". . . the spirit of my dead brother pulled me into a coffin and I suffocated. Or that's how it felt. Then, on my first LA flight, he appeared to me in the reflection of an oven and warned me about a problem on the plane. That warning saved everyone on board. Even as a child I sensed that someone was missing from our family, a boy. And when I told my mother I felt there should be someone else in our family, she just told me to shut up. But my mother absolutely hated me. And now I know why—it was because I knew the truth—or some of it. She must have been afraid of just how much I knew and *how* I could know."

"How *did* you know?" Mr. Marsten enquired softly, not missing a beat.

She blushed. Why was he not fazed by her crazy outburst? He appeared to be genuinely intrigued. She sat back in her chair. "It would seem that I have . . . a gift . . . for knowing things."

"You mean you are psychic?" he said without derision.

"In some way . . . I suppose one could explain my experiences."

She half expected him to say, "Splendid!" But he just continued to stare at her, an unfathomable expression in his eyes. Was it admiration, sorrow or amusement?

"What?" she asked.

"Well, I think you need to give yourself a big pat on the back."

"What for?" She exhaled, relaxing, allowing herself a small smile.

"Surviving this family of miscreants."

"So far," she said grimly.

"Miss Carson, Charles' death will have to be reinvestigated," he said, taking out another form. He was Mr. Professional again, Emily noticed.

"I know," she responded dully, a horrible lump forming in her stomach. *Which one of her family was the murderer?*

"Your father is still alive? And your aunt? Is that correct?"

"My aunt is alive. But . . . after Derek . . . died, my father disappeared but . . . so I'm not sure if he is alive or dead."

"Maybe your father is the one who . . .? Maybe that's why he disappeared? He would have had motive and leaving like that speaks to his guilt."

"No." Emily was emphatic. Her father had disappointed her, but somehow she knew he wasn't capable of physical violence. After Derek's suicide, he must have realized the damage he had done and felt remorseful. His guilt is what had motivated her father to run away, she was sure. Shame speaks volumes.

"In any case, we will have to find him, alive or dead, as part of the investigation."

Emily had always imagined her father living in the South of France with some young thing. She was surprised at how she welcomed the thought of seeing him again, if that was possible.

"And your Aunt Renee?"

"I'm seeing my aunt this afternoon. She's always been a good support for me."

"Splendid." He seemed genuinely pleased that she had at least one ally.

She stood and gathered up her suede jacket. "Where do we go from here?" she asked, picking up her handbag from the floor.

"How about the *Fox and Hounds* for lunch?" He grinned at her shocked expression. "Well," he continued, "we'll need to spend some time discussing strategy." He stood up suddenly, his tall frame almost blocking the view. "And . . . it was your birthday yesterday so would you allow your solicitor to treat his new client to a light lunch so we can talk about this mysterious family of yours?"

"If you insist." She grinned.

He buzzed his secretary and asked her to reserve "his usual table." As he gathered up his papers and placed them back in the correct file folders, he said, "By the way, as my new client, I have one stipulation."

"Oh? What's that?" Emily asked.

"You must call me Alistair."

"Splendid," she responded, laughing for the first time that day. "But only if you call me Emily."

She sat across from Alistair at the Tudor-style pub and studied his profile as he ordered goose pate and toast for her and French Onion soup for himself. She exhaled. Despite all that had just been revealed, she realized how safe she felt with him. Then something nudged her memory. *A man with the letter "A" who had something to do with the law would love her*, the psychic had said. Could it be Alistair? Funny, Henry had also predicted something about coming into money. And hadn't he also claimed that *when events unfold, you will understand?*

Not bad, she thought. Two out of three.

AUNT RENEE

"Sit down," Renee instructed Emily, pointing to one of the wooden chairs in the kitchen nook. The sun was softening in the late afternoon pouring gentle golden light onto the pine table. "Would you like some tea?" she asked, bustling over to the counter and busying herself arranging cups and saucers on a silver tray. "It's made." Without turning to face her niece, she enquired, "How did it go with the solicitor?"

"It was . . . very interesting." She smiled, staring out of the window at the colourful hanging baskets on the back fence.

"Oh?" Renee carried the tea tray over to the table where her niece was sitting. Her hands shook slightly as she put a plate of chocolate-covered Jaffa cakes and a pile of iris-printed paper napkins in front of Emily.

Why was Renee so edgy? Emily wondered as she reached for a napkin.

Renee poured tea into both cups, still avoiding her niece's gaze. "So what was so interesting?" Her voice was casual but Emily saw that her jaw had set into that hard line, always a sign that her aunt was anxious. Her pink cashmere twin set didn't seem so refined on her elegant frame today as if, Emily thought, she had shrunk somehow.

Emily reached into her handbag. "I brought the letter from my mother and . . ." she laid the white envelope on the table, "one from Charles."

"Charles!" Renee let her cup clatter onto her saucer. "But . . . but. . . ." Her aunt frowned. "You mean . . . Charles Senior?"

"No," Emily responded, watching her aunt closely, instantly realizing that Renee already knew there was a Charles Junior. What else did she know? she wondered.

"Who was the letter addressed to?" Renee clasped her hands tightly in her lap.

"Miss Emily Carson," she enunciated slowly.

The older woman inhaled sharply.

"Shall I read it to you?" Emily offered.

Renee closed her eyes, grimaced and covered her mouth with a napkin as if she suddenly had toothache. "I-I should . . ." She nodded. "Oh God. I knew this day would come."

Emily frowned at her aunt. What was she so afraid of?

As she read Charles' letter aloud, she glanced up intermittently to see Renee's reactions. But her aunt just sat with her elbows on the table, her head in her hands. Emily finished reading and lay the letter down.

Her aunt kept her head bowed, her face hidden. "I know what you are here to ask," she whispered. Then she looked up at Emily, despair etched into her face. "And unfortunately," she said at last, "I know the answer. I know who killed Charles."

Emily held her breath, waiting.

Renee picked up her napkin again and with her small hands, she began to twist the paper into a tight spiral. The kitchen filled with an unfamiliar heaviness. Just like a decompression, Emily thought. She began to shake. Should she now be afraid of her aunt? Emily was tempted to get up and leave but the voice in her head said, *just wait and listen.*

She waited.

Finally Renee raised her head again "I did it!" she blurted. "I killed Charles!"

Emily pushed her chair back from the table. "What! . . . How—?"

"It was all my fault!" As if the memory was causing a bitter taste in her mouth, she spat out the next words. "I put Derek up to it." She covered her face with her hands and sobbed. Agonized moans came from deep within her.

Emily had never seen her aunt lose control before. It was frightening. But despite her fear, she persisted. "You mean . . . . You mean that . . . Derek killed Charles?"

"Yes!" Renee blurted. She gulped for air and then just as suddenly she

calmed down as if by sheer force of will, pulled herself together. Tears still crept silently down her cheeks, leaving black tramlines of watery mascara. "Derek killed your half-brother and then later . . . ," she barely whispered, "killed himself."

"But . . . why?" Emily struggled to put the jagged fragments together. She knew from Alistair that Charles had died in May 1971, four years earlier. Then Derek had committed suicide in August later that year.

Renee still clutched the napkin, turning it over and over.

A humming bird hovered at the bird feeder and pecked looking for sustenance as Emily stared vacantly at it, scanning her mind, searching for a place to settle this new version of her family's past.

"Your mother," Renee began in a low voice, "suffered a lot after she gave up her baby for adoption. It was terribly heartbreaking. Derek paid the highest price. Helen and he had enjoyed such a lovely bond when he was a baby and then suddenly she didn't seem to care about him any more. She was probably suffering from post-partum depression after Charles' birth and then she had to give him, her precious baby, away to a virtual stranger. On top of that she was so devastated at the death of her lover. All that grief. Can you imagine? "

No, Emily could not. "Is that why Derek was

always so angry?" she asked. "He had been loved and then . . .?"

"Well, yes. And you know how your father was so brutal to Derek. I believe he suspected *something*. I think he had decided that Derek wasn't his son. But he had the wrong boy."

Emily remembered with sadness her father's relentless criticism of her brother. "You'll never amount to anything," he had intoned. "You'll always be a bum." Derek could do nothing right.

"And when your father returned from the war your mother had to pretend that she was deliriously happy to see him. She couldn't tell him about any of her pain, of course. She kept all those emotions locked inside." Renee shook her head. "Almost immediately after your father returned, she was pregnant again with you. When you were born, it seemed like it might be good for her but I think there was too much grief." Renee paused, mindlessly stirring her tea.

Emily, though impatient to get to the point, refrained from urging her aunt; *just tell me what happened with Derek and Charles!"*

"Derek was even jealous of you in the beginning," she added.

Unable to wait any longer, Emily demanded, "But what do you mean, you put Derek up to it? How did Derek know about Charles Junior?"

"One day, about four months before he . . . died, Derek showed up here. Somehow he knew about the half-brother suddenly and was asking a lot of questions. So we talked."

"How had he found out about Charles?"

"I'm not sure." She frowned. "Maybe your mother called him in one of her alcoholic outbursts. You know what she was like."

Emily put down her cup. "So it was Derek who had threatened Charles!"

"In 1970," Renee continued, "Derek was living in London and doing well as an actor, or so we thought. It seemed to me he was always on the brink of poverty. But you know how he loved to . . . exaggerate."

Emily guessed her aunt really meant to say "lie" but she was being kind. It had always saddened her how Derek had told big tales in order to feel accepted.

"When Derek came here, he interrogated me about his childhood. For some reason, he had a real bee in his bonnet about Charles Junior." Her aunt put a hand over her eyes.

Everything that Emily had known of her aunt was now in question. Was Renee feeling shame or remembering the horror of Derek's death, she wondered?

"I tried to make sense of everything for him," Renee went on, "about your mother's situation, to give him some perspective about the affair, the baby, the adoption, the divorce and his rejection. I honestly thought it would help him understand what had happened so he wouldn't take it so personally. I hoped that he would feel some empathy for Charles. God help me, I even suggested that Derek get in touch with his half-brother. I thought they would have something in common— rejection. But as he left here, there was something in his eyes that made me afraid. I tried to stop him." Her aunt's eyes filled with tears again and she looked beseechingly at Emily. "I know he didn't mean to *kill* Charles."

"We don't *know* that, Renee?" Emily stood and stared through the fluted glass of the back door. The flowers formed a blurry mess of pink, blue, red and green. "Charles Junior died in that engine and Derek, who is the only suspect, didn't leave a suicide note."

"Actually . . . he did." Woodenly Renee pulled herself up from the table, walked over to the kitchen counter, then opened a drawer. She turned and Emily saw a thin piece of blue folded paper in her hand.

"My God. You had it all this time?"

"You must remember I was the one who found Derek." She squared her shoulders defiantly and raised her face to stare directly at Emily. "Would you rather I had let the police find it and it all become public? With your mother . . ."

Emily got up and snatched the piece of paper from her aunt's hand. Her heart pounded as she recognized Derek's tight, slanted writing. She stared at Renee, suddenly angry.

"How could you—?"

"There was too much at stake . . . and I felt . . . so guilty."

Her tormented expression softened Emily's wrath.

"Just read it," Renee whispered and turned her back to Emily.

Shaking and swiping away tears, Emily read her brother's suicide note.

Whoever finds me . . .

I didn't mean for this to happen. It was an accident. It was just meant to scare him. He wasn't meant to die. My existence causes everyone pain. I can't do this anymore.

I didn't know. I'm sorry for everything.

Emily exhaled. As sad as this last message was

312

from her brother, she felt a surge of relief. Derek had not meant to kill his half-brother after all. He was not a murderer. Poor Derek. Like Charlie, he had also been a victim of cruel circumstances, rejected over and over again.

She glanced at her distraught aunt leaning against the counter, her back still to her.

"Can you ever forgive me, Emily?" Renee pleaded, sniffling.

"What for?"

"For keeping Derek's note. I know it caused you pain—not knowing—but I just felt so . . . responsible." She finally turned and faced her niece. "And how could I tell my sister that her son had killed her lost baby?" Her aunt returned to her seat and sank down into her chair, spent. She appeared to have shrunk even further beneath the pink cashmere. "Believe me, the whole matter haunts me."

Emily laid Derek's note on the table and stared out of the window again. "You are not the only one, Renee. Charlie, Charles Junior, has been haunting me for years, trying to get my attention through my nightmares and . . ." She hesitated. Maybe she would tell her aunt about the haunted aircraft another day. Today had been enough. And who *was* guilty here? "It seems to me," she said, "that in this we were all victims of circumstances beyond our control."

Renee was still sniffling. Emily went to put her arms around her aunt's shoulders. "None of it is your fault," she reassured her, holding on tightly as she let her own tears come. "You were simply the messenger, and you were just trying to do the right thing." Beneath the soft wool, the older woman felt frail as if the substance had suddenly gone out of her. "Maybe now we can all find some peace." The psychic's words popped into her head again. *Peace will come to all.*

Finally, Renee spoke. "I was so sorry for the two of you being constantly rejected. Derek especially did not handle it well. Then when I kept the note," she said, touching the blue paper, "I had nightmares about the police coming to take me away."

Emily thought of Alistair. He had mentioned he would have to report this case to the police. "What *will* happen if we tell the truth?" she asked.

"No!" Renee pulled away from her niece's grasp. "We mustn't tell them about the note. I would be arrested for obstruction of justice or something like that and Derek . . ." Renee grabbed Emily's wrist. "Promise me you won't."

"Well," Emily sat down again, picked up the sheet of paper and folded it in two. "The note doesn't change the outcome," she said, needing to think out loud. "The police have already ruled Charlie's death accidental, which essentially it was. So what would be the point of raking it all up again? Maybe we should just burn the note in a kind of healing ceremony and let this tragedy be over, for all of us."

"Oh, yes." The terrorized expression on Renee's face melted into one of hope. "Let's do that ... right now." Without waiting for Emily's response, she got up, went to one of the cupboards and picked out a large cream and brown bowl. Then she foraged around in a kitchen drawer and produced a box of matches.

"There," she said, with hands shaking, as she put the bowl in the center of the table then placed the letter in the bowl. "Do we need anything else?"

"Let me think . . ." Emily suddenly wondered if she was doing the right thing. She hated lying to Alistair but if she didn't, more lives would be needlessly wasted.

Her aunt collapsed into her chair, perhaps afraid Emily would change her mind.

"No, that's good," Emily said before extending her hands toward Renee. "Before we light it, why don't we say a silent prayer for Derek and Charlie to rest in peace."

Aunt and niece held hands as they bowed heads.

When Renee finally released her niece, Emily' took a single match out of the box. "Are you ready?"

Renee nodded, expelling a large breath.

Emily struck the match and applied the flame to one corner of the folded paper.

Both women watched as the blue paper curled and slowly shrunk to a pile of blue-grey ashes in the bowl.

"Rest in peace," Renee whispered.

"Amen," Emily added quietly, wondering what she would reveal to Alistair about this afternoon's meeting with her aunt.

After putting on her jacket to leave, she gave Renee a long hug. "I think you and I both need to go and pay someone a visit next week just to make sure neither of us is haunted any more."

"Who is that?"

"Someone who talks to dead people."

THE SÉANCE

Emily's twenty-sixth year had begun with a series of shocks. She felt as if she was struggling with a large unruly jigsaw puzzle, trying to put all the pieces together, but the picture kept shifting, changing and expanding. As she drove up the A23 to meet Alistair, she repeated a habit she had developed of late, of rubbing her forehead—as if it would help make sense of everything. But pieces of the jigsaw were still missing. Until they were revealed she would not be able to grasp the complete picture.

At Alistair's request they met again at his office, where he produced Charlie's effects and details of the trust account. Even though the solicitor had shown extraordinary sensitivity in presenting her half-brother's few items to her, when Emily saw the battered Spanish eight-string guitar and two scruffy cardboard boxes, she was not prepared for her overwhelming sadness. These items were the only evidence of her brother's life—and her only physical connection to him.

"How did things go with your aunt?" Alistair asked as he placed the boxes in the boot of her blue MG. "Did she have any more information?"

Emily had been anticipating this question. "Well, Aunt Renee knew about Charlie the whole time apparently. So we did a lot of talking . . . and . . . it was interesting."

"Does she know who did it, then?" he asked, taking a handkerchief from his pocket and wiping the dust from his hands.

Damn him and his questions. She shrugged. "She feels it was probably just an accident." She hated not telling the whole truth, especially to him.

He studied her, a question in his eyes. "Where are you off to next?"

She would tell him about their appointment with Henry, the psychic, later. "New York. Not till Tuesday, though."

"Would you be able to join me for dinner Saturday night?" He slammed the boot of her car shut.

"Saturday?"

"There is . . . are . . . some details I have to discuss with you . . . and it might take a while," he responded sheepishly to Emily's curious stare. "And we have to eat," he added, grinning.

"Yes . . . Yes. That would be nice."

He took her hand to shake it. His grasp was firm and warm. "Splendid. I'll pick you up at 8.00."

Later, in the privacy of her home, with a glass of red wine in hand, Emily opened both boxes. The first one contained, to her surprise and delight, a collection of Charlie's writings. She picked up what appeared to be a journal but chose not to open it just yet. There were also sheaves of lined papers; short stories, pages of sayings and lots and lots of poems. She found *Broken Wing* and read the whole poem. Tears flowed freely when she understood the loneliness and bitter rejection he must have felt. She glanced over a few more but then put them back in the box. His writings weren't the most heartrending evidence of his short existence though, Emily thought, as she pored over the contents of the second box.

She found a well-thumbed progress report on the hunt for his family, newspaper clippings from World War ll, a picture of his tall, young father in his Air Force uniform. Then something fell out of the pages and floated to the floor. She leaned over to pick it up, turned it over and gasped.

"Oh!" she exclaimed aloud at seeing the photo. Though she hadn't seen Charlie's smile before, Emily didn't need any confirmation of who the young, handsome man in the green coverall was. She recognized him instantly from the ghostly appearances on Charlie Echo and in the oven reflection in BELO's galley. "I'm so sorry, Charlie, for all your pain," she murmured as she lay the photo carefully to the side.

There was one more envelope to open. It contained no papers—just something small and hard. When Emily tipped the envelope to empty it onto her table, a small object fell out. She instantly recognized the metal piece. It was the other half of the dog tag. On it was written WRIGHT with the first stroke of the 'W" missing. Emily sat back. Her mother must have sent it to him as proof of his birthright. Hardly a consolation prize, she mused, but at least her mother gave her son something—his father's name.

After reading a few more of Charles' poems, his intelligence, sensitivity and dry, witty sense of humour emerged. Charlie had been right. They would have enjoyed being brother and sister.

"I'm going to learn to play that guitar," she announced to Renee as they drove the scenic A23 towards Brighton on Saturday. "Maybe even try and put those poems to music."

"That's a good idea," Renee replied absently. She stared out of the window at the lush green undulating hills.

Renee hadn't said much on their one hour journey today. Her aunt just sat quietly in her camel coat, listening to her niece as she narrated the ghostly encounters of Charlie on her flights. Emily knew that her aunt was not totally on board with the idea of talking to a spirit medium but she wasn't sure whether Renee was a believer and afraid of the psychic knowing too much— or that she was a disbeliever and thought this expedition and Emily's stories were just a silly waste of time.

Emily was about to push Henry's doorbell when Renee suddenly grabbed her wrist. "Do you think this is a good idea, dear?"

"If he knows too much, we can always shoot him afterwards." She smiled, but her attempt at humour did not amuse Renee.

Suddenly the door opened as if Henry had psychically heard the bell. "Good morning!" He beamed at the two women. "And you must be Renee," he said, extending a boney hand. "Come in, come in." As they stepped inside, the musty smell assaulted Emily's nostrils again.

Henry led them through the dark hallway past his office, and opened a door into a bright living room. A mismatched collection of dining chairs were arranged in a semi-circle around a faded floral sofa against the side wall. Beyond French doors, a small garden was bursting with unruly purple and white hydrangeas.

"Please, take a seat." He waved an arm to indicate the circle of chairs. Then he left the room. Renee and Emily both opted for the sofa. Without taking off their coats, they sat in silence, peering around the lounge. An abundance of white and black china cats adorned the yellow tiled mantelpiece and hearth. Shelves containing dusty books filled every wall.

Henry reappeared clutching his tape recorder. He gathered a chair from the circle and placed it in front of the two women. "This is the room I use for sittings," he explained to Emily, plunking himself down. He plugged the machine into the wall, laid the device on another chair and inserted a cassette tape. The machine whirred as he hit the record button.

"Emily tells me that you wish to contact some of your family who are passed?"

Renee regarded Henry warily.

"Let's join hands and ask them to come forth, shall we? However, I must warn you," he stated, observing

Renee, "that just because we are sending them an invitation doesn't mean we can force them to come to the party."

Renee barely nodded but took Henry's proffered hand, then took Emily's in her other. When all three were joined, Henry sat back in his chair and exhaled. His body appeared to lose its life force and his tall frame slumped back in his chair.

The women waited, watching the psychic's face. His eyes were closed but his facial muscles twitched as if hearing a private conversation. Emily suppressed a huge impulse to giggle.

"I feel a mother or sister energy," Henry began.

Emily sat up.

"Your Mother. . . she knows she was not a good mother to you in life so she wants to help you from spirit."

The younger woman shifted uncomfortably on the couch.

Sensing her resistance, Henry opened his eyes. "Spirits often come back to make amends to their children," he explained. "She cannot interfere in your life but her message is that she does not want you to waste love like she did. And there is someone who loves you."

"Who could that be?" Renee asked Emily.

"You already know him," Henry added.

Her niece simply shrugged. "I do?" She thought of Alistair and their dinner appointment in a few hours, but he was all business. While he had been very kind, and sometimes she caught him staring at her, he had made no moves.

"Wait." Henry held up one of his hands as if stopping traffic. "Someone else is coming through."

Both women sat still.

"I'm sensing two male energies, young men. "D . .. Der.. . No. . . That's strange. Dustbin? Does that mean anything?"

Renee let out a sharp cry.

"My brother," Emily whispered.

"And," Henry continued, ". . . . I also get the letters CE . . . but they feel like initials, whatever that stands for."

"Charlie Echo" Emily supplied.

"Emily," Henry turned in his chair, his energy suddenly lightening. "One of these young men wants you to learn to play his guitar." His eyes were still closed, but he was smiling and listening like a blind man overhearing a delightful dialogue. "If you do learn, he will help you put his poems to music."

Both women exchanged wide-eyed stares, remembering their conversation in the car less than an hour ago.

"How could you . . ." Renee began and then discarded the question, realizing it was redundant.

"What is your question?" Henry suddenly said, opening his eyes wide, intent on Renee.

Flustered, the aunt glanced furtively at her niece. "Well . . . I want to know if . . . if . . . Derek is at peace."

Henry shook his head. "No. Not yet."

Renee's face crumpled and a deep moan came from her throat.

"You are not at fault, Renee. The brothers tell me it was an accident. Derek says someone else was to blame."

Emily and Renee exchanged knowing looks. Derek had often blamed his lack of luck on others.

"When the fourth letter is in the open, you will understand. Then they can both be at peace."

"Fourth letter!" Aunt and niece both exclaimed.

Mother and Charlie's letters and then Derek's suicide note had been bad enough, Emily thought. What more could there be?

"Who has the fourth letter?" Renee enquired.

Henry spoke as if in a trance again. "It will be revealed very soon."

Renee sighed. "Does it ever end?"

ENDING OR BEGINNING?

In the soft light emanating from the lamp on their restaurant table, Emily glanced over at the contours of Alistair's features as he concentrated on the wine list. His veiled expression puzzled her. The usual twinkle in his eyes had dulled as if a cloud had descended over him. He had bad news for her, she was sure. Maybe he had thought that a nice dinner in this quaint haute cuisine restaurant would soften the blow. But what more bad news could there be? Had he somehow discovered Derek's part in Charlie's demise? Would Aunt Renee have to go through a criminal investigation after all?

"I don't know if you would prefer red or white wine but the filet mignon is supposed to be very good here," Alistair suggested.

With the lump of dread sitting in her stomach, Emily wasn't that hungry. "I think I'll have the salmon," she responded, "so I would prefer white. Maybe a Riesling?"

The small cozy restaurant, with its low ceilings and velvet draped windows—which was only half-filled with patrons—reminded Emily of a private living room. Everyone spoke in hushed voices as if they all knew what her dinner companion was about to impart.

After the waiter had taken their drinks order, Alistair leaned back in his chair and adjusted his tie, then sat forward again and played with the silver cutlery sitting atop the linen napkin.

"You said you had some things to discuss with me," Emily ventured. "Are you going to keep me in suspense?"

He smiled then. "Yes . . . you're right. I should get on with it." He stared at Emily as if memorizing the way she looked and then glanced around at the handful of other diners.

"First, I'll give you the good news. At least, I hope it's good news for you."

"That will make a change. What is it?"

"I've located your father. He's living in the South of France . . . Aixe-en-Provence . . . with a new wife. And he said he would love you to go and visit if you would like to."

Emily smiled at him, surprised at how much joy that gave her. She had a parent again and a step-mother. "Thank you," she said huskily. "Now tell me the bad news."

He shuffled in his seat as if he wanted to wriggle out of his elegant jacket—and this situation.

A waiter appeared and placed a cloth-covered basket between them. Emily recognized the divine aroma of just baked bread. Alistair gave him the wine list and ordered.

"Well," he began, leaning his arms on the table and gazing intently into Emily's eyes, "what I have to say to you is complicated so I would appreciate it if you would just listen and wait until I'm finished before you say anything."

"Keeping quiet is not my forte but if you insist," she

said, attempting to lighten his mood.

"I do," he said glumly.

Emily, though curious, nodded and taking a pat of butter on her knife, began to spread it on her warm bread. *Why was this so painful for him?* she wondered.

Alistair paused while the waiter placed glasses on the table and then, with a flourish, poured first Emily's, then Alistair's wine and left.

"I should first tell you that I have very recently become aware of what really happened to Charlie," he said, picking up his wine and taking a mouthful.

Uh-oh. Emily halted her butter knife in mid-air. She felt her face blush with shame as she stared at Alistair. But there was no accusation in his intense stare. In fact, Emily thought, he appeared to be the guilty one. "How . . .?"

"Today, a . . . document came into my possession." He patted his jacket pocket.

"Document?"

"Well, a letter actually."

Could this be the fourth letter that Henry mentioned? "Who?"

"We'll get to the 'who' but first I wanted to tell you the content of the letter."

Emily put down her knife and took a sip of chilled wine. "I'm listening."

"Let's just say that a certain gentleman brought this letter to my attention and it outlines in detail what happened to Charlie."

Oh no. Could Derek have sent another suicide letter? Emily wondered.

"As your Aunt Renee accurately surmised, his death was an accident. However, this gentleman has taken full responsibility for Charlie's death. He has been haunted by it for a long time."

Join the club, Emily thought.

Alistair sat back as the waiter arrived with menus.

"This gentleman," he continued, after the waiter left, "was apparently a very good friend of your mother's. When Charlie didn't stop harassing her and she couldn't cope, he offered to help take care of the situation."

Emily was running through all the possible "gentlemen" who could have become her mother's ally. There had been rumors of potential suitors, but by that time Emily was out of her mother's life and didn't know of any additions to her social circle.

"This is where it gets . . . sticky." Alistair toyed with the stem of his wine glass, twisting it from side to side. "This person had assumed that Derek was aware of Charlie's existence so he paid Derek a substantial sum to—in his words—make Charlie stay away from the family . . . for good."

Emily gasped. "For good?"

"He meant for Charlie to stay away for the rest of his life, not to be murdered." After swallowing another mouthful of wine, Alistair continued. "It was Derek who suggested that Charlie get a serious scare at his place of work—the air force base. Apparently he had a friend who worked on the ground there."

Emily couldn't take her eyes off Alistair.

The waiter hovered and seeing their menus still open, retreated.

"But just a scare," he added, as if this would comfort Emily. "Derek couldn't get past the air base security so he offered to pay his friend some of the money to do the deed. This young engineer got Charlie to do a ground check two hours early on a plane that was going to be used later that afternoon."

"Charlie Echo," Emily murmured.

"As you know, after Charlie climbed in the engine, Derek's friend put a cover on it, trapping Charlie inside. He believed that the cover would be removed later before they took off but it would give Charlie enough time to get a scare. Then the engineer was sent off shift earlier than expected and unbeknownst to him the plane's training flight was cancelled, leaving Charlie stuck in the engine for the whole weekend. They discovered him on the Monday." Alistair exhaled and sat back. "I think you know the rest."

Emily shuddered. The coffin nightmare and others over the years where she had struggled for breath still haunted her. Poor Charlie!

"I also have to tell you," Alistair leaned forward, almost whispering, "that it's debatable whether Derek really knew that Charlie was his half-brother *before* the incident. He was only told that this man was stalking your mother and that he might be dangerous. I suspect Derek only got the whole truth from your Aunt Renee afterwards. That's why he was so devastated because then he *knew* he had killed his half-brother."

Emily wanted to weep for Derek. How he had been lied to! But she also felt some relief that Derek wasn't the sole perpetrator.

"So will you charge this friend?" she asked finally. "And the gentleman?"

"That will be up to you." Alistair stared into his wine glass while twisting it. "But there's more."

Emily waited.

Her solicitor took another gulp of wine. "You may not like what I am proposing so," he said as he leaned forward, "I apologize in advance. And you can just say no if you don't . . . want to. I would understand." He was grinning with his mouth but there was a strange mixture of hopefulness and sadness in his eyes.

What *was* he talking about? she wondered. The suspense was unbearable.

"I will tell you who the gentleman is in a second but first I have to tell you that I can't be your solicitor any more."

"What? Oh." It surprised her how much that hurt, making her forget momentarily that she was just about to learn the architect of Charlie's death. That meant she would never see Alistair again. Emily glanced down at her lap and readjusted her napkin. "Am I that bad a client?"

"No." He laughed out loud, breaking the somber mood. "I . . . I . . . the truth is, I would rather date you . . . but under the circumstances . . ."

Emily looked up. "*Date* me?"

"Yes . . . and I can't do both. One or the other, solicitor or . . ."

She put her napkin up to her mouth to conceal a wide grin.

"But I don't want you to decide until I've finished talking," he added.

"Typical lawyer," she joked. "Shouldn't this be a happy thing? You look so serious."

"Please." He held up a hand to silence her.

Emily sensed a deep painful conflict within him. Should she arm herself against this new truth? "The way you're talking you would think that *you* killed Charlie."

He didn't smile back.

"Do you remember when we first spoke on the phone," he said, "and I told you that at that time my father had health problems and that's why he couldn't act as your solicitor?"

Emily nodded, frowning.

"Well, that was only part of the truth. Now my father's health issues are much worse than was previously thought."

"Oh . . . I'm so sorry . . ." That's why Alistair wasn't his normal cheery self, Emily thought, relieved but still confused.

"Is he . . ?"

"Dying? Yes. He doesn't have very long . . . just weeks." Alistair paused. She was still clutching the stem of her wine glass as he leaned forward and with one finger stroked Emily's hand. Tingles shimmied up and down her spine. "Now my father is dying," he said, "he's had to retire from the bar, of course. He has nothing left to lose so he was able to reveal the whole truth to you— and me—through this letter." Alistair reached into his jacket pocket and placed a piece of folded white bond paper on the table between them. He slid the letter slowly toward her.

"You mean . . . your father!" Emily just stared at its folds, not wanting to read the older man's words. Oh my God. Henry's reading echoed in her mind. *When the fourth letter is in the open, all will be revealed.*

"I'm so sorry." Alistair blew out a large exhalation and leaned back, as if he had set down a huge sack of cement. "He just gave this to me today." He studied Emily. "It is up to you, of course, to present charges . . . or not."

The waiter reappeared. "Have you decided . . .?"

Alistair waved a hand at him. "Could you give us a few minutes . . .?"

The waiter nodded and backed away.

Alistair topped up their glasses.

Emily was grateful for the small delay. The final

328

pieces of this jigsaw puzzle were sinking into her consciousness and coalescing into one final big picture. Emily picked up her wine and took a mouthful.

"You can speak any time now." Alistair peered anxiously into her eyes. "I'm done."

"But where does that leave us?" Emily asked finally.

He shook his head. "With two broken families . . . ." Alistair leaned over, took her left hand in his and gently squeezed it, ". . . that could potentially become one happy one." He waited, examining her expression. "Emily, you know what I want, but I would understand if you never wished to see me again."

"What do you think?" she asked. "Would Charlie want his echo to be one of old pain or new love?"

"You're the psychic," he murmured, a small grin on his face. "Why don't you ask Charlie?"

Emily laid her hand on the folded paper. She closed her eyes and thought of her half-brother and Derek. "I think he just wants love—for everyone," she said.

Slowly she slid the letter unopened back to his side of the table.

Alistair squeezed her hand tighter and with his other hand, tucked the letter back into his jacket pocket.

LEST WE FORGET

Your physical body

is home to your Spirit

while it is on this physical earth.

The Spirit is just one piece

of your Soul

and the parameter

through which your spirit's personality can learn its

soul's lessons.

This life journey is to remind you

of what you already know

and what you haven't yet accepted

about love.

Your spirit will return home

to your soul

having remembered,

having evolved,

having loved

and been loved

forever coming closer

to the God- Goddess,

of Love, Light, and Power

that you truly are.

And your spirit is always free to refuse growth

AFTER BOOK AFTERLIFE

My intention in writing is always to help the reader understand how we can face the challenges and perceived limitations of being a spirit encased in a human body.

The veil that separates the world of the living and the dead, I believe, is lifting. Perhaps *our* frequency is *rising,* allowing us mere mortals to become more and more attuned to the higher vibration of deceased spirits and other invisible forces. Becoming more transparent, enlightened, truthful, compassionate, and loving beings is the most exciting aspect of this shift into the higher realms.

In the meantime, these ghostly stories remind us that there are ghosts. And if some of us are willing to admit, we also carry our own ghosts in the form of past traumas, old grievances, misguided deeds and the ensuing guilt for things we did or didn't do. We don't have to be dead to look or feel like a ghost. In this life, we can set ourselves free from all the emotions that contribute to becoming a ghost — dead or alive.

Ghosts are spirits who are not able-or who refuse — to move on after a traumatic event and/or physical death. Alive or dead ghosts cling to people, objects, places or events like a long playing record reenacting the same old events until they get tired of going around in circles. Once ghosts choose to become unstuck, they often need support to get

331

out of the loop. To get help, ghosts attract our attention anyway they can.

If you see ghosts, you might believe the spirits or visions you see are the product of too much cheese or a wild imagination. But most of us know that our positive or negative thoughts magnetize like or complementary energies to us. How we think determines our outcomes and affects our perceptions. If we are attracting ghosts, therefore, maybe we also are carrying stuck energy? Or ghosts sense our light and are asking us for help?

When intentionally communing with spirit and other dimensions, it is important to remain in charge of your own energy field by defining healthy psychic boundaries, keeping an open mind and staying in a frequency of love and compassion for yourself and the departed. Even as an experienced psychic medium of 40 years, I still have spirits come to me in unexpected ways, challenging and expanding my own beliefs about how the spirit world works.

My first two books tell these stories and demonstrate how you can learn how to commune with the invisible if you so choose:

Aaagh! I Think I'm Psychic (And You Can Be Too)
Aaagh! I Thought You Were Dead (And Other Psychic Adventures).

If you feel that you might be stuck, these stories will empower you in realizing and releasing your subtle negative energies—including *your*-ghosts—that might be creating a drag in your life. Once we are clear of our "stuff", we can then create a future of our own choosing, a joyous heaven on earth.

The greatest gift of communing with spirit—apart from being able to assist in a spirit healing—is that we are assured there is no death. Our souls *are* eternal and our loved ones *are very much alive* in spirit. Even in death, it is never too late to love and be loved.

ABOUT THE AUTHOR

Photo: Iqbal Ishani

After surviving life in a large, chaotic family in Oxfordshire, England, Natasha J. Rosewood, a reincarnation of a nomad, found her niche as a flight attendant and apprentice palmist. She traveled extensively and lived in Switzerland, Norway, Germany, and Libya, studying the languages of those countries and picking up a few additional languages before immigrating to British Columbia, Canada. Since 1995, when she finally surrendered to her fate as a full-time psychic and writer, Natasha has evolved from palm reader to psychic coach, facilitating spiritual healing and psychic development through corporate and private workshops, hosting her own TV and radio shows, writing books and columns, and offering private and phone consultations to people around the world. Her mission is to empower her clients to realize the full power of their consciousness so they will contribute that unleashed joy and creativity to a more enlightened evolution of humanity.

TESTIMONIALS

What other professionals say about Natasha Rosewood's writing . . .

Natasha's books are thorough and complete for the psychic student. Her down-to-earth and amusing style make spiritual learning accessible and the information easily relatable. I highly recommend all three books! - **Rochelle Sparrow, Featured Psychic Trance Channel for Shirley MacLaine.com**

Loved it! Her first book and radio show was a catalyst for me to pursue my own psychic development. Now I'm suddenly psychic! For anyone committed to their spiritual journey, *Aaagh! I Think I'm Psychic* and *Aaagh! I Thought You Were Dead* are a (mostly) fun and a "must" read! I can't wait to read **GHOSTLY.** Thank you, Natasha! ~ **Stephan Jacob, Channel Director at Voice America LIVE Internet Talk Radio (stephan.jacob@modavox.com)**

In *Aaagh! I Think I'm Psychic,* her stories brought me to tears while inspiring me to continue my own spiritual path, which for a spirit medium can be very challenging. In *Aaagh! I Thought You Were Dead,* Natasha provides above and beyond enlightenment for those who are searching. Natasha's stories are so interesting, I am always disappointed when the book comes to an end. Natasha, you are an inspiration! ~ **June Field,**

International Spirit Medium

What Natasha's clients say about her work ...

I just finished reading your book. It was an incredible adventure. Each chapter guided me to leave behind certain fears and guilts. Your book and wisdom were a gate for forgiveness and liberation of past demons. ~ Mila Grandes, Quito, Ecuador

Natasha, you are such a gift to the planet. ~ Fran, Hawaii, USA

Wouldn't it be a wonderful world if people would learn and practice the proactive approach to life that Natasha recommends in her column? The world would indeed be a better place. ~ Reader, *The Local*, Sunshine Coast, Canada.

WHERE TO FIND MORE BOOKS BY NATASHA J. ROSEWOOD:

All books are available on Amazon in Print, Kindle, additional e-stores and soon to be in Audible format. Please refer to www.natashapsychic.com for a list of bookstores near you or visit Amazon.com.

Aaagh! I Think I'm Psychic (And You Can Be Too)

Aaagh! I Thought You Were Dead (And Other Psychic Adventures)

Mostly True GHOSTLY Stories

MORE BOOKS TO COME:

My fourth book is a complete departure from the metaphysical. It's a study of humanity and will make you laugh out loud. Stay tuned to my website: www.natashapsychic.com and/or natasharosewood-energydynamics.com for updates.

STAY IN TOUCH

NEWSLETTER:

Stay inspired by subscribing to Natasha's free newsletter on **www.natshapsychic.com.**

Keep informed about:

Corporate Seminars

Books and Columns

Healing and Inspiration Downloads

Audibles -Books-on-Tape

Radio and TV Shows

Events and Tours:

Intuitive Development Workshops

Manifestation Workshops

Readings

Book Tours

Speaking Engagements.